CW01024310

SIR THOMAS ELYOT

The Book named
The Governor

EDITED WITH
AN INTRODUCTION BY
S. E. LEHMBERG,
M.A.(Kansas), PH.D.(Cantab.)
*Professor of History,
University of Minnesota*

DENT: LONDON
EVERYMAN'S LIBRARY
DUTTON: NEW YORK

© *Introduction and editing, J. M. Dent & Sons Ltd, 1962*
All rights reserved
Made in Great Britain
at the
Aldine Press · Letchworth · Herts
for
J. M. DENT & SONS LTD
Aldine House · Albemarle Street · London
This edition was first published in
Everyman's Library in 1907
New edition 1962
Last reprinted 1975

Published in the U.S.A. by arrangement
with J. M. Dent & Sons Ltd

No. 227   Hardback ISBN 0 460 00227 9
No. 1227   Paperback ISBN 0 460 01227 4

EVERYMAN, I will go with thee,

and be thy guide,

In thy most need to go by thy side

⚜ SIR THOMAS ELYOT ⚜

Born about 1490, probably in Wiltshire;
educated at home, at the Middle Temple and
at Oxford. Clerk to the Justices of Assize for
the Western Circuit, 1511–26; Chief Clerk of
the King's Council, 1526–30, in which latter
year he retired to his manor at Carlton, near
Cambridge, to write *The Book named The
Governor*. Ambassador to Charles V, 1531–2.
Died 1546.

Debbie. 11. 3. 77.

Leeds.

INTRODUCTION

SIR THOMAS ELYOT'S *Book named The Governor*, first published in 1531, is a composite treatise dealing with political theory, education and moral philosophy; it seeks to set out a way of life for members of the English governing class.

The author was himself a 'governor'. Born about 1490, probably in Wiltshire, Thomas Elyot came from a long line of west-country gentlefolk. His father, Sir Richard, served for years as a justice in the Western Assizes and later in King's Bench. Sir Richard saw to it that his son was well educated, first at home, then in the Middle Temple, one of the Inns of Court, and at Oxford, where Thomas probably took a B.A. in 1519 and a degree in Civil Law in 1524.

Of greater value to Elyot, however, was his association with Sir Thomas More's 'school', where he imbibed the New Learning, the classical humanistic studies which had as yet scarcely penetrated the universities. At More's home in Chelsea Elyot met Thomas Linacre, who taught him Greek and medicine, Hans Holbein the Younger, who made portrait drawings of Elyot and his wife Margaret, and possibly also such distinguished scholars as Erasmus, Colet, Vives and Lily.

As early as 1511 Sir Richard Elyot had contrived to have his son named Clerk to the Justices of Assize for the Western Circuit, a position which Thomas held for fifteen years. By 1523 he had come to the notice of Cardinal Wolsey, through whose influence he was made Chief Clerk of the King's Council. After Wolsey's fall in 1530 Elyot was ejected from the clerkship on the grounds that his predecessor had not legally relinquished the office. In fact Elyot was never paid for his work with the Council, but (as he wrote) 'rewarded only with the order of knighthood, honourable and onerous, having much less to live on than before'.

Free from governmental duties for the first time in his adult life, Elyot retired to his manor of Carlton, near Cambridge, to write the *Governor*.

The Book named The Governor falls, topically, into three sections. Its first three chapters enunciate a monarchical political theory; the remainder of the first book presents a programme of education for the minds and bodies of prospective governors; Books II and III describe virtues appropriate to rulers.

In many ways Elyot's political theory is the most significant part of the *Governor*. He defines a public weal (a term which he prefers to common weal) as a society made up of 'sundry estates and degrees of men'. (A classless society was unthinkable in the sixteenth century.) At the apex of the hierarchical pyramid there must be a single ruler, the king. Monarchy is the only natural and proper form of government; God has ordained it, as the Bible makes clear, and history has shown that it can preserve peace and order while other systems bring only chaos. Elyot even makes the novel claim that Rome was well ruled by its Tarquin kings, after whose expulsion 'much discord was ever in the city for lack of one governor'. Though he thinks that kings should rule for the welfare of their subjects, he implies that royal power is unlimited: a king in his realm is like God in His universe.

But kings cannot rule unaided. They need the help of inferior governors, or magistrates, as Elyot calls them, and these governors must be properly trained. Since England has suffered a deplorable 'decay of learning among gentlemen', Elyot thinks it necessary to institute a radically improved educational system. He would have aspiring governors thoroughly grounded in the classics. They are to begin the study of Latin and Greek when they are seven and continue until they have read virtually all the standard authors of antiquity: Homer, Virgil, Lucian, Aristophanes, Ovid, Cicero, Quintilian, Livy, Xenophon, Caesar, Aristotle and Plato. Although such an arduous course of study might seem to require stern discipline, Elyot insists that students can be 'sweetly allured thereto' if their masters point out the 'incomparable delectation, utility, and commodity' of the classics, which teach how to manage civil and military affairs as well as 'the good sequel of virtue' and 'the evil conclusion of vicious licence'.

Lest the student be worn out with strenuous study, he is permitted various avocations. He may practise music, painting or sculpture, but only 'for recreation after tedious or laborious affairs'. He should, too, develop his body, particularly by hunting, shooting with the long bow (which 'incomparably excelleth all other exercise') and dancing (which should allegorically teach moral lessons). Elyot approves of most sports save football, 'wherein is nothing but beastly fury and extreme violence, whereof proceedeth hurt, and consequently rancour and malice do remain with them that be wounded; wherefore it is to be put in perpetual silence'.

Governors so trained will 'seem to all men worthy to be in authority, honour, and nobleness, and all that is under their governance shall prosper and come to perfection'.

The last two books of the *Governor* discuss virtues which Elyot thinks essential in members of the ruling class. His procedure is generally to define each virtue, then to give historical examples of its operation; he often seems rather more concerned with the histories than the virtues themselves. Two of his illustrative tales are especially notable: the 'wonderful history of Titus and Gisippus', taken from the *Decameron* and constituting the earliest known translation of Boccaccio into English, shows Elyot at his engaging best as a story-teller and stylist; and the account of Prince Hal's wrath (Book II, Chapter VI), repeated by Hall, Holinshed and Shakespeare, has not been traced to a source earlier than the *Governor* and may reveal Elyot transcribing a bit of traditional lore.

Several years after the publication of the *Governor*, Elyot wrote that in it one of his aims had been 'to augment our English tongue, whereby men should as well express most abundantly the thing that they conceive in their hearts (wherefore language was ordained), having words apt for the purpose, as also interpret out of Greek, Latin, or any other tongue into English as sufficiently as out of any one of the said tongues into another'. The *Governor*'s importance in the development of English prose is worth underlining; it is easy to forget how little the vernacular had been used for serious writing before the days of More and Elyot.

The *Governor* remained a work of considerable influence for a century after its publication. It had been reprinted at least seven times by 1580. It was one of the books purchased by the tutors of James VI for the young king to study and may possibly have helped shape his ideas about the power of monarchs. Shakespeare almost certainly knew and used it, for the passages on political theory in *Henry V* and *Troilus and Cressida* include remarkably close verbal echoes of Elyot's first chapters. The writers of the courtesy books so popular in Elizabethan and Jacobean England —Peacham, for instance—also owe much to the *Governor*, for it was the first English work in the *genre* and set the tone for its successors.

Probably on account of the success of the *Governor*, which was dedicated to Henry VIII, and because of his friendship with

Thomas Cromwell, Elyot was appointed ambassador to the Emperor Charles V in 1531. Ostensibly he was sent to attend a meeting of the Order of the Golden Fleece, an imperial chivalric society, but in fact his duty was (as Henry VIII's instructions said) 'to fish out and know in what opinion the Emperor is of us' and to persuade Charles that Henry's divorce case could not be tried at Rome. Since the emperor was Catherine of Aragon's nephew and adamant in his support of her cause, Elyot was unable to accomplish much. He was recalled in the spring of 1532 and never again held a governmental position of more than local significance.

Elyot was distressed at the imminent ecclesiastical Reformation, which he described as 'a great cloud . . . likely to be a great storm when it falleth'. He sympathized with Catherine—in 1540 he praised her in a thinly veiled encomium—and he supplied the Spanish ambassador with information and encouragement. He disapproved of doctrinal innovations but acquiesced in the dissolution of the monasteries, helping in the visitation of Oxfordshire religious houses and later receiving monastic lands in Cambridgeshire.

Besides the *Governor*, Elyot's most important works are *The Castle of Health* (1534?), a hygienic manual, and the first Latin-English dictionary to embody the principles of the New Learning (1538). He also wrote two dialogues on the problem of counsel, a biography of Alexander Severus and an other-worldly *Preservative Against Death*. He published translations from Plutarch, Isocrates (probably the earliest translation into English made directly from a Greek text), Cyprian and Pico della Mirandola. He endeavoured throughout his life to make the ideas and ideals of Renaissance Humanism available to Englishmen in their vernacular.

Elyot died on 26th March 1546 and was buried at Carlton, Cambridgeshire.

S. E. LEHMBERG.

1962.

S. E. Lehmberg's *Sir Thomas Elyot, Tudor Humanist* (University of Texas Press, 1960) is the most comprehensive study of Elyot's life and writings. It contains a full bibliography of Elyot's works and of writings about them. The standard critical edition of the *Governor* is that by H. H. S. Croft, 2 vols., 1880. The present Everyman edition is the first to adopt modernized spelling.

THE TABLE

THE TABLE OF THE SECOND BOOK

The Table of the Third Book

In this edition Elyot's spelling is modernized, but obsolete and archaic words are retained, and glossed in footnotes.

THE PROEM

The Proem of Thomas Elyot, knight, unto the most noble and victorious prince King Henry the Eighth, King of England and France, Defender of the True Faith, and Lord of Ireland.

I LATE considering (most excellent prince and mine only redoubted sovereign lord) my duty that I owe to my natural country with my faith also of allegiance and oath, wherewith I am double bounden unto your majesty, moreover the account that I have to render for that one little talent delivered to me to employ (as I suppose) to the increase of virtue, I am (as God judge me) violently stirred to divulgate [1] or set forth some part of my study, trusting thereby to acquit me of my duties to God, your Highness, and this my country. Wherefore taking comfort and boldness, partly of your Grace's most benevolent inclination toward the universal weal of your subjects, partly inflamed with zeal, I have now enterprised to describe in our vulgar tongue the form of a just public weal: which matter I have gathered as well of the sayings of most noble authors (Greeks and Latins) as by mine own experience, I being continually trained in some daily affairs of the public weal of this your most noble realm almost from my childhood. Which attempt is not of presumption to teach any person, I myself having most need of teaching, but only to the intent that men which will be studious about the weal public may find the thing thereto expedient compendiously written. And for as much as this present book treateth of the education of them that hereafter may be deemed worthy to be governors of the public weal under your Highness (which Plato affirmeth to be the first and chief part of a public weal; Solomon saying also, where governors be not the people shall fall into ruin), I therefore have named it *The Governor*, and do now dedicate it unto your Highness as the first fruits of my study, verily trusting that your most excellent wisdom will therein

---

[1] Promulgate.

esteem my loyal heart and diligent endeavour by the example of Artaxerxes, the noble King of Persia, who rejected not the poor husbandman which offered to him his homely hands full of clean water, but most graciously received it with thanks, esteeming the present not after the value but rather to the will of the giver. Semblably [1] King Alexander retained with him the poet Cherilus honourably for writing his history, although that the poet was but of a small estimation. Which that prince did not for lack of judgment, he being of excellent learning as disciple to Aristotle, but to the intent that his liberality employed on Cherilus should animate or give courage to others much better learned to contend with him in a semblable enterprise.

And if, most virtuous Prince, I may perceive your Highness to be herewith pleased, I shall soon after (God giving me quietness) present your Grace with the residue of my study and labours, wherein your Highness shall well perceive that I nothing esteem so much in this world as your royal estate (my most dear sovereign Lord) and the public weal of my country. Protesting unto your excellent Majesty that where I commend herein any one virtue or dispraise any one vice I mean the general description of the one and the other without any other particular meaning to the reproach of any one person. To the which protestation I am now driven through the malignity of this present time all disposed to malicious detraction. Wherefore I most humbly beseech your Highness to deign to be patron and defender of this little work against the assaults of malign interpreters which fail not to rend and deface the renown of writers, they themselves being in nothing to the public weal profitable. Which is by no man sooner perceived than by your Highness, being both in wisdom and very nobility equal to the most excellent princes, whom, I beseech God, ye may surmount in long life and perfect felicity. Amen.

[1] Similarly.

THE FIRST BOOK

I. The signification of a public weal, and why it is called in Latin
   Respublica.

A PUBLIC weal is in sundry wise defined by philosophers; but
knowing by experience that the often repetition of anything of
grave or sad importance will be tedious to the readers of this
work, who perchance for the more part have not been trained in
learning containing semblable [1] matter, I have compiled one
definition out of many, in as compendious form as my poor wit
can devise, trusting that in those few words the true signification
of a public weal shall evidently appear to them whom reason can
satisfy.

A public weal is a body living, compact or made of sundry
estates and degrees of men, which is disposed by the order of
equity and governed by the rule and moderation of reason. In the
Latin tongue it is called *Respublica*, of the which the word *Res*
hath divers significations, and doth not only betoken that that is
called a thing which is distinct from a person, but also signifieth
estate, condition, substance, and profit. In our old vulgar, profit
is called weal. And it is called a wealthy country wherein is all
thing that is profitable. And he is a wealthy man that is rich in
money and substance. Public (as Varro saith) is derived of people,
which in Latin is called *Populus*; wherefore it seemeth that men
have been long abused in calling *Rempublicam* a common weal.
And they which do suppose it so to be called for that, that everything should be to all men in common, without discrepance [2] of
any estate or condition, be thereto moved more by sensuality
than by any good reason or inclination to humanity. And that
shall soon appear unto them that will be satisfied either with
authority or with natural order and example.

[1] Similar.   [2] Distinction.

1

First, the proper and true signification of the words public and common, which be borrowed of the Latin tongue for the insufficiency of our own language, shall sufficiently declare the blindness of them which have hitherto holden and maintained the said opinions. As I have said, public took his beginning of people, which in Latin is *Populus*, in which word is contained all the inhabitants of a realm or city, of what estate or condition so ever they be.

Plebs in English is called the commonalty, which signifieth only the multitude, wherein be contained the base and vulgar inhabitants not advanced to any honour or dignity, which is also used in our daily communication. For in the city of London and other cities they that be none aldermen or sheriffs be called commoners; and in the country, at a sessions or other assembly, if no gentlemen be thereat, the saying is that there was none but the commonalty, which proveth in mine opinion that *Plebs* in Latin is in English commonalty, and *Plebeii* be commoners. And consequently there may appear like diversity to be in English between a public weal and a common weal, as should be in Latin between *Res publica* and *Res plebeia*. And after that signification, if there should be a common weal either the commoners only must be wealthy, and the gentle and noble men needy and miserable, or else, excluding gentility, all men must be of one degree and sort, and a new name provided. For as much as *Plebs* in Latin, and commoners in English, be words only made for the discrepance of degrees, whereof proceedeth order; which in things as well natural as supernatural hath ever had such a preeminence that thereby the incomprehensible majesty of God, as it were by a bright leam [1] of a torch or candle, is declared to the blind inhabitants of this world. Moreover take away order from all things, what should then remain? Certes [2] nothing finally, except some man would imagine eftsoons [3] *Chaos*, which of some is expound a confuse mixture. Also where there is any lack of order needs must be perpetual conflict, and in things subject to nature nothing of himself only may be nourished; but when he had destroyed that wherewith he doth participate by the order of his creation, he himself of necessity must then perish, whereof ensueth universal dissolution.

But now to prove, by example of those things that be within

[1] Gleam.   [2] Certainly.
[3] Again.

the compass of man's knowledge, of what estimation order is, not only among men but also with God, albeit His wisdom, bounty, and magnificence can be with no tongue or pen sufficiently expressed. Hath not He set degrees and estates in all His glorious works?

First in His heavenly ministers, whom, as the Church affirmeth, He hath constituted to be in divers degrees called hierarchs.

Also Christ saith by His evangelist that in the house of His Father (which is God) be many mansions. But to treat of that which by natural understanding may be comprehended. Behold the four elements whereof the body of man is compact, how they be set in their places called spheres, higher or lower according to the sovereignty of their natures, that is to say, the fire as the most pure element, having in it nothing that is corruptible, in his place is highest and above other elements. The air, which next to the fire is most pure in substance, is in the second sphere or place. The water, which is somewhat consolidate, and approacheth to corruption, is next unto the earth. The earth, which is of substance gross and ponderous, is set of all elements most lowest.

Behold also the order that God hath put generally in all His creatures, beginning at the most inferior or base, and ascending upward. He made not only herbs to garnish the earth, but also trees of a more eminent stature than herbs, and yet in the one and the other be degrees of qualities: some pleasant to behold, some delicate or good in taste, other wholesome and medicinable, some commodious and necessary. Semblably in birds, beasts, and fishes, some be good for the sustenance of man, some bear things profitable to sundry uses, other be apt to occupation and labour; in diverse is strength and fierceness only; in many is both strength and commodity; some other serve for pleasure; none of them hath all these qualities; few have the more part or many, specially beauty, strength, and profit. But where any is found that hath many of the said properties, he is more set by than all the other, and by that estimation the order of his place and degree evidently appeareth; so that every kind of trees, herbs, birds, beasts, and fishes, beside their diversity of forms, have (as who saith) a peculiar disposition appropered [1] unto them by God their creator: so that in everything is order, and without order may be nothing stable or permanent; and it may not be called order,

---

[1] Proper, appropriated.

except it do contain in it degrees, high and base, according to the merit or estimation of the thing that is ordered.

Now to return to the estate of mankind, for whose use all the said creatures were ordained of God, and also excelleth them all by prerogative of knowledge and wisdom. It seemeth that in him should be no less providence of God declared than in the inferior creatures, but rather with a more perfect order and disposition. And therefore it appeareth that God giveth not to every man like gifts of grace, or of nature, but to some more, some less, as it liketh His Divine Majesty.

Ne they be not in common (as fantastical fools would have all things), nor one man hath not all virtues and good qualities. Notwithstanding for as much as understanding is the most excellent gift that man can receive in his creation, whereby he doth approach most nigh unto the similitude of God, which understanding is the principal part of the soul, it is therefore congruent and according that as one excelleth another in that influence, as thereby being next to the similitude of his maker, so should the estate of his person be advanced in degree or place where understanding may profit; which is also distributed into sundry uses, faculties, and offices, necessary for the living and governance of mankind. And like as the angels which be most fervent in contemplation be highest exalted in glory (after the opinion of holy doctors), and also the fire, which is the most pure of elements and also doth clarify the inferior elements, is deputed to the highest sphere or place, so in this world they which excel other in this influence of understanding, and do employ it to the detaining of other within the bounds of reason, and show them how to provide for their necessary living, such ought to be set in a more high place than the residue where they may see and also be seen, that by the beams of their excellent wit, showed through the glass of authority, other of inferior understanding may be directed to the way of virtue and commodious living. And unto men of such virtue by very equity appertaineth honour, as their just reward and duty, which by other men's labours must also be maintained according to their merits. For as much as the said persons, excelling in knowledge whereby other be governed, be ministers for the only profit and commodity of them which have not equal understanding; where they which do exercise artificial science or corporal labour do not travail for their superiors only, but also for their own necessity. So the husbandman feedeth himself and the cloth maker; the cloth maker apparelleth himself and the husband; they both succour other artificers; other artificers them; they and other artificers them that be governors. But they that be governors (as I before said) nothing do acquire by the said influence of knowledge for their own necessities, but do employ all the powers of their wits and their diligence to the only preservation of other their inferiors; among which inferiors also behoveth to be a disposition and order according to reason, that is to say, that the slothful or idle person do not participate with him that is industrious and taketh pain, whereby the fruits of his labours should be diminished, wherein should be none equality, but thereof should proceed discourage, and finally dissolution for lack of provision. Wherefore it can none other wise stand with reason but that the estate of the person in pre-eminence of living should be esteemed with his understanding, labour, and policy; whereunto must be added an augmentation of honour and substance, which not only impresseth a reverence, whereof proceedeth due obedience among subjects, but also inflameth men naturally inclined to idleness or sensual appetite to covet like fortune, and for that cause to dispose them to study or occupation. Now to conclude my first assertion or argument: where all thing is common there lacketh order, and where order lacketh there all thing is odious and uncomely. And that have we in daily experience; for the pans and pots garnisheth well the kitchen, and yet should they be to the chamber none ornament. Also the beds, testers, and pillows beseemeth not the hall, no more than the carpets and cushions becometh the stable. Semblably the potter and tinker, only perfect in their craft, shall little do in the ministration of justice. A ploughman or carter shall make but a feeble answer to an ambassador. Also a weaver or fuller should be an unmeet captain of an army, or in any other office of a governor. Wherefore, to conclude, it is only a public weal where, like as God hath disposed the said influence of understanding, is also appointed degrees and places according to the excellency thereof; and thereto also would be substance convenient and necessary for the ornament of the same, which also impresseth a reverence and due obedience to the vulgar people or commonalty; and without that, it can be no more said that there is a public weal than it may be affirmed that a house without his proper and necessary ornaments is well and sufficiently furnished.

II. That one sovereign governor ought to be in a public weal. And what damage hath happened where a multitude hath had equal authority without any sovereign.

LIKE AS to a castle or fortress sufficeth one owner or sovereign, and where any more be of like power and authority seldom cometh the work to perfection; or being already made, where the one diligently overseeth and the other neglecteth, in that contention all is subverted and cometh to ruin. In semblable wise doth a public weal that hath more chief governors than one. Example we may take of the Greeks, among whom in divers cities were divers forms of public weals governed by multitudes. Wherein one was most tolerable where the governance and rule was always permitted to them which excelled in virtue, and was in the Greek tongue called *Aristocratia*, in Latin *Optimorum Potentia*, in English the rule of men of best disposition, which the Thebans of long time observed.

Another public weal was among the Athenians, where equality was of estate among the people, and only by their whole consent their city and dominions were governed: which might well be called a monster with many heads. Nor never it was certain nor stable; and often times they banished or slew the best citizens, which by their virtue and wisdom had most profited to the public weal. This manner of governance was called in Greek *Democratia*, in Latin *Popularis Potentia*, in English the rule of the commonalty. Of these two governances none of them may be sufficient. For in the first, which consisteth of good men, virtue is not so constant in a multitude, but that some, being once in authority, be incensed with glory, some with ambition, other with covetousness and desire of treasure or possessions. Whereby they fall into contention; and finally, where any achieveth the superiority, the whole governance is reduced unto a few in number, which fearing the multitude and their mutability, to the intent to keep them in dread to rebel, ruleth by terror and cruelty, thinking thereby to keep themselves in surety. Notwithstanding, rancour, coarcted [1] and long detained in a narrow room, at the last bursteth out with intolerable violence and bringeth all to confusion. For the power that is practised to the hurt of many cannot continue. The popular estate, if it anything do vary from equality

[1] Confined.

of substance or estimation, or that the multitude of people have over much liberty, of necessity one of these inconveniences must happen: either tyranny, where he that is too much in favour would be elevate and suffer none equality, or else into the rage of a commonalty, which of all rules is most to be feared. For like as the commons, if they feel some severity, they do humbl serve and obey, so where they embracing a license refuse to be bridled, they fling and plunge; and if they once throw down their governor, they order everything without justice, only with vengeance and cruelty, and with incomparable difficulty and unneth [1] by any wisdom be pacified and brought again into order. Wherefore undoubtedly the best and most sure governance is by one king or prince, which ruleth only for the weal of his people to him subject; and that manner of governance is best approved, and hath longest continued, and is most ancient. For who can deny but that all thing in heaven and earth is governed by one God, by one perpetual order, by one providence? One sun ruleth over the day, and one moon over the night; and to descend down to the earth, in a little beast, which of all other is most to be marvelled at, I mean the bee, is left to man by nature, as it seemeth, a perpetual figure of a just governance or rule: who hath among them one principal bee for their governor, who excelleth all other in greatness, yet hath he no prick or sting, but in him is more knowledge than in the residue. For if the day following shall be fair and dry, and that the bees may issue out of their stalls without peril of rain or vehement wind, in the morning early he calleth them, making a noise as it were the sound of a horn or a trumpet; and with that all the residue prepare them to labour, and flyeth abroad, gathering nothing but that shall be sweet and profitable, although they sit often times on herbs and other things that be venomous and stinking.

The captain himself laboureth not for his sustenance, but all the other for him; he only seeth that if any drone or other unprofitable bee entereth into the hive, and consumeth the honey gathered by other, that he be immediately expelled from that company. And when there is another number of bees increased, they semblably have also a captain, which be not suffered to continue with the other. Wherefore this new company gathered into a swarm, having their captain among them, and environing

---

[1] Scarcely.

him to preserve him from harm, they issue forth seeking a new
habitation, which they find in some tree, except with some
pleasant noise they be lured and conveyed unto another hive. I
suppose who seriously beholdeth this example, and hath any
commendable wit, shall thereof gather much matter to the forming of a public weal. But because I may not be long therein,
considering my purpose, I would that if the reader hereof be
learned, that he should repair to the *Georgics* of Virgil, or to
Pliny, or Columella, where he shall find the example more ample
and better declared. And if any desireth to have the governance
of one person proved by histories, let him first resort to the
Holy Scripture, where he shall find that Almighty God commanded Moses only to bring his elected people out of captivity,
giving only to him that authority without appointing to him any
other assistance of equal power or dignity, except in the message
to King Pharaoh, wherein Aaron, rather as a minister than a
companion, went with Moses. But only Moses conducted the
people through the Red Sea; he only governed them forty years
in desert. And because Dathan and Abiram disdained his rule
and coveted to be equal with him, the earth opened, and fire
issued out, and swallowed them in with all their whole family and
confederates to the number of 14,700.

And although Jethro, Moses' father-in-law, counselled him to
depart [1] his importable [2] labours, in continual judgments, unto
the wise men that were in his company, he notwithstanding still
retained the sovereignty by God's commandment, until, a little
before he died, he resigned it to Joshua, assigned by God to be
ruler after him. Semblably after the death of Joshua by the space
of 246 years succeeded from time to time one ruler among the
Jews, which was chosen for his excellency in virtue and specially
justice, wherefore he was called the judge, until the Israelites
desired of Almighty God to let them have a king as other people
had: who appointed to them Saul to be their king, who exceeded
all other in stature. And so successively one king governed all the
people of Israel unto the time of Rehoboam, son of the noble
King Solomon, who, being unlike to his father in wisdom,
practised tyranny among his people, wherefore nine parts of
them which they called Tribes forsook him and elected Jeroboam,
late servant to Solomon, to be their king, only the tenth part
remaining with Rehoboam.

[1] Delegate.   [2] Unbearable.

And so in that realm were continually two kings until the King of Mede had depopulated the country and brought the people in captivity to the city of Babylon, so that during the time that two kings reigned over the Jews was ever continual battle among themselves: where if one king had always reigned like to David or Solomon, of likelihood the country should not so soon have been brought in captivity.

Also in the time of the Maccabees, as long as they had but one bishop which was their ruler, and was in the stead of a prince at that day, they valiantly resisted the Gentiles; and as well the Romans, then great lords of the world, as Persians and divers other realms desired to have with them amity and alliance; and all the inhabitants of that country lived in great weal and quietness. But after that by simony and ambition there happened to be two bishops which divided their authorities, and also the Romans had divided the realm of Judea to four princes called *tetrarchas* and also constituted a Roman captain or president over them, among the heads there never ceased to be sedition and perpetual discord, whereby at the last the people was destroyed and the country brought to desolation and horrible barrenness.

The Greeks, which were assembled to revenge the reproach of Menelaus that he took of the Trojans by the ravishing of Helen, his wife, did not they by one assent elect Agamemnon to be their emperor or captain, obeying him as their sovereign during the siege of Troy? Although that they had divers excellent princes, not only equal to him, but also excelling him: as in prowess, Achilles and Ajax Thelemonius; in wisdom, Nestor and Ulysses, and his own brother Menelaus, to whom they might have given equal authority with Agamemnon; but those wise princes considered that, without a general captain, so many persons as were there of divers realms gathered together, should be by no means well governed: wherefore Homer calleth Agamemnon the shepherd of the people. They rather were contented to be under one man's obedience, than severally to use their authorities or to join in one power and dignity; whereby at the last should have sourded [1] dissension among the people, they being separately inclined toward their natural sovereign lord, as it appeared in the particular contention that was between Achilles and Agamemnon for their concubines, where Achilles, renouncing the obedience

---

[1] Raised up.

that he with all other princes had before promised, at the battle first enterprised against the Trojans. For at that time no little murmur and sedition was moved in the host of the Greeks, which notwithstanding was wonderfully pacified, and the army unscattered by the majesty of Agamemnon, joining to him counsellors Nestor and the witty Ulysses.

But to return again. Athens and other cities of Greece, when they had abandoned kings and concluded to live as it were in a commonalty which abusively they called equality, how long time did any of them continue in peace? Yea what vacation had they from the wars, or what noble man had they which advanced the honour and weal of their city, whom they did not banish or slay in prison? Surely it shall appear to them that will read Plutarch, or Aemilius Probus, in the lives of Milciades, Cimon, Themistocles, Aristides, and divers other noble and valiant captains: which is too long here to rehearse.

In like wise the Romans, during the time that they were under kings, which was by the space of 144 years, were well governed, nor never was among them discord or sedition. But after that by the persuasion of Brutus and Colatinus, whose wife (Lucretia) was ravished by Aruncius, son of Tarquin, King of Romans, not only the said Tarquin and all his posterity were exiled out of Rome for ever, but also it was finally determined amongst the people that never after they would have a king reign over them.

Consequently the commonalty more and more encroached a license, and at the last compelled the Senate to suffer them to choose yearly among them governors of their own estate and condition, whom they called Tribunes: under whom they received such audacity and power that they finally obtained the highest authority in the public weal, in so much that often times they did repeal the acts of the Senate, and to those Tribunes might a man appeal from the Senate or any other office or dignity.

But what came thereof in conclusion? Surely when there was any difficult war imminent, then were they constrained to elect one sovereign and chief of all other, whom they named *Dictator*, as it were commander, from whom it was not lawful for any man to appeal. But because there appeared to be in him the pristine authority and majesty of a king, they would no longer suffer him to continue in that dignity than by the space of six months, except he then resigned it, and by the consent of the people eftsoons did resume it. Finally, until Octavius Augustus had destroyed

Anthony, and also Brutus, and finished all the Civil Wars (that were so called because they were between the same self Roman citizens), the city of Rome was never long quiet from factions or seditions among the people. And if the nobles of Rome had not been men of excellent learning, wisdom, and prowess, and that the Senate, the most noble council in all the world, which was first ordained by Romulus and increased by Tullus Hostilius, the third King of Romans, had not continued and with great difficulty retained their authority, I suppose verily that the city of Rome had been utterly desolate soon after the expelling of Tarquin; and if it had been eftsoons renewed it should have been twenty times destroyed before the time that Augustus reigned: so much discord was ever in the city for lack of one governor.

But what need we to search so far from us, since we have sufficient examples near unto us? Behold the estate of Florence and Genoa, noble cities of Italy, what calamity have they both sustained by their own factions, for lack of a continual governor. Ferrara and the most excellent city of Venice, the one having a duke, the other an earl, seldom suffereth damage except it happen by outward hostility. We have also an example domestical, which is most necessary to be noted. After that the Saxons by treason had expelled out of England the Britons, which were the ancient inhabitants, this realm was divided into sundry regions or kingdoms. O what misery was the people then in! O how this most noble Isle of the world was decerpt[1] and rent in pieces; the people pursued and hunted like wolves or other beasts savage; none industry availed, no strength defended, no riches profited. Who would then have desired to have been rather a man than a dog, when men either with sword or with hunger perished, having no profit or sustenance of their own corn or cattle, which by mutual war was continually destroyed? Yet the dogs, either taking that that men could not quietly come by or feeding on the dead bodies which on every part lay scattered plenteously, did satisfy their hunger.

Where find ye any good laws that at that time were made and used, or any commendable monument of science or craft in this realm occupied? Such iniquity seemeth to be then, that by the multitude of sovereign governors all things had been brought to confusion, if the noble King Edgar had not reduced the monarch to his pristine estate and figure: which brought to pass, reason

[1] Plucked off.

was revived, and people came to conformity, and the realm began to take comfort and to show some visage of a public weal, and so (lauded be God) have continued: but not being alway in like estate or condition. Albeit it is not to be despaired, but that the King our sovereign lord now reigning, and this realm alway having one prince like unto his Highness, equal to the ancient princes in virtue and courage, it shall be reduced (God so disposing) unto a public weal excelling all other in pre-eminence of virtue and abundance of things necessary. But for as much as I do well perceive that to write of the office or duty of a sovereign governor or prince far exceedeth the compass of my learning, Holy Scripture affirming that the hearts of princes be in God's own hands and disposition, I will therefore keep my pen within the space that is described to me by the three noble masters, reason, learning, and experience; and by their ensignment or teaching I will ordinately treat of the two parts of a public weal, whereof the one shall be named Due Administration, the other Necessary Occupation, which shall be divided into two volumes. In the first shall be comprehended the best form of education or bringing up of noble children from their nativity, in such manner as they may be found worthy and also able to be governors of a public weal. The second volume, which, God granting me quietness and liberty of mind, I will shortly after send forth, it shall contain all the remnant, which I can either by learning or experience find apt to the perfection of a just public weal: in the which I shall so endeavour myself, that all men, of what estate or condition soever they be, shall find therein occasion to be alway virtuously occupied; and not without pleasure, if they be not of the schools of Aristippus or Apicius, of whom the one supposed felicity to be only in lechery, the other in delicate feeding and gluttony: from whose sharp talons and cruel teeth, I beseech all gentle readers to defend these works, which for their commodity is only compiled.

III. *That in a public weal ought to be inferior governors called magistrates, which shall be appointed or chosen by the sovereign governor.*

THERE BE both reasons and examples, undoubtedly infinite, whereby may be proved that there can be no perfect public weal without one capital and sovereign governor which may long endure or continue. But since one mortal man cannot have knowledge of all things done in a realm or large dominion, and at one time discuss all controversies, reform all transgressions, and exploit all consultations, concluded as well for outward as inward affairs, it is expedient and also needful that under the capital governor be sundry mean authorities, as it were aiding him in the distribution of justice in sundry parts of a huge multitude; whereby his labours being levigate [1] and made more tolerable, he shall govern with the better advice, and consequently with a more perfect governance. And, as Jesus Sirach saith, the multitude of wise men is the wealth of the world. They which have such authorities to them committed may be called inferior governors, having respect to their office or duty, wherein is also a representation of governance. Albeit they be named in Latin *Magistratus*. And hereafter I intend to call them magistrates, lacking another more convenient word in English; but that will I do in the second part of this work, where I purpose to write of their sundry offices or effects of their authority. But for as much as in this part I intend to write of their education and virtue in manners, which they have in common with princes, inasmuch as thereby they shall, as well by example as by authority, order well them which by their capital governor shall be to their rule committed, I may without annoyance of any man name them governors at this time, appropriating to the sovereigns names of kings and princes, since of a long custom these names in common form of speaking be in a higher pre-eminence and estimation than governors. That in every common weal ought to be a great number of such manner of persons it is partly proved in the chapter next before written, where I have spoken of the commodity of order. Also reason and common experience plainly declareth that where the dominion is large and populous there is it convenient that a prince have many inferior governors, which be named of Aristotle his eyes, ears, hands, and legs; which if they be of the best sort (as he furthermore saith), it seemeth impossible a country not to be well governed by good laws. And except [2] excellent virtue and learning do enable a man of the base estate of the commonalty to be thought of all men worthy to be so much advanced, else [3] such governors would be chosen out of that estate of men which be called worshipful, if among them may

[1] Lightened.   [2] Unless.
Otherwise.

be found a sufficient number, ornate with virtue and wisdom, meet for such purpose, and that for sundry causes.

First it is of good congruence that they which be superior in condition or haviour [1] should have also pre-eminence in administration, if they be not inferior to other in virtue. Also they having of their own revenues certain whereby they have competent substance to live without taking rewards, it is likely that they will not be so desirous of lucre (whereof may be engendered corruption), as they which have very little or nothing so certain.

Moreover where virtue is in a gentleman it is commonly mixed with more sufferance, more affability, and mildness, than for the more part it is in a person rural or of a very base lineage; and when it happeneth otherwise, it is to be accounted loathsome and monstrous. Furthermore, where the person is worshipful, his governance, though it be sharp, is to the people more tolerable, and they therewith the less grutch [2] or be disobedient. Also such men, having substance in goods by certain and stable possessions which they may apportionate to their own living and bringing up of their children in learning and virtues, may (if nature repugn not) cause them to be so instructed and furnished toward the administration of a public weal, that a poor man's son only by his natural wit, without other adminiculation [3] or aid, never or seldom may attain to the semblable. Toward the which instruction I have, with no little study and labours, prepared this work, as Almighty God be my judge, without arrogance or any spark of vainglory; but only to declare the fervent zeal that I have to my country; and that I desire only to employ that poor learning that I have gotten to the benefit thereof and to the recreation of all the readers that be of any noble or gentle courage, giving them occasion to eschew idleness, being occupied in reading this work, enforced [4] throughly with such histories and sentences whereby they shall take, they themselves confessing, no little commodity if they will more than once or twice read it. The first reading being to them new, the second delicious, and every time after more and more fruitful and excellent profitable.

[1] Property.
[2] Murmur, complain.
[3] Support.
[4] Stuffed, filled.

*IV. The education or form of bringing up of the child of a gentle-
man, which is to have authority in a public weal.*

FOR AS much as all noble authors do conclude and also common
experience proveth that where the governors of realms and cities
be found adorned with virtues and do employ their study and
mind to the public weal, as well to the augmentation thereof as to
the establishing and long continuance of the same, there a public
weal must needs be both honourable and wealthy. To the intent
that I will declare how such personages may be prepared, I will
use the policy of a wise and cunning gardener: who purposing to
have in his garden a fine and precious herb that should be to
him and all other repairing thereto excellently commodious or
pleasant, he will first search throughout his garden where he can
find the most mellow and fertile earth, and therein will he put the
seed of the herb to grow and be nourished, and in most diligent
wise attend that no weed be suffered to grow or approach nigh
unto it; and to the intent it may thrive the faster, as soon as the
form of an herb once appeareth, he will set a vessel of water by it,
in such wise that it may continually distil on the root sweet drops;
and as it springeth in stalk, underset it with something that it
break not, and always keep it clean from weeds. Semblable order
will I ensue in the forming the gentle wits of noblemen's children,
who, from the wombs of their mother, shall be made propise [1] or
apt to the governance of a public weal.

First, they unto whom the bringing up of such children
appertaineth ought, against the time that their mother shall be of
them delivered, to be sure of a nurse which should be of no
servile condition or vice notable. For, as some ancient writers do
suppose, often times the child sucketh the vice of his nurse with
the milk of her pap. And also observe that she be of mature or
ripe age, not under twenty years or above thirty, her body also
being clean from all sickness or deformity, and having her
complexion most of the right and pure sanguine, forasmuch as
the milk thereof coming excelleth all other both in sweetness and
substance. Moreover to the nurse should be appointed another
woman of approved virtue, discretion, and gravity, who shall not
suffer in the child's presence to be shown any act or tache [2] dishonest, or any wanton or unclean word to be spoken; and for

[1] Proper, fit.   [2] Trait, characteristic.

that cause all men, except physicians only, should be excluded and kept out of the nursery. Perchance some will scorn me for that I am so serious, saying that there is no such damage to be feared in an infant, who for tenderness of years hath not the understanding to discern good from evil. And yet no man will deny but in that innocency he will discern milk from butter, and bread from pap, and ere he can speak he will with his hand or countenance signify which he desireth. And I verily do suppose that in the brains and hearts of children, which be members spiritual, whiles they be tender and the little slips of reason begin in them to burgeon,[1] there may hap by evil custom some pestiferous dew of vice to pierce the said members and infect and corrupt the soft and tender buds, whereby the fruit may grow wild, and some time contain in it fervent and mortal poison, to the utter destruction of a realm.

And we have in daily experience that little infants assayeth to follow, not only the words, but also the facts and gesture of them that be provect [2] in years. For we daily hear, to our great heaviness, children swear great oaths and speak lascivious and unclean words, by the example of other whom they hear, whereat the lewd parents do rejoice, soon after, or in this world, or elsewhere, to their great pain and torment. Contrariwise we behold some children, kneeling in their game before images and holding up their little white hands, do move their pretty mouths, as they were praying; other going and singing as it were in procession; whereby they do express their disposition to the imitation of those things, be they good or evil, which they usually do see or hear. Wherefore not only princes, but also all other children, from their nurses' paps, are to be kept diligently from the hearing or seeing of any vice or evil tache. And incontinent [3] as soon as they can speak, it behoveth, with most pleasant allurings, to instil in them sweet manners and virtuous custom. Also to provide for them such companions and play-fellows which shall not do in his presence any reproachable act or speak any unclean word or oath, nor to advaunt [4] him with flattery, remembering his nobility, or any other like thing wherein he might glory; unless it be to persuade him to virtue, or to withdraw him from vice, in the remembering to him the danger of his evil example. For noble men more grievously offend by their example than by their deed.

Yet often remembrance to them of their estate may happen to radicate[1] in their hearts intolerable pride, the most dangerous poison to nobleness: wherefore there is required to be therein much cautel[2] and soberness.

V. The order of learning that a nobleman should be trained in before he come to the age of seven years.

SOME OLD authors hold opinion that, before the age of seven years, a child should not be instructed in letters; but those writers were either Greeks or Latins, among whom all doctrine and sciences were in their maternal tongues, by reason whereof they saved all that long time which at this day is spent in understanding perfectly the Greek or Latin. Wherefore it requireth now a longer time to the understanding of both. Therefore that infelicity of our time and country compelleth us to encroach somewhat upon the years of children, and specially of noblemen, that they may sooner attain to wisdom and gravity than private persons, considering, as I have said, their charge and example, which above all things is most to be esteemed. Notwithstanding, I would not have them enforced by violence to learn, but according to the counsel of Quintilian to be sweetly allured thereto with praises and such pretty gifts as children delight in. And their first letters to be painted or limned in a pleasant manner, wherein children of gentle courage have much delectation. And also there is no better allective[3] to noble wits than to induce them into a contention with their inferior companions: they sometime purposely suffering the more noble children to vanquish and, as it were, giving to them place and sovereignty, though indeed the inferior children have more learning. But there can be nothing more convenient than by little and little to train and exercise them in speaking of Latin: informing them to know first the names in Latin of all things that cometh in sight, and to name all the parts of their bodies, and giving them somewhat that they covet or desire, in most gentle manner to teach them to ask it again in Latin. And if by this means they may be induced to understand and speak Latin, it shall afterwards be less grief to them, in a

---

[1] Root.   [2] Caution.

[3] Enticement.

manner, to learn anything, where they understand the language wherein it is written. And, as touching grammar, there is at this day better introductions, and more facile, than ever before were made, concerning as well Greek as Latin, if they be wisely chosen. And it shall be no reproach to a nobleman to instruct his own children, or at the leastways to examine them, by the way of dalliance or solace, considering that the Emperor Octavius Augustus disdained not to read the works of Cicero and Virgil to his children and nephews. And why should not noblemen rather so do than teach their children how at dice and cards they may cunningly lose and consume their own treasure and substance? Moreover teaching representeth the authority of a prince; wherefore Dionysius, King of Sicily, when he was for tyranny expelled by his people, he came into Italy, and there in a common school taught grammar, wherewith when he was of his enemies embraided [1] and called a schoolmaster, he answered them that although Sicilians had exiled him, yet in despite of them all he reigned, noting thereby the authority that he had over his scholars. Also when it was of him demanded what availed him Plato or philosophy, wherein he had been studious, he answered that they caused him to sustain adversity patiently, and made his exile to be to him more facile and easy: which courage and wisdom considered of his people, they eftsoons restored him unto his realm and estate royal, where if he had procured against them hostility or wars, or had returned into Sicily with any violence, I suppose the people would have always resisted him and have kept him in perpetual exile: as the Romans did the proud King Tarquin whose son ravished Lucretia. But to return to my purpose, it shall be expedient that a nobleman's son, in his infancy, have with him continually only such as may accustom him by little and little to speak pure and elegant Latin. Semblably the nurses and other women about him, if it be possible, to do the same; or at the leastways, that they speak none English but that which is clean, polite, perfectly and articulately pronounced, omitting no letter or syllable, as foolish women often times do of a wantonness, whereby divers noblemen and gentlemen's children (as I do at this day know) have attained corrupt and foul pronunciation.

This industry used in forming little infants, who shall doubt

[1] Reproved.

but that they (not lacking natural wit) shall be apt to receive learning when they come to more years? And in this wise may they be instructed, without any violence or enforcing: using the more part of the time until they come to the age of seven years in such disport, as do appertain to children, wherein is no resemblance or similitude of vice.

VI. At what age a tutor should be provided, and what shall appertain to his office to do.

AFTER THAT a child is come to seven years of age, I hold it expedient that he be taken from the company of women, saving that he may have one year, or two at the most, an ancient and sad matron attending on him in his chamber, which shall not have any young woman in her company; for though there be no peril of offence in that tender and innocent age, yet in some children nature is more prone to vice than to virtue, and in the tender wits be sparks of voluptuosity which, nourished by any occasion or object, increase often times into so terrible a fire that therewith all virtue and reason is consumed. Wherefore, to eschew that danger, the most sure counsel is to withdraw him from all company of women, and to assign unto him a tutor, which should be an ancient and worshipful man, in whom is approved to be much gentleness, mixed with gravity, and, as nigh as can be, such one as the child by imitation following may grow to be excellent. And if he be also learned, he is the more commendable. Peleus, the father of Achilles, committed the governance of his son to Phenix, which was a stranger born; who, as well in speaking elegantly as in doing valiantly, was master to Achilles (as Homer saith). How much profited it to King Philip, father to the great Alexander, that he was delivered in hostage to the Thebans, where he was kept and brought up under the governance of Epaminondas, a noble and valiant captain; of whom he received such learning, as well in acts martial as in other liberal sciences, that he excelled all other kings that were before his time in Greece, and finally, as well by wisdom as prowess, subdued all that country. Semblably he ordained for his son Alexander a noble tutor called Leonidas, unto whom, for his wisdom, humanity, and learning, he committed the rule and pre-eminence over all the masters and servants of Alexander. In whom, notwithstanding, was such a familiar vice, which Alexander apprehending in childhood could never abandon: some suppose it to be fury and hastiness, other superfluous drinking of wine. Which of them it were, it is a good warning for gentlemen to be the more serious, insearching not only for the virtues, but also for the vices of them unto whose tuition and governance they will commit their children.

The office of a tutor is first to know the nature of his pupil, that is to say, whereto he is most inclined or disposed and in what thing he setteth his most delectation or appetite. If he be of nature courteous, piteous, and of a free and liberal heart, it is a principal token of grace (as it is by all Scripture determined). Then shall a wise tutor purposely commend those virtues, extolling also his pupil for having of them; and therewith he shall declare them to be of all men most fortunate, which shall happen to have such a master. And moreover shall declare to him what honour, what love, what commodity shall happen to him by these virtues. And, if any have been of disposition contrary, then to express the enormities of their vice, with as much detestation as may be. And if any danger have thereby ensued, misfortune, or punishment, to aggrieve it [1] in such wise, with so vehement words, as the child may abhor it, and fear the semblable adventure.

VII. In what wise music may be to a nobleman necessary, and what modesty ought to be therein.

THE DISCRETION of a tutor consisteth in temperance: that is to say, that he suffer not the child to be fatigued with continual study or learning, wherewith the delicate and tender wit may be dulled or oppressed; but that there may be therewith interlaced and mixed some pleasant learning and exercise, as playing on instruments of music, which moderately used and without diminution of honour, that is to say without wanton countenance and dissolute gesture, is not to be contemned. For the noble King and Prophet David, King of Israel (whom Almighty God said that He had chosen as a man according to His heart or desire), during his life, delighted in music; and with the sweet harmony that he made on his harp he constrained the evil spirit that vexed King Saul to forsake him, continuing the time that he harped.

---

[1] Show its seriousness.

The most noble and valiant princes of Greece oftentimes, to recreate their spirits and in augmenting their courage, embraced instruments musical. So did the valiant Achilles (as Homer saith), who after the sharp and vehement contention between him and Agamemnon for the taking away of his concubine: whereby he, being set in a fury, had slain Agamemnon, Emperor of the Greek army, had not Pallas, the goddess, withdrawn his hand; in which rage he, all inflamed, departed with his people to his own ships that lay at rode,[1] intending to have returned into his country; but after that he had taken to him his harp (whereon he had learned to play of Chiron the Centaur, which also had taught him feats of arms, with physic and surgery), and playing thereon had sung the gests and acts martial of the ancient prince of Greece, as Hercules, Perseus, Perithous, Theseus, and his cousin Jason, and divers other of semblable value and prowess, he was therewith assuaged of his fury and reduced into his first estate of reason: in such wise, that in redoubling his rage, and that thereby should not remain to him any note of reproach, he retaining his fierce and sturdy countenance, so tempered himself in the entertainment and answering the messengers that came to him from the residue of the Greeks, that they, reputing all that his fierce demeanour to be (as it were) a divine majesty, never embraided [2] him with any inordinate wrath or fury. And therefore the great King Alexander, when he had vanquished Ilion, where some time was set the most noble city of Troy, being demanded of one if he would see the harp of Paris Alexander, who ravished Helen, he thereat gently smiling answered that it was not the thing that he much desired, but that he had rather see the harp of Achilles, whereto he sang, not the illecebrous [3] delectations of Venus, but the valiant acts and noble affairs of excellent princes.

But in this commendation of music I would not be thought to allure noblemen to have so much delectation therein, that in playing and singing only they should put their whole study and felicity; as did the Emperor Nero, which all a long summer's day would sit in the theatre (an open place where all the people of Rome beheld solemn acts and plays) and in the presence of all the noblemen and senators would play on his harp and sing without ceasing. And if any man happened, by long sitting, to sleep, or by any other countenance to show himself to be weary, he was

---

[1] Harbour.   [2] Upbraided, reproached.
                    [3] Enticing.

suddenly bobbed on the face by the servants of Nero, for that purpose attending; or if any person were perceived to be absent, or were seen to laugh at the folly of the Emperor, he was forthwith accused, as it were, of misprision; whereby the Emperor found occasion to commit him to prison or to put him to tortures. O what misery was it to be subject to such a minstrel, in whose music was no melody, but anguish and dolour!

It were therefore better that no music were taught to a nobleman, than by the exact knowledge thereof he should have therein inordinate delight, and by that be elected to wantonness, abandoning gravity and the necessary cure and office in the public weal to him committed. King Philip, when he heard that his son Alexander did sing sweetly and properly, he rebuked him gently, saying, 'But, Alexander, be ye not ashamed that ye can sing so well and cunningly?' whereby he meant that the open profession of that craft was but of a base estimation. And that it sufficed a nobleman, having therein knowledge, either to use it secretly, for the refreshing of his wit, when he hath time of solace; or else, only hearing the contention of noble musicians, to give judgment in the excellency of their cunning. These be the causes whereunto having regard, music is not only tolerable but also commendable. For, as Aristotle saith, music in the old time was numbered among sciences, for as much as nature seeketh not only how to be in business well occupied, but also how in quietness to be commendably disposed.

And if the child be of a perfect inclination and towardness to virtue, and very aptly disposed to this science, and ripely doth understand the reason and concordance of tunes, the tutor's office shall be to persuade him to have principally in remembrance his estate, which maketh him exempt from the liberty of using this science in every time and place: that is to say, that it only serveth for recreation after tedious or laborious affairs, and to show him that a gentleman, playing or singing in a common audience, appaireth [1] his estimation: the people forgetting reverence when they behold him in the similitude of a common servant or minstrel. Yet notwithstanding, he shall commend the perfect understanding of music, declaring how necessary it is for the better attaining the knowledge of a public weal; which, as I before have said, is made of an order of estates and degrees, and

---

[1] Impairs.

by reason thereof containeth in it a perfect harmony; which he shall afterward more perfectly understand, when he shall happen to read the books of Plato and Aristotle of public weals, wherein be written divers examples of music and geometry. In this form may a wise and circumspect tutor adapt the pleasant science of music to a necessary and laudable purpose.

VIII. *That it is commendable in a gentleman to paint and carve exactly, if nature thereto doth induce him.*

IF THE child be of nature inclined (as many have been) to paint with a pen, or to form images in stone or tree, he should not be therefrom withdrawn, or nature be rebuked, which is to him benevolent; but putting one to him, which is in that craft wherein he delighteth most excellent, in vacant times from other more serious learning, he should be in the most pure wise instructed in painting or carving.

And now, perchance, some envious reader will hereof apprehend occasion to scorn me, saying that I have will hied me to make of a nobleman a mason or painter. And yet, if either ambition or voluptuous idleness would have suffered that reader to have seen histories, he should have founden excellent princes as well in painting as in carving equal to noble artificers; such were Claudius, Titus, the son of Vespasian, Hadrian, both Antonines, and divers other emperors and noble princes; whose works of long time remained in Rome and other cities, in such places where all men might behold them, as monuments of their excellent wits and virtuous occupation in eschewing of idleness.

And not without a necessary cause princes were in their childhood so instructed, for it served them afterwards for devising of engines for the war, or for making them better that be already devised. For, as Vitruvius (which writeth of building to the Emperor Augustus) saith, all torments of war, which we call ordnance, were first invented by kings or governors of hosts, or if they were devised by other, they were by them made much better. Also by the feat of portraiture or painting a captain may describe the country of his adversary, whereby he shall eschew the dangerous passages with his host or navy; also perceive the places of advantage, the form of embattling of his enemies, the situation of his camp for his most surety, the strength or weakness of the town or fortress which he intendeth to assault. And that which is most specially to be considered, in visiting his own dominions, he shall set them out in figure, in such wise that at his eye shall appear to him where he shall employ his study and treasure, as well for the safeguard of his country, as for the commodity and honour thereof, having at all times in his sight the surety and feebleness, advancement and hindrance, of the same. And what pleasure and also utility is it to a man which intendeth to edify himself to express the figure of the work that he purposeth, according as he hath conceived it in his own fantasy? Wherein, by often amending and correcting, he finally shall so perfect the work unto his purpose that there shall neither ensue any repentance, nor in the employment of his money he shall be by other deceived. Moreover the feat of portraiture shall be an allective[1] to every other study or exercise. For the wit thereto disposed shall always covet congruent matter, wherein it may be occupied. And when he happeneth to read or hear any fable or history, forthwith he apprehendeth it more desirously, and retaineth it better, than any other that lacketh the said feat; by reason that he hath found matter apt to his fantasy. Finally, every thing that portraiture may comprehend will be to him delectable to read or hear. And where the lively spirit, and that which is called the grace of the thing, is perfectly expressed, that thing more persuadeth and stirreth the beholder, and sooner instructeth him, than the declaration in writing or speaking doth the reader or hearer. Experience we have thereof in learning of geometry, astronomy, and cosmography, called in English the description of the world. In which studies I dare affirm a man shall more profit in one week by figures and charts well and perfectly made, than he shall by the only reading or hearing the rules of that science by the space of half a year at the least; wherefore the late writers deserve no small commendation which added to the authors of those sciences apt and proper figures.

And he that is perfectly instructed in portraiture and happeneth to read any noble and excellent history, whereby his courage is inflamed to the imitation of virtue, he forthwith taketh his pen or pencil, and with a grave and substantial study, gathering to him all the parts of imagination, endeavoureth himself to express

---

[1] Enticement.

lively and (as I might say) actually in portraiture, not only the fact or affair, but also the sundry affections of every personage in the history recited, which might in any wise appear or be perceived in their visage, countenance, or gesture; with like diligence as Lysippus made in metal King Alexander, fighting and struggling with a terrible lion of incomprehensible magnitude and fierceness, whom after long and difficult battle with wonderful strength and clean might at the last he overthrew and vanquished; wherein he so expressed the similitude of Alexander and of his lords standing about him that they all seemed to live. Among whom the prowess of Alexander appeared, excelling all others; the residue of his lords after the value and estimation of their courage, every man set out in such forwardness, as they then seemed more prompt to the helping of their master, that is to say, one less afeared than another. Phidias the Athenian, whom all writers do commend, made of ivory the simulacrum or image of Jupiter, honoured by the Gentiles on the high hills of Olympus; which was done so excellently that Pandenus, a cunning painter, thereat admiringly required the draftsman to show him where he had the example or pattern of so noble a work. Then Phidias answered that he had taken it out of three verses of Homer the poet, the sentence whereof ensueth, as well as my poor wit can express it in English:

> Then Jupiter the father of them all
> Thereto assented with his browés black,
> Shaking his hair, and therewith did let fall
> A countenance that made all heaven to quake,

where it is to be noted that immediately before Thetis the mother of Achilles desired Jupiter importunately to incline his favour to the part of the Trojans.

Now (as I have before said) I intend not, by these examples, to make of a prince or nobleman's son a common painter or carver which shall present himself openly stained or imbrued [1] with sundry colours, or powdered with the dust of stones that he cutteth, or perfumed with tedious savours of the metals by him wrought.

But verily mine intent and meaning is only that a noble child, by his own natural disposition, and not by coercion, may be induced to receive perfect instruction in these sciences. But

---

[1] Dirtied.

although for purposes before expressed they shall be necessary, yet shall they not be by him exercised but as a secret pastime or recreation of the wits late occupied in serious studies, like as did the noble princes before named. Although they, once being attained, be never much exercised, after that the time cometh concerning business of greater importance. Nevertheless the exquisite knowledge and understanding that he hath in these sciences hath impressed in his ears and eyes an exact and perfect judgment, as well in discerning the excellency of them which either in music or in statuary or painters' craft professeth any cunning, as also adapting their said knowledge to the adminicula- tion [1] of other serious studies and business, as I have before re- hearsed: which I doubt not shall be well approved by them that either have read and understand old authors, or advisedly will examine my considerations.

The sweet writer Lactantius saith in his first book to the Emperor Constantine against the Gentiles: 'Of cunning cometh virtue, and of virtue perfect felicity is only engendered.'

And for that cause the Gentiles supposed those princes which in virtue and honour surmounted other men to be gods. And the Romans in like wise did consecrate their emperors which excelled in virtuous example, in preserving or augmenting the public weal, and ampliating [2] of the empire, calling them *Divi*, which word representeth a signification of divinity, they thinking that it was exceeding man's nature to be both in fortune and goodness of such perfection.

IX. *What exact diligence should be in choosing masters.*

AFTER THAT the child hath been pleasantly trained and induced to know the parts of speech, and can separate one of them from another in his own language, it shall then be time that his tutor or governor do make diligent search for such a master as is excellently learned both in Greek and Latin, and therewithal is of sober and virtuous disposition, specially chaste of living, and of much affability and patience: lest by any unclean example the tender mind of the child may be infected, hard afterwards to be recovered. For the natures of children be not so much or soon

[1] Support.   [2] Enlarging.

advanced by things well done or spoken, as they be hindered and corrupted by that which in acts or words is wantonly expressed. Also by a cruel and irous [1] master the wits of children be dulled, and that thing for the which children be often times beaten is to them ever after fastidious; whereof we need no better author for witness than daily experience. Wherefore the most necessary things to be observed by a master in his disciples or scholars (as Licon the noble grammarian said) is shamefacedness and praise. By shamefacedness, as it were with a bridle, they rule as well their deeds as their appetites. And desire of praise addeth to a sharp spur to their disposition toward learning and virtue. According thereunto Quintilian, instructing an orator, desireth such a child to be given unto him whom commendation fervently stirreth, glory provoketh, and being vanquished weepeth. That child (saith he) is to be fed with ambition, him a little chiding sore biteth, in him no part of sloth is to be feared. And if nature disposeth not the child's wit to receive learning, but rather otherwise, it is to be applied with more diligence, and also policy, as choosing some book whereof the argument or matter approacheth most nigh to the child's inclination or fantasy, so that it be not extremely vicious, and therewith by little and little, as it were with a pleasant sauce, provoke him to have good appetite to study. And surely that child, whatsoever he be, is well blessed and fortunate that findeth a good instructor or master; which was considered by noble King Philip, father to the great King Alexander, who immediately after that his son was born wrote a letter to Aristotle, the prince of philosophers, the tenor whereof ensueth.

'Aristotle, we greet you well. Letting you wit [2] that we have a son born, for the which we give due thanks unto God, not for that he is born only, but also for as much as it happeneth him to be born, you living. Trusting that it shall happen that he, by you taught and instructed, shall be hereafter worthy to be named our son, and to enjoy the honour and substance that we now have provided. Thus fare ye well.'

The same Alexander was wont to say openly, that he ought to give as great thanks to Aristotle his master as to King Philip his father, for of him he took the occasion to live, of the other he received the reason and way to live well. And what manner a prince Alexander was made by the doctrine of Aristotle, it shall

---

[1] Wrathful.   [2] Know.

appear in divers places of this book, where his example to
princes shall be declared. The incomparable benefit of masters
have been well remembered of divers princes. Insomuch as
Marcus Antoninus, which among the emperors was commended
for his virtue and sapience, had his master Proculus (who taught
him grammar) so much in favour that he advanced him to be pro-
consul, which was one of the highest dignities among the Romans.

Alexander the Emperor caused his master Julius Fronto to be
consul, which was the highest office and in estate next the
emperor, and also obtained of the Senate that the statue or image
of Fronto was set up among the noble princes.

What caused Trajan to be so good a prince, insomuch that of
late days when an emperor received his crown at Rome, the
people with a common cry desired of God that he might be as
good as was Trajan, but that he happened to have Plutarch, the
noble philosopher, to be his instructor? I agree me that some be
good of natural inclination to goodness: but where good instruction and example is thereto added, the natural goodness must
therewith needs be amended and be more excellent.

X. *What order should be in learning and which authors should be*
first read.

NOW LET us return to the order of learning apt for a gentleman.
Wherein I am of the opinion of Quintilian that I would have him
learn Greek and Latin authors both at one time; or else to begin
with Greek, forasmuch as that it is hardest to come by, by reason
of the diversity of tongues, which be five in number, and all must
be known, or else scarcely any poet can be well understood. And
if a child do begin therein at seven years of age, he may continually learn Greek authors three years, and in the meantime use
the Latin tongue as a familiar language; which in a nobleman's
son may well come to pass, having none other persons to serve
him or keeping him company but such as can speak Latin
elegantly. And what doubt is there but so may he as soon speak
good Latin as he may do pure French, which now is brought into
as many rules and figures and as long a grammar as is Latin or
Greek. I will not contend who among them that do write gram-
mars of Greek (which now almost be innumerable) is the best,
but that I refer to the discretion of a wise master. Alway I would

advise him not to detain the child too long in that tedious labour, either in the Greek or Latin grammar. For a gentle wit is therewith soon fatigued.

Grammar being but an introduction to the understanding of authors, if it be made too long or exquisite to the learner, it in a manner mortifieth his courage. And by that time he cometh to the most sweet and pleasant reading of old authors, the sparks of fervent desire of learning is extinct with the burden of grammar, like as a little fire is soon quenched with a great heap of small sticks, so that it can never come to the principal logs where it should long burn in a great pleasant fire.

Now to follow my purpose: after a few and quick rules of grammar, immediately, or interlacing it therewith, would be read to the child Aesop's fables in Greek, in which argument children much do delight. And surely it is a much pleasant lesson and also profitable, as well for that it is elegant and brief (and notwithstanding it hath much variety in words, and therewith much helpeth to the understanding of Greek) as also in those fables is included much moral and politic wisdom. Wherefore, in the teaching of them, the master diligently must gather together those fables which may be most accommodate to the advancement of some virtue whereto he perceiveth the child inclined, or to the rebuke of some vice whereto he findeth his nature disposed. And therein the master ought to exercise his wit, as well to make the child plainly to understand the fable as also declaring the signification thereof compendiously and to the purpose, foreseen alway that as well this lesson as all other authors which the child shall learn, either Greek or Latin, verse or prose, be perfectly had without the book: whereby he shall not only attain plenty of the tongues called *Copia*,[1] but also increase and nourish remembrance wonderfully.

The next lesson would be some quick and merry dialogues elect out of Lucian, which be without ribaldry or too much scorning, for either of them is exactly to be eschewed, specially for a nobleman, the one annoying the soul, the other his estimation concerning his gravity. The comedies of Aristophanes may be in the place of Lucian, and by reason that they be in metre they be the sooner learned by heart. I dare make none other comparison between them for offending the friends of them both, but this

[1] Abundance. Elyot alludes to Erasmus's *De copia verborum*; he means that the child will learn the elegance of variety in expression.

much dare I say, that it were better that a child should never read any part of Lucian than all Lucian.

I could rehearse divers other poets which for matter and eloquence be very necessary, but I fear me to be too long from noble Homer, from whom as from a fountain proceeded all eloquence and learning. For in his books be contained and most perfectly expressed, not only the documents martial and discipline of arms, but also incomparable wisdom, and instructions for politic governance of people, with the worthy commendation and laud of noble princes; wherewith the readers shall be so all inflamed that they most fervently shall desire and covet, by the imitation of their virtues, to acquire semblable glory. For the which occasion, Aristotle, most sharpest witted and excellent learned philosopher, as soon as he had received Alexander from King Philip his father, he before any other thing taught him the most noble works of Homer; wherein Alexander found such sweetness and fruit that ever after he had Homer not only with him in all his journeys but also laid him under his pillow when he went to rest, and often times would purposely wake some hours of the night to take as it were his pastime with that most noble poet.

For by the reading of his work called *Iliad*, where the assembly of the most noble Greeks against Troy is recited with their affairs, he gathered courage and strength against his enemies, wisdom, and eloquence for consultation and persuasions to his people and army. And by the other work called *Odyssey*, which recounteth the sundry adventures of the wise Ulysses, he by the example of Ulysses apprehended many noble virtues, and also learned to escape the fraud and deceitful imaginations of sundry and subtle crafty wits. Also there shall he learn to ensearch and perceive the manners and conditions of them that be his familiars, sifting out (as I might say) the best from the worst, whereby he may surely commit his affairs, and trust to every person after his virtues. Therefore I now conclude that there is no lesson for a young gentleman to be compared with Homer, if he be plainly and substantially expounded and declared by the master.

Notwithstanding, forasmuch as the said works be very long, and do require therefore a great time to be all learned and conned, some Latin author would be therewith mixed, and specially Virgil; which, in his work called *Aeneid*, is most like to Homer and almost the same Homer in Latin. Also, by the joining

together of those authors, the one shall be the better understood
by the other. And verily (as I before said) none one author
serveth to so divers wits as doth Virgil. For there is not that
affect or desire whereto any child's fantasy is disposed, but in
some of Virgil's works may be found matter thereto apt and
propise.[1]

For what thing can be more familiar than his *Bucolics*? Nor no
work so nigh approacheth to the common dalliance and manners
of children, and the pretty controversies of the simple shepherds
therein contained wonderfully rejoiceth the child that heareth it
well declared, as I know by mine own experience. In his *Georgics*,
Lord, what pleasant variety there is; the divers grains, herbs, and
flowers that be there described, that, reading therein, it seemeth
to a man to be in a delectable garden or paradise. What ploughman knoweth so much of husbandry as there is expressed? Who,
delighting in good horses, shall not be thereto more inflamed,
reading there of the breeding, choosing, and keeping of them?
In the declaration whereof Virgil leaveth far behind him all
breeders, hackneymen, and skosers.[2]

Is there any astronomer that more exactly setteth out the order
and course of the celestial bodies, or that more truly doth divine
in his prognostications of the times of the year, in their qualities,
with the future estate of all things provided by husbandry, than
Virgil doth recite in that work?

If the child have a delight in hunting, what pleasure shall he
take of the fable of Aristeus; semblably in the hunting of Dido
and Aeneas, which is described most elegantly in his book of
Aeneid. If he have pleasure in wrestling, running, or other like
exercise, where shall he see any more pleasant esbatements [3] than
that which was done by Eurealus and other Trojans, which
accompanied Aeneas? If he take solace in hearing minstrels,
what minstrel may be compared to Jopas, which sang before Dido
and Aeneas, or to blind Demodocus, that played and sang most
sweetly at the dinner that the King Alcinous made to Ulysses,
whose ditties and melody excelled as far the songs of our minstrels
as Homer and Virgil excel all other poets?

If he be more desirous (as the most part of children be) to hear
things marvellous and exquisite, which hath in it a visage of some
things incredible, whereat shall he more wonder than when he

---

[1] Suitable.   [2] Horse dealers.   [3] Amusements.

shall behold Aeneas follow Sibyl into Hell? What shall he more
dread than the terrible visages of Cerberus, Gorgon, Megera, and
other furies and monsters? How shall he abhor tyranny, fraud,
and avarice, when he doth see the pains of Duke Theseus,
Prometheus, Sisyphus, and such other tormented for their
dissolute and vicious living? How glad soon after shall he be
when he shall behold in the pleasant fields of Elysium the souls of
noble princes and captains which, for their virtue and labours in
advancing the public weals of their countries, do live eternally in
pleasure inexplicable? And in the last books of *Aeneid* shall he
find matter to minister to him audacity, valiant courage, and
policy, to take and sustain noble enterprises, if any shall be
needful for the assailing of his enemies.

Finally (as I have said) this noble Virgil, like to a good nurse,
giveth to a child, if he will take it, everything apt for his wit and
capacity; wherefore he is in the order of learning to be preferred
before any other author Latin. I would set next unto him two
books of Ovid, the one called *Metamorphosis*, which is as much
to say as changing of men into other figure or form; the other is
entitled *De fastis*, where the ceremonies of the Gentiles, and
specially the Romans, be expressed: both right necessary for the
understanding of other poets. But because there is little other
learning in them concerning either virtuous manners or policy, I
suppose it were better that as fables and ceremonies happen to
come in a lesson, it were declared abundantly by the master than
that in the said two books a long time should be spent and almost
lost: which might be better employed on such authors that do
minister both eloquence, civil policy, and exhortation to virtue.
Wherefore in his place let us bring in Horace, in whom is contained much variety of learning and quickness of sentence.

This poet may be interlaced with the lesson of *Odyssey* of
Homer, wherein is declared the wonderful prudence and fortitude
of Ulysses in his passage from Troy. And if the child were
induced to make verses by the imitation of Virgil and Homer, it
should minister to him much delectation and courage to study;
ne the making of verses is not discommended in a nobleman,
since the noble Augustus and almost all the old emperors made
books in verses.

The two noble poets Silius and Lucan be very expedient to be
learned; for the one setteth out the emulation in qualities and
prowess of two noble and valiant captains, one enemy to the

other, that is to say, Silius writeth of Scipio the Roman, and
Hannibal Duke of Carthage; Lucan declareth a semblable matter,
but much more lamentable: forasmuch as the wars were civil,
and, as it were, in the bowels of the Romans, that is to say, under
the standards of Julius Caesar and Pompey.

Hesiod, in Greek, is more brief than Virgil, where he writeth of
husbandry, and doth not rise so high in philosophy, but is fuller
of fables: and therefore is more illecebrous.[1]

And here I conclude to speak any more of poets, necessary for
the childhood of a gentleman; for as much as these I doubt not
will suffice until he pass the age of thirteen years. In which time
childhood declineth, and reason waxeth ripe, and deprehendeth [2]
things with a more constant judgment. Here I would should be
remembered that I require not that all these works should be
thoroughly read of a child in this time, which were almost impossible. But I only desire that they have, in every of the said
books, so much instruction that they may take thereby some
profit.

Then the child's courage, inflamed by the frequent reading of
noble poets, daily more and more desireth to have experience in
those things that they so vehemently do commend in them that
they write of.

Leonidas, the noble King of Sparta, being once demanded of
what estimation in poetry Tirtaeus (as he supposed) was, it is
written that he answering said that for stirring the minds of
young men he was excellent, forasmuch as they, being moved
with his verses, do run into the battle, regarding no peril, as men
all inflamed in martial courage.

And when a man is come to mature years, and that reason in
him is confirmed with serious learning and long experience, then
shall he, in reading tragedies, execrate and abhor the intolerable
life of tyrants, and shall contemn the folly and dotage expressed
by poets lascivious.

Here will I leave to speak of the first part of a nobleman's
study; and now will I write of the second part, which is more
serious, and containeth in it sundry manners of learning.

[1] Alluring.   [2] Understands.

*XI. The most commodious and necessary studies succeeding
ordinately the lesson of poets.*

AFTER THAT fourteen years be passed of a child's age, his master
if he can, or some other studiously exercised in the art of an
orator, shall first read to him somewhat of that part of logic that
is called *Topica*, either of Cicero, or else of that noble clerk of
Almaine,[1] which late flowered, called Agricola: whose work
prepareth invention, telling the places from whence an argument
for the proof of any matter may be taken with little study; and
that lesson, with much and diligent learning, having mixed therewith none other exercise, will in the space of half a year be
perfectly conned. Immediately after that, the art of rhetoric
would be semblably taught, either in Greek, out of Hermogines,
or of Quintilian in Latin, beginning at the third book, and
instructing diligently the child in that part of rhetoric principally
which concerneth persuasion, forasmuch as it is most apt for
consultations. There can be no shorter instruction of rhetoric
than the treatise that Tully[2] wrote into his son, which book is
named the partition of rhetoric. And in good faith, to speak
boldly that I think, for him that needeth not or doth not desire to
be an exquisite orator, the little book made by the famous
Erasmus (whom all gentle wits are bound to thank and support), which he calleth *Copiam Verborum et Rerum*, that is to
say, plenty of words and matters, shall be sufficient.

Isocrates, concerning the lesson of orators, is everywhere
wonderful profitable, having almost as many wise sentences as he
hath words, and with that is so sweet and delectable to read that,
after him, almost all other seem unsavoury and tedious; and in
persuading as well a prince as a private person to virtue, in two
very little and compendious works, whereof he made the one to
King Nicocles, the other to his friend Demonicus, would be
perfectly conned and had in continual memory.

Demosthenes and Tully by the consent of all learned men have
pre-eminence and sovereignty over all orators, the one reigning in
wonderful eloquence in the public weal of the Romans, who had
the empire and dominion of all the world, the other, of no less
estimation, in the city of Athens, which of long time was
accounted the mother of Sapience, and the palace of Muses and

---

[1] Germany.   [2] Cicero.

all liberal sciences. Of which two orators may be attained not only eloquence, excellent and perfect, but also precepts of wisdom, and gentle manners, with most commodious examples of all noble virtues and policy. Wherefore the master in reading them must well observe and express the parts and colours of rhetoric in them contained, according to the precepts of that art before learned.

The utility that a nobleman shall have by reading these orators is that when he shall hap to reason in counsel, or shall speak in a great audience or to strange ambassadors of great princes, he shall not be constrained to speak words sudden and disordered, but shall bestow them aptly and in their places. Wherefore the most noble Emperor Octavius is highly commended, for that he never spake in the Senate, or to the people of Rome, but in an oration prepared and purposely made.

Also to prepare the child to understanding of histories, which, being replenished with the names of countries and towns unknown to the reader, do make the history tedious or else the less pleasant, so if they be in any wise known, it increaseth an inexplicable delectation. It shall be therefore, and also for refreshing the wit, a convenient lesson to behold the old tables of Ptolemy, wherein all the world is painted, having first some introduction into the sphere, whereof now of late be made very good treatises, and more plain and easy to learn than was wont to be.

Albeit there is none so good learning as the demonstration of cosmography of material figures and instruments, having a good instructor. And surely this lesson is both pleasant and necessary. For what pleasure is it in one hour to behold those realms, cities, seas, rivers, and mountains, that unneth [1] in an old man's life cannot be journeyed and pursued; what incredible delight is taken in beholding the diversities of people, beasts, fowls, fishes, trees, fruits, and herbs: to know the sundry manners and conditions of people, and the variety of their natures, and that in a warm study or parlour, without peril of the sea or danger of long and painful journeys: I cannot tell what more pleasure should happen to a gentle wit, than to behold in his own house everything that within all the world is contained. The commodity thereof knew the great King Alexander, as some writers do remember. For he caused the countries whereunto he purposed any enterprise diligently and

---

[1] Scarcely.

cunningly to be described and painted, that beholding the picture, he might perceive which places were most dangerous, and where he and his host might have most easy and covenable[1] passage.

Semblable did the Romans in the rebellion of France and the insurrection of their confederates, setting up a table openly, wherein Italy was painted, to the intent that the people looking in it should reason and consult in which places it were best to resist or invade their enemies.

I omit, for length of the matter, to write of Cyrus, the great King of Persia, Crassus the Roman, and divers other valiant and expert captains, which have lost themselves and all their army by ignorance of this doctrine.

Wherefore it may not be of any wise man denied but that cosmography is to all noblemen, not only pleasant, but profitable also, and wonderful necessary.

In the part of cosmography wherewith history is mingled Strabo reigneth, which took his argument of the divine poet Homer. Also Strabo himself (as he saith) laboured a great part of Africa and Egypt, where undoubtedly be many things to be marvelled at. Solinus writeth almost in like form, and is more brief, and hath much more variety of things and matters, and is therefore marvellous delectable; yet Mela is much shorter, and his style (by reason that it is of a more antiquity) is also more clean and facile. Wherefore he, or Dionysius, shall be sufficient.

Cosmography being substantially perceived, it is then time to induce a child to the reading of histories: but first to set him in a fervent courage, the master in the most pleasant and elegant wise expressing what incomparable delectation, utility, and commodity shall happen to emperors, kings, princes, and all other gentlemen by reading of histories, showing to him that Demetrius Phalareus, a man of excellent wisdom and learning, and which in Athens had been long exercised in the public weal, exhorted Ptolemy, King of Egypt, chiefly above all other studies to haunt and embrace histories, and such other books wherein were contained precepts made to kings and princes: saying that in them he should read those things which no man durst report unto his person. Also Cicero, father of the Latin eloquence, calleth an history the witness of times, mistress of life, the life of remembrance, of truth the light, and messenger of antiquity.

[1] Convenient.

Moreover, the sweet Isocrates exhorteth the King Nicocles, whom he instructeth, to leave behind him statues and images that shall represent rather the figure and similitude of his mind than the features of his body, signifying thereby the remembrance of his acts written in histories.

By semblable advertisements shall a noble heart be trained to delight in histories. And then, according to the counsel of Quintilian, it is best that he begin with Titus Livius, not only for his elegancy of writing, which floweth in him like a fountain of sweet milk, but also forasmuch as by reading that author he may know how the most noble city of Rome, of a small and poor beginning, by prowess and virtue little and little came to the empire and dominion of all the world.

Also in that city he may behold the form of a public weal: which, if the insolency and pride of Tarquin had not excluded kings out of the city, it had been the most noble and perfect of all other.

Xenophon, being both a philosopher and an excellent captain, so invented and ordered his work named *Paedia Cyri*, which may be interpreted *The Childhood* or *Discipline of Cyrus*, that he leaveth to the readers thereof an incomparable sweetness and example of living, specially for the conducting and well ordering of hosts or armies. And therefore the noble Scipio, who was called Africanus, as well in peace as in war was never seen without this book of Xenophon.

With him may be joined Quintus Curtius, who writeth the life of King Alexander elegantly and sweetly. In whom may be found the figure of an excellent prince, as he that incomparably excelled all other kings and emperors in wisdom, hardiness, strength, policy, agility, valiant courage, nobility, liberality, and courtesy, wherein he was a spectacle or mark for all princes to look on. Contrariwise when he was once vanquished with volupty [1] and pride his tyranny and beastly cruelty abhorreth all readers. The comparison of the virtues of these two noble princes, equally described by two excellent writers, well expressed, shall provoke a gentle courage to contend to follow their virtues.

Julius Caesar and Salust for their compendious writing, to the understanding whereof is required an exact and perfect judgment, and also for the exquisite order of battle and continuing of the

[1] Voluptuousness.

history without any variety, whereby the pain of study should be alleviate: they two would be reserved until he that shall read them shall see some experience in semblable matters. And then shall he find in them such pleasure and commodity as therewith a noble and gentle heart ought to be satisfied. For in them both it shall seem to a man that he is present and heareth the counsels and exhortations of captains, which be called *Conciones*, and that he seeth the order of hosts when they be embattled, the fierce assaults and encounterings of both armies, the furious rage of that monster called war. And he shall wene [1] that he heareth the terrible dints of sundry weapons and ordnance of battle, the conduct and policies of wise and expert captains, specially in the commentaries of Julius Caesar, which he made of his exploiture in France and Britain and other countries now reckoned among the provinces of Germany; which book is studiously to be read of the princes of this realm of England and their counsellors, considering that thereof may be taken necessary instructions concerning the wars against Irishmen or Scots, who be of the same rudeness and wild disposition that the Swiss and Britons were in the time of Caesar. Semblable utility shall be found in the history of Titus Livius, in his third Decades, where he writeth of the battles that the Romans had with Hannibal and the Carthaginians.

Also there be divers orations, as well in all the books of the said authors as in the history of Cornelius Tacitus, which be very delectable, and for counsels very expedient to be had in memory. And in good faith I have often thought that the consultations and orations written by Tacitus do import a majesty with a compendious eloquence therein contained.

In the learning of these authors a young gentleman shall be taught to note and mark, not only the order and elegancy in declaration of the history, but also the occasion of the wars, the counsels and preparations on either part, the estimation of the captains, the manner and form of their governance, the continuance of the battle, the fortune and success of the whole affairs. Semblably out of the wars in other daily affairs, the estate of the public weal, if it be prosperous or in decay, what is the very occasion of the one or of the other, the form and manner of the governance thereof, the good and evil qualities of them that be rulers, the commodities and good sequel of virtue, the discommodities and evil conclusion of vicious license.

[1] Think.

Surely if a nobleman do thus seriously and diligently read histories, I dare affirm there is no study or science for him of equal commodity and pleasure, having regard to every time and age.

By the time that the child do come to seventeen years of age, to the intent his courage be bridled with reason, it were needful to read unto him some works of philosophy; specially that part that may inform him unto virtuous manners, which part of philosophy is called moral. Wherefore there would be read to him, for an introduction, two the first books of the work of Aristotle called *Ethicae*, wherein is contained the definitions and proper significations of every virtue; and that to be learned in Greek; for the translations that we yet have be but a rude and gross shadow of the eloquence and wisdom of Aristotle. Forthwith would follow the work of Cicero, called in Latin *De officiis*, whereunto yet is no proper English word to be given; but to provide for it some manner of exposition, it may be said in this form: 'Of the duties and manners appertaining to men.' But above all other, the works of Plato would be most studiously read when the judgment of a man is come to perfection, and by the other studies is instructed in the form of speaking that philosophers used. Lord God, what incomparable sweetness of words and matter shall he find in the said works of Plato and Cicero; wherein is joined gravity with delectation, excellent wisdom with divine eloquence, absolute virtue with pleasure incredible, and every place is so enforced [1] with profitable counsel joined with honesty, that those three books be almost sufficient to make a perfect and excellent governor. The proverbs of Solomon with the books of Ecclesiastes and Ecclesiasticus be very good lessons. All the historical parts of the Bible be right necessary for to be read of a nobleman, after that he is mature in years. And the residue (with the New Testament) is to be reverently touched, as a celestial jewel or relic, having the chief interpreter of those books true and constant faith, and dreadfully to set hands thereon, remembering that Uzza, for putting his hand to the holy shrine that was called *Archa federis*, when it was brought by King David from the city of Gaba, though it were wavering and in danger to fall, yet was he stricken of God, and fell dead immediately. It would not be forgotten that the little book of the most excellent doctor Erasmus

---

[1] Stuffed, filled.

Roterodamus (which he wrote to Charles, now being Emperor and then Prince of Castile), which book is entitled *The Institution of a Christian Prince*, would be as familiar alway with gentlemen at all times and in every age as was Homer with the great King Alexander, or Xenophon with Scipio; for as all men may judge that have read that work of Erasmus, that there was never book written in Latin that in so little a portion contained of sentence, eloquence, and virtuous exhortation, a more compendious abundance. And here I make an end of the learning and study whereby noblemen may attain to be worthy to have authority in a public weal. Alway I shall exhort tutors and governors of noble children, that they suffer them not to use ingurgitations of meat or drink, nor to sleep much, that is to say, above eight hours at the most. For undoubtedly both repletion and superfluous sleep be capital enemies to study, as they be semblably to health of body and soul. Aulus Gellius saith that children, if they use of meat and sleep over much, be made therewith dull to learn, and we see that thereof slowness is taken, and the children's personages do wax uncomely, and less grow in stature. Galen will not permit that pure wine, without allay of water, should in any wise be given to children, forasmuch as it humecteth [1] the body, or maketh it moister and hotter than is convenient, also it filleth the head with fume, in them specially, which be like as children of hot and moist temperature. These be well nigh the words of the noble Galen.

XII. Why gentlemen in this present time be not equal in doctrine to the ancient noblemen.

NOW WILL I somewhat declare of the chief causes why, in our time, noblemen be not as excellent in learning as they were in old time among the Romans and Greeks. Surely, as I have diligently marked in daily experience, the principal causes be these: the pride, avarice, the negligence of parents, and the lack or fewness of sufficient masters or teachers.

As I said, pride is the first cause of this inconvenience. For of those persons be some which without shame dare affirm that to a great gentleman it is a notable reproach to be well learned and to

[1] Moistens.

be called a great clerk: which name they account to be of so base estimation that they never have it in their mouths but when they speak anything in derision, which perchance they would not do if they had once leisure to read our own chronicle of England, where they shall find that King Henry the First, son of William Conqueror and one of the most noble princes that ever reigned in this realm, was openly called Henry beau clerk, which is in English, fair clerk, and is yet at this day so named. And whether that name be to his honour or to his reproach, let them judge that do read and compare his life with his two brethren, William called Rouse,[1] and Robert le Courtoise, they both not having semblable learning with the said Henry; the one for his dissolute living and tyranny being hated of all his nobles and people, finally was suddenly slain by the shot of an arrow, as he was hunting in a forest,[2] which to make larger and to give his deer more liberty, he did cause the houses of fifty-two parishes to be pulled down, the people to be expelled, and all being desolate to be turned into desert, and made only pasture for beasts savage; which he would never have done if he had as much delighted in good learning as did his brother.

The other brother, Robert le Courtoise, being Duke of Normandy and the eldest son of William Conqueror, albeit that he was a man of much prowess, and right expert in martial affairs, wherefore he was elect before Godfrey of Boulogne to have been king of Jerusalem; yet notwithstanding when he invaded this realm with sundry puissant armies, also divers noble men aiding him, yet his noble brother Henry beau clerk, more by wisdom than power, also by learning, adding policy to virtue and courage, often times vanquished him, and did put him to flight. And after sundry victories finally took him and kept him in prison, having none other means to keep his realm in tranquillity.

It was for no rebuke, but for an excellent honour, that the Emperor Antoninus was surnamed philosopher, for by his most noble example of living and industry incomparable he during all the time of his reign kept the public weal of the Romans in such a perfect state that by his acts he confirmed the saying of Plato, that blessed is that public weal wherein either philosophers do reign, or else kings be in philosophy studious.

These persons that so much contemn learning, that they would

---

[1] William Rufus.   [2] The New Forest.

that gentlemen's children should have no part or very little thereof, but rather should spend their youth alway (I say not only in hunting and hawking, which moderately used, as solaces ought to be, I intend not to dispraise) but in those idle pastimes, which, for the vice that is therein, the commandment of the prince and the universal consent of the people expressed in statutes and laws do prohibit, I mean, playing at dice, and other games named unlawful. These persons, I say, I would should remember, or else now learn, if they never else heard it, that the noble Philip, King of Macedonia, who subdued all Greece, above all the good fortunes that ever he had, most rejoiced that his son Alexander was born in the time that Aristotle the philosopher flourished, by whose instruction he might attain to most excellent learning.

Also the same Alexander often times said that he was equally as much bound to Aristotle as to his father King Philip, for of his father he received life, but of Aristotle he received the way to live nobly.

Who dispraiseth Epaminondas, the most valiant captain of Thebes, for that he was excellently learned and a great philosopher? Who ever discommended Julius Caesar for that he was a noble orator, and, next to Tully, in the eloquence of the Latin tongue excelled all other? Who ever reproved the Emperor Hadrian for that he was so exquisitely learned, not only in Greek and Latin, but also in all sciences liberal, that openly at Athens, in the universal assembly of the greatest clerks of the world, he by a long time disputed with philosophers and rhetoricians which were esteemed most excellent, and by the judgment of them that were present had the palm or reward of victory? And yet, by the governance of that noble emperor, not only the public weal flourished but also divers rebellions were suppressed, and the majesty of the empire hugely increased. Was it any reproach to the noble Germanicus (who by the assignment of Augustus should have succeeded Tiberius in the empire, if traitorous envy had not in his flourishing youth bereft him his life) that he was equal to the most noble poets of his time, and, to the increase of his honour and most worthy commendation, his image was set up at Rome, in the habit that poets at those days used? Finally how much excellent learning commendeth, and not dispraiseth, nobility, it shall plainly appear unto them that do read the lives of Alexander called Severus, Tacitus, Probus Aurelius, Constantine, Theodosius, and Charles the Great, surnamed Charlemagne, all being emperors, and do compare them with other, which lacked or had not so much of doctrine. Verily they be far from good reason, in mine opinion, which covet to have their children goodly in stature, strong, deliver,[1] well singing, wherein trees, beasts, fishes, and birds be not only with them equal, but also far do exceed them. And cunning, whereby only man excelleth all other creatures in earth, they reject, and account unworthy to be in their children. What unkind appetite were it to desire to be father rather of a piece of flesh, that can only move and feel, than of a child that should have the perfect form of a man? What so perfectly expresseth a man as doctrine? Diogenes the philosopher seeing one without learning sit on a stone, said to them that were with him, 'Behold where one stone sitteth on another'; which words, well considered and tried, shall appear to contain in it wonderful matter for the approbation of doctrine, whereof a wise man may accumulate inevitable arguments, which I of necessity, to avoid tediousness, must needs pass over at this time.

XIII. The second and third decay of learning among gentlemen.

THE SECOND occasion wherefore gentlemen's children seldom have sufficient learning is avarice. For where their parents will not adventure to send them far out of their proper countries partly for fear of death, which perchance dare not approach them at home with their father; partly for expense of money, which they suppose would be less in their own houses or in a village, with some of their tenants or friends; having seldom any regard to the teacher, whether he be well learned or ignorant. For if they hire a schoolmaster to teach in their houses, they chiefly inquire with how small a salary he will be contented, and never do ensearch how much good learning he hath, and how among well learned men he is therein esteemed, using therein less diligence than in taking servants, whose service is of much less importance, and to a good schoolmaster is not in profit to be compared. A gentleman, ere he take a cook into his service, he will first diligently examine him, how many sorts of meats, pottages, and sauces, he can perfectly make, and how well he can season them, that they may be both pleasant and nourishing; yea

[1] Agile.

and if it be but a falconer, he will scrupulously inquire what skill
he hath in feeding, called diet, and keeping of his hawk from all
sickness, also how he can reclaim her and prepare her to flight.
And to such a cook or falconer, whom he findeth expert, he
spareth not to give much wages with other bounteous rewards.
But of a schoolmaster, to whom he will commit his child, to be
fed with learning and instructed in virtue, whose life shall be the
principal monument of his name and honour, he never maketh
further enquiry but where he may have a schoolmaster; and with
how little charge; and if one be perchance found, well learned,
but he will not take pains to teach without he may have a great
salary, he then speaketh nothing more, or else saith, 'What, shall
so much wages be given to a schoolmaster which would keep me
two servants?' To whom may be said these words, that by his son
being well learned he shall receive more commodity and also
worship than by the service of a hundred cooks and falconers.

The third cause of this hindrance is negligence of parents,
which I do specially note in this point: there have been divers, as
well gentlemen as of the nobility, that delighting to have their
sons excellent in learning have provided for them cunning
masters, who substantially have taught them grammar and very
well instructed them to speak Latin elegantly, whereof the
parents have taken much delectation; but when they have had of
grammar sufficient and be come to the age of fourteen years, and
do approach or draw toward the estate of man, which age is
called mature or ripe (wherein not only the said learning continued by much experience shall be perfectly digested, and confirmed in perpetual remembrance, but also more serious learning
contained in other liberal sciences, and also philosophy, would
then be learned), the parents, that thing nothing regarding, but
being sufficed that their children can only speak Latin properly,
or make verses without matter or sentence, they from thenceforth
do suffer them to live in idleness, or else, putting them to service
do, as it were, banish them from all virtuous study or exercise of
that which they before learned; so that we may behold divers
young gentlemen, who in their infancy and childhood were
wondered at for their aptness to learning and prompt speaking of
elegant Latin, which now, being men, not only have forgotten
their congruity [1] (as in the common word), and unneth [2] can

---

[1] Agreement, grammar.   [2] Scarcely.

speak one whole sentence in true Latin, but, that worse is, hath all learning in derision, and in scorn thereof will, of wantonness, speak the most barbarously that they can imagine.

Now some man will require me to show mine opinion if it be necessary that gentlemen should after the age of fourteen years continue in study. And to be plain and true therein, I dare affirm that, if the elegant speaking of Latin be not added to other doctrine, little fruit may come of the tongue; since Latin is but a natural speech, and the fruit of speech is wise sentence, which is gathered and made of sundry learning.

And who that hath nothing but language only may be no more praised than a popinjay, a pie, or a starling, when they speak fitly. There be many nowadays in famous schools and universities which be so much given to the study of tongues only, that when they write epistles, they seem to the reader that, like to a trumpet, they make a sound without any purpose, whereunto men do hearken more for the noise than for any delectation that thereby is moved. Wherefore they be much abused that suppose eloquence to be only in words or colours of rhetoric, for, as Tully saith, what is so furious or mad a thing as a vain sound of words of the best sort and most ornate, containing neither cunning nor sentence? Undoubtedly very eloquence is in every tongue where any matter or act done or to be done is expressed in words clean, proper, ornate, and comely: whereof sentences be so aptly compact that they by a virtue inexplicable do draw unto them the minds and consent of the hearers, they being therewith either persuaded, moved, or to delectation induced. Also every man is not an orator that can write an epistle or a flattering oration in Latin; whereof the last (as God help me) is too much used. For a right orator may not be without a much better furniture, Tully saying that to him belongeth the explicating or unfolding of sentence, with a great estimation in giving counsel concerning matters of great importance, also to him appertaineth the steering and quickening of people languishing or despairing, and to moderate them that be rash and unbridled. Wherefore noble authors do affirm that, in the first infancy of the world, men wandering like beasts in woods and on mountains, regarding neither the religion due unto God, nor the office pertaining unto man, ordered all thing by bodily strength: until Mercurius (as Plato supposeth) or some other man helped by sapience and eloquence, by some apt or proper oration, assembled them

together and persuaded to them what commodity was in mutual
conversation and honest manners. But yet Cornelius Tacitus
describeth an orator to be of more excellent qualities, saying that
an orator is he that can or may speak or reason in every question
sufficiently elegantly: and to persuade properly, according to the
dignity of the thing that is spoken of, the opportunity of time, and
pleasure of them that be hearers. Tully before him affirmed that
a man may not be an orator heaped with praise, but if he have
gotten the knowledge of all things and arts of greatest importance.
And how shall an orator speak of that thing that he hath not
learned? And because there may be nothing but it may happen to
come in praise or dispraise, in consultation or judgment, in
accusation or defence; therefore an orator, by other instruction
perfectly furnished, may, in every matter and learning, commend
or dispraise, exhort or dissuade, accuse or defend eloquently, as
occasion happeneth. Wherefore inasmuch as in an orator is required to be a heap of all manner of learning, which of some is
called the world of science, of other the circle of doctrine, which is
in one word of Greek *Encyclopedia*; therefore at this day may be
found but a very few orators. For they that come in message
from princes be, for honour, named now orators, if they be in any
degree of worship; only poor men having equal or more of
learning being called messengers. Also they which do only teach
rhetoric, which is the science whereby is taught an artificial form
of speaking, wherein is the power to persuade, move, and delight,
or by that science only do speak or write, without any adminiculation[1] of other sciences, ought to be named rhetoricians,
declamators, artificial speakers (named in Greek *Logodedali*),
or any other name than orators. Semblably they that make
verses expressing thereby none other learning but the craft of
versifying be not of ancient writers named poets, but only called
versifiers. For the name of a poet, whereat now (specially in this
realm) men have such indignation that they use only poets and
poetry in the contempt of eloquence, was in ancient time in high
estimation: insomuch that all wisdom was supposed to be therein
included, and poetry was the first philosophy that ever was
known: whereby men from their childhood were brought to the
reason how to live well, learning thereby not only manners and
natural affections, but also the wonderful works of nature,

[1] Support.

mixing serious matter with things that were pleasant; as it shall
be manifest to them that shall be so fortunate to read the noble
works of Plato and Aristotle, wherein he shall find the authority
of poets frequently alleged: yea and that more is, in poets was
supposed to be science mystical and inspired, and therefore in
Latin they were called *Vates*, which word signifieth as much as
prophets. And therefore Tully in his *Tusculan Questions* supposeth that a poet cannot abundantly express verses sufficient
and complete, or that his eloquence may flow without labour
words well sounding and plenteous, without celestial instinction,
which is also by Plato ratified.

But since we be now occupied in the defence of poets, it shall
not be incongruent to our matter to show what profit may be
taken by the diligent reading of ancient poets, contrary to the
false opinion, that now reigneth, of them that suppose that in the
works of poets is contained nothing but bawdry (such is their
foul word of reproach) and unprofitable leasing.[1]

But first I will interpret some verses of Horace, wherein he
expresseth the office of poets, and after will I resort to a more
plain demonstration of some wisdom and counsel contained in
some verses of poets. Horace, in his second book of epistles, saith
in this wise or much like:

> The poet fashioneth by some pleasant mean
> The speech of children tender and unsure:
> Pulling their ears from words unclean,
> Giving to them precepts that are pure:
> Rebuking envy and wrath if it 'dure:
> Things well done he can by example commend:
> The needy and sick he doth also his cure
> To recomfort, if aught he can amend.

But they which be ignorant in poets will perchance object, as is
their manner, against these verses, saying that in Terence and
other that were writers of comedies, also Ovid, Catullus, Martial,
and all that rout of lascivious poets that wrote epistles and
ditties of love, some called in Latin *Elegiae* and some *Epigram-
mata*, is nothing contained but incitation to lechery.

First, comedies, which they suppose to be a doctrinal of
ribaldry, they be undoubtedly a picture or as it were a mirror of
man's life, wherein evil is not taught but discovered; to the intent

[1] Lying.

that men beholding the promptness of youth unto vice, the snares
of harlots and bawds laid for young minds, the deceit of servants,
the chances of fortune contrary to men's expectation, they being
thereof warned may prepare themself to resist or prevent occasion.
Semblably remembering the wisdom, advertisements, counsels,
dissuasion from vice, and other profitable sentences most
eloquently and familiarly shown in those comedies, undoubtedly
there shall be no little fruit out of them gathered. And if the vices
in them expressed should be cause that minds of the readers
should be corrupted, then by the same argument not only interludes in English, but also sermons, wherein some vice is declared,
should be to the beholders and hearers like occasion to increase
sinners.

And that by comedies good counsel is ministered, it appeareth
by the sentence of Parmeno, in the second comedy of Terence:

> In this thing I triumph in mine own conceit,
> That I have found for all young men the way
> How they of harlots shall know the deceit,
> Their wits, their manners, that thereby they may
> Them perpetually hate; for so much as they
> Out of their own houses be fresh and delicate,
> Feeding curiously; at home all the day
> Living beggarly in most wretched estate.

There be many more words spoken which I purposely omit to
translate, notwithstanding the substance of the whole sentence is
herein comprised. But now to come to other poets, what may be
better said than is written by Plautus in his first comedy?

> Verily virtue doth all things excel.
> For if liberty, health, living and substance,
> Our country, our parents and children do well
> It happeneth by virtue; she doth all advance.
> Virtue hath all thing under governance,
> And in whom of virtue is found great plenty,
> Anything that is good may never be dainty.

Also Ovid, that seemeth to be most of all poets lascivious, in
his most wanton books hath right commendable and noble
sentences; as for proof thereof I will recite some that I have taken
at adventure.

> Time is in medicine if it shall profit;
> Wine given out of time may be annoyance.

A man shall irritate vice if he prohibit
When time is not mete unto his utterance.
Therefore, if thou yet by counsel art recuperable,
Flee thou from idleness and alway be stable.

Martial, which, for his dissolute writing, is most seldom read
of men of much gravity, hath notwithstanding many commendable sentences and right wise counsels, as among divers I will
rehearse one which is first come to my remembrance.

If thou wilt eschew bitter adventure,
And avoid the gnawing of a pensive heart,
Set in no one person all wholly thy pleasure,
The less joy shalt thou have but the less shalt thou smart.

I could recite a great number of semblable good sentences out
of these and other wanton poets, who in the Latin do express
them incomparably with more grace and delectation to the
reader than our English tongue may yet comprehend.

Wherefore since good and wise matter may be picked out of
these poets, it were no reason for some light matter that is in their
verses to abandon therefore all their works, no more than it were
to forbear or prohibit a man to come into a fair garden lest the
redolent savours of sweet herbs and flowers shall move him to
wanton courage, or lest in gathering good and wholesome herbs
he may happen to be stung with a nettle. No wise man entereth
into a garden but he soon espieth good herbs from nettles, and
treadeth the nettles under his feet whiles he gathereth good herbs,
whereby he taketh no damage, or if he be stung he maketh light
of it and shortly forgetteth it. Semblably if he do read wanton
matter mixed with wisdom, he putteth the worst under foot and
sorteth out the best, or if his courage be stirred or provoked, he
remembereth the little pleasure and great detriment that should
ensue of it, and withdrawing his mind to some other study or
exercise shortly forgetteth it.

And therefore among the Jews, though it were prohibited to
children until they came to ripe years to read the books of
Genesis, of the Judges, *Cantica Canticorum*, and some part of the
book of Ezekiel the Prophet, for that in them was contained some
matter which might happen to incense the young mind, wherein
were sparks of carnal concupiscence, yet after certain years of
men's ages it was lawful for every man to read and diligently
study those works. So although I do not approve the lesson of

wanton poets to be taught unto all children, yet think I convenient and necessary that, when the mind is become constant and courage is assuaged, or that children of their natural disposition be shamefaced and continent, none ancient poet would be excluded from the lesson of such one as desireth to come to the perfection of wisdom.

But in defending of orators and poets I had almost forgotten where I was. Verily there may no man be an excellent poet nor orator unless he have part of all other doctrine, specially of noble philosophy. And to say the truth, no man can apprehend the very delectation that is in the lesson of noble poets unless he have read very much and in divers authors of divers learning. Wherefore, as I late said, to the augmentation of understanding, called in Latin *intellectus et mens*, is required to be much reading and vigilant study in every science, specially of that part of philosophy named moral, which instructeth men in virtue and politic governance. Also no noble author, specially of them that wrote in Greek or Latin before twelve hundred years passed, is not for any cause to be omitted. For therein I am of Quintilian's opinion, that there is few or none ancient work that yieldeth not some fruit or commodity to the diligent readers. And it is a very gross or obstinate wit that by reading much is not somewhat amended.

Concerning the election of other authors to be read I have (as I trust) declared sufficiently my concept and opinion in the tenth and eleventh chapters of this little treatise.

Finally, like as a delicate tree that cometh of a kernel, which, as soon as it burgeoneth out leaves, if it be plucked up or it be sufficiently rooted, and laid in a corner, it becometh dry or rotten and no fruit cometh of it, if it be removed and set in another air or earth, which is of contrary qualities where it was before, it either semblably dieth or beareth no fruit, or else the fruit that cometh of it loseth his verdure and taste, and finally his estimation. So the pure and excellent learning whereof I have spoken, though it be sown in a child never so timely, and springeth and burgeoneth never so pleasantly, if, before it take a deep root in the mind of the child, it be laid aside, either by too much solace or continual attendance in service, or else is translated to another study which is of a more gross or unpleasant quality before it be confirmed or stablished by often reading or diligent exercise, in conclusion it vanisheth and cometh to nothing.

Wherefore let men reply as they list, but in mine opinion men be wonderfully deceived nowadays (I dare not say with the persuasion of avarice) that do put their children at the age of fourteen or fifteen years to the study of the laws of the realm of England. I will show to them reasonable causes why, if they will patiently hear me, informed partly by mine own experience.

XIV. How the students in the laws of this realm may take excellent commodity by the lessons of sundry doctrines.

IT MAY not be denied but that all laws be founded on the deepest part of reason, and, as I suppose, no one law so much as our own; and the deeper men do investigate reason the more difficult or hard must needs be the study. Also that reverend study is involved in so barbarous a language, that it is not only void of all eloquence, but also being separate from the exercise of our law only, it serveth to no commodity or necessary purpose, no man understanding it but they which have studied the laws.

Then children at fourteen or fifteen years old, in which time springeth courage, set all in pleasure, and pleasure is in nothing that is not facile or elegant, being brought to the most difficult and grave learning which hath nothing illecebrous [1] or delicate to tickle their tender wits and allure them to study (unless it be lucre, which a gentle wit little esteemeth), the more part, vanquished with tediousness, either do abandon the laws and unwares to their friends do give them to gaming and other (as I might say) idle business now called pastimes; or else if they be in any wise thereto constrained, they apprehending a piece thereof, as if they being long in a dark dungeon only did see by the light of a candle, then if after twenty or thirty years' study they happen to come among wise men, hearing matters commented of concerning a public weal or outward affairs between princes, they no less be astonished than of coming out of a dark house at noonday they were suddenly stricken in the eyes with a bright sunbeam. But I speak not this in reproach of lawyers, for I know divers of them which in consultation will make a right vehement reason, and so do some other which hath neither law nor other learning, yet the one and the other, if they were furnished with excellent doctrine, their reason should be the more substantial and certain.

[1] Alluring.

There be some also which by their friends be courted to apply the study of the law only, and for lack of plenteous exhibition be let of their liberty, wherefore they cannot resort unto pastime; these of all other be most cast away, for nature repugning, they unneth [1] taste anything that may be profitable, and also their courage is so mortified (which yet by solace perchance might be made quick or apt to some other study or laudable exercise) that they live ever after out of all estimation.

Wherefore Tully saith we should so endeavour ourselves that we strive not with the universal nature of man, but that being conserved, let us follow our own proper natures, that though there be studied more grave and of more importance, yet ought we to regard the studies whereto we be by our own nature inclined. And that this sentence is true we have daily experience in this realm specially. For how many men be there that having their sons in childhood aptly disposed by nature to paint, to carve, or grave, to embroider, or do other like things, wherein is any art commendable concerning invention, but that, as soon as they espy it, they be therewith displeased, and forthwith bindeth them apprentices to tailors, to weavers, to tuckers, and sometime to cobblers, which have been the inestimable loss of many good wits, and have caused that in the said arts Englishmen be inferiors to all other people, and be constrained, if we will have anything well painted, carved, or embroidered, to abandon our own countrymen and resort unto strangers, but more of this shall I speak in the next volume.

But to resort unto lawyers. I think verily if children were brought up as I have written, and continually were retained in the right study of very philosophy until they passed the age of twenty-one years, and then set to the laws of this realm (being once brought to a more certain and compendious study, and either in English, Latin, or good French, written in a more clean and elegant style) undoubtedly they should become men of so excellent wisdom that throughout all the world should be found in no common weal more noble counsellors, our laws not only comprehending most excellent reasons, but also being gathered and compact (as I might say) of the pure meal or flour sifted out of the best laws of all other countries, as somewhat I do intend to prove evidently in the next volume, wherein I will render mine

[1] Scarcely.

office or duty to that honourable study whereby my father was advanced to a judge, and also I myself have attained no little commodity.

I suppose divers men there be that will say, that the sweetness that is contained in eloquence and the multitude of doctrines should utterly withdraw the minds of young men from the more necessary study of the laws of this realm. To them will I make a brief answer, but true it shall be, and I trust sufficient to wise men. In the great multitude of young men, which alway will repair, and the law being once brought into a more certain and perfect language, will also increase in the reverent study of the law, undoubtedly there shall never lack but some by nature inclined, divers by desire of sundry doctrines, many for hope of lucre or some other advancement, will effectually study the laws, nor will be therefrom withdrawn by any other lesson which is more eloquent. Example we have at this present time of divers excellent learned men, both in the laws civil as also in physic, which being exactly studied in all parts of eloquence, both in the Greek tongue and Latin, have notwithstanding read and perused the great fardels and trusses of the most barbarous authors, stuffed with innumerable glosses, whereby the most necessary doctrines of law and physic be minced into fragments, and in all wise men's opinions, do perceive no less in the said learning than they which never knew eloquence, or never tasted other but the feces or dregs of the said noble doctrines. And as for the multitude of sciences cannot endamage any student, but if he be moved to study the law by any of the said motions by me before touched, he shall rather increase therein than be hindered, and that shall appear manifestly to them that either will give credence to my report, or else will read the works that I will allege; which if they understand not, to desire some learned man by interpreting to cause them perceive it. And first I will begin at orators, who bear the principal title of eloquence.

It is to be remembered that in the learning of the laws of this realm, there is at this day an exercise wherein is a manner, a shadow, or figure of the ancient rhetoric. I mean the pleading used in Court and Chancery called moots, where first a case is appointed to be mooted by certain young men, containing some doubtful controversy, which is instead of the heed of a declamation called *thema*. The case being known, they which be appointed to moot do examine the case, and investigate what they therein

can espy, which may make a contention, whereof may rise a
question to be argued, and that of Tully is called *constitutio*, and
of Quintilian *status causae*.

Also they consider what pleas on every part ought to be made,
and how the case may be reasoned, which is the first part of
rhetoric, named *invention*; then appoint they how many pleas
may be made for every part, and in what formality they should
be set, which is the second part of rhetoric, called *disposition*,
wherein they do much approach unto rhetoric; then gather they
all into perfect remembrance, in such order as it ought to be
pleaded, which is the part of rhetoric named *memory*. But forasmuch as the tongue wherein it is spoken is barbarous, and the
stirring of affections of the mind in this realm was never used,
therefore there lacketh *elocution* and *pronunciation*, two the
principal parts of rhetoric. Notwithstanding some lawyers, if they
be well retained, will in a mean cause pronounce right vehemently. Moreover there seemeth to be in the said pleadings
certain parts of an oration, that is to say for *narrations*, *partitions*,
confirmations, and *confutations*, named of some *reprehensions*,
they have *declarations*, *bars*, *replications*, and *rejoinders*, only they
lack pleasant form of beginning, called in Latin *exordium*, nor it
maketh thereof no great matter; they that have studied rhetoric
shall perceive what I mean. Also in arguing their cases, in my
opinion, they very little do lack of the whole art; for therein they
do diligently observe the rules of confirmation and confutation,
wherein resteth proof and disproof, having almost all the places
whereof they shall fetch their reasons, called of orators *loci
communes*, which I omit to name, fearing to be too long in this
matter. And verily I suppose, if there might once happen some
man, having an excellent wit, to be brought up in such form as I
have hitherto written, and may also be exactly or deeply learned
in the art of an orator, and also in the laws of this realm, the
prince so willing and thereto assisting, undoubtedly it should not
be impossible for him to bring the pleading and reasoning of the
law to the ancient form of noble orators; and the laws and exercise thereof being in pure Latin or doulce [1] French, few men in
consultations should (in my opinion) compare with our lawyers,
by this means being brought to be perfect orators, as in whom
should then be found the sharp wits of logicians, the grave

Sweet, pure.

sentences of philosophers, the elegancy of poets, the memory of civilians, the voice and gesture of them that can pronounce comedies, which is all that Tully, in the person of the most eloquent man Marcus Antonius, could require to be in an orator.

But now to conclude mine assertion, what let was eloquence to the study of the law in Quintus Scaevola, which being an excellent author in the laws civil, was called of all lawyers most eloquent? Or how much was eloquence diminished by knowledge of the laws in Crassus, which was called of all eloquent men the best lawyer?

Also Servus Sulpitius, in his time one of the most noble orators next unto Tully, was not so let by eloquence but that on the civil laws he made notable comments, and many noble works by all lawyers approved. Who readeth the text of civil, called the *Pandectes* or *Digests*, and hath any commendable judgment in the Latin tongue, but he will affirm that Ulpian, Scaevola, Claudius, and all the other there named, of whose sayings all the said texts be assembled, were not only studious of eloquence, but also wonderful exercised: forasmuch as their style doth approach nearer to the antique and pure eloquence, than any other kind of writers that wrote about that time?

Semblably Tully, in whom it seemeth that Eloquence hath set her glorious throne, most richly and preciously adorned for all men to wonder at, but no man to approach it, was not let from being an incomparable orator, nor was not by the exact knowledge of other sciences withdrawn from pleading infinite causes before the Senate and judges, and they being of most weighty importance. Insomuch as Cornelius Tacitus, an excellent orator, historian, and lawyer, saith, 'Surely in the books of Tully men may deprehend [1] that in him lacked not the knowledge of geometry, nor music, nor grammar, finally of no manner of art that was honest: he of logic perceived the subtlety, of that part that was moral all the commodity, and of all things the chief motions and causes.'

And yet for all this abundance, and as it were a garner heaped with all manner sciences, there failed not in him substantial learning in the laws civil, as it may appear as well in the books which he himself made of laws, as also and most specially in many of his most eloquent orations; which if one well learned in the laws of this realm did read and well understand, he should find, specially

---

[1] Understand.

in his orations called *Actiones* again Verres, many places where he
should espy, by likelihood, the fountains from whence proceeded
divers grounds of our common laws. But I will now leave to speak
any more thereof at this time.

All that I have written well considered, it shall seem to wise
men, that neither eloquence, nor knowledge of sundry doctrines,
shall utterly withdraw all men from study of the laws. But
although many were allected [1] unto those doctrines by natural
disposition, yet the same nature, which will not (as I might say)
be circumscribed within the bounds of a certain of studies, may
as well dispose some man, as well to desire the knowledge of the
laws of this realm, as she did incline the Romans, excellently
learned in all sciences, to apprehend the laws civil; since the laws
of this realm, being well gathered and brought in good Latin, shall
be worthy to have like praise as Tully gave to the laws comprehended in the twelve tables, from whence all civil law flowed,
which praise was in this wise. 'Although men will abraid [2] at it, I
will say as I think, the one little book of the twelve tables seemeth
to me to surmount the libraries of all the philosophers in weighty
authority, and abundance of profit, behold who so will the
fountains and heads of the laws.'

Moreover, when young men have read laws expounded in the
orations of Tully, and also in histories of the beginning of laws,
and in the works of Plato, Xenophon, and Aristotle, of the
diversities of laws and public weals, if nature (as I late said) will
dispose them to that manner study, they shall be thereto the more
incensed, and come unto it the better prepared and furnished.
And they whom nature thereto nothing moveth have not only
saved all that time which many nowadays do consume in idleness,
but also have won such a treasure whereby they shall alway be
able to serve honourably their prince, and the public weal of their
country, principally if they confer all their doctrines to the most
noble study of moral philosophy, which teacheth both virtues,
manners, and civil policy: whereby at the last we should have in
this realm sufficiency of worshipful lawyers, and also a public
weal equivalent to the Greeks or Romans.

[1] Drawn.   [2] Object.

XV. For what cause at this day there be in this realm few perfect
schoolmasters.

LORD GOD, how many good and clean wits of children be nowadays perished by ignorant schoolmasters! How little substantial
doctrine is apprehended by the fewness of good grammarians!
Notwithstanding I know that there be some well learned, which
have taught, and also do teach, but God knoweth a few, and they
with small effect, having thereto no comfort, their aptest and
most proper scholars, after they be well instructed in speaking
Latin, and understanding some poets, being taken from their
school by their parents, and either be brought to the court, and
made lackeys or pages, or else are bounden prentices; whereby
the worship that the master, above any reward, coveteth to have
by the praise of his scholar, is utterly drowned; whereof I have
heard schoolmasters, very well learned, of good right complain.
But yet (as I said) the fewness of good grammarians is a great
impediment of doctrine. (And here I would the readers should
mark that I note to be few good grammarians, and not none.) I
call not them grammarians which only can teach or make rules
whereby a child shall only learn to speak congrue [1] Latin, or to
make six verses standing in one foot, wherein perchance shall be
neither sentence nor eloquence. But I name him a grammarian,
by the authority of Quintilian, that speaking Latin elegantly, can
expound good authors, expressing the invention and disposition
of the matter, their style or form of eloquence, explicating the
figures as well of sentences as words, leaving no thing, person, or
place named by the author undeclared or hidden from his
scholars. Wherefore Quintilian saith, it is not enough for him to
have read poets, but all kinds of writing must also be sought for;
not for the histories only, but also for the propriety of words,
which commonly do receive their authority of noble authors.
Moreover without music grammar may not be perfect; forasmuch as therein must be spoken of metres and harmonies, called
rythmi in Greek. Neither if he have not the knowledge of stars, he
may understand poets, which in description of times (I omit other
things) they treat of the rising and going down of planets. Also he
may not be ignorant in philosophy, for many places that be

---

[1] Grammatical, correct.

almost in every poet fetched out of the most subtle part of
natural questions. These be well nigh the words of Quintilian.

Then behold how few grammarians after this description be in
this realm.

Undoubtedly there be in this realm many well learned, which if
the name of a schoolmaster were not so much had in contempt,
and also if their labours with abundant salaries might be requited,
were right sufficient and able to induce their hearers to excellent
learning, so they be not plucked away green, and ere they be in
doctrine sufficiently rooted. But nowadays, if to a bachelor or
master of art study of philosophy waxeth tedious, if he have a
spoonful of Latin, he will show forth a hogshead without any
learning, and offer to teach grammar and expound noble writers,
and to be in the room of a master; he will, for a small salary, set a
false colour of learning on proper wits, which will be washed away
with one shower of rain. For if the children be absent from school
by the space of one month, the best learned of them will unneth [1]
tell whether *Fato*, whereby Aeneas was brought into Italy, were
either a man, a horse, a ship, or a wild goose. Although their
master will perchance avaunt himself to be a good philosopher.

Some men peradventure do think that at the beginning of
learning it forceth not, although the masters have not so exact
doctrine as I have rehearsed; but let them take good heed what
Quintilian saith, that it is so much the better to be instructed by
them that are best learned, forasmuch as it is difficult to put out
of the mind that which is once settled, the double burden being
painful to the masters that shall succeed, and verily much more to
unteach than to teach. Wherefore it is written that Timotheus,
the noble musician, demanded alway a greater reward of them
whom other had taught, than of them that never anything learned.
These be the words of Quintilian or like.

Also common experience teacheth that no man will put his son
to a butcher to learn, or he bind him prentice to a tailor; or if he
will have him a cunning goldsmith, will bind him first prentice to
a tinker: in these things poor men be circumspect, and the nobles
and gentlemen, who would have their sons by excellent learning
come unto honour, for sparing of cost or for lack of diligent
search for a good schoolmaster wilfully destroy their children,
causing them to be taught that learning which would require six

---

[1] Scarcely.

or seven years to be forgotten; by which time the more part of that age is spent, wherein is the chief sharpness of wit called in Latin *acumen*, and also then approacheth the stubborn age, where the child brought up in pleasure disdaineth correction.

Now have I all declared (as I do suppose) the chief impeachments of excellent learning; of the reformation I need not to speak, since it is apparent, that by the contraries, men pursuing it earnestly with discreet judgment and liberality, it would soon be amended.

XVI. Of sundry forms of exercise necessary for every gentleman.

ALTHOUGH I have hitherto advanced the commendation of learning, specially in gentlemen, yet it is to be considered that continual study without some manner of exercise shortly exhausteth the spirits vital and hindereth natural decoction and digestion, whereby man's body is the sooner corrupted and brought into divers sicknesses, and finally the life is thereby made shorter; where contrariwise by exercise, which is a vehement motion (as Galen prince of physicians defineth), the health of man is preserved, and his strength increased, forasmuch as the members of moving and mutual touching do wax more hard, and natural heat in all the body is thereby augmented. Moreover it maketh the spirits of a man more strong and valiant, so that by the hardness of the members all labours be more tolerable; by natural heat the appetite is the more quick; the change of the substance received is the more ready; the nourishing of all parts of the body is the more sufficient and sure. By valiant motion of the spirits all things superfluous be expelled, and the conduits of the body cleansed. Wherefore this part of physic is not to be condemned or neglected in the education of children, and specially from the age of fourteen years upward, in which time strength with courage increaseth. Moreover there be divers manners of exercises; whereof some only prepareth and helpeth digestion; some augmenteth also strength and hardness of body; other serveth for agility and nimbleness; some for celerity or speediness. There be also which ought to be used for necessity only. All these ought he that is a tutor to a nobleman to have in remembrance, and, as opportunity serveth, to put them in experience. And specially them which with health do join commodity (and as I might say) necessity; considering that be he never so noble or valiant, some time he is subject to peril, or (to speak it more pleasantly) servant to fortune. Touching such exercises as may be used within the house or in the shadow (as is the old manner of speaking), as deambulations,[1] labouring with poises [2] made of lead or other metal called in Latin *alteres*, lifting and throwing the heavy stone or bar, playing at tennis, and divers semblable exercises, I will for this time pass over; exhorting them which do understand Latin and do desire to know the commodities of sundry exercises, to resort to the book of Galen, of the governance of health, called in Latin *De sanitate tuenda*, where they shall be in that matter abundantly satisfied, and find in the reading much delectation; which book is translated into Latin wonderful eloquently by Doctor Linacre, late most worthy physician to our most noble sovereign lord King Henry the VIII.

And I will now only speak of those exercises, apt to the furniture of a gentleman's personage, adapting his body to hardness, strength, and agility, and to help therewith himself in peril, which may happen in wars or other necessity.

XVII. Exercises whereby should grow both recreation and profit.

WRESTLING is a very good exercise in the beginning of youth, so that it be with one that is equal in strength, or somewhat under, and that the place be soft, that in falling their bodies be not bruised.

There be divers manners of wrestlings, but the best, as well for health of body as for exercise of strength, is when laying mutually their hands one over another's neck, with the other hand they hold fast each other by the arm, and clasping their legs together, they enforce themselves with strength and agility to throw down each other, which is also praised by Galen. And undoubtedly it shall be found profitable in wars, in case that a captain shall be constrained to cope with his adversary hand to hand, having his weapon broken or lost. Also it hath been seen that the weaker person, by the sleight of wrestling, hath overthrown the stronger, almost ere he could fasten on the other any violent stroke.

Also running is both a good exercise and a laudable solace. It

---

[1] Walks.   [2] Weights.

is written of Epaminondas the valiant captain of Thebes, who as
well in virtue and prowess as in learning surmounted all noblemen of his time, that daily he exercised himself in the morning
with running and leaping, in the evening in wrestling, to the intent
that likewise in armour he might the more strongly, embracing
his adversary, put him in danger. And also that in the chase,
running and leaping, he might either overtake his enemy, or being
pursued, if extreme need required, escape him. Semblably before
him did the worthy Achilles, for while his ships lay at rode,[1] he
suffered not his people to slumber in idleness, but daily exercised
them and himself in running, wherein he was most excellent and
passed all other, and therefore Homer, throughout all his work,
calleth him swift-foot Achilles.

The great Alexander being a child, excelled all his companions
in running; wherefore on a time one demanded of him if he would
run at the great game of Olympus, whereto, out of all parts of
Greece, came the most active and valiant persons to assay
mastery; whereunto Alexander answered in this form, 'I would
very gladly run there, if I were sure to run with kings, for if I
should contend with a private person, having respect to our both
estates, our victories should not be equal.' Needs must running
be taken for a laudable exercise, since one of the most noble
captains of all the Romans took his name of running and was
called Papirius Cursor, which is in English, Papirius the Runner.
And also the valiant Marius the Roman, when he had been seven
times consul, and was of the age of four score years, exercised
himself daily among the young men of Rome, in such wise that
there resorted people out of far parts to behold the strength and
agility of that old Consul, wherein he compared with the young
and lusty soldiers.

There is an exercise which is right profitable in extreme danger
of wars, but because there seemeth to be some peril in the learning thereof, and also it hath not been of long time much used,
specially among noblemen, perchance some readers will little
esteem it, I mean swimming. But notwithstanding, if they revolve
the imbecility of our nature, the hazards and dangers of battle,
with the examples which shall hereafter be shown, they will (I
doubt not) think it as necessary to a captain or man of arms, as
any that I have yet rehearsed. The Romans, who above all things

[1] Harbour.

had most in estimation martial prowess, they had a large and
spacious field without the city of Rome, which was called Mars'
field, in Latin *Campus Martius*, where the youth of the city was
exercised. This field adjoined to the river of Tiber, to the intent
that as well men as children should wash and refresh them in the
water after their labours, as also learn to swim. And not men and
children only, but also the horses, that by such usage they should
more aptly and boldly pass over great rivers, and be more able to
resist or cut the waves, and not be afraid of pirries [1] or great
storms. For it hath been often times seen that, by the good
swimming of horses, many men have been saved, and contrariwise, by a timorous royle [2] where the water hath unneth [3] come
to his belly, his legs hath faltered, whereby many a good and
proper man hath perished. What benefit received the whole city
of Rome by the swimming of Horatius Cocles, which is a noble
history and worthy to be remembered. After the Romans had
expelled Tarquin their king, as I have before remembered, he
desired aid of Porsena, King of Tuscany, a noble and valiant
prince, to recover eftsoons [4] his realm and dignity; who with a
great and puissant host besieged the city of Rome, and so
suddenly and sharply assaulted it, that it lacked but little that he
ne had entered into the city with his host over the bridge called
Sublicius; where encountered with him this Horatius with a few
Romans. And while this noble captain, being alone, with an
incredible strength resisted all the host of Porsena that were on
the bridge, he commanded the bridge to be broken behind him,
wherewith all the Tuscans thereon standing fell into the great
river of Tiber, but Horatius all armed leapt into the water and
swam to his company, albeit that he was stricken with many
arrows and darts, and also grievously wounded. Notwithstanding
by his noble courage and feat of swimming he saved the city of
Rome from perpetual servitude, which was likely to have ensued
by the return of the proud Tarquin.

How much profited the feat in swimming to the valiant Julius
Caesar, who at the battle of Alexandria, on a bridge being
abandoned of his people for the multitude of his enemies, which
oppressed them, when he might no longer sustain the shot of
darts and arrows, he boldly leapt into the sea, and, diving under
the water, escaped the shot and swam the space of two hundred

---

[1] Whirlwinds.   [2] Horse.
[3] Scarcely.   [4] Again.

paces to one of his ships, drawing his coat armour with his teeth after him, that his enemies should not attain it. And also that it might somewhat defend him from their arrows. And that more marvel was, holding in his hand above the water certain letters which a little before he had received from the Senate.

Before him Sertorius, who of the Spaniards was named the second Hannibal for his prowess in the battle that Scipio fought against the Cimbri, which invaded France. Sertorius, when, by negligence of his people, his enemies prevailed and put his host to the worse, he being sore wounded, and his horse being lost, armed as he was in a gesseron,[1] holding in his hands a target, and his sword, he leapt into the river Rhône, which is wonderful swift, and, swimming against the stream, came to his company, not without great wondering of all his enemies, which stood and beheld him.

The great King Alexander lamented that he had not learned to swim. For in India when he went against the puissant King Porus, he was constrained, in following his enterprise, to convey his host over a river of wonderful greatness; then caused he his horsemen to gauge the water, whereby he first perceived that it came to the breasts of the horses, and in the middle of the stream the horses went in water to the neck, wherewith the footmen being afraid, none of them durst adventure to pass over the river. That perceiving Alexander with a dolorous manner in this wise lamented, 'O how most unhappy am I of all other that have not ere this time learned to swim!' And therewith he pulled a target from one of his soldiers, and casting it into the water, standing on it, with his spear conveyed himself with the stream, and governing the target wisely, brought himself unto the other side of the water; whereof his people being abashed, some assayed to swim. holding fast by the horses, other by spears and other like weapons, many upon fardels and trusses,[2] got over the river; insomuch as nothing was perished save a little baggage, and of that no great quantity lost.

What utility was shown to be in swimming at the first wars which the Romans had against the Carthaginians? It happened a battle to be on the sea between them, where they of Carthage being vanquished would have set up their sails to have fled, but that perceiving divers young Romans, they threw themselves into

---

[1] Coat of mail.   [2] Packs.

the sea, and swimming unto the ships they enforced their enemies to strike on land, and there assaulted them so asprely [1] that the captain of the Romans, called Luctatius, might easily take them.

Now behold what excellent commodity is in the feat of swimming; since no king, be he never so puissant or perfect in the experience of wars, may assure himself from the necessities which fortune soweth among men that be mortal. And since on the health and safeguard of a noble captain often times dependeth the weal of a realm, nothing should be kept from his knowledge, whereby his person may be in every jeopardy preserved.

Among these exercises it shall be convenient to learn to handle sundry weapons, specially the sword and the battle-axe, which be for a nobleman most convenient. But the most honourable exercise, in mine opinion, and that beseemeth the estate of every noble person, is to ride surely and clean on a great horse and a rough, which undoubtedly not only importeth a majesty and dread to inferior persons, beholding him above the common course of other men, daunting a fierce and cruel beast, but also is no little succour, as well in pursuit of enemies and confounding them, as in escaping imminent danger, when wisdom thereto exhorteth. Also a strong and hardy horse doth some time more damage under his master than he with all his weapon: and also setteth forward the stroke, and causeth it to light with more violence.

Bucephalus, the horse of great King Alexander, who suffered none on his back save only his master, at the battle of Thebes being sore wounded, would not suffer the King to depart from him to another horse, but persisting in his furious courage, wonderfully continued out the battle, with his feet and teeth beating down and destroying many enemies. And many semblable marvels of his strength he showed. Wherefore Alexander, after the horse was slain, made in remembrance of him a city in the country of India and called it Bucephal, in perpetual memory of so worthy a horse, which in his life had so well served him.

What wonderful enterprises did Julius Caesar achieve by the help of his horse? Which not only did excel all other horses in fierceness and swift running, but also was in some part discrepant in figure from other horses, having his fore hooves like to the feet of a man. And in that figure Pliny writeth that he saw him carved before the temple of Venus.

[1] Fiercely.

Other remembrance there is of divers horses by whose monstrous power men did exploit incredible affairs: but because the report of them containeth things impossible, and is not written by any approved author, I will not in this place rehearse them: saving that it is yet supposed that the castle of Arundel in Sussex was made by one Beauvize, Earl of Southampton, for a monument of his horse called Arundel, which in far countries had saved his master from many perils. Now considering the utility in riding great horses, it shall be necessary (as I have said) that a gentleman do learn to ride a great and fierce horse whilst he is tender and the brawn and sinew of his thighs not fully consolidate. There is also a right good exercise which is also expedient to learn, which is named the vaunting of a horse: that is to leap on him at every side without stirrup or other help, specially whilst the horse is going. And being therein expert, then armed at all points to assay the same; the commodity whereof is so manifest that I need no further to declare it.

XVIII. The ancient hunting of Greeks and Romans.

BUT NOW will I proceed to write of exercises which be not utterly reproved of noble authors, if they be used with opportunity and in measure, I mean hunting, hawking, and dancing. In hunting may be an imitation of battle, if it be such as was used among them of Persia, whereof Xenophon, the noble and most eloquent philosopher, maketh a delectable mention in his book called the doctrine of Cyrus; and also maketh another special book, containing the whole discipline of the ancient hunting of the Greeks; and in that form being used, it is a laudable exercise, of the which I will now somewhat write.

Cyrus and other ancient kings of Persia (as Xenophon writeth) used this manner in all their hunting. First, whereas it seemeth there was in the realm of Persia but one city, which as I suppose was called Persepolis, there were the children of the Persians from their infancy unto the age of seventeen years brought up in the learning of justice and temperance, and also to observe continence in meat and drink; insomuch that, whithersoever they went, they took with them for their sustenance but only bread and herbs, called kerses,[1] in Latin *nasturtium*, and for their drink,

[1] Cress.

a dish to take water out of the rivers as they passed. Also they learned to shoot and to cast the dart or javelin. When they came to the age of seventeen years, they were lodged in the palaces that were there ordained for the king and his nobles, which was as well for the safeguard of the city, as for the example of temperance that they daily had at their eyes given to them by the nobles, which also might be called peers, by the significance of the Greek word, wherein they were called, *omotimi*. Moreover they were accustomed to rise alway in the first spring of the day, and patiently to sustain alway both cold and heat. And the king did see them exercised in going and also in running. And when he intended in his own person to hunt, which he did commonly every month, he took with him the one half of the company of young men that were in the palace. Then took every man with him his bow and quiver with arrows, his sword or hatchet of steel, a little target, and two darts. The bow and arrows served to pursue beasts that were swift, and the darts to assail them and all other beasts. And when their courage was chafed, or that by fierceness of the beast they were in danger, then force constrained them to strike with the sword or hatchet, and to have good eye at the violent assault of the beast, and to defend them if need were with their targets, wherein they accounted to be the truest and most certain meditation of wars. And to this hunting the king did conduct them, and he himself first hunted valiantly, and reforming them whom he saw negligent or slothful. But ere they went forth to this hunting they dined no more: for if, for any occasion, their hunting continued above one day, they took the said dinner for their supper, and the next day, if they killed no game, they hunted until supper time, accounting those two days but for one. And if they took anything, they ate it at their supper with joy and pleasure. If nothing were killed, they ate only bread and kerses, as I before rehearsed, and drank thereto water. And if any man will dispraise this diet, let him think what pleasure there is in bread, to him that is hungry, and what delectation is in drinking water, to him that is thirsty. Surely this manner of hunting may be called a necessary solace and pastime, for therein is the very imitation of battle, for not only it doth show the courage and strength as well of the horse as of him that rideth, traversing over mountains and valleys, encountering and overthrowing great and mighty beasts, but also it increaseth in them both agility and quickness, also sleight and policy to find such passages and

straits, where they may prevent or entrap their enemies. Also by
continuance therein they shall easily sustain travail in wars,
hunger and thirst, cold and heat. Hitherto be the words of
Xenophon, although I have not set them in like order as he wrote
them.

The chief hunting of the valiant Greeks was at the lion, the
leopard, the tiger, the wild swine, and the bear, and sometime the
wolf and the hart. Theseus, which was companion to Hercules,
attained the greatest part of his renown for fighting with the great
boar, which the Greeks called *phera*, that wasted and consumed
the fields of a great country.

Meleager likewise for slaying of the great boar in Caledonia,
which in greatness and fierceness exceeded all other boars, and
had slain many noble and valiant persons.

The great Alexander, in times vacant from battle, delighted in
that manner hunting. On a time he fought alone with a lion
wonderful great and fierce, being present among other strangers,
the ambassador of Lacedaemonia, and after long travail with
incredible might he overthrew the lion and slew him; whereat the
said ambassador wondering marvellously said to the King, 'I
would to God (noble prince) ye should fight with a lion for some
great empire.' By which words it seemed that he nothing approved the valiantness of a prince by fighting with a wild beast,
wherein much more was adventured than might be by the
victory gotten.

Albeit Pompey, Sertorius, and divers other noble Romans,
when they were in Numidia, Libia, and such other countries,
which now be called Barbary and Morisco, in the vacation
season from wars, they hunted lions, leopards, and such other
beasts, fierce and savage, to the intent thereby to exercise themselves and their soldiers. But Almighty God be thanked, in this
realm be no such cruel beasts to be pursued. Notwithstanding in
the hunting of red deer and fallow might be a great part of
semblable exercise used by noblemen, specially in forests which
be spacious, if they would use but a few number of hounds, only
to harbour or rouse the game, and by their yorning [1] to give
knowledge which way it fleeth; the remnants of the disport to be
in pursuing with javelins and other weapons, in manner of war.
And to them which, in this hunting, do show most prowess and

---

[1] Crying, barking.

activity, a garland or some other like token to be given, in sign of victory, and with a joyful manner to be brought in the presence of him that is chief in the company; there to receive condign praise for their good endeavour. I dispraise not the hunting of the fox with running hounds, but it is not to be compared to the other hunting in commodity of exercise. Therefore it would be used in the deep winter, when the other game is unseasonable.

Hunting of the hare with greyhounds is a right good solace for men that be studious, of them to whom nature hath not given personage or courage apt for the wars. And also for gentlewomen, which fear neither sun nor wind for impairing their beauty. And peradventure they shall be thereat less idle than they should be at home in their chambers.

Killing of deer with bows or greyhounds serveth well for the pot (as is the common saying), and therefore it must of necessity be sometimes used. But it containeth therein no commendable solace or exercise, in comparison to the other forms of hunting, if it be diligently perceived.

As for hawking, I can find no notable remembrance that it was used of ancient time among noble princes. I call ancient time before a thousand years passed, since which time virtue and nobleness hath rather decayed than increased. Nor I could never know who found first that disport.

Pliny maketh mention, in his eighth book of the history of nature, that in the parts of Greece called Thrace men and hawks, as it were by a confederacy, took birds together in this wise. The men sprang the birds out of the bushes, and the hawks, soaring over them, beat them down, so that the men might easily take them. And then did the men depart equally the prey with the falcons, which being well served, eftsoons [1] and of a custom repaired to such places where, being aloft, they perceived men to that purpose assembled. By which rehearsal of Pliny we may conject, that from Thrace came this disport of hawking. And I doubt not but many other, as well as I, have seen a semblable experience of wild hobbies,[2] which, in some countries that be champine,[3] will soar and lie aloft, hovering over larks and quails, and keep them down on the ground, whilst they which await on the prey do take them. But in what wise, or wheresoever, the beginning of hawking was, surely it is a right delectable solace,

[1] Again.   [2] Hawks.
                [3] Having fields.

though thereof cometh not so much utility (concerning exercise) as there doth of hunting. But I would our falcons might be satisfied with the division of their prey, as the falcons of Thrace were; that they needed not to devour and consume the hens of this realm in such number, that unneth [1] it be shortly considered, and that falcons be brought to a more homely diet, it is right likely that, within a short space of years, our familiar poultry shall be as scarce as be now partridge and pheasant. I speak not this in dispraise of the falcons, but of them which keepeth them like coknayes.[2] The mean gentlemen and honest householders, which care for the gentle entertainment of their friends, do find in their dish that I say truth, and noblemen shall right shortly espy it, when they come suddenly to their friends' house, unpurveyed for lack of long warning.

But now to return to my purpose: undoubtedly hawking, measurably used, and for a pastime, giveth to a man good appetite to his supper. And at the least way withdraweth him from other dalliance, or disports dishonest and to body and soul perchance pernicious.

Now I purpose to declare something concerning dancing, wherein is merit of praise and dispraise, as I shall express it in such form, as I trust the reader shall find therein a rare and singular pleasure, with also good learning in things not yet commonly known in our vulgar. Which if it be read of him that hath good opportunity and quiet silence, I doubt not, but he shall take thereby such commodity, as he looked not to have found in that exercise, which of the more part of sad men is so little esteemed.

XIX. That all dancing is not to be reproved.

I AM not of that opinion that all dancing generally is repugnant unto virtue; although some persons excellently learned, specially divines, so do affirm it, which alway have in their mouths (when they come into the pulpit) the saying of the noble doctor Saint Augustine, that better it were to delve or to go to plough on the Sunday than to dance: which might be spoken of that kind of dancing which was used in the time of St Augustine, when

---

[1] Unless. [2] Pampered pets.

everything with the Empire of Rome declined from their perfection, and the old manner of dancing was forgotten, and none remained but that which was lascivious, and corrupted the minds of them that danced, and provoked sin, as semblably some do at this day. Also at that time idolatry was not clearly extinct, but divers fragments thereof remained in every region. And perchance solemn dances, which were celebrate unto the pagans' false gods, were yet continued; forasmuch as the pure religion of Christ was not in all places consolidate, and the pastors and curates did wink at such recreations, fearing that if they should hastily have removed it, and induced suddenly the severity of God's laws, they should stir the people thereby to a general sedition; to the imminent danger and subversion of Christ's whole religion, late sown among them, and not yet sufficiently rooted. But the wise and discreet doctor St Augustine, using the art of an orator, wherein he was right excellent, omitting all rigorous menace or terror, dissuaded them by the most easy way from that manner ceremony belonging to idolatry; preferring before it bodily occupation; thereby aggravating the offence to God that was in that ceremony, since occupation, which is necessary for man's sustenance and in due times virtuous, is notwithstanding prohibited to be used on the Sundays. And yet in these words of this noble doctor is not so general dispraise to all dancing as some men do suppose. And that for two causes. First in his comparison he preferreth not before dancing or joineth thereto any vicious exercise, but connecteth it with tilling and digging of the earth, which be labours incident to man's living, and in them is contained nothing that is vicious. Wherefore the pre-eminence thereof above dancing qualifying the offence, they being done out of due time, that is to say, in an holy day, concludeth not dancing to be at all times and in every manner unlawful or vicious, considering that in certain cases of extreme necessity men might both plough and delve without doing to God any offence. Also it shall seem to them that seriously do examine the said words that therein St Augustine doth not prohibit dancing so generally as it is taken, but only such dances which (as I late said) were superstitious and contained in them a spice of idolatry, or else did with unclean motions of countenances irritate the minds of the dancers to venereal lusts, whereby fornication and avoutry [1] were daily

[1] Adultery.

increased. Also in those dances were interlaced ditties of wanton love or ribaldry, with frequent remembrance of the most vile idols Venus and Bacchus, as it were that the dance were to their honour and memory, which most of all abhorred from Christ's religion, savouring the ancient error of paganism. I would to God those names were not at this day used in ballads and ditties in the courts of princes and noblemen, where many good wits be corrupted with semblable fantasies, which in better wise employed might have been more necessary to the public weal and their prince's honour. But now will I leave this serious matter to divines to persuade or dissuade herein according to their offices. And since in mine opinion St Augustine that blessed clerk reproveth not so generally all dancing, but that I may lawfully rehearse some kind thereof which may be necessary and also commendable, taking it for an exercise, I shall now proceed to speak of the first beginning thereof, and in how great estimation it was had in divers regions.

XX. Of the first beginning of dancing and the old estimation thereof.

THERE be sundry opinions of the original beginning of dancing. The poets do feign that when Saturn, which devoured divers his children, and semblably would have done with Jupiter, Rhea the mother of Jupiter devised that *Curetes* (which were men of arms in that country) should dance in armour, playing with their swords and shields, in such form as by that new and pleasant device they should assuage the melancholy of Saturn, and in the meantime Jupiter was conveyed into Phrygia, where Saturn also pursuing him, Rhea semblably taught the people there called *Coribantes* to dance in another form, wherewith Saturn was eftsoons [1] demulced [2] and appeased, which fable hath a resemblance to the history of the Bible in the First Book of Kings, where it is remembered that Saul (whom God chose from a keeper of asses to be King of Jews, who in stature excelled and was above all other men by the head), declining from the laws and precepts of God, was possessed of an evil spirit which oftentimes tormented and vexed him, and other remedy found he none

[1] Again. [2] Stroked.

but that David, which after him was king, being at that time a proper child and playing sweetly on a harp, with his pleasant and perfect harmony reduced his mind into his pristine estate, and during the time that he played the spirit ceased to vex him, which I suppose happened not only of the efficiency of music (albeit therein is much power, as well in repressing as exciting natural affects), but also of the virtue ingenerate in the child David that played, whom God also had predestined to be a great king, and a great prophet. And for the sovereign gifts of grace and of nature that he was endowed with, Almighty God said of him that he had found a man after his heart and pleasure. But now to return to speak of dancing.

Some interpreters of poets do imagine that Proteus, who is supposed to have turned himself into sundry figures, as sometime to show himself like a serpent, sometime like a lion, other whiles like water, another time like the flame of fire, signifieth to be none other but a deliver and crafty dancer, which in his dance could imagine the inflexions of the serpent, the soft and delectable flowing of the water, the swiftness and mounting of the fire, the fierce rage of the lion, the violence and fury of the leopard; which exposition is not to be dispraised, since it discordeth not from reason. But one opinion there is which I will rehearse, more for the merry fantasy that therein is contained, than for any faith or credit that is to be given thereto.

Over Syracuse (a great and ancient city in Sicily) there reigned a cruel tyrant called Hiero, which by horrible tyrannies and oppressions brought himself into the indignation and hatred of all his people, which he perceiving, lest by mutual communication they should conspire against him any rebellion, he prohibited all men under terrible menaces that no man or woman should speak unto another, but instead of words they should use in their necessary affairs countenances, tokens, and movings with their feet, hands, and eyes, which for necessity first used, at the last grew to a perfect and delectable dancing. And Hiero, notwithstanding his foolish curiosity, at the last was slain of his people most miserably. But although this history were true, yet was not dancing at this time first begun, for Orpheus and Museus, the most ancient of poets, and also Homer, which were long afore Hiero, do make mention of dancing. And in Delos, which was the most ancient temple of Apollo, no solemnity was done without dancing.

Also in India, where the people honoureth the sun, they assemble together, and when the sun first appeareth, joined all in a dance they salute him, supposing that forasmuch as he moveth without sensible noise, it pleaseth him best to be likewise saluted, that is to say with a pleasant motion and silence. The interpreters of Plato do think that the wonderful and incomprehensible order of the celestial bodies, I mean stars and planets, and their motions harmonical, gave to them that intensity and by the deep search of reason behold their courses, in the sundry diversities of number and time, a form of imitation of a semblable motion, which they called dancing or saltation; wherefore the more near they approached to that temperance and subtle modulation of the said superior bodies, the more perfect and commendable is their dancing, which is most like to the truth of any opinion that I have hitherto found.

Other fables there be which I omit for this present time. And now I will express in what estimation dancing was had in the ancient time. And also sundry forms of dancing, not all, but such as had in them a semblance of virtue or cunning.

When the Ark of God (wherein was put the Tables of the Commandments, the yard wherewith Moses divided the Red Sea, and did the miracles in the presence of Pharaoh, King of Egypt, also a part of manna, wherewith the children of Israel were fed forty years in desert), was recovered of the Philistines, and brought unto the city of Gaba, the holy King David, wearing on him a linen surplice, danced before the said Ark, following him a great number of instruments of music. Whereat his wife Michal, the daughter of King Saul, disdained and scorned him, wherewith (as Holy Scripture saith) Almighty God was much displeased. And David, not ceasing, danced joyously through the city, in that manner honouring that solemn feast, which among the Jews was one of the chief and principal, wherewith God was more pleased than with all the other observances that then were done unto Him at that time.

I will not trouble the readers with the innumerable ceremonies of the Gentiles, which were comprehended in dancing, since they ought to be numbered among superstitions. But I will declare how wise men and valiant captains embraced dancing for a sovereign and profitable exercise.

Lycurgus, that gave first laws to the Lacedaemons (a people of Greece), ordained that the children there should be taught as diligently to dance in armour as to fight. And that in time of wars, they should move them in battle against their enemies in form and manner of dancing.

Semblably the old inhabitants of Ethiopia, at the joining of their battles, and when the trumpets and other instruments sounded, they danced; and instead of a quiver, they have their darts set about their heads, like to rays or beams of the sun, wherewith they believe that they put their enemies in fear. Also it was not lawful for any of them to cast any dart at his enemy but dancing. And not only this rude people esteemed so much dancing, but also the most noble of the Greeks, which for their excellency in prowess and wisdom were called half gods. As Achilles, and his son Pyrrhus, and divers other. Wherefore Homer, among the high benefits that God giveth to man, he reciteth dancing. For he saith in the first book of *Iliad*:

> God granteth to some man prowess martial,
> To another dancing, with song harmonical.

Suppose ye that the Romans, which in gravity of manners passed the Greeks, had not great pleasure in dancing? Did not Romulus, the first King of Romans and builder of the city of Rome, ordain certain priests and ministers to the god Mars (whom he advaunted to be his father)? Which priests, forasmuch as certain times they danced about the city with targets that they imagined to fall from heaven, were called in Latin *Salii*, which into English may be translated dancers, who continued so long time in reverence among the Romans that unto the time that they were christened,[1] the noblemen and princes' children there, using much diligence and suit, coveted to be of the college of the said dancers.

Moreover the emperors that were most noble delighted in dancing, perceiving therein to be a perfect measure, which may be called modulation, wherein some dancers of old time so wonderfully excelled, that they would plainly express in dancing, without any words or ditty, histories, with the whole circumstance of affairs in them contained, whereof I shall rehearse two marvellous experiences. At Rome, in the time of Nero, there was a philosopher called Demetrius, which was of that sect, that forasmuch as they abandoned all shamefastness in their words and acts, they were called *Cinici*, in English doggish. This Demetrius, often

[1] Became Christians.

reproving dancing, would say that there was nothing therein of any importance, and that it was none other but a counterfeiting with the feet and hands of the harmony that was shown before in the rebeck, shawm, or other instrument, and that the motions were but vain and separate from all understanding and of no purpose or efficacy. Whereon hearing a famous dancer, and one, as it seemed, that was not without good learning, and had in remembrance many histories, he came to Demetrius and said unto him, 'Sir, I humbly desire you refuse not to do me that honesty with your presence, in beholding me dance, which ye shall see me do without sound of any instrument. And then if it shall seem to you worthy dispraise, utterly banish and confound my science.' Whereunto Demetrius granted. The young man danced the advoutry [1] of Mars and Venus, and therein expressed how Vulcan, husband of Venus, thereof being advertised by the sun, laid snares for his wife and Mars; also how they were wound and tied in Vulcan's net; moreover how all the gods came to the spectacle; finally how Venus, all ashamed and blushing, fearfully desired her lover Mars to deliver her from that peril, and the residue contained in the fable; which he did with so subtle and crafty gesture, with such perspicuity and declaration of every act in the matter (which of all thing is most difficult) with such a grace and beauty, also with a wit so wonderful and pleasant, that Demetrius, as it seemed, thereat rejoicing and delighting, cried with a loud voice: 'O man, I do not only see, but also hear, what thou doest, and it seemeth also to me that with thy hands thou speakest.' Which saying was confirmed by all them that were at that time present.

The same young man sang and danced on a time before the Emperor Nero, when there was also present a strange king, which understood none other language but of his own country; yet notwithstanding the man danced so aptly and plainly, as his custom was, that the strange king, although he perceived not what he said, yet he understood every deal of the matter. And when he had taken his leave of the emperor to depart, the emperor offered to give him anything that he thought might be to his commodity. Ye may (said the king) bounteously reward me, if ye lend me the young man that danced before your majesty. Nero wondering and requiring of him why he so importunately desired the dancer,

[1] Adultery.

or what commodity the dancer might be unto him, 'Sir,' said the king, 'I have divers confines and neighbours that be of sundry languages and manners, wherefore I have often times need of many interpreters. Wherefore if I had this man with me and should have anything to do with my neighbours, he would so with his fashion and gesture express everything to me, and teach them to do the same, that from henceforth I should not have need of any interpreter.' Also the ancient philosophers commended dancing; insomuch as Socrates, the wisest of all the Greeks in his time, and from whom all the sects of philosophers as from a fountain were derived, was not ashamed to account dancing among the serious disciplines, for the commendable beauty, for the apt and proportionate moving, and for the crafty disposition and fashioning of the body. It is to be considered that in the said ancient time there were divers manners of dancing, which varied in the names, likewise as they did in tunes of the instrument, as semblably we have at this day. But those names, some were general, some were special; the general names were given of the universal form of dancing, whereby was represented the qualities or conditions of sundry estates; as the majesty of princes was shown in that dance which was named *Eumelia*, and belonged to tragedies; dissolute motions and wanton countenances in that which was called *Cordax*, and pertained to comedies, wherein men of base behaviour only danced. Also the form of battle and fighting in armour was expressed in those dances which were called *Enopliae*. Also there was a kind of dancing called *Hormus*, of all the other most like to that which is at this time used; wherein danced young men and maidens, the man expressing in his motion and countenance fortitude and magnanimity apt for the wars, the maiden moderation and shamefastness which represented a pleasant connection of fortitude and temperance. Instead of these we have now base dances, bargenettes, pavions, turgions, and rounds. And as for the special names, they were taken as they be now, either of the names of the first inventors or of the measure and number that they do contain or of the first words of the ditty, which the song comprehendeth whereof the dance was made. In every of the said dances, there was a concinnity [1] of moving the foot and body, expressing some pleasant or profitable affects or motions of the mind.

[1] Fitness.

Here a man may behold what artifice and craft there was in the ancient times in dancing, which at this day no man can imagine or conject. But if men would now apply the first part of their youth, that is to say from seven years to twenty, effectually in the sciences liberal and knowledge of histories, they should revive the ancient form as well of dancing, as of other exercises, whereof they might take not only pleasure, but also profit and commodity.

XXI. Wherefore in the good order of dancing a man and a woman danceth together.

IT IS diligently to be noted that the associating of man and woman in dancing, they both observing one number and time in their movings, was not begun without a special consideration, as well for the necessary conjunction of those two persons, as for the intimation of sundry virtues which be by them represented. And forasmuch as by the association of a man and a woman in dancing may be signified matrimony, I could in declaring the dignity and commodity of that sacrament make entire volumes, if it were not so commonly known to all men, that almost every friar limiter [1] carrieth it written in his bosom. Wherefore, lest in repeating a thing so frequent and common my book should be as fastidious or fulsome to the readers as such merchant preachers be now to their customers, I will reverently take my leave of divines. And for my part I will endeavour myself to assemble, out of the books of ancient poets and philosophers, matter as well apt to my purpose as also new or at the leastways infrequent, or seldom heard of them that have not read very many authors in Greek and Latin.

But now to my purpose. In every dance, of a most ancient custom, there danceth together a man and a woman, holding each other by the hand or the arm, which betokeneth concord. Now it behoveth the dancers and also the beholders of them to know all qualities incident to a man, and also all qualities to a woman likewise apperraining.

A man in his natural perfection is fierce, hardy, strong in opinion, covetous of glory, desirous of knowledge, appetiting by generation to bring forth his semblable. The good nature of a

[1] A friar allowed to beg only within the limits of a certain district.

woman is to be mild, timorous, tractable, benign, of sure remembrance, and shamefast. Divers other qualities of each of
them might be found out, but these be most apparent, and for
this time sufficient.

Wherefore, when we behold a man and a woman dancing
together, let us suppose there to be a concord of all the said
qualities, being joined together, as I have set them in order. And
the moving of the man would be more vehement, of the woman
more delicate, and with less advancing of the body, signifying the
courage and strength that ought to be in a man, and the pleasant
soberness that should be in a woman. And in this wise *fierceness*
joined with *mildness* maketh *severity*; *audacity* with *timorosity*
maketh *magnanimity*; wilful opinion and *tractability* (which is to
be shortly persuaded and moved) maketh *constancy* a virtue;
covetousness of glory adorned with *benignity* causeth *honour*;
desire of knowledge with *sure remembrance* procureth *sapience*;
shamefastness joined to *appetite of generation* maketh *continence*,
which is a mean between *chastity* and *inordinate lust*. These
qualities, in this wise being knit together and signified in the
personages of man and woman dancing, do express or set out the
figure of very nobility; which in the higher estate it is contained,
the more excellent is the virtue in estimation.

*XXII. How dancing may be an introduction unto the first moral
virtue, called prudence.*

As I have already affirmed, the principal cause of this my little
enterprise is to declare an induction or mean, how children of
gentle nature or disposition may be trained into the way of virtue
with a pleasant facility. And forasmuch as it is very expedient
that there be mixed with study some honest and moderate disport,
or at the leastway recreation, to recomfort and quicken the vital
spirits, lest they long travailing, or being much occupied in contemplation or remembrance of things grave and serious, might
happen to be fatigued, or perchance oppressed. And therefore
Tully, who unneth [1] found ever any time vacant from study, per-
mitteth in his first book of offices that men may use play and
disport, yet notwithstanding in such wise as they do use sleep and

[1] Scarcely.

other manner of quiet, when they have sufficiently disposed earnest matters and of weighty importance.

Now because there is no pastime to be compared to that wherein may be found both recreation and meditation of virtue, I have among all honest pastimes, wherein is exercise of the body, noted dancing to be of an excellent utility, comprehending in it wonderful figures, or, as the Greeks do call them, *ideae*, of virtues and noble qualities, and specially of the commodious virtue called prudence, whom Tully defineth to be the knowledge of things which ought to be desired and followed, and also of them which ought to be fled from or eschewed. And it is named of Aristotle the mother of virtues; of other philosophers it is called the captain or mistress of virtues; of some the housewife, forasmuch as by her diligence she doth investigate and prepare places apt and convenient, where other virtues shall execute their powers or offices. Wherefore, as Solomon saith, like as in water be shown the visages of them that behold it, so unto men that be prudent the secrets of men's hearts be openly discovered. This virtue being so commodious to man, and, as it were, the porch of the noble palace of man's reason, whereby all other virtues shall enter, it seemeth to me right expedient, that as soon as opportunity may be found, a child or young man be thereto induced. And because that the study of virtue is tedious for the more part to them that do flourish in young years, I have devised how in the form of dancing, now late used in this realm among gentlemen, the whole description of this virtue prudence may be found out and well perceived, as well by the dancers as by them which standing by will be diligent beholders and markers, having first mine instruction surely graven in the table of their remembrance. Wherefore all they that have their courage stirred toward very honour or perfect nobility, let them approach to this pastime, and either themselves prepare them to dance, or else at the leastway behold with watching eyes other that can dance truly, keeping just measure and time. But to the understanding of this instruction, they must mark well the sundry motions and measures, which in true form of dancing is to be specially observed.

The first moving in every dance is called honour, which is a reverent inclination or curtsey, with a long deliberation or pause, and is but one motion, comprehending the time of three other motions, or setting forth of the foot. By that may be signified that at the beginning of all our acts, we should do due honour to

God, which is the root of prudence; which honour is compact of these three things, fear, love, and reverence. And that in the beginning of all things we should advisedly, with some tract of time, behold and foresee the success of our enterprise.

By the second motion, which is two in number, may be signified celerity and slowness: which two, albeit they seem to discord in their effects and natural properties, and therefore they may be well resembled to the brawl in dancing (for in our English tongue we say men do brawl, when between them is altercation in words), yet of them two springeth an excellent virtue whereunto we lack a name in English.

Wherefore I am constrained to usurp a Latin word, calling it maturity: which word, though it be strange and dark, yet by declaring the virtue in a few more words, the name once brought in custom, shall be facile to understand as other words late coming out of Italy and France, and made denizens among us.

Maturity is a mean between two extremities, wherein nothing lacketh or exceedeth, and is in such estate that it may neither increase nor minish without losing the denomination of maturity. The Greeks in a proverb do express it properly in two words, which I can none otherwise interpret in English, but speed thee slowly.

Also of this word maturity sprang a noble and precious sentence, recited by Salust in the battle against Cataline, which is in this manner or like, 'Consult before thou enterprise anything, and after thou hast taken counsel, it is expedient to do it maturely.'

Maturum in Latin may be interpreted ripe or ready, as fruit when it is ripe, it is at the very point to be gathered and eaten. And every other thing, when it is ready, it is at the instant after to be occupied. Therefore that word maturity is translated to the acts of man, that when they be done with such moderation that nothing in the doing may be seen superfluous or indigent, we may say that they be maturely done: reserving the words ripe and ready to fruit and other things separate from affairs, as we have now in usage. And this do I now remember for the necessary augmentation of our language.

In the most excellent and most noble emperor Octavius Augustus, in whom reigned all nobility, nothing is more commended than that he had frequently in his mouth this word *Matura*, do maturely. As he should have said, do neither too much nor too little, too soon nor too late, too swiftly nor slowly, but in due time and measure.

Now I trust I have sufficiently expounded the virtue called maturity, which is the mean or mediocrity between sloth and celerity, commonly called speediness; and so have I declared what utility may be taken of a brawl in dancing.

XXIII. The third and fourth branches of prudence.

THE THIRD motion, called singles, is of two unities separate in passing forward; by whom may be signified providence and industry; which after everything maturely achieved, as is before written, maketh the first pass forward in dancing. But it shall be expedient to expound what is the thing called Providence, forasmuch as it is not known to every man.

Providence is, whereby a man not only foreseeth commodity and incommodity, prosperity and adversity, but also consulteth and therewith endeavoureth as well to repel annoyance, as to attain and get profit and advantage. And the difference between it and consideration is that consideration only consisteth in pondering and examining things conceived in the mind, providence in helping them with counsel and act. Wherefore to consideration pertaineth excogitation and avisement, to providence provision and execution. For like as the good husband, when he hath sown his ground, setteth up clouts or threads, which some call shailes, some blenchars, or other like shows, to fear away birds, which he foreseeth ready to devour and hurt his corn. Also perceiving the improfitable weeds appearing, which will annoy his corn or herbs, forthwith he weedeth them clean out of his ground, and will not suffer them to grow or increase. Semblably it is the part of a wise man to foresee and provide, that either in such things as he hath acquired by his study or diligence, or in such affairs as he hath in hand, he be not endamaged or impeached by his adversaries.

In like manner a governor of a public weal ought to provide as well by menaces, as by sharp and terrible punishments, that persons evil and improfitable do not corrupt and devour his good subjects. Finally there is in providence such an admiration and majesty, that not only it is attributed to kings and rulers, but also to God, creator of the world.

Industry hath not been so long time used in the English tongue as providence; wherefore it is the more strange, and requireth the more plain exposition. It is a quality proceeding of wit and experience, by the which a man perceiveth quickly, inventeth freshly, and counselleth speedily. Wherefore they that be called industrious, do most craftily and deeply understand in all affairs what is expedient, and by what means and ways they may soonest exploit them. And those things in whom other men travail, a person industrious lightly and with facility speedeth, and findeth new ways and means to bring to effect that he desireth.

Among divers other remembered in histories, such one among the Greeks was Alcibiades, who being in childhood most amiable of all other, and of most subtle wit, was instructed by Socrates. The said Alcibiades, by the sharpness of his wit, the doctrine of Socrates, and by his own experience in sundry affairs in the common weal of the Athenians, became so industrious, that were it good or evil that he enterprised, nothing almost escaped that he achieved not, were the thing never so difficult (or as who saith) impenetrable, and that many sundry things, as well for his country as also against it, after that he for his inordinate pride and lechery was out of Athens exiled.

Among the Romans, Caius Julius Caesar, which first took upon him the perpetual rule and governance of the Empire, is a noble example of industry, for in his incomparable wars and business incredible (if the authority and faith of the writers were not of long time approved) he did not only excogitate most excellent policies and devices to vanquish or subdue his enemies, but also prosecuted them with such celerity and effect that divers and many times he was in the camp of his enemies, or at the gates of their towns or fortresses, when they supposed that he and his host had been two days' journey from thence, leaving to them no time or leisure to consult or prepare against him sufficient resistance. And over that, this quality industry so reigned in him that he himself would minister to his secretaries at one time and instant the contents of three sundry epistles or letters. Also it is a thing wonderful to remember that he, being a prince of the most ancient and noble house of the Romans, and from the time that he came to man's estate almost continually in wars, also of glory insatiable, of courage invincible, could in affairs of such importance and difficulty, or (which is much more to be marvelled at now) would so exactly write the history of his own acts and gests, that for the native and inimitable eloquence in expressing the counsels, devices, conventions, progressions, enterprises, exploitures, forms, and fashions of embattling, he seemeth to put all other writers of like matter to silence.

Here is the perfect pattern of industry, which I trust shall suffice to make the proper signification thereof to be understood of the readers. And consequently to incend them to approach to the true practising thereof.

So is the singles declared in these two qualities, Providence and Industry; which, seriously noted and often remembered of the dancers and beholders, shall acquire to them no little fruit and commodity, if there be in their minds any good and laudable matter for virtue to work in.

XXIV. Of the fifth branch, called circumspection, shown in reprinse.

COMMONLY next after singles in dancing is a reprinse, which is one moving only, putting back the right foot to his fellow. And that may be well called circumspection, which signifieth as much as beholding on every part what is well and sufficient, what lacketh, how and from whence it may be provided. Also what hath caused profit or damage in the time passed, what is the estate of the time present, what advantage or peril may succeed or is imminent. And because in it is contained a deliberation, in having regard to that that followeth, and is also of affinity with providence and industry, I make him in the form of a retreat.

In this motion a man may, as it were on a mountain or place of espial, behold on every side far off, measuring and esteeming everything, and either pursue it, if it be commendable, or abandon it or eschew it, if it be noyful.[1] This quality (like as providence and industry be) is a branch of prudence, which some call the princess of virtues; and it is not only expedient but also needful to every estate and degree of men, that do continue in the life called active.

In the *Iliad* of Homer, the noble Duke Nestor, a man of marvellous eloquence and long experience, as he that lived three men's lives, as he there avaunteth in the counsel that he gave to

[1] Evil, noxious.

Agamemnon, to reconcile to him Achilles, the most strong of all
the Greeks, he persuaded Agamemnon specially to be circumspect; declaring how that the private contention between them
should replenish the host of the Greeks with much dolour,
whereat King Priam and his children should laugh, and the
residue of the Trojans in their minds should rejoice and take
courage.

Among the Romans Quintus Fabius for this quality is sove-
reignly extolled among historians; and for that cause he is often
times called of them *Fabius Cunctator*, that is to say the tarrier or
delayer, for in the wars between the Romans and Hannibal, he
knowing all coasts of the country, continually kept him and his
host on mountains and high places, within a small distance of
Hannibal's army; so that neither he would abandon his enemies
nor yet join with them battle. By which wonderful policy he
caused Hannibal so to travail, that some time for lack of victual
and for weariness, great multitudes of his host perished. Also he
oftentimes awaited them in dangerous places, unready, and then
he skirmished with them, as long as he was sure to have of them
advantage; and after he repaired to the high places adjoining,
using his accustomed manner to behold the passage of Hannibal.
And by this means this most circumspect captain Fabius wonderfully enfeebled the power of the said Hannibal; which is no less
esteemed in praise, than the subduing of Carthage by the valiant
Scipio. For if Fabius had not so fatigued Hannibal and his host,
he had shortly subverted the city of Rome, and then could not
Scipio have been able to attain that enterprise.

What more clear mirror or spectacle can we desire of circumspection than King Henry the Seventh, of most noble memory,
father unto our most dread sovereign lord, whose worthy
renown, like the sun in the midst of his sphere, shineth and ever
shall shine in men's remembrance? What incomparable circumspection was in him alway found, that notwithstanding his long
absence out of this realm, the disturbance of the same by sundry
seditions among the nobility, civil wars and battles, wherein
infinite people were slain, beside skirmishes and slaughters in the
private contentions and factions of divers gentlemen, the laws laid
in water (as is the proverb), affection and avarice subduing
justice and equity; yet by his most excellent wit he in few years
not only brought this realm in good order and under due
obedience revived the laws, advanced justice, refurnished his

dominions, and repaired his manors, but also with such circumspection treated with other princes and realms, of leagues, of alliance, and amities, that during the more part of his reign he was little or nothing inquieted with outward hostility or martial business. And yet all other princes either feared him or had him in a fatherly reverence. Which praise, with the honour thereunto due, as inheritance descendeth by right unto his most noble son, our most dear sovereign lord that now presently reigneth. For, as Tully saith, the best inheritance that the fathers leave to their children, excelling all other patrimony, is the glory or praise of virtue and noble acts. And of such fair inheritance his highness may compare with any prince that ever reigned: which he daily augmenteth, adding thereto other sundry virtues, which I forbear now to rehearse, to the intent I will exclude all suspicion of flattery, since I myself in this work do specially reprove it. But that which is presently known and is in experience needeth no monument. And unto so excellent a prince there shall not lack hereafter condign [1] writers to register his acts, with most eloquent style in perpetual remembrance.

XXV. Of the sixth, seventh, and eighth branches of prudence.

A DOUBLE in dancing is compact of the number of three, whereby may be noted these three branches of prudence: election, experience, and modesty. By them the said virtue of prudence is made complete, and is in her perfection. Election is of an excellent power and authority, and hath such a majesty, that she will not be approached unto of every man. For some there be to whom she denieth her presence, as children, natural fools, men being frantic, or subdued with affects, also they that be subjects to flatterers and proud men. In these persons reason lacketh liberty, which should prepare their entry unto election. This election, which is a part, and as it were a member, of prudence, is best described by opportunity, which is the principal part of counsel, and is compact of these things following.

The importance of the thing consulted. The faculty and power of him that consulteth. The time when. The form how. The substance wherewith to do it. The dispositions and usages of the

----

[1] Worthy, appropriate.

countries. For whom and against whom it ought to be done. All these things prepensed [1] and gathered together seriously and, after a due examination, every of them justly pondered in the balance of reason, immediately cometh the authority of election, who taketh on her to appoint what is to be effectually followed or pursued, rejecting the residue. And then ought experience to be at hand, to whom is committed the actual execution. For without her election is frustrate, and all invention of man is but a fantasy. And therefore who advisedly beholdeth the estate of man's life shall well perceive that all that ever was spoken or written was to be by experience executed; and to that intent was speech specially given to man, wherein he is most discrepant from brute beasts, in declaring what is good, what vicious, what is profitable, what improfitable, by them which by clearness of wit do excel in knowledge, to these that be of a more inferior capacity. And what utility should be acquired by such declaration, if it should not be experienced with diligence?

The philosopher Socrates had not been named of Apollo the wisest man of all Greece, if he had not daily practised the virtues which he in his lessons commended. Julius Caesar, the first Emperor, although there were in him much hid learning; insomuch as he first found the order of our calendar, with the cycle and bisext, called the leap year; yet is he not so much honoured for his learning as he is for his diligence, wherewith he exploited or brought to conclusion those counsels, which as well by his excellent learning and wisdom, as by the advice of other expert counsellors were before treated, and (as I might say) ventilated.

Who will not repute it a thing vain and scornful, and more like to a May game than a matter serious or commendable, to behold a personage, which in speech or writing expresseth nothing but virtuous manners, sage and discreet counsellors, and holy advertisements, to be resolved into all vices, following in his acts nothing that he himself in his words approveth and teacheth to other?

Who shall anything esteem their wisdom, which with great studies find out remedies and provisions necessary for things disordered or abused; and where they themselves may execute it, they leave it untouched; whereby their devices, with the sound that pronounced them, be vanished and come to nothing?

[1] Considered.

Semblably it is to be thought in all other doctrine. Wherefore, as it seemed, it was not without consideration affirmed by Tully, that the knowledge and contemplation of Nature's operations were lame and in a manner imperfect, if there followed none actual experience. Of this shall be more spoken in the later end of this work.

Herewith would be conjoined, or rather mixed with it, the virtue called Modesty, which by Tully is defined to be the knowledge of opportunity of things to be done or spoken, in appointing and setting them in time or place to them convenient and proper. Wherefore it seemeth to be much like to that which men commonly call discretion. Albeit *discretio* in Latin signifieth separation, wherein it is more like to election; but as it is commonly used, it is not only like to modesty, but it is the self modesty. For he that forbeareth to speak, although he can do it both wisely and eloquently, because neither in the time nor in the hearers he findeth opportunity, so that no fruit may succeed of his speech, he therefore is vulgarly called a discreet person. Semblably they name him discreet, that punisheth an offender less than his merits do require, having regard to the weakness of his person, or to the aptness of his amendment. So do they in the virtue called Liberality, where in giving is had consideration as well of the condition and necessity of the person that receiveth, as of the benefit that cometh of the gift received. In every of these things and their semblable is Modesty; which word not being known in the English tongue, nor of all them which understood Latin, except they had read good authors, they improperly named this virtue discretion. For if a man have a sad countenance at all times, and yet not being moved with wrath, but patient and of much gentleness, they which would be seen to be learned will say that the man is of a great modesty; where they should rather say that he were of a great mansuetude; which term, being semblably before this time unknown in our tongue, may be by the sufferance of wise men now received by custom, whereby the term shall be made familiar. That like as the Romans translated the wisdom of Greece into their city, we may, if we list, bring the learning and wisdom of them both into this realm of England, by the translation of their works; since like enterprise hath been taken by Frenchmen, Italians, and Germans, to our no little reproach for our negligence and sloth.

And thus I conclude the last part of dancing, which diligently beholden shall appear to be as well a necessary study as a noble and virtuous pastime, used and continued in such form as I hitherto have declared.

XXVI. Of other exercises, which if they be moderately used be to every estate of man expedient.

I HAVE shown how hunting and dancing may be in the number of commendable exercises, and pastimes, not repugnant to virtue. And undoubted it were much better to be occupied in honest recreation than to do nothing. For it is said of a noble author, 'In doing nothing men learn to do evil'; and Ovid the poet saith:

> If thou flee idleness Cupid hath no might;
> His bow lieth broken, his fire hath no light.

It is not only called idleness, wherein the body or mind ceaseth from labour, but specially idleness is an omission of all honest exercise. The other may be better called a vacation from serious business, which was some time embraced of wise men and virtuous.

It is written to the praise of Xerxes, King of Persia, that in time vacant from the affairs of his realm, he with his own hands planted innumerable trees, which long ere he died brought forth abundance of fruit; and for the crafty and delectable order in the setting of them, it was to all men beholding the prince's industry exceeding marvellous.

But who abhorreth not the history of Sardanapalus, King of the same realm, which having in detestation all princely affairs, and leaving all company of men, enclosed himself in chambers with a great multitude of concubines? And for that he would seem to be some time occupied, or else that wanton pleasures and quietness became to him tedious, he was found by one of his lords in a woman's attire, spinning in a distaff among persons defamed; which known abroad, was to the people so odious, that finally by them he was burned, with all the place whereto he fled for his refuge. And I suppose there is not a more plain figure of idleness than playing at dice. For besides that, that therein is no manner of exercise of the body or mind, they which do play thereat must seem to have no portion of wit or cunning, if they will be called fair players, or in some company avoid the stab of a dagger, if they be taken with any crafty conveyance. And because alway wisdom is therein suspected, there is seldom any playing at dice, but thereat is vehement chiding and brawling, horrible oaths, cruel, and sometime mortal, menaces. I omit strokes, which now and then do happen often times between brethren and most dear friends, if fortune bring alway to one man evil chances, which maketh the play of the other suspected. O why should that be called a play, which is compact of malice and robbery? Undoubtedly they that write of the first inventions of things have good cause to suppose Lucifer, prince of devils, to be the first inventor of dice playing, and hell the place where it was founded, although some do write that it was first invented by Attalus. For what better allective could Lucifer devise to allure or bring men pleasantly into damnable servitude, than to purpose to them in form of a play, his principal treasury; wherein the more part of sin is contained and all goodness and virtue confounded?

The first occasion to play is tediousness of virtuous occupation. Immediately succeedeth coveting of another man's goods, which they call playing; thereto is annected [1] avarice and straight keeping, which they call winning; soon after cometh swearing in rending the members of God, which they name nobleness (for they will say he that sweareth deep, sweareth like a lord); then followeth fury or rage, which they call courage; among them cometh inordinate watch, which they name painfulness; he bringeth in gluttony, and that is good fellowship; and after cometh sleep superfluous, called among them natural rest; and he sometime bringeth in lechery, which is now named dalliance. The name of this treasury is verily idleness, the door whereof is left wide open to dice players; but if they happen to bring in their company, learning, virtuous business, liberality, patience, charity, temperance, good diet, or shamefastness, they must leave them without the gates. For Evil Custom, which is the porter, will not suffer them to enter.

Alas what pity is it that any Christian man should by wanton company be trained, I will no more say into this treasury, but into this loathsome dungeon where he shall lie fettered in gyves [2] of ignorance, and bound with the strong chain of obstinacy, hard to be loosed but by grace?

---

[1] Connected.   [2] Fetters, chains.

The most noble Emperor Octavius Augustus, who hath among writers in divers of his acts an honourable remembrance, only for playing at dice and that but seldom, sustaineth note of reproach.

The Lacedaemons sent an ambassador to the city of Corinth, to have with them alliance; but when the ambassadors found the princes and counsellors playing at dice, they departed without exploiting their message, saying that they would not maculate [1] the honour of their people with such a reproach, to be said that they had made alliance with dicers.

Also to Demetrius the King of Parthians sent golden dice in the rebuke of his lightness.

Everything is to be esteemed after his value. But who hearing a man, whom he knoweth not, to be called a dicer, anyone supposeth him not to be of light credence, dissolute, vain, and remiss? Who almost trusteth his brother, whom he knoweth a dice player? Yea among themselves they laugh, when they perceive or hear any doctrine or virtuous word proceed from any of their companions, thinking that it becometh not his person, much more when he doth anything with devotion or wisdom. How many gentlemen, how many merchants, have in this damnable pastime consumed their substance, as well by their own labours, as by their parents', with great study and painful travail in a long time acquired, and finished their lives in debt and penury? How many goodly and bold yeomen hath it brought unto theft, whereby they have prevented the course of nature, and died by the order of laws miserably? These be the fruits and revenues of that devilish merchandise, beside the final reward, which is more terrible; the report whereof I leave to divines, such as fear not to show their learning, or fill not their mouths so full with sweet meats, or benefices, that their tongues be not let to speak truth; for that is their duty and office, except I with many other be much deceived.

Playing at cards and tables is somewhat more tolerable, only forasmuch as therein wit is more used, and less trust is in fortune, albeit therein is neither laudable study nor exercise. But yet men delighting in virtue might with cards and tables devise games, wherein might be much solace, and also study commodious; as devising a battle, or contention between virtue and vice, or other like pleasant and honest invention.

[1] Stain.

The chess, of all games wherein is no bodily exercise, is most to be commended; for therein is right subtle engine, whereby the wit is made more sharp and remembrance quickened. And it is the more commendable and also commodious if the players have read the moralization of the chess, and when they play do think upon it; which books be in English. But they be very scarce, because few men do seek in plays for virtue or wisdom.

XXVII. That shooting in a long bow is principal of all other exercises.

TULLY saith in his first book of offices, we be not to that intent brought up by Nature, that we should seem to be made to play and disport, but rather to gravity and studies of more estimation. Wherefore it is written of Alexander, Emperor of Rome, for his gravity called Severus, that in his childhood and before he was taught the letters of Greek or Latin, he never exercised any other play or game, but only one, wherein was a similitude of justice, and therefore it was called in Latin *Ad Judices*, which is in English to the judges. But the form thereof is not expressed by the said author, nor none other that I have yet read; wherefore I will repair again to the residue of honest exercise.

And forasmuch as Galen, in his second book of the preservation of health, declareth to be in them these qualities or diversities, that is to say, that some be done with extending of might, and as it were violently, and that is called valiant exercise; some with swift or hasty motion, other with strength and celerity, and that may be called vehement. The particular kinds of every of them he describeth, which were too long here to be rehearsed.

But inasmuch as he also saith that he that is of good estate in his body ought to know the power and effect of every exercise, but he needeth not to practise any other but that which is moderate and mean between every extremity; I will now briefly declare in what exercise now in custom among us may be most found of that mediocrity, and may be augmented or minished at the pleasure of him that doth exercise, without thereby appearing any part of delectation or commodity thereof.

And in mine opinion none may be compared with shooting in the long bow, and that for sundry utilities that come thereof, wherein it incomparably excelleth all other exercise. For in drawing a bow, easy and congruent to his strength, he that shooteth doth moderately exercise his arms and the over part of his body; and if his bow be bigger, he must add to more strength; wherein is no less valiant exercise than in any other whereof Galen writeth.

In shooting at butts, or broad arrow marks, is a mediocrity of exercise of the lower parts of the body and legs, by going a little distance a measurable pace.

At rovers or pricks,[1] it is at his pleasure that shooteth how fast or softly he listeth to go. And yet is the praise of the shooter neither more nor less, for as far or nigh the mark is his arrow, when he goeth softly, as when he runneth.

Tennis, seldom used, and for a little space, is a good exercise for young men, but it is more violent than shooting, by reason that two men do play. Wherefore neither of them is at his own liberty to measure the exercise. For if the one strike the ball hard, the other that intendeth to receive him is then constrained to use semblable violence if he will return the ball from whence it came to him. If it trill fast on the ground, and he intendeth to stop, or if it rebound a great distance from him, and he would eftsoons return it, he cannot then keep any measure of swiftness of motion.

Some men would say, that in mediocrity, which I have so much praised in shooting, why should not bowling, clash,[2] pins, and quoiting be as much commended? Verily as for two the last, be to be utterly abjected of all noblemen, in like wise football, wherein is nothing but beastly fury and extreme violence; whereof proceedeth hurt, and consequently rancour and malice do remain with them that be wounded; wherefore it is to be put in perpetual silence.

In clash is employed too little strength; in bowling oftentimes too much; whereby the sinews be too much strained, and the veins much chafed. Whereof often times is seen to ensue ache, or the decrease of strength or agility in the arms: where, in shooting, if the shooter use the strength of his bow within his own tiller, he shall never be therewith grieved or made more feeble.

Also in shooting is a double utility, wherein it excelleth all other exercises and games incomparably. The one is that it is, and alway

---

[1] Kinds of targets.
[2] A game played with a ball or bowl.

hath been, the most excellent artillery for wars, whereby this realm of England hath been not only best defended from outward hostility, but also in other regions a few English archers have been seen to prevail against people innumerable, also won impregnable cities and strongholds, and kept them in the midst of the strength of their enemies. This is the feat whereby Englishmen have been most dread and had in estimation with outward princes, as well enemies as allies. And the commodity thereof hath been approved as far as Jerusalem; as it shall appear in the lives of Richard the First and Edward the First, Kings of England, who made several journeys to recover that holy city of Jerusalem into the possession of Christian men, and achieved them honourably, the rather by the power of this feat of shooting.

The premisses considered, O what cause of reproach shall the decay of archers be to us now living? Yea what irrecuperable damage either to us or them in whose time needs of semblable defence shall happen? Which decay, though we already perceive, fear, and lament, and for the restoring thereof cease not to make ordinances, good laws, and statutes, yet who effectually putteth his hand to continual execution of the same laws and provisions, or beholding them daily broken, winketh not at the offenders? O merciful God, how long shall we be mockers of ourselves? How long shall we scorn at our own calamity, which, both with the eyes of our mind, and also our bodily eyes, we see daily imminent, by neglecting our public weal, and condemning the due execution of laws and ordinances? But I shall hereof more speak in another place; and return now to the second utility found in shooting in the long bow, which is killing of deer, wild fowl, and other game, wherein is both profit and pleasure above any other artillery.

And verily I suppose that before crossbows and hand guns were brought into this realm, by the sleight of our enemies, to the intent to destroy the noble defence of archery, continual use of shooting in the long bow made the feat so perfect and exact among Englishmen, that they then as surely and soon killed such game which they listed to have as they now can do with the crossbow or gun, and more expeditely, and with less labour they did it. For being therein industrious, they killed their game further from them (if they shot a great strength) than they can with a crossbow, except it be of such weight that the arm shall repent the bearing thereof twenty years after. Moreover in the long bow may be shot more arrows, and in less time, nor by the breaking thereof ensueth so much harm as by the breaking of the cross-bow. Besides that all times in bending the crossbow is in peril of breaking.

But this sufficeth for the declaration of shooting, whereby it is sufficiently proved that it incomparably excelleth all other exercise, pastime, or solace. And hereat I conclude to write of exercise, which appertaineth as well to princes and noblemen as to all other by their example, which determine to pass forth their lives in virtue and honesty. And hereafter, with the assistance of God, unto whom I render this mine account (for the talent I have of Him received), I purpose to write of the principal and (as I might say) the particular study and affairs of him, that by the providence of God, is called to the most difficult cure of a public weal.

THE SECOND BOOK

I. What things he that is elected or appointed to be a governor of a public weal ought to premeditate.

IN THE book preceding I have (as I trust) sufficiently declared as well what is to be called a very and right public weal, as also that there should be thereof one prince and sovereign above all other governors. And I have also expressed my conception and opinion touching not only the studies, but also the exercises concerning the necessary education of noblemen and other, called to the governance of a public weal, in such form as, by the noble example of their lives and the fruit thereof coming, the public weal that shall happen to be under their governance shall not fail to be accounted happy, and the authority on them to be employed well and fortunately. Now will I treat of the preparation of such personages, when they first receive any great dignity, charge, or governance of the weal public.

First, such persons being now adult, that is to say, passed their childhood as well in manners as in years, if for their virtues and learning they happen to be called to receive any dignity, they should first move[1] all company from them; and in a secret oratory or privy chamber, by themself assemble all the powers of their wits to remember these seven articles, which I have not of mine own head devised, but excerpted or gathered as well out of Holy Scriptures as out of the works of other excellent writers of famous memory, as they shall soon perceive which have read and perused good authors in Greek and Latin.

First, and above all thing, let them consider that from God only proceedeth all honour, and that neither noble progeny, succession, nor election be of such force, that by them any estate or dignity may be so established that God being stirred to vengeance shall not shortly resume it, and perchance translate it where it shall like him. And forasmuch as examples greatly do profit in the stead of experience, here shall it be necessary to

---

[1] Remove.

remember the history of Saul, whom God Himself elected to be the first King of Israel; that where God commanded him by the mouth of Samuel the Prophet, that forasmuch as the people called Amalech had resisted the children of Israel when they first departed from Egypt, he should therefore destroy all the country, and slay men, women, and children, all beasts and cattle, and that he should nothing save or keep thereof. But Saul after that he had vanquished Amalech, and taken Agag, King thereof, prisoner, he having on him compassion saved his life only. Also he preserved the best oxen, cattle, and vestures, and all other thing that was fairest and of most estimation, and would not consume it according as God had commanded him, saying to Samuel that the people kept it to the intent that they would make therewith to Almighty God a solemn sacrifice. But Samuel, reproving him, said, 'Better is obedience than sacrifice', with other words that do follow in the history. Finally, for that offence only, Almighty God abjected Saul, that he should no more reign over Israel, and caused Samuel forthwith to anoint David king, the youngest son of a poor man of Bethlehem, named Jesse, which was keeping his father's sheep. Since for once neglecting the commandment of God, and that neither natural pity, nor the intent to do sacrifice with that which was saved, might excuse the transgression of God's commandment nor mitigate his grievous displeasure. How vigilant ought a Christian man being in authority—how vigilant (I say), industrious, and diligent ought he to be in the administration of a public weal? Dreading alway the words that be spoken by eternal sapience to them that be governors of public weals: 'All power and virtue is given of the Lord that of all other is highest, who shall examine your deeds, and insearch your thoughts. For when ye were the ministers of his realm ye judged not uprightly, nor observed the law of justice, nor ye walked not according to his pleasure. He shall shortly and terribly appear unto you. For most hard and grievous judgment shall be on them that have rule over other. To the poor man mercy is granted, but the great men shall suffer great torments. He that is Lord of all excepteth no person, nor he shall fear the greatness of any man; for he made as well the great as the small, and careth for every of them equally. The stronger or of more might is the person, the stronger pain is to him imminent. Therefore to you governors be these my words, that ye may learn wisdom and fall not.'

This notable sentence is not only to be imprinted in the hearts of governors, but also to be often times revolved and called to remembrance.

They shall not think how much honour they receive, but how much care and burden. Ne they shall not much esteem their revenues and treasure, considering that it is no booty or prey, but a laborious office and travail.

Let them think the greater dominion they have, that thereby they sustain the more care and study. And that therefore they must have the less solace and pastime, and to sensual pleasures less opportunity.

Also when they behold their garments and other ornaments, rich and precious, they shall think what reproach were to them to surmount in that which be other men's works, and not theirs, and to be vanquished of a poor subject in sundry virtues, whereof they themselves be the artificers.

They that regard them of whom they have governance no more than shall appertain to their own private commodities, they no better esteem them than other men doth their horses and mules, to whom they employ no less labour and diligence, not to the benefit of the sely [1] beasts, but to their own necessities and singular advantage.

The most sure foundation of noble renown is a man to be of such virtues and qualities as he desireth to be openly published. For it is a faint praise that is gotten with fear or by flatterers given. And the fame is but fume which is supported with silence provoked by menaces.

They shall also consider that by their pre-eminence they sit as it were on a pillar on the top of a mountain, where all the people do behold them, not only in their open affairs, but also in their secret pastimes, privy dalliance, or other improfitable or wanton conditions: which soon be discovered by the conversation of their most familiar servants, which do alway embrace that study wherein their master delighteth; according to the saying of Jesus Sirach, 'As the judge of the people is, so be his ministers; and such as be the governors of the city, such be the people.' Which sentence is confirmed by sundry histories; for Nero, Caligula, Domitian, Lucius Commodus, Varius Heliogabalus, monstrous emperors, nourished about them ribalds and other voluptuous

[1] Simple.

artificers. Maximian, Diocletian, Maxentius, and other perse-
cutors of Christian men, lacked not inventors of cruel and
terrible torments. Contrariwise reigning the noble Augustus,
Nerva, Trajan, Hadrian, the two Antonines, and the wonderful
Emperor Alexander, for his gravity called Severus, the imperial
palace was always replenished with eloquent orators, delectable
poets, wise philosophers, most cunning and expert lawyers,
prudent and valiant captains. More semblable examples shall
hereof be found by them which purposely do read histories, whom
of all other I most desire to be princes and governors.

These articles well and substantially graven in a nobleman's
memory, it shall also be necessary to cause them to be delectably
written and set in a table within his bedchamber, adding to the
verses of Claudian, the noble poet, which he wrote to Theodosius and Honorius, emperors of Rome. The verses I have
translated out of Latin into English, not without great study and
difficulty, not observing the order as they stand, but the sentence
belonging to my purpose.

> Though that thy power stretcheth both far and large,
> Through Inde the rich, set at the world's end,
> And Mede with Araby be both under thy charge,
> And also Seres that silk to us both send,
> If fear thee trouble, and small things thee offend,
> Corrupt desire thine heart hath once embraced,
> Thou art in bondage, thine honour is defaced.
>
> Thou shalt be deemed then worthy for to reign,
> When of thyself thou winnest the mastery.
> Evil custom bringeth virtue in disdain,
> Licence superfluous persuadeth much folly;
> In too much pleasure set not felicity,
> If lust or anger do thy mind assail,
> Subdue occasion, and thou shalt soon prevail.
>
> What thou mayst do delight not for to know,
> But rather what thing will become thee best;
> Embrace thou virtue and keep thy courage low,
> And think that alway measure is a feast.
> Love well thy people, care also for the least,
> And when thou studiest for thy commodity
> Make them all partners of thy felicity.

Be not much moved with singular appetite,
Except it profit unto thy subjects all;
At thine example the people will delight,
Be it vice or virtue, with thee they rise or fall.
No laws avail, men turn as doth a ball;
For where the ruler in living is not stable,
Both law and counsel is turned into a fable.

These verses of Claudian, full of excellent wisdom, as I have said, would be in a table, in such a place as a governor once in a day may behold them, specially as they be expressed in Latin by the said poet, unto whose eloquence no translation in English may be equivalent. But yet were it better to con them by heart; yea, and if they were made in the form of a ditty to be sung to an instrument, O what a sweet song would it be in the ears of wise men! For a mean musician might thereof make a right pleasant harmony, where almost every note should express a counsel virtuous or necessary.

Ye have now heard what premeditations be expedient before that a man take on him the governance of a public weal. These notable premeditations and remembrances should be in his mind, which is in authority, oftentimes renewed. Then shall he proceed further in furnishing his person with honourable manners and qualities, whereof very nobility is compact; whereby all other shall be induced to honour him, love him, and fear him, which things chiefly do cause perfect obedience.

Now of these manners will I write in such order as in my concept they be (as it were) naturally disposed and set in a nobleman, and soonest in him noted or espied.

II. *The exposition of majesty.*

IN A governor or man having in the public weal some great authority, the fountain of all excellent manners is Majesty; which is the whole proportion and figure of noble estate, and is properly a beauty or comeliness in his countenance, language and gesture apt to his dignity, and accommodate to time, place, and company; which, like as the sun doth his beams, so doth it cast on the beholders and hearers a pleasant and terrible reverence. Insomuch as the words or countenance of a noble man should be in the stead of a firm and stable law to his inferiors. Yet is not majesty alway in haughty or fierce countenance, nor in speech outrageous or arrogant, but in honourable and sober demeanour, deliberate and grave pronunciation, words clean and facile, void of rudeness and dishonesty, without vain or inordinate jangling, with such an excellent temperance, that he, among an infinite number of other persons, by his majesty may be espied for a governor. Whereof we have a noble example in Homer of Ulysses, that when his ship and men were perished in the sea, and he unneth [1] escaped, and was cast on land upon a coast where the inhabitants were called Phaeacians, he being all naked, saving a mantle sent to him by the king's daughter, without other apparel or servant, represented such a wonderful majesty in his countenance and speech, that the king of the country, named Alcinous, in that extreme calamity, wished that Ulysses would take his daughter Nausicaa to wife, with a great part of his treasure. And declaring the honour that he bare toward him, he made for his sake divers noble esbatements [2] and pastimes. The people also wondering at his majesty, honoured him with sundry presents; and at their proper charges and expenses conveyed him into his own realm of Ithaca in a ship of wonderful beauty, well ordinanced and manned for his defence and safe conduct. The words of Alcinous, whereby he declareth the majesty that he noted to be in Ulysses, I have put in English, not so well as I found them in Greek, but as well as my wit and tongue can express it.

Alcinous to Ulysses

When I thee consider, Ulysses, I perceive
Thou dost not dissemble to me in thy speech
As other have done, which craftily can deceive,
Untruly reporting where they list to preach
Of things never done; such falsehood they do teach.
But in thy words there is a right good grace,
And that thy mind is good, it showeth in thy face.

The estimation of majesty in countenance shall be declared by two examples now ensuing.

To Scipio, being in his manor place, called *Linterium*, came divers great thieves and pirates, only to the intent to see his person of whose wonderful prowess and sundry victories they

---

[1] Scarcely.　　　　　[2] Diversions.

heard the renown. But he not knowing but that they had come to endamage him, armed himself and such servants as he then had with him, and disposed them about the embattlements of his house to make defence; which the captains of the thieves perceiving, they despatched the multitude from them, and laying apart their harness and weapons, they called to Scipio with a loud voice, saying that they came not as enemies, but wondering at his virtue and prowess desired only to see him, which if he vouched safe, they would account for an heavenly benefit. That being showed to Scipio by his servants, he caused the gates to be set wide open, and the thieves to be suffered to enter, who kissing the gates and posts with much reverence, as they had been of a temple or other place dedicate, they humbly approached to Scipio, who visaged them in such form that they, as subdued with a reverent dread in beholding his majesty, at the last joyfully kissing his hand often times, which he benignly offered to them, made humble reverence, and so departed, laying in the porch semblable offerings as they gave to their gods, and forthwith returned to their own habitations rejoicing incredibly that they had seen and touched a prince so noble and valiant.

It is no little thing to marvel at, the majesty showed in extreme fortune and misery.

The noble Roman Marius, when he had been seven times consul, being vanquished by Sulla, after that he had long hidden himself in marshes and desert places, he was finally constrained by famine to repair to a town called Minturnae, where he trusted to have been succoured. But the inhabitants, dreading the cruelty of Sulla, took Marius and put him in a dungeon, and after sent to slay him their common hangman, which was born in Cimbria, a country some time destroyed by Marius. The hangman, beholding the honourable port and majesty that remained in Marius, notwithstanding that he was out of honourable apparel and was in garments torn and filthy, he thought that in his visage appeared the terrible battle wherein Marius vanquished his countrymen; he therefore all trembling, as constrained by fear, did let fall out of his hand the sword wherewith he should have slain Marius, and leaving him untouched, fled out of the place. The cause of his fear reported to the people, they moved with reverence, afterward studied and devised how they might deliver Marius from the malice of Sulla.

In Augustus, Emperor of Rome, was a native majesty. For, as

Suetonius writeth, from his eyes proceeded rays or beams, which pierced the eyes of the beholders. The same Emperor spake seldom openly, but out of a commentary, that is to say, that he had before provided and written, to the intent that he would speak no more nor less than he had purposed.

Moreover toward the acquiring of majesty, three things be required to be in the oration of a man having authority: that it be compendious, sententious, and delectable, having also respect to the time when, the place where, and the persons to whom it is spoken. For the words perchance apt for a banquet or time of solace be not commendable in time of consultation or service of God. That language that in the chamber is tolerable, in place of judgment or great assembly is nothing commendable.

III. Of apparel belonging to a nobleman, being a governor or great counsellor.

APPAREL may be well a part of majesty. For as there hath been ever a discrepance in vesture of youth and age, men and women, and our Lord God ordained the apparel of priests distinct from seculars, as it appeareth in Holy Scripture, also the Gentiles had of ancient time sundry apparel to sundry estates, as to the senate, and dignitaries called magistrates. And what enormity should it now be thought, and a thing to laugh at, to see a judge or sergeant at the law in a short coat, garded and pounced after the galyard [1] fashion, or an apprentice of the law or pleader come to the bar with a Milan bonnet or French hat on his head, set full of plumes, powdered with spangles. So is there apparel comely to every estate and degree, and that which exceedeth or lacketh, procureth reproach, in a nobleman specially. For apparel simple or scanty reproveth him of avarice. If it be always exceeding precious, and oftentimes changed, as well into charge as strange and new fashions, it causeth him to be noted dissolute of manners.

The most noble Emperors of Rome, Augustus, Trajan, Hadrian, Anthony, Severus, and Alexander, which were of all other incomparable in honourable living, used a discreet moderation in their apparel, although they were great emperors and gentiles. How much more ought then Christian men, whose

[1] Gallant, gay.

denomination is founded on humility, and they that be not of the
estate of princes, to show a moderation and constance in vesture,
that they diminish no part of their majesty, either with new
fangleness or with over sumptuous expenses? And yet may this
last be suffered where there is a great assembly of strangers, for
then some time it is expedient that a nobleman in his apparel do
advaunt himself to be both rich and honourable. But in this as
well as in other parts of majesty time is to be highly considered.

Semblable decking ought to be in the house of a nobleman
or man of honour. I mean concerning ornaments of hall and
chambers, in arras, painted tables, and images containing histories, wherein is represented some monument of virtue, most
cunningly wrought, with the circumstance of the matter briefly
declared; whereby other men in beholding may be instructed, or
at the leastways, to virtue persuaded. In likewise his plate and
vessels would be engraved with histories, fables, or quick and
wise sentences, comprehending good doctrine or counsels;
whereby one of these commodities may happen, either that they
which do eat or drink, having those wisdoms ever in sight, shall
happen with the meat to receive some of them, or by purposing
them at the table, may suscitate [1] some disputation or reasoning;
whereby some part of time shall be saved, which else by superfluous eating and drinking would be idly consumed.

*IV. What very nobility is, and whereof it took first that denomin-
ation.*

NOW IT is to be feared that where majesty approacheth to excess,
and the mind is obsessed with inordinate glory, lest pride, of all
vices most horrible, should suddenly enter and take prisoner the
heart of a gentleman called to authority. Wherefore inasmuch as
that pestilence corrupteth all senses, and maketh them incurable
by any persuasion or doctrine, therefore such persons from their
adolescence (which is the age next to the state of man) ought to
be persuaded and taught the true knowledge of very nobility in
form following or like.

First, that in the beginning, when private possessions and
dignity were given by the consent of the people, who then had all

---

[1] Raise.

things in common, and equality in degree and condition, undoubtedly they gave the one and the other to him at whose virtue
they marvelled, and by whose labour and industry they received
a common benefit, as of a common father that with equal
affection loved them. And that promptitude or readiness in
employing that benefit was then named in English gentleness, as
it was in Latin *benignitas*, and in other tongues after a semblable
signification, and the persons were called gentlemen, more for the
remembrance of their virtue and benefit, than for discrepance of
estates. Also it fortuned by the providence of God that of those
good men were engendered good children, who being brought up
in virtue, and perceiving the cause of the advancement of their
progenitors, endeavoured themselves by imitation of virtue to be
equal to them in honour and authority; by good emulation they
retained still the favour and reverence of people. And for the
goodness that proceeded of such generation the state of them was
called in Greek *Eugenia*, which signifieth good kind or lineage,
but in a more brief manner it was after called nobility, and the
persons noble, which signifieth excellent, and in the analogy or
signification it is more ample than gentle, for it containeth as well
all that which is in gentleness, as also the honour or dignity therefore received, which be so annexed the one to the other that they
cannot be separate.

It would be moreover declared that where virtue joined with
great possessions or dignity hath long continued in the blood or
house of a gentleman, as it were an inheritance, there nobility is
most shown, and these noble men be most to be honoured; forasmuch as continuance in all thing that is good hath ever pre-
eminence in praise and comparison. But yet shall it be necessary
to advertise those persons, that do think that nobility may in no
wise be but only where men can avaunt them of ancient lineage,
an ancient robe, or great possessions, at this day very noble men
do suppose to be much error and folly. Whereof there is a
familiar example, which we bear ever with us, for the blood in our
bodies being in youth warm, pure, and lusty, it is the occasion of
beauty, which is everywhere commended and loved; but if in age
it be putrified, it loseth his praise. And the gouts, carbuncles,
cankers, leprosy, and other like sores and sicknesses, which do
proceed of blood corrupted, be to all men detestable.

And this persuasion to any gentlemen, in whom is apt disposition to very nobility, will be sufficient to withdraw him from

such vice, whereby he may impair his own estimation, and the good renown of his ancestors.

If he have an ancient robe left by his ancestor, let him consider that if the first owner were of more virtue than he is that succeedeth, the robe being worn, it diminisheth his praise to them which knew or have heard of the virtue of him that first owned it. If he that weareth it be vicious, it more detecteth how much he is unworthy to wear it, the remembrance of his noble ancestor making men to abhor the reproach given by an evil successor. If the first owner were not virtuous, it condemneth him that weareth it of much foolishness to glory in a thing of so base estimation, which, lacking beauty or gloss, can be none ornament to him that weareth it nor honourable remembrance to him that first owned it.

But now to confirm by true histories that according as I late affirmed, nobility is not only in dignity, ancient lineage, nor great revenues, lands, or possessions. Let young gentlemen have oftentimes told to them, and (as it is vulgarly spoken) laid in their laps, how Numa Pompilius was taken from husbandry which he exercised, and was made King of Romans by election of the people. What caused it suppose you but his wisdom and virtue, which in him was very nobility, and that nobility brought him to dignity? And if that were not nobility, the Romans were marvellously abused, that after the death of Romulus their king, they having among them a hundred senators, whom Romulus did set in authority, and also the blood royal, and old gentlemen of the Sabines, who, by the procurement of the wives of the Romans, being their daughters, inhabited the city of Rome, they would not of some of them elect a king, rather than advance a ploughman and stranger to that authority.

Quintius having but thirty acres of land, and being ploughman thereof, the Senate and people of Rome sent a messenger to show him that they had chosen him to be *dictator*, which was at that time the highest dignity among the Romans, and for three months had authority royal. Quintius hearing the message, let his plough stand, and went into the city and prepared his host against the Samnites, and vanquished them valiantly. And that done, he surrendered his office, and being discharged of the dignity, he repaired again to his plough, and applied it diligently.

I would demand now, if nobility were only in the dignity, or in his prowess which he showed against his enemies? If it were only in his dignity, it therewith ceased, and he was (as I might say) eft-soons [1] unnoble; and then was his prowess unrewarded, which was the chief and original cause of that dignity: which were incongruent and without reason. If it were in his prowess, prowess consisting of valiant courage and martial policy, if they still remain in the person, he may never be without nobility, which is the commendation and as it were the surname of virtue.

The two Romans called both Decii were of the base estate of the people, and not of the great blood of the Romans, yet for the preservation of their country they avowed to die, as it were in a satisfaction for all their country. And so with valiant hearts they pierced the host of their enemies, and valiantly fighting, they died there honourably, and by their example gave such audacity and courage to the residue of the Romans, that they employed so their strength against their enemies, that with little more loss they obtained victory. Ought not these two Romans which by their death gave occasion of victory be called noble? I suppose no man that knoweth what reason is will deny it.

Moreover, we have in this realm coins which be called nobles; as long as they be seen to be gold, they be so called. But if they be counterfeited, and made in brass, copper, or other vile metal, who for the print only calleth them nobles? Whereby it appeareth that the estimation is in the metal, and not in the print or figure. And in a horse or good greyhound we praise that we see in them, and not the beauty or goodness of their progeny. Which proveth that in esteeming of money and cattle we be led by wisdom, and in approving of man, to whom beasts and money do serve, we be only induced by custom.

Thus I conclude that nobility is not after the vulgar opinion of men, but is only the praise and surname of virtue; which the longer it continueth in a name or lineage, the more is nobility extolled and marvelled at.

V. Of affability and the utility thereof in every estate.

TO THAT which I before named gentleness, be incident three special qualities, affability, placability, and mercy; of whom I will now separately declare the proper significations.

---

[1] Again.

Affability is of a wonderful efficacy or power in procuring love. And it is in sundry wise, but most properly, where a man is facile or easy to be spoken unto. It is also where a man speaketh courteously, with a sweet speech or countenance, wherewith the hearers (as it were with a delicate odour) be refreshed, and allured to love him in whom is the most delectable quality. As contrariwise, men vehemently hate them that have a proud and haughty countenance, be they never so high in estate or degree. How often have I heard people say, when men in great authority have passed by without making gentle countenance to those which have done to them reverence: 'This man weeneth with a look to subdue all the world; nay, nay, men's hearts be free, and will love whom they list.' And thereto all the other do consent in a murmur, as it were bees. Lord God, how they be sore blinded which do ween that haughty countenance is a comeliness of nobility; where undoubted nothing is thereto a more greater blemish. As they have well proved which by fortune's mutability have changed their estate, when they perceive that the remembrance of their pride withdraweth all pity, all men rejoicing at the change of their fortune.

Dionysius, the proud King of Sicily, after that for his intolerable pride he was driven by his people out of his realm, the remembrance of his haughty and stately countenance was to all men so odious that he could be in no country well entertained. Insomuch as if he had not been relieved by learning, teaching a grammar school in Italy, he, for lack of friends, had been constrained to beg for his living.

Semblably, Perseus, King of Macedonia, and one of the richest kings that ever was in Greece, for his execrable pride, was at the last abandoned of all his allies and confederates, by reason whereof he was vanquished and taken prisoner by Paulus Aemilius, one of the consuls of Rome; and not only he himself bound and led as a captive, in the triumph of the said Paulus, but also the remembrance of his pride was so odious to people, that his own son, destitute of friends, was by need constrained to work in a smith's forge, not finding any man that of his hard fortune had any compassion.

The pride of Tarquin, the last King of Romans, was more occasion of his exile than the ravishing of Lucretia by his son Aruncius, for the malice that the people by his pride had long gathered, finding valiant captains, Brutus, Colatinus, Lucretius, and other nobles of the city, at the last burst out and taking occasion of the ravishment, although the King were thereto not party, they utterly expelled him forever out of the city. These be the fruits of pride, and that men do call stately countenance.

When a noble man passeth by, showing to men a gentle and familiar visage, it is a world to behold how people taketh comfort, how the blood in their visage quickeneth, how their flesh stirreth, and hearts leapeth for gladness. Then they all speak as it were in an harmony, the one saith, 'Who beholding this man's most gentle countenance, will not with all his heart love him?' Another saith, 'He is no man, but an angel; see how he rejoiceth all men that behold him.' Finally, all do grant that he is worthy all honour that may be given or wished him.

But now to resort to that which most properly (as I have said) is affability, which is facile or easy to be spoken unto.

Mark Antony, Emperor of Rome (as Lampridius writeth), ensearched who were most homely and plain men within the city, and secretly sent for them into his chamber, where he diligently inquired of them what the people conjectured of his living, commanding them upon pain of his high indignation to tell him truth, and hide nothing from him. And upon their report, if he heard anything worthy never so little dispraise, he forthwith amended it. And also by such means he corrected them that were about his person, finding them negligent, dissemblers, and flatterers. The noble Trajan, when his nobles and counsellors noted him too familiar and courteous and therefore did blame him, he answered that he would be a like emperor to other men, as if he were a subject he would wish to have over himself.

O what damage have ensued to princes and their realms where liberty of speech hath been restrained! What availed fortune incomparable to the great King Alexander, his wonderful puissance and hardiness, or his singular doctrine in philosophy, taught him by Aristotle, in delivering him from death in his young and flourishing age? Where, if he had retained the same affability that was in him in the beginning of his conquest, and had not put to silence his counsellors which before used to speak to him frankly, he might have escaped all violent death, and by similitude, have enjoyed the whole monarchy of all the world. For after that he waxed to be terrible in manners, and prohibited his friends and discreet servants to use their accustomed liberty in speech, he fell into a hateful grudge among his own people.

But I had almost forgotten Julius Caesar, who, being not able to sustain the burden of fortune, and envying his own felicity, abandoned his natural disposition, and as it were being drunk with over much wealth, sought new ways how to be advanced above the estate of mortal princes. Wherefore little by little he withdrew from men his accustomed gentleness, becoming more sturdy in language and strange in countenance than ever before had been his usage. And to declare more plainly his intent, he made an edict or decree that no man should press to come to him uncalled, and that they should have good await,[1] that they spake not in such familiar fashion to him as they before had been accustomed; whereby he so did alienate from him the hearts of his most wise and assured adherents, that, from that time forward, his life was to them tedious, and abhorring him as a monster or common enemy, they being knit in a confederacy slew him sitting in the Senate; of which conspiracy was chief captain, Marcus Brutus, whom of all other he best loved for his great wisdom and prowess. And it is of some writers suspected that he was begotten of Caesar, forasmuch as Caesar in his youth loved Servilia, the mother of Brutus, and, as men supposed, used her more familiarly than honesty required. Thus Caesar, by omitting his old affability, did incense his next friends and companions to slay him.

But now take heed what damage ensued to him by his decree, wherein he commanded that no man should be so hardy to approach or speak to him. One which knew of the conspiracy against him, and by all likelihood did participate therein, being moved either with love or pity, or otherwise his conscience remording[2] against the destruction of so noble a prince, considering that by Caesar's decree he was prohibited to have to him any familiar access, so that he might not plainly detect the conspiracy; he, thereto vehemently moved, wrote in a bill all the form thereof, with the means how it might be espied, and since he might find none other opportunity, he delivered the bill to Caesar the same day that his death was prepared, as he went toward the place where the Senate was holden. But he being radicate[3] in pride, and neglecting to look on that bill, not esteeming the person that delivered it, which perchance was but a mean haviour,[4] continued his way to the Senate, where he incontinently was slain

---

[1] Watch, guard.　　[2] Causing remorse.
[3] Rooted.　　[4] Substance, wealth.

by the said Brutus, and many more of the Senate for that purpose appointed.

Who beholding the cause of the death of this most noble Caesar, unto whom in eloquence, doctrine, martial prowess, and gentleness no prince may be compared, and the acceleration or haste to his confusion caused by his own edict or decree, will not commend affability and extol liberty of speech? Whereby only love is in the hearts of people perfectly kindled, all fear excluded, and consequently realms, dominions, and all other authorities consolidate and perpetually stablished. The sufferance of noble men to be spoken unto is not only to them an incomparable surety, but also a confounder of repentance, enemy to prudence, whereof is engendered this word, 'Had I wist', which hath been ever of all wise men reproved.

On a time King Philip, father to the great Alexander, sitting in judgment and having before him a matter against one of his soldiers, being overcome with watch fell on a slumber, and suddenly being awaked, immediately would have given a sentence against the poor soldier. But he, with a great voice and outcry, said, 'King Philip, I appeal.' 'To whom wilt thou appeal?' said the King. 'To thee' (said the soldier) 'when thou art thoroughly awaked.' With which answer the King suspended his sentence, and more diligently examining the matter, found the soldier had wrong; which being sufficiently discussed, he gave judgment for him, whom before he would have condemned.

Semblably happened by a poor woman, against whom the same King had given judgment; but she as desperate, with a loud voice, cried, 'I appeal, I appeal.' 'To whom appealest thou?' said the King. 'I appeal,' said she, 'from thee, now being drunk, to King Philip the sober.' At which words, though they were indiscreet and foolish, yet he, not being moved to displeasure, but gathering to him his wits, examined the matter more seriously; whereby, he finding the poor woman to sustain wrongs, he reversed his judgment, and according to truth and justice gave to her that she demanded. Wherein he is of noble authors commended, and put for an honourable example of affability.

The noble Emperor Antoninus, called the philosopher, was of such affability, as Herodian writeth, that to every man that came to him he gently delivered his hand; and would not permit that his guard should prohibit any man to approach him.

The excellent Emperor Augustus on a time, in the presence of many men, played on cymbals, or another like instrument. A poor man, standing with other and beholding the Emperor, said with a loud voice to his fellow, 'Seest thou not how this voluptuous lecher tempereth all the world with his finger?' Which words the Emperor so wisely noted, without wrath or displeasure, that ever after, during his life, he refrained his hands from semblable lightness.

The good Antoninus, Emperor of Rome, coming to supper to a mean gentleman, beheld in the house certain pillars of a delicate stone, called porphyry, asked of the good man, where he had bought those pillars. Who made to the Emperor this answer, 'Sir, when ye come into any other man's house than your own, ever be you both dumb and deaf.' Which liberal taunt that most gentle Emperor took in so good part that he oftentimes rehearsed that sentence to other for a wise and discreet counsel.

By these examples appeareth now evidently what good cometh of affability, or sufferance of speech, what most pernicious danger alway ensueth to them, that either do refuse counsel, or prohibit liberty of speech; since that in liberty (as it hath been proved) is most perfect surety, according as it is remembered by Plutarch of Theopompus, King of Lacedaemonia, who being demanded, how a realm might be best and most surely kept, 'If' (said he) 'the prince give to his friends liberty to speak to him things that be just, and neglecteth not the wrongs that his subject sustaineth.'

VI. How noble a virtue placability is.

PLACABILITY is no little part of benignity, and it is properly where a man is by any occasion moved to be angry, and notwithstanding, either by his own reason ingenerate or by counsel persuaded, he omitteth to be revenged, and oftentimes receiveth the transgressor once reconciled into more favour; which undoubtedly is a virtue wonderful excellent. For, as Tully saith, nothing is more to be marvelled at, or that more becometh a man noble and honourable, than mercy and placability. The value thereof is best known by the contrary, which is ire, called vulgarly wrath, a vice most ugly and farthest from humanity. For who, beholding a man in estimation of nobility and wisdom by fury changed into an horrible figure, his face enfarced [1] with rancour,

---

[1] Filled.

his mouth foul and imbossed, his eyes wide staring and sparkling like fire, not speaking, but as a wild bull, roaring and braying out words despiteful and venomous; forgetting his estate or condition, forgetting learning, yea forgetting all reason, will not have such a passion in extreme detestation? Shall he not wish to be in such a man placability? Whereby only he should be eftsoons [1] restored to the form of a man, whereof he is by wrath despoiled, as it is wondrously well described by Ovid in his craft of love.

> Man, to thy visage it is convenient
> Beastly fury shortly to assuage.
> For peace is beautiful to man only sent,
> Wrath to the beasts cruel and savage.
> For in man the face swelleth when wrath is in rage
> The blood becometh wan, the eyes fiery bright,
> Like Gorgon the monster appearing in the night.

This Gorgon that Ovid speaketh of is supposed of poets to be a fury or infernal monster, whose hairs were all in the figure of adders, signifying the abundance of mischief that is contained in wrath.

Wherewith the great King Alexander, being (as I might say) obsessed, did put to vengeable death his dear friend Clitus, his most prudent counsellor Calisthenes, his most valiant captain Philotas, with his father Parmenio, and divers others. Whereof he so sore after repented that oppressed with heaviness he had slain himself, had he not been let by his servants. Wherefore his fury and inordinate wrath is a foul and grievous blemish to his glory, which, without that vice, had incomparably excelled all other princes.

Who abhorreth or hateth not the violence or rage that was in Sulla and Marius, noble Romans, and in their time in highest authority within the city, having the governance of the more part of the world?

Sulla, for the malignity that he had toward Marius, caused the heads of a thousand and seven hundred of the chief citizens of Rome to be stricken off, and brought to him fresh bleeding and quick, and thereon fed his most cruel eyes, which to eat his mouth naturally abhorred. Marius with no less rancour inflamed, beside a terrible slaughter that he made of noblemen leaning to Sulla, he also caused Caius Caesar (who had been both

[1] Again.

consul and censor, two of the most honourable dignities in the city of Rome) to be violently drawn to the sepulchre of one Varius, a simple and seditious person, and there to be dishonestly slain. With like bestial fury he caused the head of Mark Antony, one of the most eloquent orators of all the Romans, to be brought unto him as he sat at dinner, and there took the head all bloody between his hands, and with a malicious countenance reproached him of his eloquence, wherewith he had not only defended many an innocent, but also the whole public weal had been by his wise consultation singularly profited.

O what calamity happened to the most noble city of Rome by the implacability or wrath insatiable of these two captains, or (as I might say) devils! The nobles between them exhaust, the chivalry almost consumed, the laws oppressed, and lacking but little that the public weal had not been extinct, and the city utterly desolate.

The indiscreet hastiness of the Emperor Claudius caused him to be noted for foolishness. For moved with wrath he caused divers to be slain, for whom after he demanded and would send for to supper. Notwithstanding that he was right well learned, and in divers great affairs appeared to be wise. These discommodities do happen by implacable wrath, whereof there be examples innumerable.

Contrariwise the valiant King Pyrrhus, hearing that two men at a feast, and in a great assembly and audience, had openly spoken words to his reproach, he, moved with displeasure, sent for the persons, and when they were come, he demanded where they spake of him any such words. Whereunto one of them answered, 'If' (said he) 'the wine had not the sooner failed us, all that which was told to your highness, in comparison of that which should have been spoken, had been but trifles.' The wise prince with that plain confession was mitigate,[1] and his wrath converted to laughing.

Julius Caesar, after his victory against the great Pompey, who had married his daughter, sitting in open judgment, one Sergius Galba, one of the nobles of Rome, a friend unto Pompey, said unto him, 'I was bounden for thy son-in-law, Pompey, in a great sum, when he was consul the third time, wherefore I am now sued, what shall I do? Shall I myself pay it?' By which words he

[1] Satisfied.

might seem to reproach Caesar of the selling of Pompey's goods, in defrauding his creditors. But Caesar, then having a gentle heart and a patient, was moved with no displeasure towards Galba, but caused Pompey's debts to be discharged.

We lack not of this virtue domestic examples, I mean of our own kings of England; but most specially one, which, in mine opinion, is to be compared with any that ever was written of in any region or country.

The most renowned prince, King Henry the Fifth, late King of England, during the life of his father was noted to be fierce and of wanton courage. It happened that one of his servants whom he well favoured, for felony by him committed, was arraigned at the King's Bench; whereof he being advertised, and incensed by light persons about him, in furious rage came hastily to the bar, where his servant stood as a prisoner, and commanded him to be ungyved [1] and set at liberty, whereat all men were abashed, reserved the Chief Justice, who humbly exhorted the Prince to be contented that his servant might be ordered according to the ancient laws of this realm, or if he would have him saved from the rigour of the laws, that he should obtain, if he might, of the King, his father, his gracious pardon; whereby no law or justice should be derogate. With which answer the Prince nothing appeased, but rather more inflamed, endeavoured himself to take away his servant. The judge considering the perilous example and inconvenience that might thereby ensue, with a valiant spirit and courage commanded the Prince upon his allegiance to leave the prisoner and depart his way. With which commandment the Prince, being set all in a fury, all chafed, and in a terrible manner, came up to the place of judgment—men thinking that he would have slain the judge, or have done to him some damage; but the judge sitting still, without moving, declaring the majesty of the King's place of judgment, and with an assured and bold countenance, had to the Prince these words following: 'Sir, remember yourself; I keep here the place of the King, your sovereign lord and father, to whom ye owe double obedience, wherefore eftsoons [2] in his name I charge you desist of your wilfulness and unlawful enterprise, and from henceforth give good example to those which hereafter shall be your proper subjects. And now for your contempt and disobedience, go you to the prison of the

---

[1] Unchained.   [2] Again.

King's Bench, whereunto I commit you; and remain ye there prisoner until the pleasure of the King, your father, be further known.' With which words being abashed and also wondering at the marvellous gravity of that worshipful Justice, the noble Prince, laying his weapon apart, doing reverence, departed and went to the King's Bench as he was commanded. Whereat his servants disdaining, came and showed to the King all the whole affair. Whereat he a while studying after as a man all ravished with gladness, holding his eyes and hands up toward heaven, abraided,[1] saying with a loud voice, 'O merciful God, how much am I, above all other men, bound to your infinite goodness; specially for that ye have given me a judge who feareth not to minister justice, and also a son who can suffer semblably and obey justice!'

Now here a man may behold three persons worthy excellent memory. First a judge, who being a subject, feared not to execute justice on the eldest son of his sovereign lord, and by the order of nature his successor. Also a prince and son and heir of the king, in the midst of his fury, more considered his evil example, and the judge's constancy in justice, than his own estate or wilful appetite. Thirdly, a noble king and wise father, who contrary to the custom of parents, rejoiced to see his son and the heir of his crown to be for his disobedience by his subject corrected.

Wherefore I conclude that nothing is more honourable, or to be desired in a prince or nobleman, than placability. As contrariwise, nothing is so detestable, or to be feared in such one, as wrath and cruel malignity.

VII. That a governor ought to be merciful, and the diversity of mercy and vain pity.

MERCY is and hath been ever of such estimation with mankind that not only reason persuadeth, but also experience proveth, that in whom mercy lacketh and is not found, in him all other virtues be drowned and lose their just commendation.

The vice called cruelty, which is contrary to mercy, is by good reason most odious of all other vices, inasmuch as like a poison or continual pestilence it destroyeth the generation of man. Also

---

[1] Shouted out.

the virtues being in a cruel person be not only obfuscate [1] or hid, but also likewise as nourishing meats and drinks in a sick body do lose their bounty and augment the malady, semblably divers virtues in a person malicious do minister occasion and assistance to cruelty.

But now to speak of the inestimable price and value of mercy. Let governors, which know that they have received their power from above, revolve in their minds in what peril they themselves be in daily if in God were not abundance of mercy, but that as soon as they offend Him grievously, He should immediately strike them with His most terrible dart of vengeance. Albeit unneth [2] any hour passeth that men deserve not some punishment.

The most noble emperors, which for their merits received of the Gentiles divine honours, vanquished the great hearts of their mortal enemies in showing mercy above men's expectation.

Julius Caesar, which in policy, eloquence, celerity, and prowess excelled all other captains, in mercy only he surmounted himself; that is to say, contrary to his own affects and determinate purposes, he not only spared but also received into tender familiarity his sworn enemies. Wherefore if the disdain of his own blood and alliance had not traitoriously slain him, he had reigned long and prosperously.

But among many other examples of mercy, whereof the histories of Rome do abound, there is one remembered by Seneca, which may be in the stead of a great number.

It was reported to the noble Emperor Octavius Augustus that Lucius Cinna, which was sister's son to the great Pompey, had imagined his death. Also that Cinna was appointed to execute his feat while the Emperor was doing his sacrifice. This report was made by one of the conspirators, and therewith divers other things agreed: the old hostility between the houses of Pompey and Caesar, the wild and seditious wit of Cinna, with the place and time, where and when the Emperor should be disfurnished of servants. No wonder though the Emperor's mind were inquiet, being in so perilous a conflict, considering on the one part, that if he should put to death Cinna, which came of one of the most noble and ancient houses of Rome, he should ever live in danger, unless he should destroy all that noble family, and cause the memory of them to be utterly exterminate; which might not be

---

[1] Obscured.   [2] Scarcely.

brought to pass without effusion of the blood of persons innumerable, and also peril of the subversion of the empire late
pacified. On the other part, he considered the imminent danger
that his person was in, wherefore nature stirred him to provide for
his surety, whereto he thought then to be none other remedy but
the death of his adversary. To him being thus perplexed came his
wife, Livia, the Empress, who said unto him, 'Pleaseth it you,
sir, to hear a woman's advice. Do you as physicians be wont to
do, where their accustomed remedies prove not, they do assay the
contrary. By severity ye have hitherto nothing profited, prove
therefore now what mercy may avail you. Forgive Cinna; he is
taken with the maynure,[1] and may not now endamage you;
profit he may much to the increase of your renown and perpetual
glory.' The Emperor rejoiced to himself that Cinna had found
such an advocatrice, and giving her thanks he caused his counsellors, which he had sent for, to be countermanded, and calling to
him Cinna only, he commanded the chamber to be avoided, and
another chair to be set for Cinna; and that done he said in this
manner to him: 'I desire of thee this one thing, that while I speak,
thou wilt not let or disturb me, or in the midst of my words make
any exclamation. What time, Cinna, I found thee in the host of
mine enemies, although thou were not by any occasion made
mine enemy, but by succession from thine ancestors born mine
enemy, I not only saved thee, but also gave unto thee all thine
inheritance; and at this day thou art so prosperous and rich, that
they which had with me victory do envy thee that were vanquished. Thou askest of me a spiritual promotion, and forthwith
I gave it thee before many other, whose parents had served me in
wars. And for that I have done so much for thee, thou now hast
purposed to slay me.' At that word when Cinna cried out, saying
that such madness was far from his mind, 'Cinna' (said the
Emperor), 'thou keepest not promise; it was covenanted that
thou shouldest not interrupt me. I say thou preparest to kill me.'
And thereto the Emperor named his companions, the place, time,
and order of all the conspiracy, and also to whom the sword was
committed. And when he perceived him astonished, holding then
his peace, not for because that he so promised, but that his
conscience him moved; 'For what intent didst thou thus?' (said
Augustus). 'Because thou wouldest be emperor? In good faith

---

[1] *Main œuvre;* taken with the maynure, caught in the deed.

the public weal is in an evil estate if nothing letteth thee to reign, but I only; thou canst not maintain or defend thine own house. It is not long since that thou in a private judgment were overcome of a poor man but late enfranchised; therefore thou mayst nothing do lightlier than plead against the Emperor. Say now, do I alone let thee of thy purpose? Supposest thou that Paulus, Fabius Maximus, the Cosses, and Serviliis, ancient houses of Rome, and such a sort of noblemen (not they which have vain and glorious names, but such as for their merits be adorned with their proper images) will suffer thee?' Finally, said the Emperor (after that he had talked with him by the space of two hours), 'I give to thee thy life, Cinna, the second time—first being mine enemy, now a traitor and murderer of thy sovereign lord, whom thou oughtest to love as thy father. Now from this day let amity between us two begin; and let us both contend whether I with a better heart have given to thee thy life, or that thou canst more gently recompense my kindness.' Soon after Augustus gave to Cinna the dignity of consul undesired, blaming him that he durst not ask it; whereby he had him most assured and loyal. And Cinna afterward dying, gave to the Emperor all his goods and possessions. And never after was Augustus in danger of any treason. O what sufficient praise may be given to this most noble and prudent Emperor, that in a chamber alone, without men, ordnance, or weapon, and perchance without harness, within the space of two hours, with words well couched, tempered with majesty, not only vanquished and subdued one mortal enemy, which by a malignity, engendered of a domestic hatred, had determined to slay him, but by the same feat excluded out of the whole city of Rome all displeasure and rancour toward him, so that there was not left any occasion whereof might proceed any little suspicion of treason, which otherwise could not have happened without slaughter of people innumerable.

Also the Empress Livia may not of right be forgotten, which ministered to her lord that noble counsel in such a perplexity; whereby he saved both himself and his people. Suppose ye that all the senators of Rome and counsellors of the Emperor, which were little fewer than a thousand, could have better advised him? This history therefore is no less to be remembered of women than of princes, taking thereby comfort to persuade sweetly their husbands to mercy and patience; to which counsel only they should be admitted and have free liberty. But I shall forbear to speak more of Livia now, forasmuch as I purpose to make a book only for ladies; wherein her laud shall be more amply expressed. But to resort now to mercy.

Surely nothing more entirely and fastly joineth the hearts of subjects to their prince or sovereign than mercy and gentleness. For Seneca saith, a temperate dread represseth high and sturdy minds; fear frequent and sharp, set forth with extremity stirreth men to presumption and hardiness, and constraineth them to experiment all things. He that hastily punisheth ofttimes soon repenteth. And who that over much correcteth, observeth none equity. And if ye ask me what mercy is, it is a temperance of the mind of him that hath power to be avenged, and it is called in Latin *clementia*, and is alway joined with reason. For he that for every little occasion is moved with compassion, and beholding a man punished condignly [1] for his offence lamenteth or waileth, is called piteous, which is a sickness of the mind, wherewith at this day the more part of men be diseased. And yet is the sickness much worse by adding to one word, calling it vain pity.

Some man perchance will demand of me what is vain pity? To that I will answer in a description of daily experience. Behold what an infinite number of Englishmen and women at this present time wander in all places throughout this realm, as beasts brute and savage, abandoning all occupation, service, and honesty. How many seemly personages, by outrage in riot, gaming, and excess of apparel, be induced to theft and robbery, and sometime to murder, to the inquietation of good men, and finally to their own destruction?

Now consider semblably what noble statutes, ordinances, and acts of council from time to time have been excogitate,[2] and by grave study and mature consultation enacted and decreed, as well for the due punishment of the said idle persons and vagabonds as also for the suppression of unlawful games and reducing apparel to convenient moderation and temperance. How many proclamations thereof have been divulgate [3] and not obeyed? How many commissions directed and not executed? (Mark well here, that disobedient subjects and negligent governors do frustrate good laws.) A man hearing that his neighbour is slain or robbed, forthwith hateth the offender and abhorreth his enormity, thinking him worthy to be punished according to the laws; yet when he

[1] Fitly, justly.　　　　　[2] Thought out.
[3] Promulgated.

beholdeth the transgressor, a seemly personage, also to be his servant, acquaintance, or a gentleman born (I omit now to speak of any other corruption), he forthwith changeth his opinion, and preferreth the offender's condition or personage before the example of justice, condemning a good and necessary law, for to excuse an offence pernicious and damnable; yea and this is not only done by the vulgar or common people, but much rather by them which have authority to them committed concerning the effectual execution of laws. They behold at their eye the continual increase of vagabonds into infinite numbers, the obstinate resistance of them that daily do transgress the laws made against games and apparel, which be the straight paths to robbery and semblable mischief; yet if any one commissioner, moved with zeal to his country, according to his duty do execute duly and frequently the law or good ordinance, wherein is any sharp punishment, some of his companions thereat rebelleth, infaming [1] him to be a man without charity, calling him secretly a pick-thank,[2] or ambitious of glory, and by such manner of obloquy they seek means to bring him into the hatred of people. And this may well be called vain pity; wherein is contained neither justice not yet commendable charity, but rather thereby ensueth negligence, contempt, disobedience, and finally all mischief and incurable misery.

If this sickness had reigned among the old Romans, suppose ye that the estate of their public weal had six hundred years increased, and two hundred years continued in one excellent estate and wonderful majesty? Or think ye that the same Romans might so have ordered many great countries, with fewer ministers of justice than be now in one shire of England? But of that matter, and also of rigour and equality of punishment, I will treat more amply in a place more propitious for that purpose.

And here I conclude to write any more at this time of mercy.

VIII. *The three principal parts of humanity.*

THE NATURE and condition of man, wherein he is less than God Almighty, and excelling notwithstanding all other creatures in earth, is called humanity; which is a general name to those

---

[1] Reputing.   [2] Desirer of flattery.

virtues in whom seemeth to be a mutual concord and love in the nature of man. And although there be many of the said virtues, yet be there three principal by whom humanity is chiefly compact: benevolence, beneficence, and liberality, which maketh up the said principal virtue called benignity or gentleness.

Benevolence, if it do extend to a whole country or city, it is properly called charity, and sometime zeal; and if it concern one person, then is it called benevolence. And if it be very fervent and to one singular person, then may it be named love or amity. Of that virtuous disposition proceedeth an act, whereby something is employed which is profitable and good to him that receiveth it. And that virtue, if it be in operation or (as I might say) endeavour, it is called then beneficence, and the deed (vulgarly named a good turn) may be called a benefit. If it be in money or other thing that hath substance it is then called liberality, which is not alway a virtue as beneficence is; for in well doing (which is the right interpretation of beneficence) can be no vice included. But liberality, though it proceed of a free and gentle heart, willing to do something thankful, yet may it transgress the bonds of virtue, either in excessive rewards, or expenses, or else employing treasure, promotion, or other substance on persons unworthy, or on things inconvenient, and of small importance. Albeit some think such manner of erogation not to be worthy the name of liberality. For Aristotle defineth a liberal man to be he which doth erogate [1] according to the rate of his substance and as opportunity happeneth. He saith also in the same place, that liberality is not in the multitude or quantity of that which is given, but in the habit or fashion of the giver, for he giveth according to his ability. Neither Tully approveth it to be liberality, wherein is any mixture of avarice or rapine; for it is not properly liberality to exact unjustly, or by violence or craft to take good from particular persons, and distribute them in a multitude; or to take from many unjustly and enrich therewith one person or few. For as the same author saith, the last precept concerning benefits or rewards is, to take good heed that he contend not against equity, nor that he uphold none injury.

Now will I proceed seriously and in a due form to speak more particularly of these three virtues. Notwithstanding there is such affinity between beneficence and liberality, being always a virtue,

[1] Spend.

that they tend to one conclusion or purpose, that is to say, with a free and glad will to give to another that thing which he before lacked.

IX. Of what excellence benevolence is.

WHEN I remember what incomparable goodness hath ever proceeded of this virtue benevolence, merciful God, what sweet flavour feel I piercing my spirits, whereof both my soul and body to my thinking do conceive such recreation, that it seemeth me to be in a paradise, or other semblable place of incomparable delights and pleasures. First I behold the dignity of that virtue, considering that God is thereby chiefly known and honoured both of angel and man. As contrariwise the devil is hated and reproved both of God and man for his malice, which vice is contrarious and repugnant to benevolence. Wherefore without benevolence may be no God. For God is all goodness, all charity, all love, which wholly be comprehended in the said word benevolence.

Now let us see where any other virtue may be equal in dignity with this virtue benevolence, or if any virtue remaineth, where this is excluded. For what cometh of prudence where lacketh benevolence, but deceit, rapine, avarice, and tyranny? What of fortitude, but beastly cruelty, oppression, and effusion of blood? What justice may there be without benevolence? Since the first or chief portion of justice (as Tully saith) is to endamage no man, only as thou be wrongfully vexed. And what is the cause hereof but equal and entire love; which being removed, or ceasing, who endeavoureth not himself to take from another all thing that he coveteth, or for everything that discontenteth him would not forthwith be avenged? Whereby he confoundeth the virtue called temperance, which is the moderatrice as well of all motions of the mind, called affects, as of all acts proceeding of man. Here it sufficiently appeareth (as I suppose) of what estimation benevolence is.

Now will I, according to mine accustomed manner, endeavour me to recreate the spirits of the diligent reader with some delectable histories, wherein is any noble remembrance of this virtue benevolence, that the worthiness thereof may appear in a more plain declaration; for in every discipline example is the best instructor.

But first I will advertise the reader, that I will now write of that benevolence only which is most universal, wherein is equality without singular affection or acceptance of personages. And here it is to be noted that if a governor of a public weal, judge, or any other minister of justice do give sentence against one that hath transgressed the laws, or punisheth him according to the qualities of his trespass, benevolence thereby is not anything perished; for the condemnation or punishment is either to reduce him that erreth into the train of virtue, or to preserve a multitude from damage, by putting men in fear that be prone to offend, dreading the sharp correction that they behold another to suffer. And that manner of severity is touched by the prophet David, in the fourth Psalm, saying in this wise: 'Be you angry and look that you sin not.' And Tully saith in his first book of offices, 'It is to be wished that they which in the public weal have any authority may be like to the laws, which in correcting be led only by equity and not by wrath or displeasure.' And in that manner, when Korah, Dathan, and Abiram moved a sedition against Moses, he prayed God that the earth might open and swallow them, considering that the fury of the people might not be by any other means assuaged, nor they kept in due rule or obedience.

Elijah the holy prophet of God did his own hands put to death the priests of the idol Baal, yet ceased he not with fasting, praying, long and tedious pilgrimages to pacify the displeasure that God took against the people of Israel. But to return to benevolence.

Moses being highly entertained with Pharaoh, King of Egypt, and so much in his favour by the means of the King's sister that (as Joseph saith) he being made captain of a huge army was sent by Pharaoh against the Ethiopians or Moors, where he made such exploiture that he not only achieved his enterprise but also had given unto him, for his prowess, the king's daughter of Ethiopia to be his wife, with great abundance of riches. And also for his endeavour, prowess, and wisdom, was much esteemed by Pharaoh and the nobles of Egypt; so that he might have lived there continually in much honour and wealth, if he would have preferred his singular advail [1] before the universal weal of his own kindred or family. But he inflamed with fervent benevolence or zeal toward them, to redeem them out of their miserable bondage, chose rather to be in the dangerous indignation of

[1] Profit.

Pharaoh, to commit his person to the changeable minds of a multitude, and they most unstable, to pass great and long journeys through deserts replenished with wild beasts and venomous serpents, to suffer extreme hunger and thirst, lacking often times not only victual but also fresh water to drink, than to be in the palace of Pharaoh where he should have been satisfied with honour, riches and ease, and all other things pleasant. Who that readeth the book of Exodus shall find the charity of this man wonderful. For when Almighty God, being grievously moved with the children of Israel for their ingratitude, forasmuch as they often times murmured against him, and unneth [1] might be kept by Moses from idolatry, he said to Moses that he would destroy them utterly, and make him ruler of a much greater and better people. But Moses burning in a marvellous charity towards them said unto God, 'This people, good Lord, have most grievously sinned, yet either forgive them this trespass, or, if ye do not, strike me clean out of the book that ye wrote.' And divers other times he importunately cried to God for the safeguard of them, notwithstanding that many times they concluded to have slain him, if he had not been by his wisdom, and specially by the power of God, preserved.

But peradventure some, which seek for starting holes to maintain their vices, will object, saying that Moses was a holy prophet and a person elect by predestination to deliver the children of Israel out of captivity, which he could not have done if he had not been of such patience and charity. Therefore let us see what examples of semblable benevolence we can find among the Gentiles, in whom was no virtue inspired, but that only which natural reason induced.

When a furious and wilful young man in a sedition had stricken out one of the eyes of King Lycurgus, wherefore the people would have slain the transgressor, he would not suffer them, but having him home to his house, he by such wise means corrected the young man that he at the last brought him to good manners and wisdom. Also the same Lycurgus, to the intent that the effect of his benevolence toward the common weal of his country might persist and continue, and that his excellent laws being established should never be altered, he did let swear all his people, that they should change no part of his laws until he were returned, feigning

[1] Scarcely.

to them that he would go to Delphos, where Apollo was chiefly
honoured, to consult with that god what seemed to him to be
added to or minished of those laws, which also he feigned to have
received of the said Apollo. But finally he went in to the Isle of
Crete, where he continued and died, commanding at his death
that his bones should be cast into the sea, lest if they were brought
to Lacedaemonia, his country, the people should think themselves
of their oath and promise discharged.

Semblable love Codrus, the last King of Athens, had to his
country. For where the people called Dorians (whom some think
to be now Sicilians) would avenge their old grudges against the
Athenians, they demanded of some of their gods, what success
should happen if they made any wars. Unto whom answer was
made, that if they slew not the King of Athens they should then
have the victory. When they came to the field, straight commandment was given among them that, above all thing, they should
have good await [1] of the King of Athens, which at that time was
Codrus. But he before knowing the answer made to the Dorians,
and what commandment was given to the army, did put off his
princely habit or robes, and in apparel all ragged and rent,
carrying on his neck a bundle of twigs, entered into the host of
his enemies, and was slain in the press by a soldier whom he
wounded with a hook purposely. But when it was perceived and
known to be the corpse of King Codrus, the Dorians all dismayed
departed from the field without proffering battle. And in this wise
the Athenians, by the virtue of their most benevolent king, who
for the safeguard of his country willingly died, were clearly
delivered from battle. O noble Codrus, how worthy had you been
(if God had been pleased) to have aboden the reparation of mankind, that, in the habit and religion of a Christian prince, ye
might have shown your wonderful benevolence and courage, for
the safeguard of Christian men, and to the noble example of other
princes.

Curtius, a noble knight of the Romans, had no less love to his
country than Codrus. For soon after the beginning of the city
there happened to be a great earthquake, and after there remained a great dell or pit without bottom, which to behold was
horrible and loathsome, and out of it proceeded such a damp or
air, that corrupted all the city with pestilence. Wherefore when

[1] Guard.

they had counselled with such idols as they then worshipped, answer was made that the earth should not close until there were thrown into it the most precious thing in the city; which answer received, there was thrown in rich jewels of gold and precious stone; but all availed not. At the last, Curtius, being a young and goodly gentleman, considering that no riches thrown in profited, he finally conjected that the life of man was above all things most precious; to the intent the residue of the people might be saved by his only death, he armed himself at all points, and sitting on a courser, with his sword in his hand ready drawn, with a valiant and fierce courage enforced his horse to leap into the dell or pit, and forthwith it joined together and closed, leaving only a sign where the pit was; which long after was called Curtius' Lake.

I pass over the two Decii, Marcus Regulus, and many other princes and noblemen that for the weal of their country died willingly. And now will I speak of such as in any other form have declared their benevolence.

Xenophon, condisciple of Plato, wrote the life of Cyrus, King of Persia, most elegantly, wherein he expresseth the figure of an excellent governor or captain. He showeth there that Croesus, the rich King of Lydia, whom Cyrus had taken prisoner, subdued his country, and possessed his treasure, said on a time to Cyrus, when he beheld his liberality, that such largeness as he used should bring him in poverty, where, if he listed, he might accumulate up treasure incomparable. Then Cyrus demanded of Croesus, 'What treasure suppose ye should I now have, if during the time of my reign I would have gathered and kept money as ye exhort me to do?' Then Croesus named a great sum. 'Well,' said Cyrus, 'send ye some man, whom ye best trust, with Histaspa my servant; and thou, Histaspa, go about to my friends and show them that I lack gold toward a certain business, wherefore I will they shall send me as much as they can, and that they put it in writing and send it sealed by the servant of Croesus.' In the same wise Cyrus wrote in a letter, and also that they should receive Histaspa as his counsellor and friend, and sent it by him. Histaspa, after that he had done the message of Cyrus and was returned with the servant of Croesus, who brought letters from Cyrus's friends, he said to Cyrus, 'O sir, from henceforth look that ye take me for a man of great substance. For I am highly rewarded with many great gifts for bringing your letters.' Then Cyrus, at the hour appointed, led with him King Croesus into his camp, saying to him,

'Now behold here is our treasure; account, if ye can, how much money is ready for me, if I have need of any to occupy.' When Croesus beheld and reckoned the innumerable treasure which in sundry parts were laid about the pavilion of Cyrus, he found much more than he said to Cyrus that he should have in his treasure, if he himself had gathered and kept it. And when all appeared sufficiently, Cyrus then said, 'How think you, Croesus, have I not treasure? And ye counselled me that I should gather and keep money, by occasion whereof I should be envied and hated by my people, and moreover put my trust to servants hired to have rule thereof. But I do all otherwise; for, in making my friends rich, I take them all for my treasure, and have them more sure and trusty keepers both of me and my substance, than I should do those whom I must trust only for their wages.'

Lord God, what a notable history is this, and worthy to be graven in tables of gold; considering the virtue and power of benevolence therein expressed. For the benevolent mind of a governor not only bindeth the hearts of the people unto him with the chain of love, more strong than any material bonds, but also guardeth more safely his person than any tower or garrison.

The eloquent Tully said in his offices, 'A liberal heart is cause of benevolence, although perchance that power sometime lacketh'. Contrariwise he saith, 'They that desire to be feared needs must they dread them, of whom they be feared.'

Also Pliny the Younger saith, 'He that is not environed with charity, in vain is he guarded with terror; since armour with armour is stirred.' Which is ratified by the most grave philosopher Seneca, in his book of mercy that he wrote to Nero, where he saith, 'He is much deceived that thinketh a man to be sure, where nothing from him can be safe. For with mutual assurance surety is obtained.'

Antoninus Pius, Emperor of Rome, so much tendered the benevolence of his people, that when a great number had conspired treason against him, the Senate being therewith grievously moved, endeavoured them to punish the said conspirators; but the Emperor caused the examination to cease, saying, that it should not need to seek too busily for them that intended such mischief, lest, if they found many, he should know that many him hated. Also when the people (forasmuch as on a time they lacked corn in their granaries) would have slain him with stones, rather than he would have the seditious persons to be punished, he in his own person declared to them the occasion of the scarcity, wherewith they being pacified every man held him contented.

I had almost forgotten a notable and worthy remembrance of King Philip, father to great King Alexander. It was on a time to him reported that one of his captains had menacing words towards him, whereby it seemed he intended some damage toward his person. Wherefore his council advised him to have good await [1] of the said captain, and that he were put under ward; to whom the King answered, 'If any part of my body were sick or else sore, whether should I therefore cut it from the residue, and cast it from me, or else endeavour myself that it might be healed?' And then he called for the said captain, and so entertained him with familiarity and bounteous rewards that ever after he had him more assured and loyal than ever he was.

Agesilaus, King of Lacedaemonia, to him that demanded how a king might most surely govern his realm without soldiers or a guard to his person, answered, 'If he reigned over his people, as a father doth over his children.'

The city of Athens (from whence issued all excellent doctrine and wisdom) during the time that it was governed by those persons unto whom the people might have a familiar access, and boldly expound their griefs and damages, prospered marvellously, and during a long season reigned in honour and weal. Afterwards the Lacedaemons, by the mutability of fortune, vanquished them in battle and committed the city of Athens to the keeping of thirty of their own captains, which were for their pride and avarice called tyrants. But now see how little surety is in great number or strength, where lacketh benevolence. These thirty tyrants were continually environed with sundry garrisons of armed men, which was a terrible visage to people that before lived under the obedience of their laws only. Finally the Athenians, by fear being put from their accustomed access to their governors to require justice, and therewith being fatigued as men oppressed with continual injury, took to them a desperate courage, and in conclusion expelled out of the city all the said tyrants, and reduced it unto his pristine governance.

What misery was in the life of Dionysius, the tyrant of Sicily? Who knowing that his people desired his destruction, for his

[1] Guard.

rapine and cruelty, would not be of any man shaven, but first caused his own daughters to clip his beard, and afterward he also mistrusted them, and then he himself with a burning coal seared the hairs of his beard, and yet finally was he destroyed.

In like wretchedness was one Alexander, prince of a city called Pherae, for he, having an excellent fair wife, not only excluded all men from her company, but also, as often as he would lie with her, certain persons should go before him with torches, and he following with his sword ready drawn would therewith ensearch the bed, coffers, and all other places of his chamber, lest any man should be there hid, to the intent to slay him. And that notwithstanding by the procurement of his said wife (who at the last, fatigued with his most foolish jealousy, converted her love into hatred) he was slain by his own subjects. Now doth it appear that this reverend virtue benevolence is of all men, most specially of governors and men of honour, incomparably before other to be embraced.

King Philip, when he heard that his son Alexander used a marvellous liberality among the people, he sent to him a letter, wherein he wrote in this wise: 'Alexander, what perverse opinion hath put thee in such hope, that thou thinkest to make them loyal unto thee, whom thou with money corruptest, considering that the receiver thereof is thereby appaired, being trained by thy prodigality to look and gape alway for a semblable custom?' And therefore the treasure of a gentle countenance, sweet answers, aid in adversity, not with money only but also with study and diligent endeavour, can never be wasted, nor the love of good people, thereby acquired, can be from their hearts in any wise separate. And here I make an end to speak any more at this time of benevolence.

X. *Of beneficence and liberality.*

ALTHOUGH philosophers in the description of virtues have devised to set them as it were in degrees, having respect to the quality and condition of the person which is with them adorned; as applying magnificence to the substance and estate of princes, and to private persons beneficence and liberality, yet be not these in any part defalcate [1] of their condign [2] praises. For if virtue be

---

[1] Cut off, diminished.　　　　[2] Fit, appropriate.

an election annexed unto our nature, and consisteth in a mean which is determined by reason, and that mean is the very midst of two things vicious, the one in surplusage, the other in lack, then needs must beneficence and liberality be capital virtues. And magnificence proceedeth from them, approaching to the extreme parts; and may be turned into vice if he lack the bridle of reason. But beneficence can by no means be vicious and retain still his name. Semblably liberality (as Aristotle saith) is a measure, as well in giving as in taking of money and goods. And he is only liberal, which distributeth according to his substance, and where it is expedient. Therefore he ought to consider to whom he should give, how much, and when. For liberality taketh his name of the substance of the person from whom it proceedeth; for it resteth not in the quantity or quality of things that be given, but in the natural disposition of the giver.

The great Alexander on a time, after that he had vanquished Darius in battle, one of his soldiers brought unto him the head of an enemy that he had slain, which the King thankfully and with sweet countenance received, and taking a cup of gold filled with good wine, said unto the soldier, 'In old time a cup of gold was the reward of such virtue as thou hast now shown, which semblably thou shalt receive.' But when the soldier for shamefulness refused the cup, Alexander added unto it these words: 'The custom was to give the cup empty, but Alexander giveth to thee full of wine with good handsel.' [1] Wherewith he expressed his liberal heart, and as much comforted the soldier as if he had given him a great city.

Moreover he that is liberal neglecteth not his substance or goods, nor giveth it to all men, but useth it so as he may continually help therewith other, and giveth when, and where, and on whom it ought to be employed. Therefore it may be said that he useth everything best that exerciseth the virtue which is to the thing most appropriate. For riches is of the number of things that may be either good or evil, which is in the arbitrament of the giver. And for that cause liberality and beneficence be of such affinity that the one may never from the other be separate. For the employment of money is not liberality if it be not for a good end or purpose.

The noble Emperors Antonine and Alexander Severus gave of

[1] A gift expressing good wishes.

the revenues of the Empire innumerable substance, to the re-edifying of cities and common houses decayed for age, or by earthquakes subverted, wherein they practised liberality and also beneficence.

But Tiberius, Nero, Caligula, Heliogabalus and other semblable monsters, which exhausted and consumed infinite treasures in bordel [1] houses, and places where abominations were used, also in enriching slaves, concubines and bawds, were not therefore named liberal, but suffereth therefore perpetual reproach of writers, being called devourers and wasters of treasure. Wherefore inasmuch as liberality wholly resteth in the giving of money, it sometime coloureth a vice. But beneficence is never taken but in the better part, and (as Tully saith) is taken out of virtue, where liberality cometh out of the coffer. Also where a man distributeth his substance to many persons, the less liberality shall he use to other; so with bounteousness bounty is minished. Only they that be called beneficial, and do use the virtue of beneficence, which consisteth in counselling and helping other with any assistance in time of need, shall alway find coadjutors and supporters of their gentle courage. And doubtless that manner of gentleness that consisteth in labour, study, and diligence, is more commendable, and extendeth further, and also may more profit persons, than that which resteth in rewards and expenses. But to return to liberality.

What greater folly may be, than that thing that a man most gladly doth, to endeavour him with all study that it may no longer be done? Wherefore Tully calleth them prodigal, that in inordinate feasts and banquets, vain plays, and huntings do spend all their substance, and in those things whereof they shall leave but a short or no remembrance. Wherefore to resort to the counsel of Aristotle before expressed. Notwithstanding that liberality, in a nobleman specially, is commended, although it somewhat do exceed the terms of measure; yet if it be well and duly employed, it acquireth perpetual honour to the giver, and much fruit and singular commodity thereby increaseth. For where honest and virtuous personages be advanced, and well rewarded, it stirreth the courages of men, which have any spark of virtue, to increase therein, with all their force and endeavour. Wherefore next to the helping and relieving of a commonalty, the

[1] Brothel.

great part of liberality is to be employed on men of virtue and
good qualities. Wherein is required to be a good election and
judgment, that, for hope of reward or favour, under the cloak of
virtue be not hid the most mortal poison of flattery.

XI. *The true description of amity or friendship.*

I HAVE already treated of benevolence and beneficence generally.
But forasmuch as friendship, called in Latin *amicitia*, comprehendeth both those virtues more specially and in an higher degree,
and is now so infrequent or strange among mortal men, by the
tyranny of covetise and ambition, which have long reigned, and
yet do, that amity may now unneth [1] be known or found throughout the world, by them that seek for her as diligently as a maiden
would seek for a small silver pin in a great chamber strawed with
white rushes, I will therefore borrow so much of the gentle
reader though he be nigh weary of this long matter, barren of
eloquence and pleasant sentence, and declare somewhat by the
way of very and true friendship. Which perchance may be an
allective [2] to good men to seek for their semblable, on whom they
may practise amity. For as Tully saith, 'Nothing is more to be
loved or to be joined together, than similitude of good manners
or virtues'; wherein be the same or semblable studies, the same
wills or desires, in them it happeneth that one in another as much
delighteth as in himself.

But now let us ensearch what friendship or amity is. Aristotle
saith that friendship is a virtue, or joineth with virtue; which is
affirmed by Tully, saying, that friendship cannot be without
virtue, nor but in good men only. Who be good men, he after
declareth to be those persons, which do so bear themselves and
in such wise do live, that their faith, surety, equality and liberality
be sufficiently proved. Nor that there is in them any covetise, wilfulness, or fool-hardiness, and that in them is great stability or
constance; them suppose I (as they be taken) to be called good
men, which do follow (as much as men may) nature, the chief
captain or guide of man's life. Moreover the same Tully defineth
friendship in this manner, saying that it is none other thing but a
perfect consent of all things appertaining as well to God as to

---

[1] Scarcely.   [2] Enticement.

man, with benevolence and charity; and that he knoweth nothing given of God (except sapience) to man more commodious. Which definition is excellent and very true. For in God, and all thing that cometh of God, nothing is of more great estimation than love, called in Latin *amor*, whereof *amicitia* cometh, named in English friendship or amity; the which taken away from the life of man, no house shall abide standing, no field shall be in culture. And that is lightly perceived, if a man do remember what cometh of dissension and discord. Finally he seemeth to take the sun from the world, that taketh friendship from man's life.

Since friendship cannot be but in good men, nor may not be without virtue, we may be assured that thereof none evil may proceed, or therewith any evil thing may participate. Wherefore inasmuch as it may be but in a few persons (good men being in a small number), and also it is rare and seldom (as all virtues be commonly), I will declare after the opinion of philosophers, and partly by common experience, who among good men be of nature most apt to friendship.

Between all men that be good cannot alway be amity, but it also requireth that they be of semblable or much like manners. For gravity and affability be every of them laudable qualities, so be severity and placability, also magnificence and liberality be noble virtues, and yet frugality, which is a soberness or moderation in living is, and that for good cause, of all wise men extolled. Yet where these virtues and qualities be separately in sundry persons assembled, may well be perfect concord, but friendship is there seldom or never; for that, which the one delighteth, it is to the other repugnant unto his nature; and where is any repugnance, may be none amity, since friendship is an entire consent of wills and desires. Therefore it is seldom seen that friendship is between these persons, a man sturdy, of opinion inflexible, and of sour countenance and speech, with him that is tractable, and with reason persuaded, and of sweet countenance and entertainment. Also between him which is elevated in authority and another of a very base estate or degree. Yea and if they be both in an equal dignity, if they be desirous to climb, as they do ascend, so friendship for the more part decayeth. For as Tully saith in his first book of offices, what thing so ever it be, in the which many cannot excel or have therein superiority, therein oftentimes is such a contention that it is a thing of all other most difficult to keep among them good or virtuous company; that is as much to say as to retain among them friendship and amity. And it is often-times seen that divers, which before they came in authority, were of good and virtuous conditions, being in their prosperity were utterly changed, and despising their old friends set all their study and pleasure on their new acquaintance. Wherein men shall per-ceive to be a wonderful blindness, or (as I might say) a madness, if they note diligently all that I shall hereafter write of friendship. But now to resort to speak of them in whom friendship is most frequent, and they also thereto be most aptly disposed. Un-doubtedly it be specially they which be wise and of nature inclined to beneficence, liberality, and constance. For by wisdom is marked and substantially discerned the words, acts, and demeanour of all men between whom happeneth to be any inter-course or familiarity, whereby is engendered a favour or dis-position of love. Beneficence, that is to say, mutually putting to their study and help in necessary affairs, induceth love. They that be liberal do withhold or hide nothing from them whom they love, whereby love increaseth. And in them that be constant is never mistrust or suspicion, nor any surmise or evil report can withdraw them from their affection, and hereby friendship is made perpetual and stable. But if similitude of study or learning be joined unto the said virtues, friendship much rather happeneth, and the mutual interview and conversation is much more pleasant, specially if the studies have in them any delectable affection or motion. For where they be too serious or full of contention, friendship is oftentimes assaulted, whereby it is often in peril. Where the study is elegant and the matter illecebrous, that is to say, sweet to the reader, the course whereof is rather gentle persuasion and quick reasonings than over-subtle argu-ments or litigious controversies, there also it happeneth that the students do delight one in another and be without envy or malicious contention.

Now let us try out what is that friendship that we suppose to be in good men. Verily it is a blessed and stable connection of sundry wills, making of two persons one in having and suffering. And therefore a friend is properly named of philosophers the other I. For that in them is but one mind and one possession and that which more is, a man more rejoiceth at his friend's good fortune than at his own.

Orestes and Pylades, being wonderful like in all features, were taken together and presented unto a tyrant who deadly hated

Orestes, but when he beheld them both, and would have slain Orestes only, he could not discern the one from the other. And also Pylades, to deliver his friend, affirmed that he was Orestes; on the other part Orestes, to save Pylades, denied and said that he was Orestes (as the truth was). Thus a long time they together contending, the one to die for the other, at the last so relented the fierce and cruel heart of the tyrant, that wondering at their marvellous friendship he suffered them freely to depart, without doing them any damage.

Pytheas and Damon, two Pythagoreans, that is to say, students of Pythagoras' learning, being joined together in a perfect friendship, for that one of them was accused to have conspired against Dionysius, King of Sicily, they were both taken and brought to the King, who immediately gave sentence that he that was accused should be put to death. But he desired the King that ere he died, he might return home to set his household in order and to distribute his goods; whereat the King laughing demanded of him scornfully what pledge he would leave him to come again. At the which words his companion stepped forth and said that he would remain there as a pledge for his friend, that in case he came not again at the day to him appointed, that he willingly would lose his head; which condition the tyrant received. The young man that should have died was suffered to depart home to his house, where he set all thing in order and disposed his goods wisely. The day appointed for his return was come, the time much passed; wherefore the King called for him that was pledge, who came forth merely without semblance of dread, offering to abide the sentence of the tyrant, and without grudging to die for the saving the life of his friend. But as the officer of justice had closed his eyes with a kerchief, and had drawn his sword to have stricken off his head, his fellow came running and crying that the day of his appointment was not yet past; wherefore he desired the minister of justice to loose his fellow, and to prepare to do execution on him that had given the occasion. Whereat the tyrant being all abashed, commanded both to be brought in his presence, and when he had enough wondered at their noble hearts and their constance in very friendship, he offering to them great rewards desired them to receive him into their company; and so, doing them much honour, did set them at liberty. Undoubtedly that friendship which doth depend either on profit or else in pleasure, if the ability of the person, which might be profitable, do fail or diminish, or the disposition of the person, which should be pleasant, do change or appair,[1] the ferventness of love ceaseth, and then is there no friendship.

XII. The wonderful history of Titus and Gisippus, and whereby is fully declared the figure of perfect amity.

BUT NOW in the midst of my labour, as it were to pause and take breath, and also to recreate the readers, which, fatigued with long precepts, desire variety of matter, or some new pleasant fable or history, I will rehearse a right goodly example of friendship. Which example, studiously read, shall minister to the readers singular pleasure and also incredible comfort to practise amity.

There was in the city of Rome a noble senator named Fulvius, who sent his son called Titus, being a child, to the city of Athens in Greece (which was the fountain of all manner of doctrine), there to learn good letters, and caused him to be hosted with a worshipful man of that city called Chremes. This Chremes happened to have also a son named Gisippus, who not only was equal to the said young Titus in years, but also in stature, proportion of body, favour, and colour of visage, countenance and speech. The two children were so like that without much difficulty it could not be discerned of their proper parents which was Titus from Gisippus, or Gisippus from Titus. These two young gentlemen, as they seemed to be one in form and personage, so, shortly after acquaintance, the same nature wrought in their hearts such a mutual affection, that their wills and appetites daily more and more so confederated themselves, that it seemed none other, when their names were declared, but that they had only changed their places, issuing (as I might say) out of the one body, and entering into the other. They together and at one time went to their learning and study, at one time to their meals and refection; they delighted both in one doctrine, and profited equally therein; finally they together so increased in doctrine, that within a few years, few within Athens might be compared unto them. At the last died Chremes, which was not only to his son, but also to Titus, cause of much sorrow and heaviness. Gisippus, by the goods of his father, was known to be a man of

---

[1] Deteriorate.

great substance, wherefore there were offered to him great and rich marriages. And he then being of ripe years and of an habile [1] and goodly personage, his friends, kin, and allies exhorted him busily to take a wife, to the intent he might increase his lineage and progeny. But the young man, having his heart already wedded to his friend Titus and his mind fixed to the study of philosophy, fearing that marriage should be the occasion to sever him both from the one and the other, refused of long time to be persuaded; until at the last, partly by the importunate calling on of his kinsmen, partly by the consent and advise of his dear friend Titus, thereto by other desired, he assented to marry such one as should like him. What shall need many words? His friends found a young gentlewoman, which in equality of years, virtuous conditions, nobility of blood, beauty, and sufficient riches, they thought was for such a young man apt and convenient. And when they and her friends upon the covenants of marriage were thoroughly accorded, they counselled Gisippus to repair unto the maiden, and to behold how her person contented him. And he so doing found her in every form and condition according to his expectation and appetite; whereat he much rejoiced and became of her amorous, insomuch as many and often times he leaving Titus at his study secretly repaired unto her. Notwithstanding the fervent love that he had to his friend Titus, at the last surmounted shamefastness. Wherefore he disclosed to him his secret journeys, and what delectation he took in beholding the excellent beauty of her whom he purposed to marry, and how, with her good manners and sweet entertainment, she had constrained him to be her lover. And on a time he, having with him his friend Titus, went to his lady, of whom he was received most joyously. But Titus forthwith, as he beheld so heavenly a personage adorned with beauty inexplicable, in whose visage was most amiable countenance, mixed with maidenly shamefastness, and the rare and sober words, and well couched, which issued out of her pretty mouth, Titus was thereat abashed, and had the heart through pierced with the fiery dart of blind Cupid. Of the which wound the anguish was so exceeding and vehement, that neither the study of philosophy, neither the remembrance of his dear friend Gisippus, who so much loved and trusted him, could anything withdraw him from that unkind appetite, but that of force

[1] Suitable.

he must love inordinately that lady, whom his said friend had determined to marry. Albeit with incredible pains he kept his thoughts secret, until that he and Gisippus were returned unto their lodgings. Then the miserable Titus, withdrawing him as it were to his study, all tormented and oppressed with love, threw himself on a bed, and there rebuking his own most despiteful unkindness, which, by the sudden sight of a maiden, he had conspired against his most dear friend Gisippus, against all humanity and reason, he cursed his fate or constellation, and wished that he had never come to Athens. And therewith he sent out from the bottom of his heart deep and cold sighs, in such plenty that it lacked but little that his heart ne was riven in pieces. In dolour and anguish tossed he himself by a certain space, but to no man would he discover it. But at the last the pain became so intolerable, that, would he or no, he was enforced to keep his bed, being for lack of sleep and other natural sustenance brought in such feebleness that his legs might not sustain his body. Gisippus missing his dear friend Titus was much abashed, and hearing that he lay sick in his bed had forthwith his heart pierced with heaviness, and with all speed came to him where he lay. And beholding the rosial colour, which was wont to be in his visage, turned into sallow, the residue pale, his ruddy lips wan, and his eyes leaden and hollow, Gisippus might unneth [1] keep himself from weeping; but, to the intent he would not discomfort his friend Titus, he dissimulated his heaviness, and with a comfortable countenance demanded of Titus what was the cause of his disease, blaming him of unkindness that he so long had sustained it without giving him knowledge, that he might for him have provided some remedy, if any might have been gotten, though it were with the dispending of all his substance. With which words the mortal sighs renewed in Titus, and the salt tears burst out of his eyes in such abundance, as it had been a land flood running down of a mountain after a storm. That beholding Gisippus, and being also resolved into tears, most heartily desired him and (as I might say) conjured him that for the fervent and entire love that had been, and yet was, between them, he would no longer hide from him his grief, and that there was nothing to him so dear or precious (although it were his own life) that might restore Titus to health, but that he should gladly and without grudging employ

---

[1] Scarcely.

it. With which words, obtestations,[1] and tears of Gisippus, Titus
constrained, all blushing and ashamed, holding down his head,
brought forth with great difficulty his words in this wise. 'My
dear and most loving friend, withdraw your friendly offers, cease
of your courtesy, refrain in your tears and regrettings, take rather
your knife and slay me here where I lie, or otherwise take
vengeance on me, most miserable and false traitor unto you, and
of all other most worthy to suffer most shameful death. For
whereas God of nature, like as he hath given to us similitude in
all the parts of our body, so had he conjoined our wills, studies,
and appetites together in one, so that between two men was never
like concord and love, as I suppose. And now notwithstanding,
only with the look of a woman, those bonds of love be dissolved,
reason oppressed, friendship is excluded; there availeth no
wisdom, no doctrine, no fidelity or trust; yea, your trust is the
cause that I have conspired against you this treason. Alas,
Gisippus, what envious spirit moved you to bring me with you to
her whom ye have chosen to be your wife, where I received this
poison? I say, Gisippus, where was then your wisdom, that ye
remembered not the fragility of our common nature? What
needed you to call me for a witness of your private delights? Why
would ye have me see that, which you yourself could not behold
without ravishing of mind and carnal appetite? Alas, why forget
ye that our minds and appetites were ever one? And that also
what so ye liked was ever to me in like degree pleasant? What will
ye more? Gisippus, I say your trust is the cause that I am en-
trapped; the rays or beams issuing from the eyes of her whom ye
have chosen, with the remembrance of her incomparable virtues,
hath thrilled throughout the midst of my heart, and in such wise
burneth it, that above all things I desire to be out of this wretched
and most unkind life, which is not worthy the company of so
noble and loving a friend as ye be.' And therewith Titus concluded his confession with so profound and bitter a sigh, received
with tears, that it seemed that all his body should be dissolved and
relented into salt drops.

But Gisippus, as he were therewith nothing astonished or
discontented, with an assured countenance and merry regard
embracing Titus and kissing him, answered in this wise. 'Why,
Titus, is this your only sickness and grief that ye so uncourteously

_____
[1] Supplications.

have so long concealed, and with much more unkindness kept it from me than ye have conceived it? I acknowledge my folly, wherewith ye have with good right upbraided me, that, in showing to you her whom I loved, I remembered not the common estate of our nature, nor the agreeableness, or (as I might say) the unity of our two appetites, surely that default can be no reason excused. Wherefore it is only I that have offended. For who may by right prove that ye have trespassed, that by the inevitable stroke of Cupid's dart are thus bitterly wounded? Think ye me such a fool or ignorant person that I know not the power of Venus, where she listeth to show her importable violence? Have not ye well resisted against such a goddess, that for my sake ye have striven with her almost to the death? What more loyalty or troth can I require of you? Am I of that virtue that I may resist against celestial influence preordinate by providence divine? If I so thought, what were my wits? Where were my study so long time spent in noble philosophy? I confess to you, Titus, I love that maiden as much as any wise man might possible, and take in her company more delight and pleasure than of all the treasure and lands that my father left to me, which ye know was right abundant. But now I perceive that the affection of love toward her surmounteth in you above measure, what, shall I think it of a wanton lust or sudden appetite in you, whom I have ever known of grave and sad disposition, inclined alway to honest doctrine, fleeing all vain dalliance and dishonest pastime? Shall I imagine to be in you any malice or fraud, since from the tender time of our childhood I have alway found in you, my sweet friend Titus, such a conformity with all my manners, appetites, and desires, that never was seen between us any manner of contention? Nay, God forbid that in the friendship of Gisippus and Titus should happen any suspicion, or that any fantasy should pierce my head, whereby that honourable love between us should be the mountenance[1] of a crumb perished. Nay, nay, Titus, it is (as I have said) the only providence of God. She was by him from the beginning prepared to be your lady and wife. For such fervent love entereth not into the heart of a wise man and virtuous, but by a divine disposition; whereat if I should be discontented or grudge, I should not only be unjust to you, withholding that from you which is undoubtedly yours, but also obstinate and repugnant against the determination

[1] Amount.

of God; which shall never be found in Gisippus. Therefore, gentle friend Titus, dismay you not at the chance of love, but receive it joyously with me, that am with you nothing discontented, but marvellous glad, since it is my hap to find for you such a lady, with whom ye shall live in felicity, and receive fruit to the honour and comfort of all your lineage. Here I renounce to you clearly all my title and interest that I now have or might have in that fair maiden. Call to you your pristine courage, wash clean your visage and eyes thus bewept, and abandon all heaviness. The day appointed for our marriage approacheth; let us consult how without difficulty ye may wholly attain your desires. Take heed, this is mine advice; ye know well that we two be so like, that, being apart and in one apparel, few men do know us. Also ye do remember that the custom is, that, notwithstanding any ceremony done at the time of the espousal, the marriage notwithstanding is not confirmed, until at night that the husband putteth a ring on the finger of his wife, and unlooseth her girdle. There I myself will be present with my friends and perform all the parts of a bride. And ye shall abide in a place secret, where I shall appoint you, until it be night. And then shall ye quickly convey yourself into the maiden's chamber, and for the similitude of our personages and of our apparel, ye shall not be espied of the women, which have with none of us any acquaintance, and shortly get you to bed, and put your own ring on the maiden's finger, and undo her girdle of virginity, and do all other thing that shall be to your pleasure. Be now of good cheer, Titus, and comfort yourself with good refections and solace, that this wan and pale colour, and your cheeks meagre and lean, be not the cause of your discovering. I know well that, ye having your purpose, I shall be in obloquy and derision of all men, and so hated of all my kindred, that they shall seek occasion to expel me out of this city, thinking me to be a notable reproach to all my family. But let God therein work. I force not what pain that I abide, so that ye, my friend Titus, may be safe, and pleasantly enjoy your desires, to the increasing of your felicity.'

With these words Titus began to move, as it were, out of a dream, and doubting whether he heard Gisippus speak, or else saw but a vision, lay still as a man abashed. But when he beheld the tears trickling down by the face of Gisippus, he then recomforted him, and thanking him for his incomparable kindness, refused the benefit that he offered, saying that it were better that a hundred such unkind wretches, as he was, should perish, than so noble a man as was Gisippus should sustain reproach or damage. But Gisippus eftsoons [1] comforted Titus, and therewith swore and protested that with free and glad will he would that this thing should be in form aforesaid accomplished, and therewith embraced and sweetly kissed Titus. Who perceiving the matter sure and not feigned, as a man not sick but only awaked out of his sleep, he set himself up in his bed, the quick blood somewhat resorted unto his visage, and, after a little good meats and drinks taken, he was shortly and in a few days restored into his old fashion and figure. To make the tale short. The day of marriage was come. Gisippus accompanied with his allies and friends came to the house of the damsel, where they were honourably and joyously feasted. And between him and the maiden was a sweet entertainment, which to behold all that were present took much pleasure and comfort, praising the beauty, goodliness, virtue, and courtesy which in those couples were excellent above all other that they had ever seen. What shall I say more? The covenants were read and sealed, the dower appointed, and all other bargains concluded, and the friends of either part took their leave and departed, the bride with a few women (as was the custom) brought into her chamber. Then (as it was before agreed) Titus conveyed himself after Gisippus returned to his house, or perchance to the chamber appointed for Titus, nothing sorrowful, although that he heartily loved the maiden, but with a glad heart and countenance, that he had so recovered his friend from death, and so well brought him to the effect of his desire. Now is Titus in bed with the maiden, not known of her, nor of any other, but for Gisippus. And first he sweetly demanded her, if that she loved him, and deigned to take him for her husband, forsaking all other, which she all blushing with an eye half laughing half mourning (as in point to depart from her maidenhood, but supposing it to be Gisippus that asked her) affirmed. And then he eftsoons asketh her, if she in ratifying that promise would receive his ring, which he had there all ready, whereto she consenting putteth the ring on her finger and unlooseth her girdle. What thing else he did, they two only knew it. Of one thing I am sure, that night was to Titus more comfortable than ever was the longest day of the year, yea, and I suppose a whole year of days.

---

[1] Again.

The morrow is come. And Gisippus, thinking it to be expedient that the truth should be discovered, assembled all the nobility of the city at his own house, where also by appointment was Titus, who among them had these words that do follow.

'My friends Athenians, there is at this time shown among you an example almost incredible of the divine power of honourable love, to the perpetual renown and commendation of this noble city of Athens, whereof ye ought to take excellent comfort, and therefore give due thanks to God, if there remain among you any token of the ancient wisdom of your most noble progenitors. For what more praise may be given to people, than benevolence, faithfulness, and constance? Without whom all countries and cities be brought unto desolation and ruin, like as by them they become prosperous and in most high felicity. What shall I long tarry you in conjecting mine intent and meaning? Ye all know from whence I came unto this city, that of adventure I found in the house of Chremes his son Gisippus, of mine own age, and in everything so like to me, that neither his father nor any other man could discern of us the one from the other, but by our own ensignment or showing, insomuch as there were put about our necks laces of sundry colours to declare our personages. What mutual agreement and love have been alway between us, during the eight years that we have been together, ye all be witnesses, that have been beholders and wonderers of our most sweet conversation and consent of appetites, wherein was never any discord or variance. And as for my part, after the decease of my father, notwithstanding that there was descended and happened unto me great possessions, fair houses, with abundance of riches; also I being called home by the desirous and importunate letters of mine allies and friends, which be of the most noble of all the senators, offered the advancement to the highest dignities in the public weal; I will not remember the lamentations of my most natural mother, expressed in her tender letters, all besprent[1] and blotted with abundance of tears, wherein she accuseth me of unkindness for my long tarrying, and specially now in her most discomfort; but all this could not remove me the breadth of my nail from my dear friend Gisippus. And but by force could not I, nor yet may be drawn from his sweet company, but if he thereto will consent I choosing rather to live with him as his companion and fellow,

---

[1] Sprinkled.

yea, and as his servant, rather than to be consul of Rome. Thus my kindness hath he well acquitted, or (as I might say) redoubled, delivering me from the death, yea, from the most cruel and painful death of all other. I perceive ye wonder hereat, noble Athenians, and no marvel; for what person should be so hardy to attempt any such thing against me, being a Roman, and of the noble blood of the Romans? Or who should be thought so malicious to slay me, who (as all ye be my judges) never trespassed against any person within this city? Nay, nay, my friends, I have none of you all therein suspected. I perceive ye desire and harken to know what he was that presumed to do so cruel and great an enterprise. It was love, noble Athenians, the same love which (as your poets do remember) did wound the more part of all the gods that ye do honour, that constrained Jupiter to transform himself in a swan, a bull, and divers other likenesses; the same love that caused Hercules, the vanquisher and destroyer of monsters and giants, to spin on a rock, sitting among maidens in a woman's apparel; the same love that caused to assemble all the noble princes of Asia and Greece in the fields of Troy; the same love, I say, against whose assaults may be found no defence or resistance, hath suddenly and unaware stricken me unto the heart with such vehemence and might, that I had in short space died with most fervent torments, had not the incomparable friendship of Gisippus helped me. I see you would fain know who she is that I loved. I will no longer delay you, noble Athenians. It is Sophronia, the lady whom Gisippus had chosen to have to his wife, and whom he most entirely loved. But when his most gentle heart perceived that my love was in a much higher degree than his toward that lady, and that it proceeded neither of wantonness, neither of long conversation, nor of any other corrupt desire or fantasy but in an instant, by only one look, and with such fervence that immediately I was so cruciate,[1] that I desired, and, in all that I might, provoked death to take me, he by his wisdom soon perceived (as I doubt not but that ye do) that it was the very provision of God, that she should be my wife, and not his. Whereto he giving place, and more esteeming true friendship than the love of a woman, whereunto he was induced by his friends, and not by violence of Cupid constrained, as I am, hath willingly granted to me the interest that he had in the damsel;

---

[1] Tormented.

and it is I, Titus, that have verily wedded her, I have put the ring on her finger, I have undone the girdle of shamefastness. What will ye more? I have lain with her, and confirmed the matrimony, and made her a wife.'

At these words all they that were present began to murmur and to cast a disdainful and grievous look upon Gisippus. Then spake again Titus. 'Leave your grudgings and menacing countenance toward Gisippus; he hath done to you all honour and no deed of reproach. I tell you, he hath accomplished all the parts of a friend; that love which was most certain that he continued: he knew that he might find in Greece another maiden as fair and as rich as this that he had chosen, and one perchance that he might love better. But such a friend as I was (having respect to our similitude, the long approved concord, also mine estate and condition) he was sure to find never none. Also the damsel suffereth no disparagement in her blood, or hindrance in her marriage, but is much rather advanced (no dispraise to my dear friend Gisippus). Also consider, noble Athenians, that I took her not my father living, when ye might have suspected that as well her riches as her beauty should have thereto allured me, but soon after my father's decease, when I far exceeded her in possessions and substance, when the most noble men of Rome and of Italy desired mine alliance. Ye have therefore all cause to rejoice and thank Gisippus, and not to be angry, and also to extol his wonderful kindness toward me, whereby he hath won me and all my blood such friends to you and your city, that ye may be assured to be by us defended against all the world. Which being considered, Gisippus hath well deserved a statue or image of gold to be set on a pillar in the midst of your city, for an honourable monument in the remembrance of our incomparable friendship, and of the good that thereby may come to your city. But if this persuasion cannot satisfy you, but that ye will imagine anything to the damage of my dear friend Gisippus after my departing, I make mine avow unto God, creator of all thing, that as I shall have knowledge thereof, I shall forthwith resort hither with the invincible power of the Romans, and revenge him in such wise against his enemies, that all Greece shall speak of it to their perpetual dishonour, shame, and reproach.' And therewith Titus and Gisippus rose; but the other, for fear of Titus, dissembled their malice, making semblance as they had been with all thing contented.

Soon after, Titus, being sent for by the authority of the Senate and people of Rome, prepared to depart out of Athens, and would fain have had Gisippus to have gone with him, offering to divide with him all his substance and fortune. But Gisippus, considering how necessary his counsel should be to the city of Athens, would not depart out of his country, notwithstanding that above all earthly things he most desired the company of Titus. Which abode also for the said consideration Titus approved. Titus with his lady is departed towards the city of Rome, where at their coming they were of the mother of Titus, his kinsmen, and of all the senate and people joyously received. And there lived Titus with his lady in joy inexplicable, and had by her many fair children, and for his wisdom and learning was so highly esteemed that there was no dignity or honourable office within the city that he had not with much favour and praise achieved and occupied.

But now let us resort to Gisippus, who immediately upon the departing of Titus was so maligned at, as well by his own kinsmen as by the friends of the lady, that he to their seeming shamefully abandoned, leaving her to Titus, that they spared not daily to vex him with all kinds of reproach that they could devise or imagine. And first they excluded him out of their counsel, and prohibited from him all honest company. And yet not being therewith satisfied, finally they adjudged him unworthy to enjoy any possessions or goods left to him by his parents, whom he (as they supposed), by his indiscreet friendship had so distained. Wherefore they despoiled him of all things, and almost naked expelled him out of the city. Thus is Gisippus, late wealthy and one of the most noble men of Athens, for his kind heart banished his own country for ever, and as a man dismayed wandering hither and thither, findeth no man that would succour him. At the last, remembering in what pleasure his friend Titus lived with his lady, for whom he suffered these damages, concluded that he would go to Rome and declare his infortune to his said friend Titus. What shall need a long tale? In conclusion, with much pain, cold, hunger, and thirst, he is come to the city of Rome, and diligently inquiring for the house of Titus, at the last he came to it, but beholding it so beauteous, large, and princely, he was ashamed to approach nigh to it, being in so simple estate and unclad; but standeth by, that in case that Titus came forth out of his house he might then present himself to him. He being in this thought, Titus holding his lady by the hand issued out from his door, and taking their

horses to solace themselves, beheld Gisippus; but beholding his
vile apparel regarded him not, but passed forth on their way.
Wherewith Gisippus was so wounded to the heart, thinking that
Titus had condemned his fortune, that oppressed with mortal
heaviness he fell in a swoon, but being recovered by some that
stood by, thinking him to be sick, he forthwith departed, intending not to abide any longer, but as a wild beast to wander abroad
in the world. But for weariness he was constrained to enter into
an old barn, without the city, where he casting himself on the bare
ground, with weeping and dolorous crying bewailed his fortune.
But most of all accusing the ingratitude of Titus, for whom he
suffered all that misery, the remembrance whereof was so intolerable that he determined no longer to live in that anguish and
dolour. And therewith drew his knife, purposing to have slain
himself. But ever wisdom (which he by the study of philosophy
had attained) withdrew him from that desperate act. And in this
contention between wisdom and will, fatigued with long journeys
and watch, or as God would have it, he fell into a dead sleep, his
knife (wherewith he would have slain himself) falling down by
him. In the meantime a common and notable ruffian or thief,
which had robbed and slain a man, was entered into the barn
where Gisippus lay, to the intent to sojourn there all that night.
And seeing Gisippus bewept, and his visage replenished with
sorrow, and also the naked knife by him, perceived well that he
was a man desperate, and suppressed with heaviness of heart
was weary of his life. Which the said ruffian taking for a good
occasion to escape, took the knife of Gisippus, and putting it in
the wound of him that was slain, put it all bloody in the hand of
Gisippus, being fast asleep, and so departed. Soon after the dead
man being found, the officers made diligent search for the
murderer. At the last they entering into the barn, and finding
Gisippus on sleep, with a bloody knife in his hand, they awaked
him; wherewith he entered again into his old sorrows, complain-
ing his evil fortune. But when the officers laid unto him the death
of the man, and the having of the bloody knife, he thereat rejoiced, thanking God that such occasion was happened, whereby
he should suffer death by the laws and escape the violence of his
own hands. Wherefore he denied nothing that was laid to his
charge, desiring the officers to make haste that he might be
shortly out of his life. Whereat they marvelled. Anon report came
to the Senate that a man was slain and that a stranger and a

Greek born was found in such form as is before mentioned. They forthwith commanded him to be brought unto their presence, sitting there at that time Titus, being then consul or in other like dignity. The miserable Gisippus was brought to the bar with bills and staves like a felon, of whom it was demanded, if he slew the man that was found dead. He nothing denied, but in most sorrowful manner cursed his fortune, naming himself of all other most miserable. At the last one demanding him of what country he was, he confessed to be an Athenian, and therewith he cast his sorrowful eyes upon Titus with much indignation, and burst out into sighs and tears abundantly. That beholding Titus, and espying by a little sign in his visage, which he knew, that it was his dear friend Gisippus, and anon considering that he was brought unto despair by some misadventure, he anon rose out of his place where he sat, and falling on his knees before the judges, said that he had slain the man for old malice that he bare toward him, and that Gisippus being a stranger was guiltless, and that all men might perceive that the other was a desperate person; wherefore to abbreviate his sorrows he confessed the act, whereof he was innocent, to the intent that he would finish his sorrows with death. Wherefore Titus desired the judges to give sentence on him according to his merits. But Gisippus perceiving his friend Titus (contrary to his expectation) to offer himself to the death, for his safeguard, more importunately cried to the Senate to proceed in their judgment on him that was the very offender. Titus denied it, and affirmed with reasons and arguments that he was the murderer and not Gisippus. Thus they of long time with abundance of tears contended which of them should die for the other. Whereat all the Senate and people were wonderly abashed, not knowing what it meant. There happened to be in the press at that time he which indeed was the murderer, who perceiving the marvellous contention of these two persons, which were both innocent, and that it proceedeth of an incomparable friendship, was vehemently provoked to discover the truth. Wherefore he broke through the press, and coming before the Senate he spoke in this wise. 'Noble fathers, I am such a person whom ye know have been a common barrator [1] and thief by a long space of years. Ye know also that Titus is of noble blood, and is approved to be alway a man of excellent virtue and wisdom, and never was

---

[1] Brawler.

malicious. This other stranger seemeth to be a man full of simplicity, and, that more is, desperate for some grievous sorrow that he hath taken, as it is to you evident. I say to you, fathers, they both be innocent. I am that person that slew him that is found dead by the barn, and robbed him of his money. And when I found in the barn this stranger lying on sleep, having by him a naked knife, I, the better to hide mine offence, did put the knife into the wound of the dead man, and so all bloody laid it again by this stranger. This was my mischievous device to escape your judgment. Whereunto now I remit me wholly, rather than this nobleman Titus and this innocent stranger should unworthily die.'

Hereat all the Senate and people took comfort, and the noise of rejoicing hearts filled all the court. And when it was further examined, Gisippus was discovered. The friendship between him and Titus was throughout the city published, extolled, and magnified. Wherefore the Senate consulted of this matter, and finally, at the instance of Titus and the people, discharged the felon. Titus recognized his negligence in forgetting Gisippus, and Titus being advertised of the exile of Gisippus, and the despiteful cruelty of his kindred, he was therewith wonderful wrath, and having Gisippus home to his house (where he was with incredible joy received of the lady, whom some time he should have wedded) he was honourably apparelled and there Titus offered to him to use all his goods and possessions at his own pleasure and appetite. But Gisippus desiring to be again in his proper country, Titus by the consent of the Senate and people assembled a great army and went with Gisippus unto Athens. Where he having delivered to him all those which were causers of banishing and despoiling of his friend Gisippus, he did on them sharp execution, and restoring to Gisippus his lands and substance stablished him in perpetual quietness, and so returned to Rome.

This example in the affects of friendship expresseth (if I be not deceived) the description of friendship engendered by the similitude of age and personage, augmented by the conformity of manners and studies, and confirmed by the long continuance of company.

Seneca saith that very friendship is induced neither with hope nor with reward. But it is to be desired for the estimation of itself, which estimation is honesty, and what thing is more honest than to be kind, like as nothing is so dishonest as to be unkind?

Perchance some will say that friendship is not known but by receiving of benefits. Hear what Seneca saith: 'Like as of all other virtues, semblably of friendship, the estimation is referred to the mind of a man. For if a friend persist in his office and duty, whatsoever lacketh in benefit, the blame is in fortune. Like as a man may be a good singing man, though the noise of the standers about letteth him to be heard. Also he may be eloquent, though he be let to speak, and a strong man, though his hands be bound. Also there may happen to fail no part of cunning, though there be a let so that it is not expressed. So kindness may be in will, although there lacketh power to declare it.'

Perchance some will demand this question, if friendship may be in will without exterior signs, whereby shall it be perceived or known? That I shall now declare.

How do we know the virtues of Socrates, Plato, Tully, Agesilaus, Titus, Trajan, the two Antonines, and other like emperors and noble captains and counsellors? But only by the fame of their nobility; and for those virtues we love them, although they were strangers, nor we hope to receive any benefit by them. Much more if we be naturally inclined to favour one of our own country, of whom the assured fame is, and also we ourself have convenient experience that in him is such virtue where we delight, who also, for some semblable opinion that he hath in us, useth us with some special familiarity, on such one shall we employ all manner of beneficence.

It would be remembered that friendship is between good men only, and is engendered of an opinion of virtue. Then may we reason in this form: a good man is so named, because that all that he willeth or doeth is only good; in good can be none evil, therefore nothing that a good man willeth or doeth can be evil. Likewise virtue is the affection of a good man, which neither willeth nor doeth anything that is evil. And vice is contrary unto virtue, for in the opinion of virtue is neither evil nor vice. And very amity is in friendship. Therefore in the first election of friends resteth all the importance; wherefore it would not be without a long deliberation and proof, and, as Aristotle saith, in as long time as by them both being together conversant a whole bushel of salt might be eaten.

For often times with fortune (as I late said) is changed, or at the least minished, the ferventness of that affection; according as the sweet poet Ovid affirmeth, saying in this sentence:

Whiles fortune thee favoureth friends thou hast plenty,
The time being troublous thou art all alone;
Thou seest colvers [1] haunt houses made white and dainty,
To the ruinous tower almost cometh none.
Of emmets [2] innumerable, unneth [3] thou findest one
In empty barns, and where faileth substance
Happeneth no friend in whom is assurance.

But if any happeneth in every fortune to be constant in friendship he is to be made of above all things that may come unto man and above any other that be of blood or kindred (as Tully saith), for from kindred may be taken benevolence, from friendship it can never be severed. Wherefore benevolence taken from kindred yet the name of kinsman remaineth. Take it from friendship and the name of friendship is utterly perished.

But since this liberty of speech is now usurped by flatterers, where they perceive that assentation and praises be abhorred, I am therefore not well assured how nowadays a man shall know or discern such admonition from flattery, but by one only means, that is to say, to remember that friendship may not be but between good men. Then consider, if he that doth admonish thee be himself voluptuous, ambitious, covetous, arrogant, or dissolute, refuse not his admonition, but, by the example of the Emperor Antonine, thankfully take it, and amend such default as thou perceivest doth give occasion of obloquy, in such manner as the reporter also by thine example may be corrected. But for that admonition only, account him not immediately to be thy friend, until thou have of him a long and sure experience, for undoubtedly it is wonderfully difficult to find a man very ambitious or covetous to be assured in friendship. For where findest thou him (saith Tully) that will not prefer honours, great offices, rule, authority, and riches before friendship? Therefore (saith he) it is very hard to find friendship in them that be occupied in acquiring honour or about the affairs of the public weal. Which saying is proved true by daily experience. For disdain and contempt be companions with ambition, like as envy and hatred be also her followers.

[1] Doves.   [2] Ants.   [3] Scarcely.

XIII. The division of ingratitude and the dispraise thereof.

THE MOST damnable vice and most against justice, in mine opinion, is ingratitude, commonly called unkindness. Albeit, it is in divers forms and of sundry importance, as it is described by Seneca in this form. He is unkind which denyeth to have received any benefit that indeed he hath received. He is unkind that dissimuleth,[1] he is unkind that recompenseth not. But he is most unkind that forgetteth. For the other, if they render not again kindness, yet they owe it, and there remaineth some steps or tokens of deserts enclosed in an evil conscience, and at the last by some occasion may hap to return to yield again thanks, when either shame thereto provoketh them, or sudden desire of thing that is honest, which is wont to be for a time in stomachs though they be corrupted, if a light occasion do move them. But he that forgetteth kindness may never be kind, since all the benefit is quite fallen from him. And where lacketh remembrance there is no hope of any recompense. In this vice men be much worse than beasts. For divers of them will remember a benefit long after that they have received it. The courser, fierce and courageous, will gladly suffer his keeper, that dresseth and feedeth him, to vaunt him easily, and stirreth not, but when he listeth to provoke him; where if any other should ride him, though he were a king, he will stir and plunge and endeavour himself to throw him.

Such kindness have been found in dogs, that they have not only died in defending their masters, but also some, after that their masters have died or been slain, have abstained from meat, and for famine have died by their masters.

Pliny remembereth of a dog, which in Epirus (a country in Greece) so assaulted the murderer of his master in a great assembly of people, that, with barking and biting him, he compelled him at the last to confess his offence. The dog also of one Jason, his master being slain, would never eat meat but died for hunger. Many semblable tokens of kindness Pliny rehearseth, but principally one of his own time worthy to be here remembered.

When execution should be done on one Titus Habinius and his servants, one of them had a dog, which might never be driven from the prison, nor never would depart from his master's body, and, when it was taken from the place of execution, the dog

---

[1] Dissembles.

howled most lamentably, being compassed with a great number of people; of whom when one of them had cast meat to the dog, he brought and laid it to the mouth of his master. And when the corpse was thrown into the river of Tiber the dog swam after it, and, as long as he might, he enforced himself to bear and sustain it, the people scattering abroad to behold the faithfulness of the beast.

Also the lion, which of all other beasts is accounted most fierce and cruel, hath been found to have in remembrance benefit shown unto him. As Gellius remembereth out of the history of Appian how a lion, out of whose foot a young man had once taken a stub and cleansed the wound, whereby he waxed whole, after knew the same man being cast to him to be devoured, and would not hurt him, but licking the legs and hands of the man, which lay dismayed looking for death, took acquaintance of him, and ever after followed him, being led in a small lyam; [1] whereat wondered all they that beheld it. Which history is wonderful pleasant but for the length thereof I am constrained now to abridge it.

How much be they repugnant, and (as I might say) enemies both to nature and reason, that such one whom they have long known to be to them benevolent, and joined to them in a sincere and assured friendship, approved by infallible tokens, ratified also with sundry kinds of beneficence, they will condemn or neglect, being advanced by any good fortune. I require not such excellent friendship as was between Pytheas and Damon, between Orestes and Pylades, or between Gisippus and Titus, of whom I have before written (for I firmly believe they shall never happen in pairs or couples). Nor I seek not for such as will alway prefer the honour or profit of their friend before their own, nor (which is the least part of friendship) for such one as desirously will participate with his friend all his good fortune or substance. But where at this day may be found such friendship between two, but that where fortune is more benevolent to the one than to the other, the friendship waxeth tedious, and he that is advanced desireth to be matched with one having semblable fortune? And if any damage happeneth to his old friend, he pitieth him but he sorroweth not, and though he seem to be sorrowful, yet he helpeth not, as though he would be seen to help him, yet travaileth he not, and though he would be seen to travail, yet he suffereth

[1] Leash.

not. For (let us lay apart assistance with money, which is a very small portion of friendship) who will so much esteem friendship, that therefore will enter into the displeasure, not of his prince, but of them whom he supposeth may minish his estimation towards his prince, yea and that much less is, will displease his new acquaintance, equal with him in authority or fortune, for the defence, help, or advancement of his ancient and well approved friend? O the most miserable estate at this present time of mankind, that, for the thing which is most proper unto them, the example thereof must be found among the savage and fierce beasts.

But alas such perverse constellation now reigneth over men that where some be aptly and naturally disposed to amity, and findeth one, in similitude of study and manners, equal to his expectation, and therefore kindleth a fervent love toward that person, putting all his joy and delight in the praise and advancement of him that he loveth, it happeneth that he which is loved, being promoted in honour, either of purpose neglecteth his friend, thereby suppressing liberty of speech or familiar resort; or else esteeming his mind with his fortune only, and not with the surety of friendship, hideth from him the secrets of his heart, and either trusteth no man, or else him whom prosperous fortune hath late brought in acquaintance. Whereby do ensue two great inconveniences: one is, that he which so entirely loved, perceiving his love to be vainly employed, withdraweth by little and little the fire which serveth to no use, and so amity, the greatest treasure that may be, finally perisheth. The other inconvenience is that he which neglecteth such a friend either consumeth himself with solicitude, if he be secret, or in sundry affairs for lack of counsel is after with repentance attached, or disclosing his mind to his new acquaintance is sooner betrayed than well counselled. Wise men know this to be true, and yet will they unneth be content to be thus warned.

XIV. The election of friends and the diversity of flatterers.

A NOBLEMAN above all things ought to be very circumspect in the election of such men as should continually attend upon his person at times vacant from busy affairs, whom he may use as his familiars, and safely commit to them his secrets. For as Plutarch saith, whatsoever he be that loveth, he doteth and is blind in that thing which he doth love, except by learning he can accustom himself to ensue and set more price by those things that be honest and virtuous than by them that he seeth in experience and be familiarly used. And surely as the worms do breed most gladly in soft wood and sweet, so the most gentle and noble wits, inclined to honour, replenished with most honest and courteous manners, do soonest admit flatterers, and be by them abused. And it is no marvel. For like as the wild corn, being in shape and greatness like to the good, if they be mingled, with great difficulty will be tried out, but either in a narrow-holed sieve they will still abide with the good corn, or else, where the holes be large, they will issue out with the other; so flattery from friendship is hardly severed, forasmuch as in every motion and affect of the mind they be mutually mingled together.

Of this perverse and cursed people be sundry kinds, some which apparently do flatter, praising and extolling everything that is done by their superior, and bring him on hand that in him it is of every man commended, which of truth is of all men abhorred and hated. To the affirmance thereof they add to oaths, adjurations, and horrible curses, offering themselves to eternal pains except their report be true. And if they perceive any part of their tale mistrusted, then they set forth suddenly an heavy and sorrowful countenance, as if they were abject and brought into extreme desperation. Other there be, which in a more honest term may be called assenters or followers, which do await diligently what is the form of the speech and gesture of their master, and also other his manners, and fashion of garments, and to the imitation and resemblance thereof they apply their study, that for the similitude of manners they may the rather be accepted into the more familiar acquaintance. Like to the servants of Dionysius, King of Sicily, which although they were inclined to all unhappiness and mischief, after the coming of Plato they perceiving that for his doctrine and wisdom the King had him in high estimation, they then counterfeited the countenance and habit of the philosopher, thereby increasing the King's favour towards them, who then was wholly given to study of philosophy. But after that Dionysius by their incitation had expelled Plato out of Sicily, they abandoned their habit and severity, and eftsoons returned to their mischievous and voluptuous living.

The great Alexander bore his head some part on the one side

more than the other, which divers of his servants did counterfeit. Semblably did the scholars of Plato, the most noble philosopher, which forasmuch as their master had a broad breast and high shoulders, and for that cause was named Plato, which signifieth broad and large, they stuffed their garments and made on their shoulders great bolsters, to seem to be of like form as he was; whereby he should conceive some favour towards them for the demonstration of love that they pretended in the ostentation of his person. Which kind of flattery I suppose Plato could right well laugh at. But these manner of flatterers may be well found out and perceived by a good wit, which sometimes by himself diligently considereth his own qualities and natural appetite. For the company or communication of a person familiar, which is alway pleasant and without sharpness, inclining to inordinate favour and affection, is alway to be suspected. Also there is in that friend small commodity which followeth a man like his shadow, moving only when he moveth, and abiding where he list to tarry. These be the mortal enemies of noble wits and specially in youth, when commonly they be more inclined to glory than gravity. Wherefore that liberality, which is on such flatterers employed, is not only perished but also spilled and devoured. Wherefore in mine opinion it were a right necessary law that should be made to put such persons openly to tortures, to the fearful example of other; since in all princes' laws (as Plutarch saith) not only he that hath slain the king's son and heir, but also he that counterfeiteth his seal, or adulterateth his coin with more base metal, shall be judged to die as a traitor. In reason how much more pain (if there were any greater pain than death) were he worthy to suffer, that with false adulation doth corrupt and adulterate the gentle and virtuous nature of a nobleman, which is not only his image, but the very man himself. For without virtue man is but in the number of beasts. And also by perverse instruction and flattery such one slayeth both the soul and good renown of his master. By whose example and negligence perisheth also an infinite number of persons, which damage to a realm neither with treasure nor with power can be redoubted.

But hard it is alway to eschew these flatterers, which, like to crows, do pick out men's eyes ere they be dead. And it is to noble men most difficult, whom all men covet to please and to displease them it is accounted no wisdom, perchance lest there should ensue thereby more peril than profit.

Also Carneades the philosopher was wont to say that the sons of noblemen learned nothing well but only to ride. For whiles they learned letters their masters flattered them, praising every word that they spake; in wrestling their teachers and companions also flattered them, submitting themselves and falling down to their feet; but the horse or courser not understanding who rideth him, nor whether he be a gentleman or yeoman, a rich man or a poor, if he sit not surely and can skill of riding, the horse casteth him quickly. This is the saying of Carneades.

There be other of this sort, which more covertly lay their snares to take the hearts of princes and noblemen. And as he which intendeth to take the fierce and mighty lion pitcheth his hay or net in the wood, among great trees and thorns, where as is the most haunt of the lion, that being blinded with the thickness of the covert, ere he be ware, he may suddenly tumble into the net; where the hunter, sealing both his eyes and binding his legs strongly together, finally daunteth his fierceness and maketh him obedient to his ensigns and tokens. Semblably there be some that by dissimulation can ostent or show a high gravity, mixed with a sturdy entertainment and fashion, exiling themselves from all pleasure and recreation, frowning and grudging at everything wherein is any mirth or solace, although it be honest; taunting and rebuking immoderately them with whom they be not contented; naming themselves therefore plain men, although they do the semblable and oftentimes worse in their own houses. And by a simplicity and rudeness of speaking, with long deliberation used in the same, they pretend the high knowledge of counsel to be in them only. And in this wise pitching their net of adulation they entrap the noble and virtuous heart, which only beholdeth their fained severity and counterfeit wisdom, and the rather because this manner of flattery is most unlike to that which is commonly used. Aristotle in his *Politics* exhorteth governors to have their friends for a great number of eyes, ears, hands, and legs; considering that no one man may see or hear all things that many men may see and hear, nor can be in all places, or do as many things well, at one time, as many persons may do. And often times a beholder or looker on espieth a default that the doer forgetteth or skippeth over. Which caused the Emperor Antoninus to inquire of many what other men spake of him; correcting thereby his defaults, which he perceived to be justly reproved.

O what an incomparable wisdom was in this noble prince that

provided such punishment, which was equal to the importance of the trespass, and terrible to all other semblably inclined to flattery and vain promises; where else he was to all men of good, and specially men of great learning, excellent bounteous.

This I trust shall suffice for the expressing of that incomparable treasure called amity, in the declaration whereof I have aboden the longer, to the intent to persuade the readers to ensearch therefor vigilantly, and being so happy to find it, according to the said description, to embrace and honour it, abhorring above all things ingratitude, which pestilence hath long time reigned among us, augmented by detraction, a corrupt and loathly sickness, whereof I will treat in the last part of this work, that men of good nature espying it need not (if they list) be therewith deceived.

THE THIRD BOOK

I. Of the noble and most excellent virtue named justice.

THE MOST excellent and incomparable virtue called justice is so
necessary and expedient for the governor of a public weal that
without it none other virtue may be commendable, nor wit or any
manner of doctrine profitable. Tully saith that at the beginning
when the multitude of people were oppressed by them that
abounded in possessions and substance, they espying someone
which excelled in virtue and strength, to him they repaired; who
ministering equity, when he had defended the poor men from
injury, finally he retained together and governed the greater
persons with the less, in an equal and indifferent order. Wherefore they called that man a king, which is as much to say as a
ruler. And as Aristotle saith, justice is not only a portion or
species of virtue, but it is entirely the same virtue. And thereof
only (saith Tully) men be called good men, as who saith that
without justice all other qualities and virtues cannot make a man
good.

The ancient civilians do say justice is a will perpetual and
constant, which giveth to every man his right. In that it is named
constant, it importeth fortitude; in discerning what is right or
wrong, prudence is required; and to proportion the sentence or
judgment in an equality, it belongeth to temperance. All these
together conglutinate and effectually executed maketh a perfect
definition of justice.

Justice although it be but one entire virtue, yet is it described in
two kinds or species. The one is named justice distributive, which
is in distribution of honour, money, benefit, or other thing
semblable; the other is called commutative or by exchange, and
of Aristotle it is named in Greek *diorthotice*, which is in English
corrective. And that part of justice is contained in intermeddling,
and sometime is voluntary, sometime involuntary intermeddling.
Voluntary is buying and selling, love, surety, letting, and taking,
and all other thing wherein is mutual consent at the beginning;
and therefore is it called voluntary. Intermeddling involuntary

sometime is privily done, as stealing, avoutry,[1] poisoning, false-hood, deceit, secret murder, false witness, and perjury; sometime it is violent, as battery, open murder and manslaughter, robbery, open reproach, and other like. Justice distributive hath regard to the person; justice commutative hath no regard to the person, but only considering the inequality whereby the one thing exceedeth the other, endeavoureth to bring them both to an equality. Now will I return again to speak first of justice distributive, leaving justice commutative to another volume, which I purpose shall succeed this work, God giving me time and quietness of mind to perform it.

II. *The first part of justice distributive.*

IT IS not to be doubted but that the first and principal part of justice distributive is, and ever was, to do to God that honour which is due to His Divine Majesty; which honour (as I before said in the First Book, where I wrote of the motion called honour in dancing) consisteth in love, fear, and reverence. For since all men grant that justice is to give to every man his own, much more to render one good deed for another, most of all to love God, of whom we have all thing, and without Him we were nothing, and being perished we were eftsoons [2] recovered, how ought we (to whom is given the very light of true faith) to embrace this part of justice more, or at the least no less, than the Gentiles; which wandering in the darkness of ignorance knew not God as He is, but dividing His majesty into sundry portions imagined idols of divers forms and names, assigned to them particular authorities, offices, and dignities. Notwithstanding, in the honouring of those gods, such as they were, they supposed alway to be the chief part of justice.

Romulus (the first King of Romans) for his fortune and benefits, which he ascribed to his gods, made to the honour of them great and noble temples, ordaining to them images, sacri-fices, and other ceremonies. And moreover (which is much to be marvelled at) he also prohibited that anything should be read or spoken reproachable or blasphemous to god. And therefore he excluded all fables made of the adulteries and other enormities

---

[1] Adultery.   [2] Again.

that the Greeks had fained their gods to have committed; inducing his people to speak and also to conjecture nothing of god but only that which was in nature most excellent, which after was also commanded by Plato in the first book of his public weal.

Numa Pompilius, which was the next king after Romulus, and thereto elect by the Senate, although he were a stranger born, and dwelling with his father in a little town of the Sabines, yet he considering from what estate he came to that dignity, he being a man of excellent wisdom and learning thought that he could never sufficiently honour his gods for that benefit by whose providence he supposed that he had attained the governance of so noble a people and city. He therefore not only increased within the city temples, altars, ceremonies, priests, and sundry religions, but also with a wonderful wisdom and policy (which is too long to be now rehearsed) he brought all the people of Rome to such a devotion, or (as I might say) a superstition, that where alway before during the time that Romulus reigned, which was thirty-seven years, they ever were continually occupied in wars and rapine, they by the space of forty-three years (so long reigned Numa) gave themselves all as it were to an observance of religion, abandoning wars, and applying in such wise their study to the honouring of their gods and increasing their public weal that other people adjoining wondering at them, and for their devotion having the city in reverence, as it were a palace of god, all that season never attempted any wars against them or with any hostility invaded their country. Many more princes and noblemen of the Romans could I rehearse who for the victories had against their enemies raised temples and made solemn and sumptuous plays in honour of their gods, rendering (as it were) unto them their duty, and always accounting it the first part of justice. And this part of justice toward God in honouring Him with convenient ceremonies is not to be condemned; example we have among us that be mortal. For if a man being made rich, and advanced by his lord or master, will provide to receive him a fair and pleasant lodging, hanged with rich arras or tapestry, and with goodly plate and other things necessary most freshly adorned, but, after that his master is once entered, he will never entertain or countenance him but as a stranger, suppose ye that the beauty and garnishing of the house shall only content him, but that he will think that his servant brought him thither only for vain glory, and as a beholder and wonderer at the riches that he himself gave him, which the other unthankfully doth attribute to his own fortune or policy? Much rather is that servant to be commended, which having a little reward of his master, will in a small cottage make him hearty cheer with much humble reverence. Yet would I not be noted that I would seem so much to extol reverence by itself, that churches and other ornaments dedicate to God should be therefore condemned. For undoubtedly such things be not only commendable, but also expedient for the augmentation and continuing of reverence. For be it either after the opinion of Plato, that all this world is the temple of God, or that man is the same temple, these material churches whereunto repaireth the congregation of Christian people, in the which is the corporal presence of the Son of God and very God, ought to be like to the said temple, pure, clean, and well adorned; that is to say, that as the heaven visible is most pleasantly garnished with planets and stars resplendent in the most pure firmament of azure colour, the earth furnished with trees, herbs, and flowers of divers colours, fashions, and savours, beasts, fowls, and fishes of sundry kinds, semblably the soul of man of his own kind being incorruptible, neat, and clear, the senses and powers wonderful and pleasant, the virtues in it contained noble and rich, the form excellent and royal, as that which was made to the similitude of God. Moreover the body of man is of all other mortal creatures in proportion and figure most perfect and elegant. What perverse or froward opinion were it to think that God, still being the same God that He ever was, would have His Majesty now condemned or be in less estimation, but rather more honoured for the benefits of His glorious Passion, which may be well perceived, whoso peruseth the holy history of the Evangelists, where he shall find in order that he desired cleanness and honour. First in preparation of His coming, which was by the washing and cleansing of the body of man by baptism in water, the soul also made clean by penance, the election of the most pure and clean Virgin to be His mother, and she also of the line of princes most noble and virtuous. It pleased Him much that Mary humbly kneeled at His feet and washed them with precious balm and wiped them with her hair. In His glorious Transfiguration His visage shone like the sun, and His garments were wonderful white, and more pure (as the Evangelist saith) that any workmen could make them. Also at His coming to Jerusalem toward His Passion, He would then be received with great routs of people, who laying their garments on the way as He rode, other casting boughs abroad went before Him in form of a triumph. All this honour would He have before His Resurrection, when He was in the form of humility. Then how much honour is due to Him now that all power is given to Him, as well in heaven as in earth, and being glorified of His Father, sitteth on His right hand, judging all the world?

In reading the Bible men shall find that the infinite number of the sturdy hearted Jews could never have been governed by any wisdom, if they had not been bridled with ceremonies. The superstition of the Gentiles preserved oftentimes as well the Greeks as the Romans from final destruction. But we will lay all those histories apart and come to our own experience.

For what purpose was it ordained that Christian kings (although they by inheritance succeeded their progenitors kings) should in an open and stately place before all their subjects receive their crown and other regalities, but that by reason of the honourable circumstances then used should be impressed in the hearts of the beholders perpetual reverence, which (as I before said) is fountain of obedience; or else might the kings be anointed and receive their charge in a place secret, with less pain to them and also their ministers? Let it be also considered that we be men and not angels, wherefore we know nothing but by outward significations. Honour, whereto reverence pertaineth, is (as I have said) the reward of virtue, which honour is but the estimation of people, which estimation is not everywhere perceived, but by some exterior sign, and that is either by laudable report, or excellence in vesture, or other things semblable. But report is not so common a token as apparel. For in old time kings wore crowns of gold, and knights only wore chains. Also the most noble of the Romans wore sundry garlands, whereby was perceived their merit. O creatures most unkind and barren of justice that will deny that thing to their God and Creator, which of very duty and right is given to Him by good reason afore all princes which in a degree incomparable be His subjects and vassals. By which opinion they seem to despoil Him of reverence, which shall cause all obedience to cease, whereof will ensue utter confusion, if good Christian princes moved with zeal do not shortly provide to extinct utterly all such opinions.

III. The three noble counsels of reason, society, and knowledge.

VERILY the knowledge of justice is not so difficult or hard to be attained unto by man as it is commonly supposed, if he would not willingly abandon the excellency of his proper nature, and foolishly apply himself to the nature of creatures unreasonable, in the stead of reason embracing sensuality, and for society and benevolence following wilfulness and malice, and for knowledge, blind ignorance and forgetfulness. Undoubtedly reason, society called company, and knowledge remaining, justice is at hand, and as she were called for, joineth herself to that company, which by her fellowship is made inseparable; whereby happeneth (as I might say) a virtuous and most blessed conspiracy. And in three very short precepts or advertisements man is persuaded to receive and honour justice. Reason bidding him do the same thing to another that thou wouldest have done to thee. Society (without which man's life is unpleasant and full of anguish) saith, 'Love thou thy neighbour as thou doest thyself.' And that sentence or precept came from heaven when society was first ordained of God, and is of such authority that the only Son of God being demanded of a doctor of law which is the great commandment in the law of God, answered, 'Thou shalt love thy Lord God with all thy heart, and in all thy soul, and in all thy mind, that is the first and great commandment. The second is like to the same, thou shalt love thy neighbour as thyself. In these two commandments do depend all the law and prophets.' Behold how our Saviour Christ joineth benevolence with the love of God, and not only maketh it the second precept, but also resembleth it unto the first.

Knowledge also, as a perfect instructrice and mistress, in a more brief sentence than yet hath been spoken, declareth by what mean the said precepts of reason and society may be well understood and thereby justice finally executed. The words be these in Latin, *nosce te ipsum*, which is in English know thyself. This sentence is of old writers supposed for to be first spoken by Chilon or some other of the seven ancient Greeks called in Latin *sapientes*, in English sages or wise men. Others do accommodate it to Apollo, whom the pagans honoured for god of wisdom. But to say the truth, were it Apollo that spake it, or Chilon, or any other, surely it proceeded of God, as an excellent and wonderful sentence. By this counsel man is induced to understand the other two precepts, and also whereby is accomplished not only the second part, but also all the residue of justice, which I before have rehearsed. For a man knowing himself shall know that which is his own and pertaineth to himself. But what is more his own than his soul? Or what thing more appertaineth to him than his body? His soul is undoubtedly and freely his own. And none other person may by any mean possess it or claim it. His body so pertaineth unto him that none other without his consent may vindicate therein any property. Of what valour or price his soul is, the similitude whereunto it was made, the immortality and life everlasting, and the powers and qualities thereof, abundantly do declare. And of that same matter and substance that his soul is of, be all other souls that now are, and have been, and ever shall be, without singularity or pre-eminence of nature. In semblable estate is his body, and of no better clay (as I might frankly say) is a gentleman made than a carter, and of liberty of will as much is given of God to the poor herdsman as to the great and mighty emperor. Then in knowing the condition of his soul and body he knoweth himself, and consequently in the same thing he knoweth every other man.

If thou be a governor, or hast over other sovereignty, know thyself, that is to say, know that thou art verily a man compact of soul and body, and in that all other men be equal unto thee. Also that every man taketh with thee equal benefit of the spirit of life, nor thou hast any more of the dew of heaven, or the brightness of the sun, than any other person. Thy dignity or authority wherein thou only differest from other is (as it were) but a weighty or heavy cloak, freshly glittering in the eyes of them that be purblind, where unto thee it is painful, if thou wear him in his right fashion, and as it shall best become thee. And from thee it may be shortly taken of him that did put it on thee, if thou use it negligently, or that thou wear it not comely, and as it appertaineth. Therefore whiles thou wearest it, know thyself, know that the name of a sovereign or ruler without actual governance is but a shadow, that governance standeth not by words only, but principally by act and example; that by example of governors men do rise or fall in virtue or vice. And, as it is said of Aristotle, rulers more grievously do sin by example than by their act. And the more they have under their governance, the greater account have they to render, that in their own precepts and ordinances they be not found negligent. Wherefore there is a noble advertisement of the Emperor Alexander, for his gravity called Severus. On a time one of his noblemen exhorted him to do a thing contrary to a law or edict, which he himself had enacted; but he firmly denied it. The other, still persisting, said that the Emperor was not bound to observe his own laws. Whereunto the said Emperor, displeasantly answering, said in this manner, 'God forbid that ever I should devise any laws whereby my people should be compelled to do anything which I myself cannot tolerate.' Wherefore ye that have any governance, by this most noble prince's example know the bounds of your authority, know also your office and duty, being yourselves men mortal among men, and instructors and leaders of men. And that as obedience is due unto you, so is your study, your labour, your industry with virtuous example due to them that be subject to your authority. Ye shall know alway yourself, if for affection or motion ye do speak or do nothing unworthy the immortality and most precious nature of your soul, and remembering that your body be subject to corruption, as all other be, and lifetime uncertain. If ye forget not this common estate, and do also remember that in nothing but only in virtue ye are better than another inferior person, according to the saying of Agesilaus King of Lacedaemons, who hearing the great King of Persia praised, asked how much that great King was more than he in justice. And Socrates being demanded if the King of Persia seemed to him happy, 'I cannot tell' (said he) 'of what estimation he is in virtue and learning.' Consider also that authority, being well and diligently used, is but a token of superiority, but in very deed it is a burden and loss of liberty.

And what governor in this wise knoweth himself he shall also by the same rule know all other men, and shall needs love them for whom he taketh labours and forsaketh liberty.

In semblable manner the inferior person or subject ought to consider that albeit (as I have spoken) he in the substance of soul and body be equal with his superior, yet for else much as the powers and qualities of the soul and body, with the disposition of reason, be not in every man equal, therefore God ordained a diversity or pre-eminence in degrees to be among men for the necessary direction and preservation of them in conformity of living. Whereof nature ministereth to us examples abundantly, as in bees (whereof I have before spoken in the First Book), cranes, red deer, wolves, and divers other fowls and beasts which herdeth or flocketh (too long here to be rehearsed), among whom is a governor or leader, towards whom all the other have a vigilant eye, awaiting his signs or tokens, and according thereto preparing themselves most diligently. If we think that this natural instinct of creatures unreasonable is necessary and also commendable, how far out of reason shall we judge them to be that would exterminate all superiority, extinct all governance and laws, and under the colours of Holy Scripture, which they do violently wrest to their purpose, do endeavour themselves to bring the life of man into a confusion inevitable, and to be in much worse estate than the afore named beasts? Since without governance and laws the persons most strong in body should by violence constrain them that be of less strength and weaker to labour as bondmen or slaves for their sustenance and other necessaries, the strong men being without labour or care. Then were all our equality dashed, and finally as beasts savage the one shall desire to slay another. I omit continual manslaughters, ravishments, avoutries [1] and enormities horrible to rehearse, which (governance lacking) must needs of necessity ensue, except these evangelical persons could persuade God or compel Him to change men into angels, making them all of one disposition and confirming them all in one form of charity. And as concerning all men in a generality, this sentence, know thyself, which of all other is most compendious, being made but of three words, every word being but one syllable, induceth men sufficiently to the knowledge of justice.

IV. Of fraud and deceit, which be against justice.

TULLY saith that the foundation of perpetual praise and renown is justice, without the which nothing may be commendable. Which sentence is verified by experience. For be a man never so valiant, so wise, so liberal or plenteous, so familiar or courteous, if he be seen to exercise injustice or wrong it is often remembered. But the other virtues be seldom reckoned without an exception, which is in this manner. As in praising a man for some good quality, where he lacketh justice, men will commonly say, he is an honourable man, a bounteous man, a wise man, a valiant man, saving that he is an oppressor, an extortioner, or is deceitful or of his promise unsure. But if he be just with the other virtues, then is

[1] Adulteries.

it said he is good and worshipful, or he is a good man and an honourable, good and gentle, or good and hardy, so that justice only beareth the name of good, and like a captain or leader precedeth all virtues in every commendation. But whereas the said Tully saith that injury, which is contrary to justice, is done by two means, that is to say, either by violence or by fraud, fraud seemeth to be properly of the fox, violence or force of the lion, the one and the other be far from the nature of man, but fraud is worthy most to be hated. That manner of injury which is done with fraud and deceit is at this present time so commonly practised, that if it be but a little it is called policy, and if it be much and with a visage of gravity, it is then named and accounted for wisdom. And of those wise men speaketh Tully, saying of all injustice none is more capital than of those persons that, when they deceive a man most, they do it as they would seem to be good men. And Plato saith that it is extreme injustice he to seem rightwise which indeed is unjust. Of those two manner of frauds will I severally speak. But first will I declare the most mischievous importance of this kind of injury in a generality. Like as the physicians call those diseases most perilous against whom is found no preservative and once entered be seldom or never recovered, semblably those injuries be most to be feared against the which can be made no resistance, and being taken, with great difficulty or never they can be redressed. Injury apparent and with power enforced either may be with like power resisted, or with wisdom eschewed, or with entreaty refrained. But where it is by crafty engine imagined, subtly prepared, covertly dissembled, and deceitfully practised, surely no man may by strength withstand it, or by wisdom escape it, or by any other manner or mean resist or avoid it. Wherefore of all injuries that which is done by fraud is most horrible and detestable, not in the opinion of man only, but also in the sight and judgment of God. For unto Him nothing may be acceptable wherein lacketh verity, called commonly truth, He Himself being all verity, and all thing containing untruth is to Him contrarious and adverse. And the devil is called a liar, and the father of leasings.[1] Wherefore all thing which in visage or appearance pretendeth to be any other than verily it is may be named a leasing; the execution whereof is fraud, which is in effect but untruth, enemy to truth, and consequently enemy to

---

[1] Lies.

God. For fraud is (as experience teacheth us) an evil deceit, craftily imagined and devised, which under a colour of truth and simplicity endamageth him that nothing mistrusteth. And because it is evil it can by no means be lawful; wherefore it is repugnant unto justice.

The Neapolitans and Nolans (people in Italy) contended together for the limits and bounds of their lands and fields. And for the discussing of that controversy either of them sent their ambassadors to the Senate and people of Rome (in whom at that time was thought to be the most excellent knowledge and execution of justice), desiring of them an indifferent arbiter and such as was substantially learned in the laws civil, to determine the variance that was between the two cities, compromising themselves in the name of all their country to abide and perform all such sentence and award as should be by him given. The Senate appointed for that purpose one named Quintus Fabius Labeo, whom they accounted to be a man of great wisdom and learning. Fabius after that he was come to the place which was in controversy, he separating the one people from the other, communed with them both apart, exhorting the one and the other that they would not do or desire anything with a covetous mind, but in treading out of their bounds rather go short thereof than over. They doing according to his exhortation there was left between both companies a great quantity of ground, which at this day we call debatable. That perceiving Fabius, he assigned to every of them the bounds that they themselves had appointed. And all that land, which was left in the middle, he adjudged it to the Senate and people of Rome. That manner of dealing (saith Tully) is to deceive and not to give judgment. And verily every good man will think that this lack of justice in Fabius, being a nobleman and well learned, was a great reproach to his honour.

It was a notable rebuke unto the Israelites that when they besieged the Gibeonites (a people of Canaan) they in conclusion received them into a perpetual league. But after that the Gibeonites had yielded them, the Jews perceiving that they were restrained by their oath to slay them or cruelly entreat them, they made of the Gibeonites, being their confederates, their scullions and drudges; wherewith Almighty God was nothing contented. For the league or truce wherein friendship and liberty was intended (which caused the Gibeonites to be yielded) was not duly observed, which was clearly against justice.

Truly in every covenant, bargain, or promise ought to be a simplicity, that is to say, one plain understanding or meaning between the parties. And that simplicity is properly justice. And where any man of a covetous or malicious mind will digress purposely from that simplicity, taking advantage of a sentence or word which might be ambiguous or doubtful or in something either superfluous or lacking in the bargain or promise, where he certainly knoweth the truth to be otherwise, this in mine opinion is damnable fraud, being as plain against justice as if it were enforced by violence. Finally all deceit and dissimulation, in the opinion of them which exactly honour justice, is nearer to dispraise than commendation, although that thereof might ensue something that were good. For in virtue may be nothing fucate [1] or counterfeit. But therein is only the image of verity, called simplicity. Wherefore Tully being of the opinion of Antipater the philosopher saith, 'To counsel anything which thou knowest, to the intent that for thine own profit thou wouldest that another who shall take any damage or benefit thereby should not know it, is not the act of a person plain or simple, or of a man honest, just, or good; but rather of a person crafty, ungentle, subtle, deceitful, malicious, and wily.' And after he saith that reason requireth that nothing be done by treason, nothing by dissimulation, nothing by deceit. Which he excellently (as he doth all thing) afterward in a brief conclusion proveth, saying, 'Nature is the fountain whereof the law springeth, and it is according to nature no man to do that whereby he should take (as it were) a prey of another man's ignorance.' Of this matter Tully writeth many proper examples and quick solutions.

But now here I make an end to write any more at this time of fraud, by which may be joined to the virtue named justice.

V. That justice ought to be between enemies.

SUCH IS the excellency of this virtue justice, that the practise thereof hath not only obtained digne [2] commendation of such persons as between whom hath been mortal hostility, but also it hath extinct often times the same hostility. And fierce hearts of mutual enemies hath been thereby rather subdued than by

---

[1] Pretended.   [2] Worthy, just.

armour or strength of people. As it shall appear by examples
ensuing.

When the valiant King Pyrrhus warred most asprely [1] against
the Romans, one Timochares, whose son was yeoman for the
mouth with the King, promised to Fabricius, then being consul,
to slay King Pyrrhus, which thing being to the Senate reported,
they by their ambassador warned the King to beware of such
manner of treason, saying that the Romans maintained their wars
with arms and not with poison. And yet notwithstanding they
discovered not the name of Timochares, so that they embraced
equity as well in that they slew not their enemy by treason, as also
that they betrayed not him which purposed them kindness. Insomuch was justice of old time esteemed, that without it none act
was allowed were it never so noble or profitable.

What time that Xerxes, King of Persia, with his army, was
expelled out of Greece, all the navy of Lacedaemonia lay at rode
in an haven called Gytheum, within the dominion of the Athenians. Themistocles, one of the princes of Athens, a much noble
captain, said unto the people that he had advised himself of an
excellent counsel, whereunto if fortune inclined, nothing might
more augment the power of the Athenians, but that it ought not
to be divulged or published; he therefore desired to have one
appointed unto him, unto whom he might secretly discover the
enterprise. Whereupon there was assigned unto him one Aristides,
who for his virtue was surnamed rightwise. Themistocles declared to him that his purpose was to put fire in the navy of the
Lacedaemons, which lay at Gytheum, to the intent that it being
burned, the dominion and whole power over the sea should be
only in the Athenians. This device heard and perceived, Aristides
coming before the people said that the counsel of Themistocles
was very profitable, but the enterprise was dishonest and against
justice. The people hearing that the act was not honest or just, all
cried with one voice, nor yet expedient. And forthwith they commanded Themistocles to cease his enterprise. Whereby this noble
people declared that in every act special regard and, above all
thing, consideration ought to be had of justice and honesty.

[1] Fiercely.

VI. Of faith or fidelity, called in Latin Fides, *which is the foundation of justice.*

THAT WHICH in Latin is called *Fides* is a part of justice and may diversely be interpreted, and yet finally it tendeth to one purpose in effect. Sometime it may be called faith, sometime credence, other whiles trust. Also in a French term it is named loyalty. And to the imitation of Latin it is often called fidelity. All which words, if they be entirely and (as I might say) exactly understood, shall appear to a studious reader to signify one virtue or quality, although they seem to have some diversity. As believing the precepts and promise of God it is called faith. In contracts between man and man it is commonly called credence. Between persons of equal estate or condition it is named trust. From the subject or servant to his sovereign or master it is properly named fidelity, and in a French term loyalty.

Wherefore to him that shall either speak or write, the place is diligently to be observed where the proper signification of the word may be best expressed.

Considering (as Plato saith) that the name of everything is none other but the virtue or effect of the same thing conceived first in the mind, and then by the voice expressed and finally in letters signified.

But now to speak in what estimation this virtue was of old time among Gentiles, which now (alas, to the lamentable reproach and perpetual infamy of this present time) is so neglected throughout Christendom that neither regard of religion or honour, solemn oaths, or terrible curses can cause it to be observed. And that I am much ashamed to write, but that I must needs now remember it. Neither seals of arms, sign manuals, subscription, nor other specialities, yea, unneth [1] a multitude of witnesses, be now sufficient to the observing of promises. O what public weal should we hope to have there, where lacketh fidelity, which as Tully saith is the foundation of justice? What marvel is it though there be in all places contention infinite, and that good laws be turned into sophisms and insolubles, since everywhere fidelity is constrained to come in trial, and credence (as I might say) is become a vagabond?

[1] Scarcely.

To Joshua, which succeeded Moses in the governance and leading of the Jews, Almighty God gave in commandment to slay as
many as he should happen to take of the people called Canaanites.
There happened to be nigh to Jerusalem a country called Gibeon,
and indeed the people thereof were Canaanites, who, hearing of
the precept given to Joshua, as men (as it seemed) of great wisdom,
they sent an ambassador to Joshua which approached their
country, saying that they were far distant from the Canaanites,
and desired to be in perpetual league with him and his people;
and to dissemble the length of their journey, as their country had
been far thence, they had on them old worn garments and torn
shoes. Joshua supposing all to be true that they spake, concluded peace with them and confirmed the league. And with a
solemn oath ratified both the one and the other. Afterward it was
discovered that they were Canaanites, which if Joshua had known
before the league made, he had not spared any of them. But when
he revolved in his mind the solemn oath that he had made, and
the honour which consisted in his promise, he presumed that
faith being observed unperished should please Almighty God
above all things. Which was then proved. For it appeareth not
that God ever did so much as in any wise upbraid him for breaking of His commandment. By this example it appeareth in what
estimation and reverence leagues and truces made by princes
ought to be had; to the breach whereof none excuse is sufficient.
But let us leave princes' affairs to their counsellors. And I will
now write of the parts of fidelity which be more frequent and
accustomed to be spoken of. And first of loyalty and trust; and
last of credence, which principally resteth in promise. In the most
renowned wars between the Romans and Hannibal (Duke of
Carthage), a noble city in Spain called Sagunto, which was in
amity and league with the Romans, was by the said Hannibal
strongly besieged; insomuch as they were restrained from victual
and all other sustenance. Of the which necessity by their privy
messages they ascertained the Romans. But they being busied
about the preparation for the defence of Italy, and also of the city
against the intolerable power of Hannibal, having also late two
of their most valiant captains, Publius Scipio and Lucius Scipio,
with a great host of Romans slain by Hannibal in Spain, deferred
to send any speedy succour to the Saguntines. But notwithstanding that Hannibal desired to have with them amity, offering
them peace with their city, and goods at liberty, considering that

they were brought into extreme necessity, lacking victuals, and despairing to have succour from the Romans, all the inhabitants comforting and exhorting each other to die rather than to violate the league and amity that they of long time had continued with the Romans, by one whole assent, after that they had made sundry great piles of wood and of other matter to burn, they laid in it all their goods and substance, and last of all, conveying themselves into the said piles or bonfires with their wives and children, set all on fire, and there were burned ere Hannibal could enter the city.

Semblable loyalty was in the inhabitants of Petilia the same time; who, being likewise besieged by Hannibal, sent for succour to Rome. But for the great loss that a little erst [1] the Romans had sustained at the battle of Cannae they could in no wise deliver them; wherefore they discharged them of their promise, and licensed them to do that thing which might be most for their safeguard. By which answer they seemed to be discharged, and lawfully might have entered into the favour of Hannibal. Yet notwithstanding, this noble people, preserving loyalty before life, putting out of their city their women and all that were of years unable for the wars, that they might more frankly sustain famine, they obstinately defended their walls, that in the defence they all perished. So that when Hannibal was entered, he found that he took not the city, but rather the sepulchre of the loyal city Petilia.

O noble fidelity, which is so much the more to be wondered at, that it was not only in one or a few persons, but in thousands of men, and they not being of the blood or alliance of the Romans, but strangers, dwelling in far countries from them, being only of gentle nature and virtuous courage, inclined to love honour, and to be constant in their assurance!

Now will I write from henceforth of particular persons which have showed examples of loyalty, which I pray God may so cleave to the minds of the readers that they may be alway ready to put the semblable in experience.

How much ought all they, in whom is any portion of gentle courage, endeavour themselves to be always trusty and loyal to their sovereign, who putteth them in trust, or hath been to them beneficial, as well reason exhorteth, as also sundry examples of

---

[1] Earlier.

noble personages, which, as compendiously as I can, I will now
bring to the readers' remembrance.

What time that Saul for his grievous offences was abandoned of
Almighty God, who of a very poor man's son did advance him to
the Kingdom of Israel, and that David, being his servant and as
poor a man's son as he, was elected by God to reign in Israel, and
was anointed king by the prophet Samuel, Saul being therefore
in a rage, having indignation at David, pursued him with a great
host to have slain him, who (as long as he might) fled and forbear
Saul, as his sovereign lord. On a time David was so enclosed by
the army of Saul, that he might by no ways escape, but was fain
to hide him and his men in a great cave which was wide and deep
in the earth. During the time that he was in the cave, Saul not
knowing thereof entered into the cave, to the intent to do his
natural easement; which the people of David perceiving, exhorted
him to slay Saul, having such opportunity; saying that God had
brought his enemy into his hands, and that Saul being slain, the
war were all at an end, considering that the people loved better
David than Saul. But David refusing their counsel, said that he
would not lay violent hands on his sovereign lord, being a king
anointed of God: but softly he approached to Saul, and did cut
off a piece of the nether part of his mantle. And after that Saul
was departed out of the cave toward his camp David called after
him saying, 'Whom pursuest thou, noble prince?' (with other
words rehearsed in the Bible in the First Book of Kings), and then
showed to him the part of his mantle. Whereat Saul being
abashed, recognized his unkindness, calling David his dear son
and trusty friend, recommending to him his children and progeny,
since by the will of God he was elected to succeed him in the
kingdom of Israel. And so departed Saul from David. Yet notwithstanding, afterwards he pursued him in Gaddy.[1] And in a
night, when Saul and his army were at rest, and that David by an
espial knew that they were all fast on sleep, he took with him a
certain of the most assured and valiant personages of his host,
and in most secret wise came to the pavilion of King Saul, where
he found him surely sleeping, having by him his spear and a cup
with water. Wherefore one of the company of David said that he
with the spear of Saul would strike him through and slay him.
'Nay,' said David, 'our Lord forbade that I suffer my sovereign

---

[1] Engedi, in the desert west of the Dead Sea.

lord to be slain, for he is anointed of God.' And therewith he took
the spear with the cup of water, and when he was a good distance
from the host of Saul, he cried with a loud voice to Abner, which
was then marshal of the army of Saul. Who answered and said,
'What art thou that thus diseasest the King, which is now at his
rest?' To whom David said, 'Abner, thou and thy company are
worthy death, that have so negligently watched your prince;
where is his spear and the cup of water that stood at his bed's
head? Surely ye be but dead men when he shall know it.' And
therewith he showed the spear and cup with water. Which Saul
perceiving and hearing the voice of David, cried unto him saying,
'Is not this the voice of my dear son David? I uncourteously do
pursue him, and he notwithstanding doth to me good for evil.'
With other words, which to abbreviate the matter I do pass over.
This noble history and other semblable, either wrought in arras
or cunningly painted, will much better beseem the houses of
noblemen than the concubines and voluptuous pleasures of the
same David and Solomon his son, which be more frequently
expressed in the hangings of houses and counterpoints than the
virtue and holiness of the one or the wise experiments of the
other. But now will I pass over to histories which be more strange,
and therefore I suppose more pleasant to the reader.

Xerxes being King of Persia, the great city of Babylon rebelled
against him, which was of such strength that the King was not of
power to subdue it; that perceiving a gentleman, one of the
counsel of King Xerxes, named Zopirus, a man of notable
wisdom, unwitting to any person, did cut off his own ears and
nose, and privily departed toward Babylon, and being known by
them of the city, was demanded who had so disfigured him. Unto
whom he answered with apparent tokens of heaviness, that forasmuch as he had given to Xerxes counsel and advice to be
reconciled unto their city, he being moved with ire and displeasure toward him in most cruel wise caused him to be so
shamefully mutilated. Adding thereunto reproachful words
against Xerxes. The Babylonians beholding his miserable estate,
and the tokens which (as it seemed to them) approved his words
to be true, much pitied him. And as well for the great wisdom
that they knew to be in him, as for the occasion which they
supposed should incense him to be shortly avenged, they made
him their chief captain, and committed wholly to him the
governance and defence of their city. Which happened in every

thing according to his expectation. Whereupon he shortly gave notice to the King of all his affairs and exploitures. And finally so endeavoured himself by his wisdom, that he accorded the King and the city, without any loss or damage to either of them. Wherefore on a time the said King Xerxes cutting an oddly great pomegranate, and beholding it fair and full of kernels, said in the presence of all his counsel, that he had liefer [1] have such one friend as Zopirus was, than as many Babylons as there were kernels in the pomegranate. And also that he rather would that Zopirus were restored again to his nose and his ears, than to have a hundred such cities as Babylon was; which by the report of writers was incomparably the greatest and fairest city of all the world.

The Parthians, in a civil discord among themselves, drove Arthabanus their king out of his realm, and elected among them one Cinnamus to be their king. Iazate, King of Adiabenes, unto whom Arthabanus was fled, sent an ambassador unto the Parthians, exhorting them to receive again Arthabanus; but they made answer that since departing of Arthabanus, they had by a whole assent chosen Cinnamus, unto whom they had done their fealty, and were sworn his subjects, which oath they might not lawfully break. Thereof hearing Cinnamus, who at that time was king over them, he wrote unto Arthabanus and Iazate that they should come, and that he would render the realm of Parthia unto Arthabanus. And when they were come, Cinnamus met with them, adorned in the robes of a king, and as he approached Arthabanus, alighting down off his horse, he said in this wise, 'Sir, when the people had expelled you out of your realm, and would have translated it unto another, at their instance and desire I took it; but when I perceived their rancour assuaged, and that with good will they would have you again, which are their natural sovereign lord, and that nothing letted, but only that they would nothing do contrary to my pleasure, with good will, and for no dread, or other occasion, as ye may perceive, do here render your realm eftsoons unto you.' And therewith taking the diadem off from his own head, did set it immediately upon the head of Arthabanus.

The fidelity of Ferdinand, King of Aragon, is not to be forgotten, whom his brother Henry, King of Castile, deceasing,

[1] Rather.

made governor of his son, being an infant. This Ferdinand with such justice ruled and ordered the realm, that in a parliament held at Castile, it was treated by the whole consent of the nobles and people, that the name or title of the kingdom of Spain should be given unto him. Which honour he feigning to receive thankfully, did put upon him a large and wide robe, wherein he secretly bore the young prince his nephew, and so came into the place, where for the said purpose the nobles and people were assembled, demanding of every man his sentence, who with one voice gave unto him the Kingdom of Spain. With that he took out his robe the little baby his nephew, and setting him on his shoulder, said all aloud unto them, 'Lo ye Castilians, behold here is your king.' And then he, confirming the hearts of the people toward his nephew, finally delivered to him his realm in peace, and in all things abundant. This is the fidelity that appertaineth to a noble and gentle heart.

In what hatred and perpetual reproach ought they to be that, corrupted with pestilential avarice or ambition, betrayeth their masters, or any other that trusteth them? O what monstrous persons have we read and heard of, which for the inordinate and devilish appetite to reign, have most tyrannously slain the children, not only of their sovereign lords, but also of their own natural brethren, committed unto their governance? Of whom purposely I leave at this time to write, to the intent that the most cursed remembrance of them shall not consume the time that the well disposed reader might occupy in examples of virtue.

This one thing I would were remembered, that by the just providence of God, disloyalty or treason seldom escapeth great vengeance, albeit that it be pretended for a necessary purpose. Example we have of Brutus and Cassius, two noble Romans, and men of excellent virtues, which, pretending an honourable zeal to the liberty and common weal of their city, slew Julius Caesar (who trusted them most of all other) for that he usurped to have the perpetual dominion of the Empire, supposing thereby to have brought the Senate and people to their pristine liberty. But it did not so succeed to their purpose. But by the death of so noble a prince happened confusion and civil battles. And both Brutus and Cassius, after long wars vanquished by Octavian, nephew and heir unto Caesar, at the last falling into extreme desperation, slew themselves. A worthy and convenient vengeance for the murder of so noble and valiant a prince. Many other like examples do remain as well in writing as in late remembrance, which I pass over for this time.

VII. Of promise and covenant.

CONCERNING that part of fidelity which concerneth the keeping of promise or covenants experience declareth how little it is now had in regard; to the notable rebuke of all us which do profess Christ's religion. Considering that the Turks and Saracens have us therefore in contempt and derision, they having fidelity of promise above all thing in reverence. Insomuch as in their contracts they seldom use any bond or oath. But, as I have heard reported of men born in those parts, after the mutual consent of the parties, the bargainer, or he that doth promise, toucheth the ground with his hand, and after layeth it on his head, as it were that he vouched all the world to bear witness. But by this little ceremony he is so bound, that if he be found to break touch willingly, he is without any redemption condemned unto the pale, that is, to have a long stake thrust in at the secret parts of his body, whereon he shall abide dying by a long space. For fear of the which most terrible execution, seldom any man under the Turks' dominion breaketh his promise. But what hope is there to have fidelity well kept among us in promises and bargains, when for the breach thereof is provided no punishment, nor yet notorious rebuke; saving if it be tried by action, such pretty damages as the jury shall assess, which perchance daily practiseth semblable lightness of purpose. I omit to speak now of attaints in the law, reserving that matter to a place more convenient.

But no marvel that a bare promise holdeth not, where an oath upon the Evangelists, solemnly and openly taken, is but little esteemed. Lord God, how frequent and familiar a thing with every estate and degree throughout Chritendom is this reverent oath on the Gospels of Christ! How it hath been hitherto kept, it is so well known and had in daily experience that I shall not need to make of the neglecting thereof any more declaration. Only I will show how the Gentiles, lacking true religion, had solemn oaths in great honour, and how terrible a thing it was among them to break their oaths or vows. Insomuch as they supposed that there was no power, victory, or profit which might be equal to the virtue of an oath.

Among the Egyptians, they which were perjured had their heads stricken off, as well for that they violated the honour due unto God, as also that thereby faith and trust among people might be decayed.

The Scythians swore only by the chair or throne of their king, which oath if they broke, they therefore suffered death.

The ancient Romans (as Tully writeth) swore in this manner. He that should swear held in his hand a stone, and said in this wise, 'The city with the goods thereof being safe, so Jupiter cast me out of it, if I deceive wittingly, as I cast from me this stone.' And this oath was so straightly observed, that it is not remembered that ever any man broke it.

Plutarch writeth that at the first Temple that Numa Pompilius, the second King of Romans made in the city of Rome, was the temple of faith. And also he declared that the greatest oath that might be was faith. Which nowadays is unneth taken for any oath, but most commonly is used in mockery, or in such things as men foresee not, though they be not believed. In daily communication the matter savoureth not, except it be as it were seasoned with horrible oaths. As by the holy blood of Christ, His wounds which for our redemption He painfully suffered, His glorious heart, as it were numbles [1] chopped in pieces. Children (which abhorreth me to remember) do play with the arms and bones of Christ, as they were cherry stones. The soul of God, which is incomprehensible, and not to be named of any creature without a wonderful reverence and dread, is not only the oath of great gentlemen, but also so indiscreetly abused, that they make it (as I might say) their guns, wherewith they thunder out threatenings and terrible menaces, when they be in their fury, though it be at the damnable play of dice. The Mass, in which honourable ceremony is left unto us the memorial of Christ's glorious Passion, with His corporal presence in form of bread, the invocation of the three divine persons in one deity, with all the whole company of blessed spirits and souls elect, is made by custom so simple an oath that it is now almost neglected, and little regarded of the nobility, and is only used among husbandmen and artificers, unless some tailor or barber, as well in his

[1] Parts of stags and swine.

oaths as in the excess of his apparel, will counterfeit and be like a gentleman. In judicial causes, be they of never so light importance, they that be no parties but strangers, I mean witnesses and jurors, which shall proceed in the trial, do make no less oath, but openly do renounce the help of God and His saints and the benefit of His Passion, if they say not true as far forth as they know. How evil that is observed where the one party in degree far exceedeth the other, or where hope of reward or affection taketh place, no man is ignorant, since it is every year more common than harvest. Alas! what hope shall we have of any public weal where such a pestilence reigneth? Doth not Solomon say, 'A man much swearing shall be filled with iniquity, and the plague shall not depart from his house?' O merciful God, how many men be in this realm which be horrible swearers and common jurors perjured? Then how much iniquity is there, and how many plagues are to be feared, whereas be so many houses of swearers? Surely I am in more dread of the terrible vengeance of God, than in hope of amendment of the public weal. And so in mine opinion ought all other to be, which believe that God knoweth all thing that is done here in earth, and as He Himself is all goodness, so loveth He all thing that is good, which is virtue; and hateth the contrary, which is vice. Also all thing that pleaseth Him, He preserveth; and that thing that He hateth, He at the last destroyeth. But what virtue may be without verity called truth, the declaration whereof is faith or fidelity? For as Tully saith, faith is a constance and truth of things spoken or covenanted. And in another place he saith, nothing keepeth so together a public weal as doth faith. Then followeth it well, that without faith a public weal may not continue, and Aristotle saith, that by the same craft or means that a public weal is first constituted, by the same craft or means is it preserved. Then since faith is the foundation of justice, which is the chief constitutor and maker of a public weal, and by the aforementioned authority, faith is conservator of the same, I may therefore conclude that faith is both the original and (as it were) principal constitutor and conservator of the public weal.

Now, like as it is more facile to repair than to new edify, and also to amend than to make all again, so more soon is a public weal reformed, than of new constitute, and by the same thing that it is constitute and conserved, by the same thing shall it be reformed and preserved. Where I say conserved I mean kept and maintained; where I say preserved, I intend corroborate and defended against annoyances. The thing that I spoke of is faith, which I by the authority of Tully do name the foundation of justice. For thereat not only dependeth all contracts, conventions, commutations, intercourses, mutual intelligence, amity, and benevolence, which be contained in the word which of Tully is called the society or fellowship of mankind; but also by due observing of faith malefactors be espied, injuries be tried out and discussed, the property of things is adjudged. Wherefore to a governor of a public weal nothing more appertaineth than he himself to have faith in reverence, and most scrupulously to observe it. And where he findeth it to be condemned or neglected, and specially with adding to perjury, most sharply, yea most rigorously and above all other offences punish it, without acceptance or favour of any person; remembering this sentence, 'Of faith cometh loyalty, and where that lacketh there is no surety.'

It is also no little reproach unto a man which esteemeth honesty to be light in making promise; or when he hath promised, to break or neglect it. Wherefore nothing ought to be promised which should be in any wise contrary to justice. On a time one remembered King Agesilaus of his promise: 'By God,' said he, 'that is truth, if it stand with justice; if not, I then spoke, but I promised not.'

But now at this present time we may make the exclamation that Seneca doth, saying, 'O the foul and dishonest confession of the fraud and mischief of mankind; nowadays seals be more set by than souls.' Alas! what reproach is it to Christian men, and rejoicing to Turks and Saracens, that nothing is so exactly observed among them as faith, consisting in lawful promise and covenant. And among Christian men it is so neglected, that it is more often times broken than kept. And not only sealing (which Seneca disdained that it should be more set by than souls) is unneth [1] sufficient, but also it is now come into such a general contempt that all the learned men in the laws of this realm, which be also men of great wisdom, cannot with all their study devise so sufficient an instrument to bind a man to his promise or covenant, but that there shall be something therein espied to bring it in argument if it be denied. And in case that both the parties be equal in estimation or credence, or else he that denieth superior

---

[1] Scarcely.

to the other, and no witnesses deposeth on knowledge of the thing in demand, the promise or covenant is utterly frustrated. Which is one of the principal decays of the public weal, as I shall treat thereof more largely hereafter. And here at this time I leave to speak any more of the parts of that most royal and necessary virtue called justice.

VIII. Of the noble virtue fortitude, and of the two extreme vices, audacity and timorosity.

IT IS to be noted that to him that is a governor of a public weal belongeth a double governance, that is to say, an interior or inward governance, and an exterior or outward governance. The first is of his affects and passions, which do inhabit within his soul, and be subjects to reason. The second is of his children, his servants, and other subjects to his authority. To the one and the other is required the virtue moral called fortitude, which as much as it is a virtue is a mediocrity or mean between two extremities, the one in surplusage, the other in lack. The surplusage is called audacity, the lack timorosity or fear. I name that audacity which is an excessive and inordinate trust to escape all dangers, and causeth a man to do such acts as are not to be jeoparded. Timorosity is as well when a man feareth such things as be not to be feared, as also when he feareth things to be feared more than needeth. For some things there be which be necessary and good to be feared, and not to fear them it is but rebuke. Infamy and reproach be of all honest men to be dread. And not to fear things that be terrible, against which no power or wit of man can resist, is foolhardiness, and worthy no praise, as earthquakes, rages of great and sudden floods, which do bear down before them mountains and great towns, also the horrible fury of sudden fire, devouring all thing that it apprehendeth. Yet a man that is valiant, called in Latin *fortis*, shall not in such terrible adventures be resolved into wailings or desperation. But where force constraineth him to abide, and neither power or wisdom assayed may suffice to escape, but, will he or no, he must needs perish, there doth he patiently sustain death, which is the end of all evils. And like as an excellent physician cureth most dangerous diseases and deadly wounds, so doth a man that is valiant advance himself as invincible in things that do seem most terrible, not unadvisedly, and as it were in a beastly rage, but of a gentle courage, and with premeditation, either by victory or by death, winning honour and perpetual memory, the just reward of their virtue. Of this manner of valiance was Horatius Cocles, an ancient Roman, of whose example I have already written in the First Book, where I commended the feat of swimming.

Pyrrhus, whom Hannibal esteemed to be the second of the most valiant captains, assaulting a strong fortress in Sicily, called Erice, he first of all other scaled the walls, where he behaved him so valiantly, that such as resisted, some he slew, and other by his majesty and fierce countenance he did put to discomfort; and finally, before any of his army, entered the walls, and there alone sustained the whole brunt of his enemies, until his people which were without, at the last missing him, stirred partly with shame that they had so lost him, partly with his courageous example, took good heart, and enforced themselves in such wise that they climbed the walls and came to the succour of Pyrrhus, and by his prowess so won the garrison. What valiant heart was in the Roman, Mutius Scaevola, that when Porsena, King of Etruscans, had by great power constrained the Romans to keep them within their city, Scaevola taking on him the habit of a beggar, with a sword hid privily under his garment, went to the enemies' camp, where he being taken for a beggar, was nothing mistrusted. And when he had espied the King's pavilion he drew him thither, where he found divers noblemen sitting. But forasmuch as he certainly knew not which of them was the King, he at the last perceiving one to be in more rich apparel than any of the other, and supposing him to be Porsena, he, ere any man espied him, stepped to the said lord, and with his sword gave him such a stroke that he immediately died. But Scaevola being taken, forasmuch as he might not escape such a multitude, he boldly confessed that his hand erred, and that his intent was to have slain King Porsena. Wherewith the King (as reason was) all chaufed, commanded a great fire forthwith to be made, wherein Scaevola should have been burned, but he nothing abashed, said to the King, 'Think not, Porsena, that by my death only thou mayest escape the hands of the Romans, for there be in the city three hundred young men, such as I am, that be prepared to slay thee by one means or other, and to the accomplishment thereof be also determined to suffer all torments, whereof thou shalt have of me an experience in thy sight.' And incontinently he went to the fire, which was made for to burn him, and with a glad countenance did put his hand into the flame, and there held it of a long time without changing of any countenance, until his said hand was burned unto ashes. In likewise he would have put his other hand into the fire, if he had not been withdrawn by Porsena, who, wondering at the valiant courage of Scaevola, licensed him to return unto the city. But when he considered that by the words of Scaevola so great a number of young men of semblable prowess were confederate to his destruction, so that, or all they could be apprehended, his life should be alway in jeopardy, he, despairing of winning the city of Rome, raised his siege and departed.

IX. In what acts fortitude is, and of the considerations thereto belonging.

BUT ALTHOUGH I have now rehearsed sundry examples to the commendation of fortitude concerning acts martial, yet by the way I would have it remembered that the praise is properly to be referred unto the virtue, that is to say, to enterprise things dreadful, either for the public weal or for winning of perpetual honour, or else for eschewing reproach or dishonour. Whereunto be annexed these considerations, what importance the enterprise is, and wherefore it is done, with the time and opportunity when it ought to be done. For (as Tully saith) to enter in battle and to fight unadvisedly, it is a thing wild and a manner of beasts, but thou shalt fight valiantly when time requireth, and also necessity. And alway death is to be preferred before servitude or any dishonesty. And therefore the acts of Hannibal against the Saguntines, which never did him displeasure, is not accounted for any prowess. Neither Cataline, which, for his singular commodity and a few other, attempted detestable wars against his own country, intending to have burned the noble city of Rome, and to have destroyed all the good men, is not numbered among valiant men, although he fought manly and with great courage until he was slain. What availed the boldness of Varro and Flaminius, noble captains of Romans, which despising the prowess and craft of Hannibal, and condemning the sober counsel of Fabius, having only trust in their own hardiness, lost two noble armies, whereby the power of the Romans was nigh utterly perished? Wherefore eftsoons [1] I say that a valiant man is he that doth tolerate or suffer that which is needful, and in such wise as is needful, and for that which is needful, and also when it is needful. And he that lacketh any of this may be called hardy, but not valiant. Moreover, although they which be hardy or persons desperate have a similitude, and seem to be valiant, yet be they not valiant, no more than kings in May games and interludes be kings. For they that be hardy, ere they come to the peril, they seem to be fierce and eager, and in beginning their enterprise wonderful hasty; but when they feel the thing more hard and grievous than they esteemed, their courage decayeth more and more, and as men abashed and unprepared, their hearts utterly do fail, and in conclusion they appear more faint than they that be cowards. Also in desperation cannot be fortitude, for that being a moral virtue is ever voluntary. Desperation is a thing as it were constrained nor hath any manner of consideration; where fortitude expendeth everything and act diligently, and doth also moderate it with reason. Here now appeareth (as I suppose) that neither they which employ their force without just cause or necessity, nor they which without forecast, or (as I might say) circumspection, will take in hand an hard enterprise, nor they which headlong will fall into dangers, from whence there is no hope to escape, nor yet men desperate, which do die willingly without any motion of honour or zeal toward the public weal, be in the number of valiant persons; but of a refuse company, and rather to be reckoned with beasts savage than among men which do participate with reason. For as Curtius saith, it appertaineth to men that be valiant, rather to despise death than to hate life.

A man is called in Latin *vir*, whereof, saith Tully, virtue is named. And the most proper virtue belonging to a man is fortitude, whereof be two excellent properties, that is to say, the contempt of death and of grief. But what very fortitude is he more plainly doth declare afterward in a more large circumspection, saying, 'Things human ought to be little esteemed, death not regarded, labours and griefs to be thought tolerable.' When this is ratified by judgment and a constant opinion, then that is a valiant and stable fortitude. But thereunto I would should be added, which opinion and judgment proceedeth of a reason, and not repugnant to justice. And then it shall accord

[1] Again.

with this saying of Aristotle, 'A valiant man sustaineth and doth that which belongeth to fortitude for cause of honesty.' And a little before he saith, 'A man that is valiant as well suffereth as doth that which agreeth with his worship, and as reason commandeth.' So no violence or sturdy mind lacking reason and honesty is any part of fortitude. Unto this noble virtue be attendant, or as it were continual adherents, divers virtues, which do ensue, and be of right great estimation.

X. Of painfulness the first companion of fortitude.

IN THEM which be either governors or captains or in other office whereunto appertaineth great cure, or dispatching of sundry great affairs, painfulness, named in Latin *tolerantia*, is wonderful commendable. For thereby things be in such wise exploited that utility proceedeth thereof, and seldom repentance. Forasmuch as thereof cometh an excellent fruit called opportunity, which is ever ripe, and never in other estate. For lack of this virtue much wisdom and many a valiant enterprise have perished and turned to none effect, for things sharply invented, prudently discussed, and valiantly enterprised, if they be not diligently followed, and without ceasing applied and pursued, as it were in a moment all thing is subverted. And the pains before taken, with the time therein spent, is utterly frustrated. The painfulness of Quintus Fabius, being dictator or principal captain of the Romans, in leading his army by mountains and other hard passages, so disappointed Hannibal of the hope of victory, wherein he so much gloried, that at the last he trained and drew Hannibal and his host into a field enclosed about with mountains and deep rivers, where Fabius had so environed him by the fortifying of two mountains with his people, that they were in jeopardy either to be famished (their victuals soon after failing them) or else in fleeing to be slain by the Romans, had not the crafty and politic wit of Hannibal delivered them; which, for the notable invention, I will borrow so much time of the reader to renew the remembrance thereof in our English tongue. Hannibal, perceiving the danger that he and his army were in, he commanded in the deep of the night, when nothing was stirring, to be brought before him about two thousand great oxen and bulls, which a little before his men had taken in foraging, and causing faggots made of dry sticks to

be fastened unto their horns, and set on fire, the beasts troubled
with the flame of fire, ran as they were woode [1] up toward the
mountains, whereas lay the host of the Romans, Hannibal, with
his whole army following in array. The Romans which kept the
mountains, being sore afraid of this new and terrible sight, forsook their places, and Fabius, dreading the deceitful wit of
Hannibal, kept the army within his trench, and so Hannibal with
his host escaped without damage. But Fabius, being painful in
pursuing Hannibal from place to place, awaiting to have him at
advantage, at the last did so fatigue him and his host that thereby
in conclusion his power minished, and also the strength of the
Carthaginians, of whom he was general captain. Insomuch as
they were at the last constrained to countermand him by sundry
messengers, willing him to abandon the wars in Italy, and to
return to the defence of his own city. Which by the opinion of
most excellent writers should never have happened if Fabius
would have left any part of his purpose, either for the tediousness
of the pain and travail, or for the intolerable rebukes given unto
him by Minutius, who upbraided him with cowardice. Among the
virtues which abounded in Julius Caesar, none was accounted
more excellent than that in his counsels, affairs, and exploitures,
he omitted no time nor forsook any pain; wherefore most soonest
of any man he achieved and brought to good pass all things that
he enterprised. Suppose ye that the same Hannibal, of whom we
late spoke, could have won from the Romans all Spain, and have
pierced the mountains called Alps, making a way for his army
where before was never any manner of passage, and also have
gotten all Italy unto Rome gates, if he had not been a man painful
and of labour incomparable?

Julius Caesar, after that he had the entire governance and
dominion of the Empire of Rome, he therefore never omitted
labour and diligence, as well in common causes as private, concerning the defence and assistance of innocents. Also he labori-
ously and studiously discussed controversies, which almost daily
he heard in his own person.

Trajan and both Antonines, Emperors of Rome, and for their
virtue worthy to be emperors of all the world, as well in exterior
affairs as in the affairs of the city, were ever so continually occupied that unneth they found any little time to have any recreation
or solace.

[1] Mad.

Alexander also, Emperor, for his incomparable gravity called Severus, being but of the age of eighteen years when he first was made Emperor, was inclined to so incredible labours, that where he found the noble city of Rome, then mistress of the world, thoroughly corrupted with most abominable vices, by the most shameful example and living of that detestable monster, Varius Heliogabalus, next Emperor before him, a great part of the Senate and nobility being resolved into semblable vices, the chivalry dispersed, martial prowess abandoned, and well nigh the majesty imperial dissolved and brought in contempt, this noble young prince Alexander, inflamed with the zeal of the pristine honour of the Romans, laying apart utterly all pleasures and quietness, wholly gave his wit and body to study and travails intolerable, and choosing out of all parts of the world men of greatest wisdom and experience, consulting with them, never ceased until he had reduced as well the Romans as all other cities and provinces unto them subject to their pristine moderation and temperance. Many other examples could I rehearse to the commendation of painfulness. But these shall suffice at this present time to prove that a governor must needs be painful in his own person, if he desire to have those things prosper that be committed to his governance.

XI. Of the noble and fair virtue named patience.

PATIENCE is noble virtue, appertaining as well to inward governance as to exterior governance, and is the vanquisher of injuries, the sure defence against all affects and passions of the soul, retaining always glad semblance in adversity and dolour.

Saint Ambrose saith in his book of offices, 'Better is he that condemneth injury, than he that sorroweth. For he that condemneth it as he nothing felt, he passeth not on it: but he that is sorrowful, he is therewith tormented as though he felt it.'

Which was well proved by Zeno Eleates, a noble philosopher, who being a man of excellent wisdom and eloquence, came to a city called Agrigentum, where reigned Phalaris, the most cruel tyrant of all the world, who kept and used his own people in most miserable servitude. Zeno first thought by his wisdom and eloquence to have so persuaded the tyrant to temperance that he should have abandoned his cruel and avaricious appetite. But custom of vice more prevailed in him than profitable counsel. Wherefore Zeno having pity at the wretched estate of the people, excited divers noblemen to deliver the city of that servile condition. This counsel was not so secretly given but that notice thereof came to the tyrant, who, causing all the people to be assembled in the market place, caused Zeno there to be cruciate [1] with sundry torments, always demanding of him who did participate with him of his said counsel. But for no pains would he confess any person, but induced the tyrant to have in mistrust his next friends and familiar servants, and reproving the people for their cowardice and dread, he at the last so inflamed them unto liberty, that suddenly, with great violence, they fell on the tyrant and pressed him with stones. The old Zeno in all his exquisite torments never made any lamentable cry or desire to be relieved. But for this form of patience this only example sufficeth at this time, since there be so frequent examples of martyrs, which for true religion sustained patiently not only equal torments with Zeno, but also far exceeding. But now will I write of that patience that pertaineth unto interior governance, whereby the natural passions of man be subdued and the malice of fortune sustained. For they which be in authority and be occupied about great affairs, their lives be not only replenished with labours and grievous displeasures, but also they be subjects to sundry chances.

The mean to obtain patience is by two things principally: a direct and upright conscience, and true and constant opinion in the estimation of goodness. Which seldom cometh only of nature, except it be wonderful excellent; but by the diligent study of very philosophy (not that which is sophisticated, and consisteth in sophisms) nature is thereto prepared and helped. This opinion is of such power that once cleaving fast to the mind, it draweth a man as it were by violence to good or evil. Therefore, Tully saith, like as when the blood is corrupted, and either phlegm or choler, black or red, is superabundant, then in the body be engendered sores and diseases, so the vexation of evil opinions and their repugnance despoileth the mind of all health, and troubleth it with griefs. Contrariwise afterward Tully describeth good opinion, and calleth it the beauty of the soul, saying in this wise, 'As of bodily members there is an apt figure, with a manner pleasantness of colour, and that is called beauty; so in the soul

---

[1] Afflicted.

the equality and constancy of opinions and judgments ensuing virtue, with a stable and steadfast purpose, or containing the self same effects that is in virtue, is named beauty.' Which sentences deeply investigated and well perceived by them that be about princes and governors, they may consider how wary and circumspect they ought to be in the inducing them to opinions. Whereof they be sufficiently admonished by the most excellent divine Erasmus Roterodamus, in his book of the *Institution of a Christian Prince*, which in mine opinion cannot be so much praised as it is worthy. Therefore I will leave now to write any more of opinion, saving that I would that it should be alway remembered, that opinion in judging things as they verily be armeth a man unto patience.

XII. *Of patience in sustaining wrongs and rebukes.*

UNTO HIM that is valiant of courage it is a great pain and difficulty to sustain injury, and not to be forthwith revenged. And yet often times is accounted more valiantness in the sufferance than in hasty revenging. As it was in Antoninus the Emperor, called the philosopher, against whom rebelled one Cassius, and usurped the imperial majesty in Syria and the East parts. Yet at the last, being slain by the captains of Antoninus next adjoining, he thereof unwitting was therewith sore grieved. And therefore taking to him the children of Cassius, entreated them honourably, whereby he acquired ever after the incomparable and most assured love of his subjects. As much dishonour and hatred his son Commodus won by his impatience, wherein he so exceeded, that forasmuch as he found not his bath hot to his pleasure, he caused the keeper thereof to be thrown into the hot burning furnace. What thing might be more odible [1] than that most devilish impatience? Julius Caesar, when Catullus the poet wrote against him contumelious or reproachable verses, he not only forgave him, but to make him his friend caused him oftentimes to sup with him. The noble Emperor Augustus, when it was shown him that many men in the city had of him unfitting words, he thought it a sufficient answer that in a free city men must have their tongues needs at liberty. Nor never was with any person that spoke evil of him in

---

[1] Hateful.

word or countenance worse discontented. Some men will not praise this manner of patience, but account it for foolishness; but if they behold on the other side what incommodity cometh of impatience, how a man is therewith abstract from reason and turned into a monstrous figure, and do confer all that with the stable countenance and pleasant regard of him that is patient, and with the commodity that doth ensue thereof, they shall affirm that that simplicity is an excellent wisdom. Moreover the best way to be avenged is so to condemn injury and rebuke, and live with such honesty that the doer shall at the last be thereof ashamed, or at the least, lose the fruit of his malice, that is to say, shall not rejoice and have glory of thy hindrance or damage.

XIII. Of patience deserved in repulse, or hindrance of promotion.

TO A MAN having a gentle courage, likewise as nothing is so pleasant or equally rejoiceth him as reward or preferment suddenly given or above his merit, so nothing may be to him more displeasant or painful than to be neglected in his painstaking, and the reward and honour that he looketh to have, and for his merit is worthy to have, to be given to one of less virtue, and perchance of no virtue or laudable quality. Plato in his Epistle to Dion, King of Sicily, 'It is' (saith he) 'good right that they which be good men, and do the semblable, obtain honour which they be worthy to have.'

Undoubtedly in a prince or nobleman may be nothing more excellent, yea nothing more necessary, than to advance men after the estimation of their goodness; and that for two special commodities that do come thereof. First, that thereby they provoke many men to apprehend virtue. Also to them which be good and already advanced do give such courage, that they endeavour themselves with all their power to increase that opinion of goodness, whereby they were brought to that advancement which needs must be to the honour and benefit of those by whom they were so promoted. Contrariwise, where men from their infancy have ensued virtue, worn the flourishing time of youth with painful study, abandoning all lusts and all other thing which in that time is pleasant, trusting thereby to profit their public weal, and to obtain thereby honour, when either their virtue and travail is little regarded, or the preferment which they look for is given to another not equal in merit, it not only pierceth his heart with much anguish, and oppresseth him with discomfort, but also mortifieth the courages of many other which be aptly disposed to study and virtue, and hoped thereby to have the proper reward thereof, which is commendation and honour, which being given to men lacking virtue and wisdom, shall be occasion for them to do evil (as Democritus saith), for who doubteth but that authority in a good man doth publish his virtue, which before lay hid? In an evil man it ministereth boldness and licence to do evil, which by dread was before covered. Surely this repulse or (as they vulgarly speak) putting back from promotion is no little pain or discomfort, but it may be withstood, or at the least remedied, with patience, which may be in this wise induced.

First, considering that the world was never so constant that at all times before good men were justly rewarded, and none but they only promoted. Cato, called Uticensis, at whose gravity as well the Senate and people of Rome as other kings and princes reverenced, looking to be one of the consuls, was openly reject. Wherewith his friends and kinsmen took no little discomfort. But Cato himself so little regarded that repulse, that where always he went very homely, he the next day following decked and trimmed himself more freshly than he was wont, and when he had shown himself so to the people, at afternoon he walked with one of his friends in the market-place, bare legged and in single apparel, as he was accustomed.

Scipio, called Nasica, who by the whole Senate was judged the best man in the city, and of an ancient house, was likewise put back for being consul. Lelius likewise, which was openly called the wise man, was semblably refused. And divers other of whom histories do make mention were abject, when they had well deserved honours, and their inferiors in merits promoted. Also a man's conscience shall well comfort him when he hath so lived that, where he is known, men do judge him worthy preferment. And then may he say to them which marvel why he is not advanced, as Cato said to a person that told to him that men wondered why among so many noble men's images as were set up in the city, Cato's image was not espied. 'By God,' said Cato, 'I had liefer that men wondered why I have none image set up, than why men should set up mine image.' So if men marvel why a man is not advanced, knowing him a good man, then judge they him to be worthy promotion, which judgment proceedeth of favour, and then though he lack promotion, yet hath he perfect glory, which every noble heart desireth.

For Tully saith, 'The perfect and most principal glory consisteth in those three things. If the multitude love us; if they put confidence in us; if also as it were marvelling at us, they think us worthy to have honour given unto us.' With this glory and cleanness of conscience shall a wise man content him, and be induced to patience, and not be grieved with his fortune, but to follow Democritus in laughing at the blind judgments of men in bestowing promotions. I omit at this time to write any more of this virtue patience, since to the institution of a governor this seemeth to be sufficient, to the residue he shall be better persuaded by the works of Plutarch, Seneca, and Pontanus, where they write of patience, which works he may hereafter read at his leisure.

XIV. Of magnanimity, which may be named valiant courage.

MAGNANIMITY is a virtue much commendable, and also expedient to be in a governor, and is, as I have said, a companion of fortitude. And may be in this wise defined, that it is an excellency of mind concerning things of great importance or estimation, doing all thing that is virtuous for the achieving of honour. But now I remember me, this word magnanimity being yet strange, as late borrowed out of the Latin, shall not content all men, and specially them whom nothing contenteth out of their accustomed Mumpsimus,[1] I will adventure to put for magnanimity a word more familiar, calling it good courage, which, having respect to the said definition, shall not seem much inconvenient.

But now concerning a more large description of the said virtue. Aristotle saith, 'That man seemeth to be of noble courage that is worthy, and also judgeth himself worthy to have things that be great.' He saith also afterward, 'Noble courage is an ornament of virtues, for it maketh them the more ample, and without them she herself may not be.' But I will for a little time leave this noble philosopher Aristotle, and reverently interpret a place in the offices of Tully, where he most eloquently and plainly setteth out this virtue, saying, 'Alway a valiant and noble courage is discerned by two things specially, whereof one is in despising things

---

[1] Obstinate adherence to old ways.

outward, when a man is persuaded neither to marvel at anything, neither to wish or desire anything but that which is honest. Moreover, that a man should not bow for any fortune or trouble of mind.' Another thing is that when thou art of that mind or courage, as I before said, then that thou practise those things not only which be great and most profitable, but also them that be very difficult, and full of labour and peril, as well concerning man's life as many other things thereunto pertaining. And afterwards the same Tully saith, 'To esteem little those things which unto the more part of men seemeth excellent, and also with reason firm and stable to condemn them, it is sign of a noble and valiant courage. Also to tolerate those things which do seem bitter or grievous (whereof there be many in the life of man and in fortune) in such wise as thou depart not from the estate of nature, neither from the worship pertaining unto a wise man, betokeneth a good courage, and also much constancy.' By this it seemeth that magnanimity or good courage is, as it were, the garment of virtue, wherewith she is set out (as I might say) to the uttermost. I mean not that thereby virtue is amended, or made more beauteous, which of herself is perfect, but likewise as a lady of excellent beauty, though that she be always fair, yet a rich and fresh garment declareth her estate, and causeth her the more to be looked on, and thereby her natural beauty to be the better perceived. Semblably doth magnanimity, joined with any virtue, set it wonderfully forth to be beholden, and (as I might say) marvelled at, as it shall appear abundantly in the examples ensuing.

Agesilaus, King of Lacedaemonia, in the beginning of his youth, perceiving that all Greece was in great fear for the fame that was spread of the coming of the Persians with an infinite army, he with a noble courage proffered not only to defend his own country, but also with a small host to pass the seas into Asia, and from thence either to bring victory of the Persians, or else a sure and honourable peace. With whose courage the Lacedaemons, highly recomforted, delivered unto him ten thousand soldiers. With the which host he went into Asia, and there vanquished the Persians, and returned joyfully into his country with his people all safe, to his perpetual renown, and also the honour and surety of all Greece.

Antigonus, King of Macedonia, being on the sea, one of his captains advised him to depart, saying that the navy of his enemy was much greater in number than his, whereunto with a noble courage he answered, 'And for how many ships account you our person?' Wherewith his people took such comfort that they boldly did set forth and vanquished their enemies.

Such noble courage was in great King Alexander, that in his wars against Darius he was seen of all his people fighting in the press of his enemies bare-headed.

I will not be so uncourteous to leave unremembered in this place the notable magnanimity of a king of England, which I happened to read late in an old chronicle.

Edgar, who in the time that the Saxons had this realm in subjection, had subdued all the other kings Saxons, and made them his tributaries. On a time he had them all with him at dinner, and after it was shown him that Rynande, King of Scots, had said that he wondered how it should happen that he and other kings, that were tall and great personages, would suffer themselves to be subdued by so little a body as Edgar was. Edgar dissembled and answered nothing, but feigning to go on hunting he took with him the Scottish King in his company, and purposely withdrew him from them that were with him; and causing by a secret servant two swords to be conveyed into a place in the forest by him appointed, as soon as he came thither he took the one sword, and delivered the other to Rynande, bidding him to prove his strength, and to assay whither his deeds would ratify his words. Whereat the Scottish King being abashed, beholding the noble courage of Edgar, with an horrible fear confessed his error, desiring pardon, which he with most humble submission at the last obtained. That noble King Edgar declaring by his magnanimity that by his virtue, and not by chance, he was elected to reign over so noble a region.

Plato, for his divine wisdom and eloquence named the god of philosophers, was sent for by Dionysius, King of Sicily, to the intent, as it seemed, that he would be of him instructed concerning the politic governance of his realm. But when he had been with him a certain space, and would not flatter with the King and uphold his tyranny, the King became weary of him, insomuch that if it had not been at the request of Archytas, prince of Tarentum, he would have put him to death. Wherefore, partly at the desire of that prince, partly for fear of the Athenians, he licensed Plato to depart without damage, but at his departing he said unto him, as it were in despite, 'O how evil wilt thou speak of me, Plato, when thou comest among thy companions and scholars.' Then Plato with a noble courage answered, 'God defend there should be in my school so much vacant time from the study of wisdom, that there might be any place left once to remember thee.'

Now will I make an end of this virtue, and proceed further to write of some vices which commonly do follow magnanimity, and with great difficulty may be eschewed.

XV. Of obstinacy, a familiar vice following magnanimity.

THE PRINCE of orators, Marcus Tullius, in his first book of offices, saith that in height and greatness of courage is most soonest engendered obstinacy, and inordinate desire of sovereignty.

Obstinacy is an affection immovable, fixed to will, abandoning reason, which is engendered of pride, that is to say, when a man esteemeth so much himself above any other, that he reputeth his own wit only to be in perfection, and condemneth all other counsel. Undoubtedly this is an horrible and perilous vice, and very familiar with them which be of most noble courage. By it many a valiant captain and noble prince have not only fallen themselves, but also brought all their countries in danger and oftentimes to subversion and ruin.

The wise King Solomon saith, 'Among proud men be alway contentions, and they that do all things with counsel, be governed by wisdom.'

I need not to rehearse examples out of old writers what damage have ensued of obstinacy, considering that every history is full thereof, and we still have it in daily experience. But one thing am I sure, where obstinacy ruleth, and reason lacketh place, there counsel availeth not, and where counsel hath not authority and franchise, there may nothing be perfect. Solomon saith, where as be many counsels, there the people is in surety. Now will I declare the residue of Tully's sentence, concerning inordinate desire of sovereignty, which is properly called ambition.

XVI. Of another vice following magnanimity, called ambition.

IT WAS NOT without a high and prudent consideration that certain laws were made by the Romans, which were named the laws of ambition, whereby men were restrained in the city to obtain offices and dignities in the public weal, either by giving rewards, or by other sinister labour or means. And they which by that law were condemned were put to death without any favour.

Verily it was a noble law, and for all places necessary, considering what inconvenience happeneth by this vain and superfluous appetite. Witnesses among the Romans Sulla, Marius, Carbo, Cinna, Pompey, and Caesar, by whose ambition more Romans were slain than in acquiring the empire of all the world. Sulla condemned, and caused to be slain, four score thousand Romans, beside many more that were slain in the battles between him and the both Marius.

Also Pompey and Julius Caesar, the one suffering no peer, the other no superior, by their ambition caused to be slain between them people innumerable, and subverted the best and most noble public weal of the world, and finally having little time of rejoicing their unlawful desire, Pompey, shamefully fleeing, had his head stricken off by the commandment of Ptolemy, King of Egypt, unto whom as unto his friend he fled for succour. Caesar, the vanquisher, was murdered in the Senate with daggers, by them whom he most specially favoured.

I could occupy a great volume with histories of them which, coveting to mount into excellent dignities, did thereby bring into extreme perils both themselves and their country. For as Tacitus saith, wonderful elegantly, with them which desire sovereignty, there is no mean place between the top and the step down. To the which words Tully agreeing, saith that high authorities should not much be desired, or rather not to be taken at some time, and oftentimes to be left and forsaken.

So did Sulla, whom I late spoke of, and Diocletian, Emperor of Rome, who after that he had governed the empire twenty-five years honourably (if he had not been polluted with the blood of innumerable Christian men) he willingly abandoned the crown and dignity imperial, and lived nine years on his private possessions. And on a time he being desired of Herculius and Galerius, unto whom he had resigned the empire, to take eftsoons [1] on him

---

[1] Again.

the governance, abhorring it as a pestilence, answered in this wise, I would ye did see the herbs that I have with mine own hands sown and set at Salonae, surely ye would not then in this wise advise me. Also Octavius Augustus, which in felicity passed all emperors, devised oftentimes with his friends to have resigned his authority. And if at that time the Senate had been as well furnished with noble and wise personages as it was before the civil wars between Caesar and Pompey, it is to be thought that he would surely have restored the public weal to his pristine glory.

But now let us see what is the cause why that ambition is so pernicious to a public weal, and in mine opinion it is for two causes principally.

First, forasmuch as they which be of that courage and appetite, when they be in authority, they suppose all thing to be lawful that liketh them, and also by reason of their pre-eminence they would so be separate from other that no man should control them or warn them of their enormities, and finally, they would do what they list without contradiction. Whereof do ensure divers injuries and subversion of justice.

And that this which I have now said is true, Tully affirmeth, saying, 'Verily it is a great difficulty, where thou wouldest be above all men, to observe equity, which is the thing most appropriate to justice.' And shortly after he saith, 'The more high of courage that a man is, and desirous of glory, the sooner is he moved to do things against right.' Seeing that it was so in the time of Tully, when almost every man that was in authority had excellent learning (the Romans bringing up their children in study of moral philosophy), what shall we then suppose in our time, when few men in authority do care for learning? Why should we think to be more justice now used in authority than was in the time of Tully? Is there not now private affection, particular favour, displeasure, and hatred, as was at that time? I would that the readers hereof be judges, examining these my words with daily experience.

The second cause that condemneth ambition is covetousness of treasure, therewith to maintain their ostentation and vainglory, which ambitious persons do call their honour. Whereby they be procured to find unjust means by their authority to provide for such substance, wherewith they may be not only satisfied (they being insatiable) but according to their own appetite fully sufficed. Wherefore the philosophers called *Stoici* used this sentence,

'Great indigence or lack cometh not of poverty, but of great plenty, for he that hath much shall need much.' But certes, such persons ambitious may well consider that the men, magnificence and pomp which they covet is not so much wondered at, as avarice and collection of money is universally hated. Wherefore Darius, King of Persia and father to Xerxes, when he had commanded a subsidy to be levied of his subjects, he demanded the chief men of the countries whether they found themselves grieved, they answering that they were in a meetly good case, he commanded the one half to be eftsoons [1] restored, lest he of any avarice should be suspected. By the which act he established his dignity and made it more perfect. Moreover Tully saith, 'To take anything from another man, and one man to increase his commodity with another man's detriment, is more repugnant to nature than death, than poverty, pain, or other thing that might happen either to the body or other goods worldly.' And this for now sufficeth to speak of ambition.

XVII. The true definition of abstinence and continence.

ABSTINENCY and continency be also companions of fortitude, and be noble and excellent virtues, and I cannot tell whether there be any to be preferred before them, specially in men having authority, they being the bridles of two capital vices, that is to say, avarice and lechery; which vices, being refrained by a noble that liveth at liberty and without controlment, procureth unto him, beside the favour of God, immortal glory. And that city or realm whereof the governors with these vices be little or nothing acquainted, do abide long in prosperity. For, as Valerius Maximus saith, wheresoever this fervent pestilence of mankind hath entry, injury reigneth, reproach or infamy is spread, and devoureth the name of nobility.

The properties of these two virtues be in this manner. Abstinence is whereby a man refraineth from anything, which he may lawfully take, for a better purpose. Continence is a virtue which keepeth the pleasant appetite of man under the yoke of reason. Aristotle in his *Ethics*, making them both but one, describeth them under the name of continence, saying, 'He that is

[1] Again.

continent, forasmuch as he knoweth that covetous desires be evil, he doth abandon them, reason persuading him.' For this time I take abstinence for the wilful abandoning of money, possessions, or other things semblable; continence the only for-bearing the unlawful company of women.

Marcius Coriolanus, a noble young man, which lineally descended from Ancus, sometime King of Romans, when he had done many valiant acts and achieved sundry enterprises, he was according to his merits commended in the army by Postumius, then being consul. And by their universal assent he was rewarded with all such honours as then appertained to a good warrior. Also with one hundred acres of arable land, the election of ten prisoners, ten horses apparelled for the wars, one hundred of oxen, and as much silver as he might bear. But of all this would he take nothing, but one only prisoner which was of his acquain-tance, and one courser, which always after he used in battle.

Manius Curius, the very rule and pattern of fortitude and moderate living, when the people called Samnites, which had wars with the Romans, found him sitting in his house by the fire upon a homely form, eating his meat in a dish of tree, they bring-ing to him a great sum of gold by the consent of the people, and wondering at his poverty, with courteous language desired him to take that they had brought him, he thereat smiling, said thus unto them: 'Ye ministers of a vain and superfluous message, show you to the Samnites that Curius had liefer have dominion over them that be rich than be himself to have riches. And as for this gold which ye account precious, take it again with you, and remember that ye can neither vanquish me in battle nor corrupt me with money.'

Quintus Tubero, surnamed Catelius, what time he was consul, the people of Greece called Aetoli sent to him by their ambassa-dors a great quantity of silver vessel curiously wrought and graven. But when they came to him they found on his table vessel only of earth. And when he saw them he exhorted them that they should not suppose that his continence, as if it were poverty, should be with their presents relieved. And with that saying, commanded them to depart.

To Epaminondas, the Theban, being in his time as well in virtue as prowess the most noble man of all Greece, Artaxerxes, King of Persia, to make him his friend, sent one of his servants to Thebes with a great quantity of treasure to give to Epaminondas.

Which servant, knowing his manners, durst not offer it unto him when he came, but speaking to a young man which was familiar with Epaminondas, gave unto him a great reward to move Epaminondas to receive the King's present. Who unneth [1] hearing the first words of the young man, commanded the King's servant to be brought unto him, unto whom he had these words. 'Friend, show to the King that he needeth not to offer me money, for if he have anything to do with the Thebans for a good purpose, he may have their assistance without any reward; if the purpose be nought, he cannot with all the treasure of the world hope to obtain it.' Which words were spoken with such a gravity that the said servant, being afraid, desired Epaminondas that he might be safely conveyed out of the city. Which he granted with good will, lest if the money were taken away he might of the receiving thereof have been suspected. Moreover, he caused the Theban, which was his friend and companion, to restore to the messenger the money that he had received.

Semblable abstinence was there in Phocion, a noble counsellor of Athens, unto whom the ambassadors of the great King Alexander brought from their master a hundred talents of gold, which were of English money twelve thousand pounds. But before that he heard them speak anything, he demanded of them why to him only the King sent so bounteous a reward. And they answered forasmuch as King Alexander judged him only to be a good man and a just. 'Then suffer ye me,' said Phocion, 'to be and to seem the same man that your King do judge me, and carry your gold again to him.' The same Phocion, the ambassador of Antipater (who succeeded the great King Alexander in Macedonia), offered to give a great sum of money, which Phocion despising, said in this wise, 'Since Antipater is not greater than Alexander nor his cause better, I do nothing perceive why I should take anything of him.' And when the orator would have had Phocion's son to have taken the money, Phocion answered, 'If his son would be like unto him he should have no need neither of that money nor of none other. If he would be unlike unto him and of dissolute manners, neither Antipater's gifts nor none others, were they never so great, should be sufficient.'

By these examples it doth appear how good men did alway flee from rewards, although they might have been lawfully taken,

[1] Scarcely.

which in them was neither foolishness nor yet rusticity, but of a prudent consideration. Forasmuch as both by wisdom and experience they knew that he which taketh a reward before anything done is no longer at liberty, but of a free man is made bond, inasmuch as he hath taken earnest for his true endeavour. Also by the taking he is become an evil man, though before he were good, for if he received it for an evil purpose, he is then a wretch, and detestable. If the matter were good, then he is not rightwise in selling a good deed, which he ought to do thankfully and without reward. And I doubt not whosoever is contented with his present estate, and supposeth felicity to be in a mean, and all excess to be perilous, will allow these sentences and think them worthy to be had in remembrance, specially of them that be governors. For that realm or city where men in authority have their hands open for money, and their houses for presents, is ever in the way to be subverted. Whether Caius Pontius, prince of Samnites, was wont to say, 'I would God' (said he) 'that fortune had reserved me unto the time, and that I had been then born when the Romans should begin to take gifts; I should then not suffer them any longer to rule.'

Paulus Aemilius, when he had vanquished King Persius, and subdued all Macedonia, he brought into the common treasury of Rome an infinite treasure, that the substance of that one prince discharged all the Romans to pay ever after any tax or subsidy. And yet of all that goods Aemilius brought nothing into his own house, but only perpetual renown.

Scipio, when he had gotten and destroyed the great city of Carthage, he was not therefore the richer one halfpenny. By this it appeareth that honour resteth not in riches, although some perchance will say that their revenues be small, and that they must take such rewards as be lawful, only to maintain their honour, but let them take heed to the saying of Tully, 'Nothing is more to be abhorred than avarice, specially in princes and them which do govern public weals.'

XVIII. The examples of continence given by noblemen.

NOW WILL I speak of continence, which is specially in refraining or forbearing the act of carnal pleasure, whereunto a man is fervently moved, or is at liberty to have it. Which undoubtedly is a thing not only difficult, but also wonderful in a man noble or of great authority, but in such one as it happeneth to be, needs must be reputed much virtue and wisdom, and to be supposed that his mind is invincible, considering that nothing so sharply assaileth a man's mind as doth carnal affection, called (by the followers thereof) love. Wherefore Plato saith that the soul of man which by love is possessed dieth in his own body, and liveth in another.

The great King Alexander, after his first victory against King Darius, having always in his host the wife of the same Darius, which incomparably excelled all other women in beauty; after that he had once seen her, he never after would have her come in his presence. Albeit that he caused her estate still to be maintained, and with as much honour as ever it was, saying to them which, wondering at the lady's beauty, marvelled why Alexander did not desire to have with her company, he answered that it should be to him a reproach to be any wise subdued by the wife of him whom he had vanquished.

Antiochus, the noble King of Asia, being in the city of Ephesus, beheld a virgin being a Mynchen [1] in the temple of Diana to be of excellent beauty, where he perceiving himself to be ravished in the love of the maiden, he hastily and immediately departed out of the city, lest love should constrain him to violate a virgin; wisely considering that it was best to abstain from doing battle with that enemy which unneth might be vanquished but with flight only.

The valiant Pompey, when he had vanquished the King Mithridates, and had taken divers of his concubines, which in beauty excelled, he would have no carnal knowledge with any of them; but when he knew that they were of noble lineage, he sent them undefiled to their parents and kinsfolk.

Semblably did Scipio when he won Carthage. For among divers women which were there taken, one most fairest of other was brought unto him to do with her his pleasure. But after that she had discovered to him that she was affianced to a gentleman, called Indibilis, he caused him to be sent for, and when he beheld the lamentation and signs of love between them, he not only delivered her to Indibilis, with her ransom, which her friends had paid for her redemption, but also added thereto an honourable portion of his own treasure. By the which continence and liberality he won the hearts of Indibilis and all his blood, whereby

---

[1] Nun, votaress.

he the sooner obtained and won all the country. Of this virtue be examples innumerable, as well of Gentiles as of Christian men. But these for this time shall suffice, saving that for the strangeness of it, I will rehearse a notable history which is remembered by the most excellent doctor, Saint Jerome.

Valerian, being Emperor of Rome, and persecuting the Church, in Egypt a Christian man was presented unto him, whom he beholding to be young and lusty, thinking therefore to remove him from the faith, rather by venereal motions, than by sharpness of torments, caused him to be laid in a bed within a fair garden, having about him all flowers of sweet odour and most delectable savours and perfumes. And then caused a fair tender young woman to be laid by him all naked, who ceased not sweetly and lovingly to embrace and kiss him, showing to him all pleasant devices, to the intent to provoke him to do fornication. There lacked little that the young man was not vanquished, and that the flesh yielded not to the service of Venus; that perceiving the young man, which was armed with grace, and seeing none other refuge, he with his teeth did gnaw of his own tongue, wherein he suffered such incredible pain, that therewith the furious burning of voluptuous appetite was utterly extinct. In this notable act, I wot not which is to be most commended, either his invincible courage in resisting so much against nature, or his wisdom in subduing the less pain with the more, and biting of that whereby he might be constrained to blaspheme God or renounce his religion. Sure I am that he therefore received immortal life and perpetual glory. And this I suppose sufficeth to persuade men of good nature to embrace continence. I mean not to live ever chaste, but to honour matrimony, and to have good await,[1] that they let not the sparks of concupiscence grow in great flames, wherewith the wits shall be dried up, and all noble virtues shall be devoured.

XIX. Of constancy or stability.

IN BUILDING of a fortress or other honourable mansion, it ought to be well considered that the cement wherewith the stones be laid be firm and well binding. For if it be brokle [2] and will moulder away with every shower of rain, the building may not

---

[1] Guard, watch.   [2] Fragile.

continue, but the stones, being not surely couched and mortared, falleth away one after another, and finally the whole house is defaced, and falleth in ruin. Semblably, that man which in childhood is brought up in sundry virtues, if either by nature, or else by custom, he be not induced to be alway constant and stable, so that he move not for any affection, grief, or displeasure, all his virtues will shortly decay, and, in the estimation of men, be but as a shadow, and be soon forgotten.

Also if a painter had wrought in a table some piece of portraiture wonderful elegant and pleasant to behold, as well for the good proportion and figure as for the fresh and delectable colours, but forasmuch as in tempering his colours, he lacked good size, wherewith they should have been bound, and made to endure; after that the image hath been a little while pleasant to the beholders, the colours being not surely wrought, either by moistness of weather relenteth or fadeth, or by some stroke or fall scaleth off, or mouldereth away, by reason whereof the image is utterly deformed, and the industry of the workman being never so excellent is perished, and accounted but for a vanity.

So he that hath all the gifts of nature and fortune, and also in his childhood is adorned with doctrine and virtue, which he hath acquired with much travail, watch, and study, if he add not to constancy, when he cometh to the time of experience, which experience is as it were the work of the craftsman, but moved with any private affection, or fear of adversity or exterior damage, will omit any part of his learning of virtue, the estimation of his person immediately ceaseth among perfect workmen, that is to say, wise men, and finally nothing being in him certain or stable, what thing in him may be commended? And in one thing meseemeth that constancy hath equal praise with justice, that is to say, that he that is himself unjust loveth that person that dealeth justly with him, and contrariwise hateth that person that dealeth unjustly, or doth him wrong. In like wise, he which is inconstant extolleth him whom he findeth constant, and desireth to have him his friend; on the other part, whom he proveth inconstant and wavering, he is angry with him, and accounteth him a beast, and unworthy the company of men, and awaiteth diligently to trust him with nothing. We note in children inconstancy, and likewise in women; the one for slenderness of wit, in rebuking a man of inconstancy, to call him a childish or womanly person. Albeit some women nowadays be found more constant than men, and specially in love towards their husbands; or else might there happen to be some wrong inheritors.

Constancy is as proper unto a man as is reason, and is of such estimation, that according as it was spoken of a wise man, it were better to have a constant enemy than an inconstant friend. Whereof I myself have had sufficient experience. But now to declare some experience of constancy, whereby the readers may be the more thereto provoked, I will rehearse some examples thereof out of old histories, as I shall happen to remember them.

After that Sulla had vanquished Marius, and destroyed the part of his adversaries, he with a great number of persons all armed, environed the Senate, intending to compel them by violence to condemn Marius for a traitor; which request none durst gainsay, Scaevola only excepted, who being thereof demanded, would give no sentence. But when Sulla did cast therefore on him a cruel countenance, he with a constant visage and noble courage, said to him, 'Sulla, although thou facest and threatenest me with thy multitude of soldiers, with whom thou hast thus besieged this court, yea and although thou dost menace me with death never so much, yet shalt thou never bring it to pass that for shedding a little old blood, I shall judge Marius a traitor, by whom this city and all Italy have been preserved.'

The constancy that great King Alexander had in trusting his friend against false report saved his life, whereof all men despaired. For after that noble battle wherein he had vanquished Darius, and taken his treasure, as he passed through Cilicia, being sore chafed with fervent heat and the length of his journey, as he came by the river called Cydnus, beholding it clear and pleasant, and thinking to assuage therein the heats that he suffered, he went thereinto naked and drank thereof. But immediately, by the exceeding cold which was in that water, his sinews shrank, and his joints became unwieldy, and as they were dead, and all his host being discomforted, he was conveyed to a city thereby, called Tarsus. Whereupon the physicians assembled and devising for the best remedy, they all were determined to give him one medicine, and that it should be ministered by one Philip, chief physician with Alexander. In the meantime, Parmenio, one of the greatest captains about Alexander, advertised him by his letters that he should beware of the treason of the said Philip, saying that he was corrupted with a great sum of money by Darius.

Wherewith he being nothing esbaied [1] held in his hands the letter, and receiving the medicine that Philip gave him, he at one time delivered the letter open to Philip, and drank also the medicine, declaring thereby the constancy that was in his friendship. Which trust not only caused nature the better to work with the medicine, but also bound so the heart of the physician toward him, that he ever after studied more diligently for the help and preservation of the noble prince that did so much trust him.

The constancy of Cato Uticensis was alway immovable, insomuch as at sundry times, when he in the Senate eagerly defended the public weal with vehement and long orations against the attempts of ambitious persons, he was by them rebuked and committed to prison. But he therefore not ceasing, but going toward prison, detected to the people, as he went, the unlawful purposes and enterprises of them by whom he was punished with the peril that was imminent to the public weal. Which he did with such courage and eloquence that as well the Senate as the people drew so about him, that his adversaries were fain for fear to discharge him. Who can sufficiently commend this noble man Cato, when he readeth in the works of Plutarch of his excellent courage and virtue? How much worthier had he been to have had Homer, the trump of his fame immortal, than Achilles, who for a little wench contended with Agamemnon only, where Cato, for the conservation of the weal public contended, and also resisted against Julius Caesar and the great Pompey, and not only against their menaces, but also against their desires and offers of alliance? Whereof I would gladly have made a remembrance in this work if the volume thereby should not too much have increased, and become unhandsome.

Undoubtedly, constancy is an honourable virtue, as inconstancy is reproachful and odious. Wherefore, that man which is mutable for every occasion must needs often repent him, and in much repentance is not only much folly, but also great detriment, which every wise man will eschew if he can. Wherefore to governors nothing is more proper than to be in their living stable and constant.

[1] Dismayed, appalled.

XX. The true signification of temperance a moral virtue.

THIS BLESSED company of virtues in this wise assembled, followeth temperance, as a sad and discreet matron and reverent governess, awaiting diligently that in any wise voluptuousness or concupiscence have no pre-eminence in the soul of man. Aristotle defineth this virtue to be a mediocrity in the pleasures of the body, specially in taste and touching. Therefore he that is temperate fleeth pleasures voluptuous, and with the absence of them is not discontented, and from the presence of them he willingly abstaineth. But in mine opinion, Plotinus, the wonderful philosopher, maketh an excellent definition of temperance, saying that the propriety or office thereof is to covet nothing which may be repented, also not to exceed the bounds of mediocrity, and to keep desire under the yoke of reason. He that practiseth this virtue is called a temperate man, and he that doeth contrary thereto is named intemperate. Between whom and a person incontinent Aristotle maketh this diversity: that he is intemperate, which by his own election is led, supposing that the pleasure that is present, or (as I might say) in use should alway be followed. But the person incontinent supposeth not so, and yet he notwithstanding doth follow it. The same author also maketh a diversity between him that is temperate and him that is continent, saying that the continent man is such one that nothing will do for bodily pleasure which shall stand against reason. The same is he which is temperate, saving that the other hath corrupt desires, which this man lacketh. Also the temperate man delighteth in nothing contrary to reason. But he that is continent delighteth, yet will he not be led against reason. Finally, to declare it in few words, we may well call him a temperate man that desireth the thing which he ought to desire, and as he ought to desire, and when he ought to desire. Notwithstanding there be divers other virtues which do seem to be as it were companions with temperance. Of whom (for the exchange of tediousness) I will speak now only of two, moderation and soberness, which no man (I suppose) doubteth to be of such efficacy, that without them no man may attain unto wisdom, and by them wisdom is soonest espied.

XXI. Of moderation a species of temperance.

MODERATION is the limits and bounds which honesty hath appointed in speaking and doing; like as in running passing the goal is accounted but rashness, so running half way is reproved for slowness. In like wise words and acts be the paces wherein the wit of man maketh his course, and moderation is instead of the goal, which if he pass over, he is noted either of presumption or of foolhardiness; if he come short of the purpose, he is condemned as dull, and unapt to affairs of great importance. This virtue shall best be perceived by rehearsing of examples shown by noble men, which is in effect but daily experience.

Fabius Maximus, being five times consul, perceiving his father, his grandfather, and great-grandfather, and divers other his ancestors to have had oftentimes that most honourable dignity, when his son, by the universal consent of the people, should be also made consul, he earnestly entreated the people to spare his son, and to give to the house of Fabius as it were a vacation time from that honour, not for that he had any mistrust in his son's virtue and honesty, but that his moderation was such that he would not that excellent dignity should alway continue in one family. Scipio Africanus the Elder, when the Senate and people had purposed that according to his merits he should have certain statues or images set in all courts and places of assembly, also they would have set his image in triumphant apparel within the capitol, and have granted to him to have been consul and dictator during his life; he, notwithstanding, would not suffer that any of them should be decreed, either by the act of the Senate, or by the people's suffrage. Wherein he showed himself to be as valiant in refusing of honours as he was in the acts wherein he had them well deserved. There is also moderation in toleration of fortune of every sort, which of Tully is called equability, which is, when there seemeth to be alway one visage and countenance never changed nor for prosperity nor for adversity.

Metellus, called Numidicus, in a common sedition being banished from Rome, and abiding in Asia, as he happened to sit with noblemen of that country in beholding a great play, there were letters delivered him, whereby he was ascertained that by the whole consent of the Senate and people his return into his country was granted; he (notwithstanding that he was of that tidings exceeding joyful) removed not until the plays were ended, nor any man sitting by him might perceive in his countenance any token of gladness.

The great King Antiochus, which long time had in his dominion all Asia, which is accounted to be the third part of the world, when at the last being vanquished by Lucius Scipio, he had lost the more part of his empire, and was assigned but to a small portion, he used his fortune so moderately that he gave great thanks to the Romans, that being delivered of so great burden and charge, he more easily might govern a little dominion. Alexander, Emperor of Rome, so in this virtue excelled, that being elect and made Emperor at sixteen years of his age, when the Senate and people for his virtue, wherein he passed all other, would have him called the great Alexander and father of the country, which of all names was highest, he with a wonderful gravity refused it, saying that it behoved that those names were obtained by merits and ripeness of years. The same prince also would not suffer his Empress to use in her apparel any richer stones than other ladies; and if any were given her, he either caused them to be sold or else gave them unto temples, affirming that the example of pomp and inordinate expenses should not proceed of the Emperor's wife. And when, for the honour that he did to the Senate and laws, his wife and his mother rebuked him, saying that he should bring the imperial majesty into too low an estate, he answered that it should be the surer and continue the longer.

There is also a moderation to be used against wrath or appetite of vengeance. Hadrian, the Emperor, while he was but a private person, bare toward a captain grievous displeasure, who afterward hearing that he was made Emperor, was in great fear lest Hadrian would be avenged. But when he came to the Emperor's presence, he nothing did or said to him, but only these words, 'Thou hast well escaped.' By which words he well declared his moderation, and also that whosoever putteth on the habit of a common person or governor, it shall not become him to revenge private displeasures.

Archytas, when he had been a long space out of his country and at his return found his possessions and goods destroyed and wasted, he said to his bailiff, 'I would surely punish thee if I should not be angry.'

Much like did Plato, for when his servant had offended him

grievously, he desired Speusippus, his friend, to punish him, 'lest' (said he) 'if I beat him, I should happen to be angry.' Wherein Plato deserved more praise than Archytas, inasmuch as he observed his patience, and yet did not suffer the offence of his servant to be unpunished. For most oftentimes the omitting of correction redoubleth a trespass.

Semblable moderation and wisdom, Aulus Gellius remembereth to be in Plutarch, the philosopher, which was master to Trajan the Emperor.

It happened that the bondman of Plutarch had committed some grievous offence, wherefore his master willed that he should be sharply punished. Wherefore commanding him to be stripped naked, caused another of his servants in his presence to beat him. But the slave who, as it seemed, was learned, while he was in beating, cried out on Plutarch, and in manner of reproach said unto him, 'How agreeth this with thy doctrine that preachest so much of patience, and in all thy lessons reprovest wrath, and now contrary to thine own teaching, thou art all inflamed with wrath, and clean from the patience which thou so much praisest?' Unto whom Plutarch without any change of countenance answered in this form. 'Thou embraidest[1] me causeless with wrath and impatience, but I pray thee what perceivest thou in me that I am angry or out of patience? I suppose (except I be much deceived) thou seest me not stare with mine eyes, or my mouth imbosed, or the colour of my face changed, or any other deformity in my person or gesture, or that my words be swift, or my voice louder than modesty requireth, or that I am unstable in my gesture or motion, which be the signs and evident tokens of wrath and impatience.' Wherefore said he to the corrector, 'Since he cannot prove that I am yet angry, in the meantime while he and I do dispute of this matter, and until he utterly do cease of his presumption and obstinacy, look that thou still beat him.' Verily, in mine opinion Plutarch herein declared his excellent wisdom and gravity, as well in his example of patience as also in subduing the stubborn courage of an obstinate servant. Which history shall be expedient for governors to have in remembrance, that when according to the laws they do punish offenders, they themselves be not chafed or moved with wrath, but (as Tully saith) be like to the laws, which be provoked to punish not by wrath or displeasure, but only by equity. And immediately the same author

[1] Reprove.

giveth another noble precept concerning moderation in punishment, saying that in correcting wrath is principally to be forbidden, for he that punisheth while he is angry, shall never keep that mean which is between too much and too little.

XXII. Of sobriety in diet.

VERILY I nothing doubt but that the more part of the readers of this work will take in good part all that is before written, considering the benefit and also the ornament that those virtues of whom I have spoken, of good reason and congruence, must be to them in whom they shall be planted and do continue. But I know well that this chapter which now ensueth shall unneth [1] be thankfully received of a few readers, nor shall be accounted worthy to be read of any honourable person, considering that the matter therein contained is so repugnant and adverse to that pernicious custom, wherein of long time men hath esteemed to be the more part of honour; insomuch as I very well know that some shall account great presumption in this mine attempt in writing against that which have been so long used. But forasmuch as I have taken upon me to write of a public weal, which taketh his beginning as the example of them that be governors, I will not let [2] for the dispraise given by them which be abused. But with all study and diligence I will describe the ancient temperance and moderation in diet, called sobriety, or, in a more general term, frugality, the act whereof is at this day as infrequent or out of use among all sorts of men, as the terms be strange unto them which have not been well instructed in Latin.

The noble Emperor Augustus, who in all the residue of his life was for his moderation and temperance excellently commended, suffered no little reproach, forasmuch as he in a secret supper or banquet, having with him six noblemen, his friends, and six noble women, and naming himself at that time Apollo, and the other men and women the names of other gods and goddesses, fared sumptuously and delicately, the city of Rome at that time being vexed with scarcity of grain. He therefore was rent with curses and rebukes of the people, insomuch as he was openly called Apollo the tormenter, saying also that he with his gods had

---

[1] Scarcely.   [2] Stay, be hindered.

devoured their corn. With which liberty of speech, being more persuaded than discontented, from thenceforth he used such a frugality or moderation of diet, that he was contented to be served at one meal with three dishes, or six at the most, which also were of a moderate price, and yet therein he used such soberness that either he himself would not sit until they which dined with him had eaten a good space, or else if he sat when they did, he would arise a great space or any of them had left eating. And for what purpose suppose ye did this Emperor in this wise, in whom was never spot of avarice or vile courage? Certes for two causes, first knowing the inconveniences that always do happen by ingurgitations and excessive feeding. Also that like as to him was committed the sovereign governance of all the world, so would he be to all men the general example of living. Now what damages do happen among men by immoderate eating and drinking we be every day taught by experience; but to bring them (as it were) to men's eyes, I will set them out evidently.

First, of satiety or fulness be engendered painful diseases and sicknesses, as squinces,[1] distillations called rheums or poses,[2] haemorrhoids, great bleedings, cramps, duskiness of sight, the tisike,[3] and the stitch, with many other that come not now to my remembrance. Of too much drinking proceedeth dropsy, wherewith the body and oftentimes the visage is swollen and defaced, beastly fury, wherewith the minds be perished, and of all other most odious, swine drunkenness, wherewith both the body and soul is deformed, and the figure of man is as it were by enchantment transformed into an ugly and loathsome image. Wherefore the Lacedaemons sometimes purposely caused their rustic servants to be made very drunk, and so to be brought in at their common dinners, to the intent that young men beholding the deformity and hasty fury of them that were drunkards should live the more soberly, and should eschew drunkenness as a thing foul and abominable. Also Pittacus (one of the seven sages of Greece) did constitute for a law that they which being drunk did offend should sustain double punishment, that men should the more diligently forbear to be drunk.

It is right evident to every wise man, who at any time hath haunted affairs whereunto was required contemplation or serious study, that to a man having due concoction and digestion as is

---

[1] Quinsy, tonsillitis.   [2] Catarrhs.
[3] Phthisis.

expedient, shall in the morning, fasting, or with a little refection, not only have his invention quicker, his judgment perfecter, his tongue readier, but also his reason fresher, his ear more attentive, his remembrance more sure, and generally all his powers and wits more effectual and in better estate, than after that he hath eaten abundantly. Which I suppose is the cause why the ancient courts of record in this realm have ever been used to be kept only before noon. And surely the consideration is wonderful excellent, and to be (as I might say) superstitiously observed; the reasons why be so apparent that they need not here to be rehearsed.

Pythagoras was never seen to eat any fish or flesh, but only herbs and fruits. Semblably did many other who exactly followed his doctrine. Wherefore it was supposed that they the rather excelled all other in finding out the secrets and hid knowledges of nature, which to other were impenetrable.

Plato (or rather Socrates, Plato inditing) in his second book of the public weal, willeth that the people of his city, which he would constitute, should be nourished with barley bread and cakes of wheat, and that the residue of their diet should be salt, olives, cheese, and leeks, and moreover worts that the fields do bring forth, for their pottage. But he addeth too, as it were to make the dinner more delicate, figs, beans, myrtle berries, and beech-mast, which they should roast on the coals, and drink to it water moderately. So (saith he) they living restfully and in health unto extreme age, shall leave the same manner of living unto their successors. I know well some readers, for this diet appointed by Socrates, will scorn him, accounting him for a fool, who not only by the answer of Apollo but also by the consent of all excellent writers that followed him, and the universal renown of all people, was approved to be the wisest man of all Greece. Certes I have known men of worship in this realm, which during their youth have drunk for the more part water. Of whom some yet liveth in great authority, whose excellency as well in sharpness of wit as in exquisite learning, is already known through all Christendom.

But here men shall not note me that I write this as who sayeth that noblemen in this realm should live after Socrates' diet, wherein having respect to this time and region, they might per-chance find occasion to reprove me. Surely like as the excess of fare is to be justly reproved, so in a nobleman much pinching and niggardship of meat and drink is to be discommended.

I cannot commend Aelius Pertinax, who being Emperor of

Rome, would have his guests served with a plant of lettuce
divided in two parts, and except something were sent him, he
would appoint nine pound weight of flesh unto three messes, and
if any dish happened to be brought to him, he caused it to be set
up until the next day. I am ashamed to remember that he would
send to his friends two morsels of meat, a piece of a pudding,
or the carcass of a capon. This was but misery and wretched
niggardship in a man of such honour.

In like manner who will not have in extreme detestation the
insatiable gluttony of Vitellius, Fabius Gurges, Apicius, and
divers other, to which cormorants neither land, water, nor air
might be sufficient.

Neither the curiosity and wanton appetite of Heliogabalus,
Emperor of Rome, is of any wise man allowed. Who being at
Rome or far from the sea, would eat only sea fish, and when he
sojourned nigh to the sea, he would touch no fish but which was
taken out of the River of Tiber or other places of equal or of
more distance. Also he would have dishes of meat made of
camels' heels, the combs of cocks newly cut, the tongues of pea-
cocks and nightingales, partridges' eggs, and other things hard
for to come by, whereto be no English names found (as I suppose)
apt to the true signification.

Moreover although I dispraised niggardship and vicious
scarcity in these number of dishes which I have commended, yet
I desire not to have therein meats for any occasion too much
sumptuous. For in one or two dishes may be employed as much
money as in twenty, perchance as good or better in eating. Whereof there remaineth a noble example of Cleopatra, daughter of
Ptolemy, late King of Egypt (whom Caesar in his life held for his
concubine), the same lady Antony (with whom Octavian divided
the Empire) loved also paramours, abandoning his wife, which
was sister to Octavian. And the wars between him and Octavian
ceasing by a little space, he (during that time) lived in most
prodigal riot, and thinking all thing in the sea, the land, and the
air to be made for satisfying his gluttony, he devoured all flesh
and fish that might be anywhere found. Cleopatra disdaining to
be vanquished in any excess by a Roman, laid a wager with
Antony that she herself would receive into her body at one
supper the value of fifty thousand pounds, which to Antony was
thought in a manner to be impossible. The wager was put into
the hands of Munatius Plancus, a noble Roman. The next day

Cleopatra prepared for Antony a right sumptuous supper, but whereat Antony nothing marvelled, knowing the value thereof by his accustomed fare, then the Queen smiling called for a goblet, whereinto she did pour a quantity of very tart vinegar, and taking a pearl which hung at one of her ears, she quickly did let it fall into the vinegar, wherein being shortly dissolved (as it is the nature of the pearl) she immediately drank it, and although she had vanquished Antony according to her wager, the pearl without any doubt being of the value of fifty thousand pounds, yet had she likewise drunk another pearl of like value, which was hanging at her other ear, had not Munatius Plancus, as an indifferent judge, forthwith given judgment that Antony was already vanquished.

I have rehearsed this history written by Macrobius and also Pliny, to the intent that the vanity in sumptuous feasting should be the better expressed.

Androcides (a man of excellent wisdom) wrote unto the great King Alexander an epistle, desiring him to refrain his intemperance, wherein he said, 'Noble prince, when thou wilt drink wine, remember then that thou drinkest the blood of the earth.' Signifying thereby (as I suppose) that the might and power of wine, and also warning Alexander of the thirst or appetite of blood which would ensue by his intemperate drinking. For Pliny (that writeth this history) saith immediately that if Alexander had obeyed the precepts of Androcides, he had never slain his friends in his drunkenness. For undoubtedly it may be said with good right that there is nothing to the strength of man's body more profitable than wine, nor to voluptuous appetites more pernicious, if measure lacketh. Also it is very truly and properly written of Propertius the poet, in this sentence following or like:

> By wine beauty fadeth, and age is defaced,
> Wine maketh forgotten that late was embraced.

Moreover Solomon, in his book named Ecclesiastes, calleth that country happy whereof the governors do eat in their time. And what shall we suppose is their time but only that which nature and the universal consent of all people hath ordained? And of what space is that time? But only that which sufficeth to the abundant sustentation and not oppression of nature, nor letteth [1] any part of their necessary affairs about the public weal.

[1] Hinders.

This meseemeth may be one exposition of Solomon's sentence. And here will I now make an end to write any more at this time of moderate diet, which I have not done of any presumption, but only to exhort gentlemen to preserve and augment their wits by this exhortation to temperance, or such like by themselves or some other better devised.

XXIII. Of sapience, and the definition thereof.

ALBEIT THAT some men which have hitherto read this book will suppose that those virtues whereof I have treated be sufficient to make a governor virtuous and excellent, nevertheless forasmuch as the effect of mine enterprise in this work is to express, as far forth as God shall instruct my poor wit, what things do belong to the making of a perfect public weal, which well nigh may no more be without an excellent governor than the universal course of nature may stand or be permanent without one chief disposer and mover, which is over all supereminent in power, understanding, and goodness. Wherefore because in governance be included disposition and order, which cannot be without sovereign knowledge, proceeding of wisdom, in a more elegant word called sapience, therefore I will now declare as much as my little wit doth comprehend of that part of sapience that of necessity must be in every governor of a just or perfect public weal.

The noble philosopher and most excellent orator, Tullius Cicero, in the fourth book of his Tusculan Questions saith in this wise, 'Sapience is the science of things divine and human, which considereth the cause of everything, by reason whereof that which is divine she followeth, that which is human she esteemeth far under the goodness of virtue.' This definition agreeth well with the gift of sapience that God gave to Solomon, King of Israel, who asked only wisdom to govern therewith his realm. But God, which is the fountain of sapience, graciously pondering the young prince's petition which proceeded of an apt inclination to virtue, with his own most bounteous liberality, which he purposed to employ on him for the entire love that he had to his father; he therefore infused in him plenty of all wisdom and cunning in things as well natural as supernatural, as it appeareth by the works of the same King Solomon, wherein be well nigh as many wisdoms as there be sentences. And in mine opinion one thing is specially to be noted. King David, father to Solomon, was a man of a rare and marvellous strength, insomuch as he himself reporteth in the Book of Kings that he, being a child and carrying to his brethren their dinner, where they kept their cattle, slew first a great bear, and after a lion, which fierce and hungry, assaulted him, although he were unarmed and whether he had any weapon or no, it is uncertain, since he maketh thereof no mention. Also of what prowess he was in arms and how valiant and good captain in battle it may sufficiently appear to them that will read his noble acts and achievances in the books before remembered. Wherein no good catholic man will anything doubt, though they be marvellous, yet notwithstanding, all his strength and puissance was not of such effect that in the long time of his reign, which was by the space of forty years, he could have any time vacant from wars. But alway had either continual battle with the Philistines, or else was molested with his own children and such as ought to have been his friends. Contrariwise, his son Solomon, of whom there is no notable mention made that he showed any commendable feat concerning martial prowess, saving the furniture of his garrisons with innumerable men of war, horses and chariots; which proveth not him to be valiant and strong, but only prudent; he after a little bickering with the Philistines in the beginning of his reign, afterward during the time that he reigned, continued in peace without any notable battle or molestation of any person. Wherefore he is named in scripture *Rex pacificus*, which is in English the peaceable king. And only by sapience so governed his realm, that though it were but a little realm in quantity, it excelled incomparably all other in honour and riches; insomuch as silver was at that time in the city of Jerusalem as stones in the street. Wherefore it is to be noted that sapience in the governance of a public weal is of more efficacy than strength and puissance. The authority of sapience is well declared by Solomon in his proverbs. 'By me' (saith sapience) 'kings do reign, and makers of laws discern things that be just. By me princes do govern, and men having power and authority do determine justice. I love all them that love me, and who that watcheth to have me shall find me. With me is both riches and honour, stately possessions, and justice. Better is the fruit that cometh of me than gold and stones that be precious.' The same King saith in his book called Ecclesiastes: 'A king without sapience shall lose his people, and cities shall be inhabited by the wit of them that be prudent.' Which sentence was verified by the son and successor of the same King Solomon, called Rehoboam, to whom the said book was written. Who neglecting the wise and virtuous doctrine of his father, condemned the sage counsel of ancient men and embraced the light persuasions of young men and flatterers; whereby he lost his honour and brought his realm in perpetual division.

The Empire of Rome (whose beginning, prosperity, and desolation seemeth to be a mirror and example to all other realms and countries) declareth to them that exactly beholdeth it, of what force and value sapience is to be esteemed, being begun with shepherds fleeing the wrath and displeasure of their masters.

Romulus during the time of his reign (which was thirty-seven years), he nothing did enterprise without the authority and consent of the fathers, whom he himself chose to be senators. And finally, as long as the Senate continued or increased in the city of Rome, and retained their authority, which they received of Romulus, and was increased by Tullus Hostilius, the third king, they wonderfully prospered, and also augmented their empire over the more part of the world. But soon after the Emperor Constantine had abandoned the city and translated the Senate from thence to Constantinople, and that, finally, the name and authority of the Senate was by little and little exhausted by the negligence and folly of ignorant emperors, not only that most noble city, head and princess of the world, and fountain of all virtue and honour, fell into most lamentable ruin; but also the majesty of the Empire decayed utterly, so that unneth [1] a little shadow thereof now remaineth; which whoso beholdeth and conferreth it with Rome when it flourished, according as it is left in remembrance by noble writers, he shall unneth keep tears out of his eyes, beholding it now as a rotten sheepcote, in comparison of that city noble and triumphant. O poor and miserable city, what sundry torments, excisions, subversions, depopulations, and other evil adventures hath happened unto thee, since thou were bereft of that noble court of sapience! Whose authority, if it had alway continued, being also confirmed in the faith and true religion of Christ, God being with thee pleased, thou couldst never have

---

[1] Scarcely.

been thus desolate unto the final consummation and end of the world. Now have I briefly and generally declared the utility of sapience, and the mischief that happeneth by the default or lack thereof. The particular effects we will declare hereafter more specially.

I doubt not but it is well known to every catholic man that hath the liberal use of reason, that all manner of understanding and knowledge, whereof proceedeth perfect operation, do take their original of that high sapience which is the operatrice of all things. And therefore Solomon, or Philo, or whoso made the book called Sapientia, made his prayer to God in this wise: 'Give to me, good Lord, sapience that sitteth by Thy throne.' And in the later end of the prayer he saith: 'Send her from the seat of Thy holiness that she may be with me, and labour with me, and that I may know what may be accepted with Thee.'

Orpheus (one of the eldest poets of Greece) affirmeth in his hymns that the Muses were gotten between Jupiter and Memory. Which saying being well understood and exactly tried, it shall appear manifestly with the saying of the wise man, contained in the said prayer late rehearsed.

Eustathius (the expositor of Homer) sayeth that *Musa* is the knowledge of the soul, and is a thing divine as the soul is. But, finally, as by old authors a man may aggregate a definition, that which is called in Greek and Latin *Musa*, is that part of the soul that induceth and moveth a man to search for knowledge, in the which motion is a secret and inexplicable delectation. Albeit because knowledge is in sundry wise distributed, and the number of nine among old authors was always rehearsed where they spoke of a multitude, as it shall appear to them that read Homer and Virgil, therefore there were devised to be nine Muses, which also for the resemblance of their disposition were feigned by the poets to be nine virgins, that first invented all liberal sciences, but the other opinion approacheth more near unto the truth, and agreeth better unto my purpose. Moreover, Jupiter was alway taken of the poets and philosophers for the supreme god, which was the giver of life and creator of all things, as it appeareth in all their works. Wherefore sometime they call him omnipotent, sometime the father of gods and of men, so that under that name they acknowledged to be a very god, though they honoured not him as one only god, as they ought to have done.

But now Orpheus' saying that the Muses proceeded of Jupiter

and Memory, may be in this wise interpreted: that God Almighty
infused sapience into the memory of man (for to the acquiring
of science belongeth understanding and memory), which, as a
treasury, hath power to retain, and also to erogate [1] and distribute, when opportunity happeneth. And for the excellency of
this thing some noted to be in man's soul a divine substance. As
Pythagoras, or some of his scholars writing his sentence, saith in
this wise speaking to man:

> Now in thyself have thou good confidence,
> Since mortal men be of the kind divine,
> In whose nature a reverent excellence
> Appeareth clear, which all thing doth define.

Which sentence of Pythagoras is not reject either of Plato, which
approached next unto the catholic writers, or of divines which
interpret Holy Scripture; taking the soul for the image and
similitude of God.

Moreover Plato (in his book called Timaeus) affirmeth that
there is set in the soul of man coming into the world certain
species, or as it were seeds of things and rules of arts or sciences.
Wherefore Socrates (in the book of Science) resembleth himself
to a midwife, saying that in teaching young men he did put into
them no science, but rather brought forth that which already was
in them, like as the midwife brought not in the child, but, being
conceived, did help to bring it forth. And like as in hounds is
a power or disposition to hunt, in horses and greyhounds an
aptitude to run swiftly, so in the souls of men is ingenerate a
leme [2] of science, which with the mixture of a terrestrial substance is obfuscate [3] or made dark; but where there is a perfect
master prepared in time, then the brightness of the science
appeareth polite and clear. Like as the power and aptitude of the
beasts before rehearsed appeareth not to the uttermost, except it
be by exercise provoked, and that sloth and dullness being
plucked from them by industry, they be induced unto the continual act. Which, as Plato affirmeth, is proved also in the master
and the disciple. Semblably the foresaid Socrates in Plato's book
of Sapience sayeth to one Theages: 'Never man learned of me
anything, although by my company he became the wiser, I only
exhorting and the good spirit inspiring.' Which wonderful

[1] Spend.   [2] Gleam.
                    [3] Obscured.

sentence, as meseemeth, may well accord with our catholic faith, and be received into the commentaries of the most perfect divines. For as well that sentence, as all other before rehearsed, do comprobate [1] with Holy Scripture that God is the fountain of sapience, like as He is the sovereign beginning of all generation.

Also it was wonderfully well expressed of whom Sapience was engendered by a poet, named Afranius, whose verses were set over the porch of the Temple where the Senate of Rome most commonly assembled. Which verses were in this manner:

> Usus me genuit, mater peperit memoria.
> Sophiam me Graii vocant, vos Sapientiam.

Which in English may be in this wise translated:

> Memory hight my mother, my father experience.
> Greeks call me Sophi, but ye name me Sapience.

By use or experience in these verses expressed the poet intended those acts which we ourself daily do practise as also them which being done by other in time passed, for the fruit or utility which thereof succeeded, were allowed, and also proved to be necessary. And the cause why that the poet conjoineth experience and memory together, as it were in a lawful matrimony, experience begetting, and memory alway producing that incomparable fruit called sapience, is for that memory in her operation properly succeedeth experience. For that which is presently done we perceive, that which is to come we conject or divine, but that which is passed only we have in our memory. For as Aristotle declareth wonderfully in an example, in the principal sense of man there is conceived an image or figure of a thing, which by the same sense is perceived as long as it is retained entire or whole, and (as I might say), consolidate, pure, manifest, or plain and without blemish, in such wise that in every part of it the mind is stirred or occupied, and by the same mind it may be thoroughly perceived and known, not as an image in itself, but as representing another thing; this is properly memory. But if the whole image or figure be not retained in the mind, but part thereof only remaineth, part is put out either by the length of time, or by some other mishap or injury, so that it neither can bring the mind eftsoons [2] unto it, nor it can be called again of the mind, as often

---

[1] Agree.   [2] Again.

as by that portion which still remaineth and hath aboden alway entire and clean, the residue that was thereto knit and adjoined and late seemed for the time dead or bereft from the mind, is revived and (as it were) returned home again, it is then had for redeemed or restored, and is properly called remembrance.

This is the exposition of the noble philosopher, which I have written principally to the intent to ornate our language with using words in their proper signification. Whereof what commodity may ensue all wise men will, I doubt not, consider.

XXIV. What is the true signification of understanding.

FORASMUCH as in the beginning of the first book of this work I endeavoured myself to prove, that by the order of man's creation, pre-eminence in degree should be among men according as they do excel in the pure influence of understanding, which cannot be denied to be the principal part of the soul, some reader perchance moved with disdain will for that one assertion immediately reject this work, saying that I am of a corrupt or foolish opinion; supposing that I do intend by the said words that no man should govern or be in authority, but only he which surmounteth all other in doctrine, which, in his hasty malice, he deemeth that I only do mean where I speak of understanding.

I suppose all men do know that man is made of body and soul, and that the soul in pre-eminence excelleth the body as much as the master or owner excelleth the house, or the artificer excelleth his instruments, or the king his subjects. And therefore Sallust in the conspiracy of Catiline sayeth, 'We use specially the rule of the soul and service of the body; the one we participate with gods, the other with beasts.' And Tully saith in Tusculan Questions: 'Man's soul, being decerpt [1] or taken of the portion of divinity called *Mens*, may be compared with none other thing (if a man might lawfully speak it) but with God Himself.' Also the noble divine Chrisostomus sayeth that the body was made for the soul, and not the soul for the body. Now it is to be further known that the soul is of three parts: the one, wherein is the power or efficacy of growing, which is also in herbs and trees as well as in man, and that part is called vegetative. Another part, wherein man doth participate with all other things living, which is called

[1] Plucked.

sensitive, by reason that thereof the senses do proceed, which be distributed into divers instrumental parts of the body; as sight into the eyes, hearing to the ears, smelling to the nose, tasting to the mouth, feeling to every part of the body wherein is blood, without the which undoubtedly may be no feeling. The third part of the soul is named the part intellectual or of understanding, which is of all the other most noble, as whereby man is most like unto God, and is preferred before all other creatures. For where other beasts by their senses do feel what thing do profit them, and what doth annoy them, only man understandeth whereof the said contrary dispositions do come, and by what means they do either help or annoy; also he perceiveth the causes of the same thing, and knoweth how to resist, where and when need doth require, and with reason and craft how to give remedy, and also with labour and industry to provide that thing which is wholesome or profitable. This most pure part of the soul, and (as Aristotle saith) divine, impassable, and incorruptible, is named in Latin *Intellectus*, whereunto I can find no proper English but understanding. For intelligence, which cometh of *Intelligentia*, is the perceiving of that which is first conceived by understanding, called *Intellectus*. Also intelligence is now used for an elegant word where there is mutual treaties or appointments, either by letters or message, specially concerning wars, or like other great affairs between princes or noblemen. Wherefore I will use this word understanding for *Intellectus*, until some other more proper English word may be found and brought in custom. But to perceive more plainly what thing it is that I call understanding. It is the principal part of the soul which is occupied about the beginning or original causes of things that may fall into man's knowledge, and his office is, before that anything is attempted, to think, consider, and prepense,[1] and, after often tossing it up and down in the mind, then to exercise that power, the property whereof is to espy, seek for, and find out; which virtue is referred to wit, which is as it were the instrument of understanding.

Moreover, after the things be invented, conjected, perceived, and by long time and often considered, and that the mind disposeth herself to execution or actual operation, then the virtue, named Prudence, first putteth herself forwards, and then appeareth her industry and labour; forasmuch as she teacheth, warneth,

[1] Anticipate.

exhorteth, ordereth, and profiteth, like to a wise captain that setteth his host in array. And therefore it is to be remembered that the office or duty of understanding precedeth the enterprise of acts, and is in the beginning of things. I call that beginning wherein, before any matter taken in hand, the mind and thought is occupied, and that a man searcheth, and doubteth whether it be to be enterprised, and by what way, and in what time it is to be executed. Who by this little introduction knowing what understanding do signify will not suppose that he which therein doth excel is not with honour to be advanced? Then it followeth not by this argument that forasmuch as he that excelleth other in understanding should be preferred in honour, that therefore no man should be preferred to honour, but only they that excel other in learning. No man having natural reason, though he never read logic, will judge this to be good argument, considering that understanding called in Latin *Intellectus* and *Mens*, is by itself sufficient and is not of any necessity annexed to doctrine, but doctrine proceedeth of understanding. But, if doctrine be alway attending upon understanding, as the daughter upon the mother, undoubtedly then understanding must be the more perfect and of a more efficacy, being increased by the inventions and experiences of many other declared by doctrine, no one man without inspiration having knowledge of all thing. I call doctrine, discipline intellective, or learning, which is either in writing or by report of things before known, which proceedeth from one man to another.

That which I have said is in this wise confirmed by Solomon, saying, 'A man that is wise by hearing shall become wiser, and he that hath understanding shall be a governor.'

Seneca saith we instruct our children in liberal sciences, not because those sciences may give any virtue, but because they prepare the mind and make it apt to receive virtue. Which being considered, no man will deny but that they be necessary to every man that coveteth very nobility; which as I have oftentimes said is in the having and use of virtue. And verily in whom doctrine hath been so found joined with virtue, there virtue had seemed excellent and as I might say triumphant.

Scipio, coming of the most noble house of the Romans, in high learning and knowledge of the nature of things wonderful studious, having alway with him the most excellent philosophers and poets that were in his time, was an example and mirror of martial prowess, continence, devotion, liberality, and of all other virtues.

Cato, called Uticensis, named the chief pillar of the public weal of the Romans, was so much inflamed in the desire of learning that (as Suetonius writeth), he could not temper himself in reading Greek books whilst the Senate was sitting.

How much it profited to the noble Augustus that until the death of his uncle Julius Caesar, he diligently applied his study in Athens, it well appeared after that the civil wars were all finished, when he, reforming the whole estate of the public weal, established the Senate, and taking unto him ten honourable personages, daily in his own person consulted with them of matters to be reported twice in a month to the Senate; in such wise aiding and helping forth that most noble court with his incomparable study and diligence.

The Emperor Titus, son of Vespasian, for his learning and virtue was named the delicate of the world.

Marcus Antonius the Emperor was in every kind of learning so excellent that he was therefore openly named the philosopher, not in reproach (as men do nowadays in despite call them philosophers and poets whom they perceive studious in sundry good disciplines), but to the augmentation of his honour. For being of his own nature aptly inclined to embrace virtue, he, adding to abundance of learning, became thereby a wonderful and perfect prince, being neither by study withdrawn from affairs of the public weal, nor by any business utterly plucked from philosophy and other noble doctrines. By the which mutual conjunction and just temperance of those two studies he attained to such a form in all his governance that he was named and taken for father of the Senate, of the people, and universally of all the whole Empire. Moreover his deeds and words were of all men had in so high estimation and reverence that both the Senate and people took of him laws and rules of their living. And in his governance and proper living, as well at home in his house as in his civil business, he was to himself the only law and example. And as he was above other highest in authority, so by the universal opinion of all men he was judged to be of all other men then living, the best and also the wisest.

XXV. Of experience which have preceded our time, with a defence of histories.

EXPERIENCE whereof cometh wisdom is in two manner of wise. The one is acts committed or done by other men, whereof profit or damage succeeding, we may (in knowing or beholding it), be thereby instructed to apprehend the thing which to the public weal, or to our own persons, may be commodious; and to eschew that thing, which either in the beginning or in the conclusion, appeareth noisome and vicious.

The knowledge of this experience is called example, and is expressed by history, which of Tully is called the life of memory. And so it agreeth well with the verses of Afranius by me late declared. And therefore to such persons as do condemn ancient histories, reputing them among leasings [1] and fantasies (these be their word of reproach), it may be said that in condemning histories they frustrate experience; which (as the said Tully saith) is the light of virtue, which they would be seen so much to favour although they do seldom embrace it. And that shall they perceive manifestly if they will a little while lay apart their accustomed obstinacy, and suffer to be distilled into their ears two or three drops of the sweet oil of remembrance. Let them revolve in their minds generally that there is no doctrine, be it either divine or human, that is not either all expressed in history or at the least mixed with history. But to the intent that there shall be left none ignorance whereby they might be detained in their error, I will declare unto them what is that that is called an history, and what it comprehendeth.

First it is to be noted that it is a Greek name, and cometh of a word or verb in Greek *historeo*, which doth signify to know, to see, to ensearch, to enquire, to hear, to learn, to tell, or expound unto other. And then must history which cometh thereof be wonderful profitable, which leaveth nothing hid from man's knowledge, that unto him may be either pleasant or necessary. For it not only reporteth the gests or acts of princes or captains, their counsels and attempts, enterprises, affairs, manners in living good and bad, descriptions of regions and cities, with their inhabitants, but also it bringeth to our knowledge the forms of sundry public weals with augmentations and decays and occasion

[1] Lies.

thereof; moreover precepts, exhortations, counsels, and good persuasions, comprehended in quick sentences and eloquent orations. Finally so large is the compass of that which is named history, that it comprehendeth all thing that is necessary to be put in memory. Insomuch as Aristotle, where he declareth the parts of man's body with their description and offices, and also the sundry forms and dispositions of all beasts, fowls, and fishes, with their generation he nameth his book an history.

Semblably Theophrastus, his scholar, a noble philosopher, describing all herbs and trees, whereof he might have the true knowledge, entitleth his book the History of Plants. And finally Pliny the Elder calleth his most excellent and wonderful work, the History of Nature; in the which book he nothing omitteth that in the bosom of nature is contained, and may be by man's wit comprehended, and is worthy to be had in remembrance. Which authorities of these three noble and excellent learned men approveth the signification of history to agree well with the exposition of the verb *historeo*, whereof it cometh.

Now let us see what book of Holy Scripture, I mean the Old Testament and the New, may be said to have no part of history. The five books of Moses, the book of Judges, the four books of Kings, Job, Esther, Judith, Ruth, Tobias, and also the history of Maccabees (which from the other is separate), I suppose no man will deny but that they be all historical, or (as I might say) entire histories. Also Esra, Nehemiah, Ezekiel, and Daniel, although they were prophets, yet be their works compact in form of narrations, which by orators be called enunciative and only pertaineth to histories, wherein is expressed a thing done, and persons named. All the other prophets, though they speak of the time future or to come, which is out of the description of an history, yet either in rebuking the sins and enormities passed, or bewailing the destruction of their country, or captivity of the people, and such like calamity or miserable estate, also in moving or persuading the people, they do recite some circumstance of a narration. But now be we come to the New Testament, and principally the books of the Evangelists, vulgarly called the Gospels, which be one context of an history, do not they contain the temporal life of our Saviour Christ, King of Kings and Lord of the world, until His glorious Ascension? And what thing lacketh therein that doth pertain to a perfect history? There lacketh not in things order and disposition, in the context or narration verity, in the sentences gravity, utility in the counsels, in the persuasions doctrine, in expositions or declarations facility.

The books of Acts of Apostles, what thing is it else but a plain history? The epistles of Saint Paul, Saint Peter, Saint John, Saint James, and Judas the Apostles do contain counsels and advertisements in the form of orations, reciting divers places as well out of the Old Testament as out of the Gospels, as it were an abbreviate, called of the Greeks and Latins, *epitoma*.

This is well known to be true of them that have had any leisure to read Holy Scripture, who, remembering themselves by this my little induction, will leave to neglect history, or condemn it with so general a dispraise as they have been accustomed. But yet some will impugn them with a more particular objection, saying that the histories of the Greeks and Romans be nothing but lies and feigning of poets (some such persons there be between whom and good authors have ever been perpetual hostility). First, how do they know that all the histories of Greeks and Romans be leasings,[1] since they find not that any scripture authentic made about that time that those histories were written, do reprove or condemn them? But the most catholic and renowned doctors of Christ's religion in the corroboration of their arguments and sentences, do allege the same histories and vouch (as I might say) to their aid the authority of the writers. And yet some of those Rabbines [2] (in God's name) which in comparison of the said noble doctors be as who saith petites [3] and unneth [4] lettered, will presume with their own silly wits to disprove that which both by anciency of time and consent of blessed and noble doctors is allowed and by their works honoured. If they will conject histories to be lies because they sometimes make report of things seen and acts done which do seem to the readers incredible, by that same reason may they not only condemn all Holy Scripture, which containeth things more wonderful than any historian writeth, but also exclude credulity utterly from the company of man. For how many things be daily seen, which being reported unto him that never saw them, should seem impossible? And if they will allege that all thing contained in Holy Scripture is approbate by the whole consent of all the clergy of Christendom at divers general councils assembled, certes the same councils never disproved or rejected the histories of Greeks or Romans;

[1] Lies.   [2] Religious authorities.
[3] Young.   [4] Scarcely.

but the most catholic and excellent learned men of those congregations embraced their examples, and sowing them in their works made of them to the Church of Christ a necessary ornament.

Admit that some histories be interlaced with leasings; why should we therefore neglect them, since the affairs there reported nothing concerneth us, we being thereof no partners, nor thereby only may receive any damage? But if by reading the sage counsel of Nestor, the subtle persuasions of Ulysses, the compendious gravity of Menelaus, the imperial majesty of Agamemnon, the prowess of Achilles, and valiant courage of Hector, we may apprehend anything whereby our wits may be amended and our personages be more apt to serve our public weal and our prince, what forceth it us [1] though Homer write leasings? I suppose no man thinketh that Aesop wrote gospels, yet who doubteth but that in his fables the fox, the hare, and the wolf, though they never spoke, do teach many good wisdoms, which being well considered, men (if they have not avowed to repugn against reason) shall confess with Quintilian that few and unneth one may be found of ancient writers which shall not bring to the readers something commodious; and specially that they do write matters historical, the lesson whereof is as it were the mirror of man's life, expressing actually, and (as it were at the eye) the beauty of virtue, and the deformity and loathliness of vice. Wherefore Lactantius saith, 'Thou must needs perish if thou know not what is to thy life profitable, that thou mayest seek for it, and what is dangerous, that thou mayest flee and eschew it.' Which I dare affirm may come soonest to pass by reading of histories, and retaining them in continual remembrance.

XXVI. The experience or practice necessary in the person of a governor of a public weal.

THE OTHER experience which is in our proper persons and is of some men called practice, is of no small moment or efficacy in the acquiring of sapience, insomuch that it seemeth that no operation or affair may be perfect, nor no science or art may be complete, except experience be thereunto added, whereby knowledge is ratified, and (as I might say) consolidate.

[1] Does it matter to us.

It is written that the great King Alexander on a time being (as it happened) unoccupied, came to the ship of Apelles, the excellent painter, and standing by him whilst he painted, the King reasoned with him of lines, adumbrations, proportions, or other like things pertaining to imagery, which the painter a little while suffering, at the last said to the King with the countenance all smiling, 'Seest thou, noble prince, how the boy that grindeth my colours doth laugh thee to scorn?' Which words the King took in good part and held him therewith justly corrected, considering by his own office in martial affairs that he then had in hand, how great a portion of knowledge faileth, where lacketh experience. And therein governors shall not disdain to be resembled unto physicians, considering their offices in curing and preserving be most like of any other. That part of physic called rational, whereby is declared the faculties or powers of the body, the causes, accidents, and tokens of sicknesses, cannot always be sure without some experience in the temperature or distemperature of the regions, in the disposition of the patient in diet, concoction, quietness, exercise, and sleep.

And Galen, prince of physicians, exhorteth them to know exactly the accustomed diet of their patients, which cannot happen without much resort into their companies, seriously noting their usage in diet. Semblably, the universal state of a country or city may be well likened to the body of man. Wherefore the governors, in the stead of physicians attending on their cure, ought to know the causes of the decay of their public weal, which is the health of their country or city, and then with expedition to proceed to the most speedy and sure remedy. But certes the very cause of decay, nor the true mean to cure it, may never be sufficiently known of governors, except they themselves will personally resort and peruse all parts of the countries under their governance, and insearch diligently as well what be the customs and manners of people good and bad, as also the commodities and discommodities, how the one may be preserved, the other suppressed, or at the leastways amended. Also among them that have ministration or execution of justice (which I may liken unto the members), to taste and feel how every of them do practise their offices, that is to say, whether they do it feebly or unprofitably, and whether it happen by negligence, discourage, corruption, or affection.

But now may the reader with good reason demand of me by

what manner experience the governors may come to the true knowledge hereof. That shall I now declare. First the governors themselves adorned with virtue, being in such wise an example of living to their inferiors, and making the people judges of them and their domestical servants and adherents, should sundry times during their governance, either purposely or by way of solace, repair into divers parts of their jurisdiction or province, and making there abode, they shall partly themselves attentively hear what is commonly or privately spoken concerning the estate of the country or persons, partly they shall cause their servants or friends, of whose honesty and truth they have good assurance, to resort in disporting themselves in divers towns and villages; and as they happen to be in company with the inhabitants privily and with some manner of circumstance, inquire what men of haviour [1] dwell nigh unto them, what is the form of their living, of what estimation they be in justice, liberality, diligence in executing the laws, and other semblable virtues; contrariwise whether they be oppressors, covetous men, maintainers of offenders, remiss or negligent, if they be officers; and what the examiners do hear the greater number of people report that they entirely and truly denounce it to the said governor. By the which intimation and their own prudent endeavour, they shall have infallible knowledge who among the inhabitants be men toward the public weal best disposed. Them shall they call for and most courteously entertain, and (as it were) lovingly embrace with thanks for their good will and endeavour toward the public weal; commending them openly for their virtue and diligence, offering to them their assistance in their semblable doings, and also their furtherance toward the due recompense of their travails. On the contrary part, when they see any of them who among their inferiors observe not justice, and likewise officers which be remiss or favourable to common offenders and breakers of laws, and negligent in the execution of their authorities, to them shall they give condign reprehensions, manifesting their defaults in omitting their duties, and in giving evil example to their companions, also boldness to transgress, to condemn the laws, declaring also that the ministering such occasion deserve not only a sharp rebuke but also right grievous punishment. And if he that thus admonisheth be a sovereign governor or prince, if, I say, he shortly hereupon doth

[1] Substance.

ratify his words by expelling some of them which I now re-hearsed from their offices, or otherwise sharply correcting them, and contrariwise advance higher some good man and whom he hath proved to be diligent in the execution of justice, undoubtedly he shall inflame the appetite and zeal of good ministers, and also suscitate or raise the courage of all men inclined to virtue, so that there shall never lack men apt and proper to be set in authority. Where the merits of men being hid and unknown to the sovereign governor, and the negligent ministers or inferior governors having not only equal thank or reward but perchance much more than they which be diligent, or would be if they might have assistance, there undoubtedly is grievous discourage and peril of conscience; forasmuch as they omit oftentimes their duties and offices, reputing it great folly and madness to acquire by the executing of justice not only an opinion of tyranny among the people, and consequently hatred, but also malignity among his equals and superiors, with a note of ambition.

This revolved and considered by a circumspect governor, Lord God, how shortly and with little difficulty shall he dispose the public weal that is grieved to receive medicine, whereby it should be soon healed and reduced to his perfection.

XXVII. Of detraction and the image thereof made by the painter Apelles.

THERE IS much conversant among men in authority a vice very ugly and monstrous, who under the pleasant habit of friendship and good counsel with a breath pestilential infecteth the wits of them that nothing mistrusteth; this monster is called in English Detraction, in Latin *Calumnia*, whose property I will now declare. If a man, being determined to equity, having the eyes and ears of his mind set only on the truth and the public weal of his country, will have no regard to any request or desire, but proceedeth directly in the administration of justice, then either he which by justice is offended, or some his favourers, abettors, or adherents, if he himself or any of them be in service or familiarity with him that is in authority, as soon as by any occasion mention happeneth to be made of him who hath executed justice exactly, forthwith they imagine some vice or default, be it never so little, whereby they may minish his credence, and craftily omitting to speak anything of his rigour in justice, they will note and touch something of his manners, wherein shall either seem to be lightness or lack of gravity, or too much sourness, or lack of civility, or that he is not benevolent to him in authority, or that he is not sufficient to receive any dignity, or to despatch matters of weighty importance, or that he is superfluous in words or else too scarce. Also if he live temperately and delighteth much in study, they embraid him with niggardship, or in derision do call him a clerk or a poet, unmeet for any other purpose. And this do they covertly and with a more gravity than any other thing that they enterprise. This evil report is called detraction, who was wonderfully well expressed in figures by the most noble painter Apelles, after that he was discharged of the crime whereof he was falsely accused to Ptolemy King of Egypt, having for his amends of the said King twelve thousand pounds sterling and his accuser to his bondman perpetually. The table wherein detraction was expressed was painted in this form. At the right hand was made sitting a man having long ears, putting forth his hand to Detraction, who far off came towards him; about this man stood two women, that is to say, Ignorance and Suspicion. On the other side came Detraction, a woman above measure well trimmed, all chafed and angry, having her aspect or look like to the fire, in showing a manner of rage or fury. In her left hand she held a burning torch or brand, and with her other hand she drew by the ear of his head a young man who held up his hands toward heaven, calling God and the saints for witness. With her came a man pale and evil favoured, beholding the young man intently, like unto one that had been with long sickness consumed, whom ye might lightly conject to be Envy. Also there followed two other women, that trimmed and apparelled Detraction; the one was Treason, the other Fraud. After followed a woman in a mourning weed, black and ragged, and she was called Repentance, who turning her back weeping and sore ashamed beheld Verity, who then approached. In this wise Apelles described detraction, by whom he himself was in peril. Which in mine opinion is a right necessary matter to be in tables or hangings set in every man's house that is in authority, considering what damage and loss hath ensued and may hereafter ensue by this horrible pestilence, false detraction. To the avoiding whereof, Lucian, who writeth of this picture, giveth a notable counsel, saying that a wise man, when he doubteth of the honesty and virtue of the person accused, he should keep close his ears and not open them hastily to them which be with this sickness infected, and put reason for a diligent porter and watch, which ought to examine and let in the reports that be good, and exclude and prohibit them that be contrary. For it is a thing to laugh at and very unfitting to ordain for thy house a keeper or porter, and thine ears and mind to leave to all men wide open. Wherefore when any person cometh to us to tell us any report or complaint, first, it shall behove us thoroughly and evenly to consider the thing, not having respect to the ears of him that reporteth, or to his form of living or wisdom in speaking. For the more vehement the reporter is in persuading, so much more diligent and exact trial and examination ought to be used. Therefore trust is not to be given to another man's judgment, much less to the malice of an accuser. But every man shall retain to himself the power to ensearch out the truth, and leaving the envy or displeasure to the detractor, he shall ponder or weigh the matter indifferently, that everything in such wise being curiously ensearched and proved, he may at his pleasure either love or hate him whom he hath so substantially tried. For in good faith to give place to detraction at the beginning, it is a thing childish and base, and to be esteemed among the most great inconveniences and mischiefs. These be well-nigh the words of Lucian; whether the counsel be good I remit it to the wise readers. Of one thing am I sure, that by detraction as well many good wits have been drowned, as also virtue and painful study have been unrewarded, and many zealators [1] or favourers of the public weal have been discouraged.

XXVIII. Of consultation and counsel, and in what form they ought to be used in a public weal.

THE GRIEFS or diseases which of Aristotle be called the decays of the public weal being investigate, examined, and tried by the experience before expressed, then cometh the time and opportunity of consultation, whereby, as I said, is provided the remedies most necessary for the healing of the said griefs or reparation of decays. This thing that is called consultation is the general denomination of the act wherein men do devise

---

[1] Zealous supporters.

together and reason what is to be done. Counsel is the sentence or advice particularly given by every man for that purpose assembled. Consultation hath respect to the time future or to come, that is to say, the end or purpose thereof is addressed to some act or affair to be practised after the consultation. And yet be not all other times excluded, but first the state of things present ought to be examined, the power, assistance, and substance to be esteemed; semblably things passed with much and long deliberation to be revolved and tossed in the mind, and to be conferred with them that be present; and being exactly weighed the one against the other, then to investigate or inquire exquisitely the form and reason of the affair, and in that study to be wholly resolved so effectually that they which be counsellors may bear with them out of the counsel house, as it were on their shoulders, not only what is to be followed and exploited, but also by what means or ways it shall be pursued, and how the affair may be honourable; also what is expedient and of necessity, and how much is needful, and what space and length of time, and finally how the enterprise being achieved and brought to effect may be kept and retained. For oftentimes after exploitures happeneth occasions, either by assaults or other encumbrances of enemies, or of too much trust in fortune's assurance, or by disobedience or presumption of some persons whom the thing toucheth, that this last part of consultation is omitted, or more rather neglected; where much study, travail, and cost have utterly perished, not only to the no little detriment of infinite persons, but also to the subversion of most noble public weals. Moreover it is to be diligently noted that every counsel is to be approved by three things principally, that it be rightwise, that it be good, and that it be with honesty. That which is rightwise is brought in by reason. For nothing is right that is not ordered by reason. Goodness cometh of virtue. Of virtue and reason proceedeth honesty. Wherefore counsel being compact of these three, may be named a perfect captain, a trusty companion, a plain and unfeigned friend. Therefore in the commendation thereof Titus Livius saith, 'Many things be impeached by nature which by counsel be shortly achieved.' And verily the power of counsel is wonderful, having authority as well over peace as martial enterprise. And therefore with good reason Tully affirmeth in his book of offices, 'Arms without the doors be of little importance, if counsel be not at home.' And he saith soon after: 'In things

most prosperous the counsel of friends must be used.' Which is
ratified by the author of the noble work named Ecclesiasticus,
saying: 'My son, without counsel see thou do nothing, and then
after thy deed thou shalt never repent thee.' The same author
giveth three noble precepts concerning this matter, which of
every wise man ought to be had in continual memory. 'Of fools
take thou no counsel, for they can love nothing but that pleaseth
themselves. Discover not thy counsel before a stranger, for thou
knowest not what thereof may happen. Unto every man disclose
not thy heart, lest peradventure he will give to thee a feigned
thank, and after report rebukefully of thee.' Fools be, as I
suppose, they which be more led with affection than reason. And
whom he calleth strangers be those of whose fidelity and wisdom
he is not assured; and in the general name of every man may be
signified the lack of election of counsellors, which would be with
a vigilant search and (as I might say) of all other most scrupulous.

XXIX. What in consultation is to be chiefly considered.

THE END of all doctrine and study is good counsel, whereunto as
unto the principal point, which geometricians do call the centre,
all doctrines (which by some authors be imagined in the form of
a circle) do send their effects like unto equal lines, as it shall
appear to them that will read the books of the noble Plato, where
he shall find that the wise Socrates, in every investigation, which
is in form of a consultation, useth his persuasions and demonstra-
tions by the certain rules and examples of sundry sciences,
proving thereby that the conclusion and (as I might say) the perfection of them is in good counsel, wherein virtue may be found,
being (as it were) his proper mansion or palace, where her power
only appeareth concerning governance, either of one person
only, and then it is called moral, or of a multitude, which for a
diversity may be called politic. Since counsel is of such an
efficacy, and in things concerning man hath such a pre-eminence,
it is therefore expedient that consultation (wherein counsel is
expressed) be very serious, substantial, and profitable. Which to
bring to effect requireth two things principally to be considered.
First, that in everything concerning a public weal no good
counsellor be omitted or passed over, but that his reason therein
be heard to an end. I call him a good counsellor, which (as Caesar

saith, in the conjuration of Cataline), whiles he consulteth in doubtful matters, is void of all hate, friendship, displeasure, or pity. How necessary to a public weal it shall be to have in any wise men's opinions declared, it is manifest to them that do remember that in many heads be divers manners of wits, some inclined to sharpness and rigour, many to pity and compassion, divers to a temperance and mean between both extremities; some have respect to tranquillity only, other more to wealth and commodity, divers to much renown and estimation in honour. There be that will speak all their mind suddenly and perchance right well; divers require to have respect and study, wherein is much more surety, many will speak warily for fear of displeasure; some more bold in virtue will not spare to show their minds plainly, divers will assent to that reasons wherewith they suppose that he which is chief in authority will be best pleased. These undoubtedly be the diversities of wits. And moreover, where there is a great number of counsellors, they all being heard needs must the counsel be the more perfect. For sometime perchance one of them, which in doctrine, wit, or experience is in least estimation, may hap to express some sentence more available to the purpose wherein they consult than any that before came to the others' remembrances; no one man being of such perfection that he can have in an instant remembrance of all thing. Which I suppose was considered by Romulus the first King of Romans in the first constitution of their public weal; for having of his own people but three thousand foot men and three hundred horsemen, he chose of the eldest and wisest of them all one hundred counsellors. But to the more assertion of divers men's sentences I will declare a notable experience which I late happened to read.

Belinger Baldasine, a man of great wit, singular learning, and excellent wisdom (who was one of the counsellors to Ferdinand, King of Aragon), when anything doubtful or weighty matter was consulted of, where he was present, afterward, when he had supped at home in his house, he would call before him all his servants, and merrily purposing to them some feigned question or fable, wherein was craftily hid the matter which remained doubtful, would merrily demand of every man his particular opinion, and giving good ear to their judgments, he would confer together every man's sentence, and with good deliberation, pondering their value, he at the last perceived which was the truest and most apt to his purpose; and being in this wise

furnished, translating japes [1] and things feigned to matter serious
and true, he among the King's counsellors in giving good and
substantial advice had alway pre-eminence.

How much commodity then suppose ye might be taken of the
sentences of many wise and expert counsellors? And like as
Calchas, as Homer writeth, knew by divination things present,
things to come, and them that were passed, so counsellors garnished with learning and also experience shall thereby consider
the places, times, and personages, examining the state of the
matter then practised, and expending the power, assistance, and
substance, also revolving long and oftentimes in their minds
things that be passed, and conferring them to the matters that be
then in experience, studiously do seek out the reason and manner,
how that which is by them approved may be brought to effect.
And such men's reasons would be thoroughly heard and at
length, for the wiser that a man is, in tarrying his wisdom
increaseth, his reason is more lively, and quick sentence aboundeth.
And to the more part of men when they be chafed in reasoning,
arguments, solutions, examples, similitudes, and experiments do
resort, and (as it were) flow unto their remembrances.

XXX. *The second consideration to be had in consultation.*

THE SECOND consideration is that the general and universal
estate of the public weal would be preferred in consultation
before any particular commodity, and the profit or damage
which may happen within our own countries would be more considered than that which may happen from other regions; which
to believe common reason and experience leadeth us.

For who commendeth those gardeners that will put all their
diligence in trimming or keeping delicately one knot or bed of
herbs, suffering all the remnant of their garden to be subverted
with a great number of moles, and do attend at no time for the
taking and destroying of them, until the herbs, wherein they have
employed all their labours, be also turned up and perished, and
the moles increased in so infinite numbers that no industry or
labour may suffice to consume them, whereby the labour is
frustrated and all the garden made unprofitable and also unpleasant? In this similitude to the garden may be resembled the

[1] Tricks.

public weal, to the gardeners the governors and counsellors, to the knots or beds sundry degrees of personages, to the moles vices and sundry enormities. Wherefore the consultation is but of a small effect wherein the universal estate of the public weal do not occupy the more part of the time, and in that generality every particular estate be not diligently ordered. For as Tully saith, they that consult for part of the people and neglect the residue, they bring into the city or country a thing most pernicious, that is to say, sedition and discord, whereof it happeneth that some will seem to favour the multitude, other be inclined to lean to the best sort, few do study for all universally. Which hath been the cause that not only Athens (which Tully doth name), but also the city and empire of Rome, with divers other cities and realms, have decayed and been finally brought in extreme desolation. Also Plato, in his book of fortitude, saith in the person of Socrates, 'Whensoever a man seeketh a thing for cause of another thing, the consultation ought to be alway of that thing for whose cause the other thing is sought for, and not of that which is sought for because of the other thing.' And surely wise men do consider that damage oftentimes happeneth by abusing the due form of consultation: men like evil physicians seeking for medicines ere they perfectly know the sicknesses; and as evil merchants do utter first the wares and commodities of strangers, whilst strangers be robbing of their own coffers.

Therefore these things that I have rehearsed concerning consultation ought to be of all men in authority substantially pondered, and most vigilantly observed, if they intend to be to their public weal profitable, for the which purpose only they be called to be governors. And this conclude I to write any more of consultation, which is the last part of moral sapience, and the beginning of sapience politic.

Now all ye readers that desire to have your children to be governors, or in any other authority in the public weal of your country, if ye bring them up and instruct them in such form as in this book is declared, they shall then seem to all men worthy to be in authority, honour, and noblesse, and all that is under their governance shall prosper and come to perfection. And as a precious stone in a rich brooch they shall be beholden and wondered at, and after the death of their body their souls for their endeavour shall be incomprehensibly rewarded of the giver of wisdom, to whom only be given eternal glory. Amen.